D1590394

816.9003
Si4L

139648

DATE DUE			

WITHDRAWN
L. R. COLLEGE LIBRARY

The Letters of William Gilmore Simms

1834-1870

SUPPLEMENT

The Letters of William Gilmore Simms

Collected and Edited
by
MARY C. SIMMS OLIPHANT
and
T. C. DUNCAN EAVES

Volume VI
Supplement (1834–1870)

CARL A. RUDISILL LIBRARY
LENOIR RHYNE COLLEGE

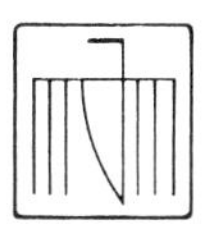

UNIVERSITY OF SOUTH CAROLINA PRESS

Publication of this work has been made possible in part by a grant from the Andrew W. Mellon Foundation and the financial support of the National Endowment for the Humanities.

816.9003
Si4L
139648
Aug. 1986

Copyright©University of South Carolina 1982

First Edition

Published by the University of South Carolina Press, Columbia, S.C., 1982
Manufactured in the United States of America

Library of Congress Cataloging in Publication Data

Simms, William Gilmore, 1806–1870. Letters.
Bibliographical footnotes.
CONTENTS: v. 1. 1830–1844.—v. 2. 1845–1849.— [etc.]—v. 6. Supplement 1834–1870.
1. Simms, William Gilmore, 1806–1870—Correspondence. 2. Authors, American—19th century—Correspondence.
PS2853.A4 1952 818'.309 [B] 52-2352
ISBN O-87249-438-1 (v. 6) AACR1

Frontispiece: William Gilmore Simms, reproduced from what is thought to be the last photograph. *Courtesy of Mrs. James C. Player, the great-great-granddaughter of Simms, descended from his eldest daughter, Anna Augusta Simms Roach.*

PREFACE

No apology is needed for the publication of a supplementary sixth volume of *The Letters of William Gilmore Simms.* When the first five volumes were published by the University of South Carolina Press in 1952–1956, Simms' reputation was perhaps at its lowest point. William Peterfield Trent's biography, published in 1892, was the only readily accessible source for the facts of Simms' life and career, and it is far from exhaustive and, in the opinion of many, equally far from giving a just estimate of Simms or of his literary works. *The Yemassee* was the only one of Simms' many books in print, and Simms was neglected or even ignored by students of American literature. *The Letters of William Gilmore Simms* enabled twentieth-century scholars to see Simms as he really was, and what they saw aroused their interest and raised their opinion of the man and of the writer. The last twenty-five years have witnessed reprints of various early editions of most of Simms' novels and of several of his other volumes. Books and articles have appeared (and will continue to appear) on Simms and his works. In 1969 the University of South Carolina Press published *Voltmeier,* the first volume of *The Centennial Edition of the Writings of William Gilmore Simms,* and this volume has been followed by several others. In 1976 the South Carolina Committee for the Humanities in conjunction with the Southern Studies Program of the University of South Carolina sponsored for the South Carolina American Revolution Bicentennial the reissuance of all eight of Simms' Revolutionary War novels, *Joscelyn, The Partisan, Mellichampe, Katharine Walton, The Scout, The Forayers, Eutaw,* and *Woodcraft.* Moreover, writers on the social, political, and literary history of nineteenth-century America have found Simms' letters an invaluable source of information. An exhaustive biography of Simms will someday be written, but, even so, Simms will perhaps still remain through his letters his own best and most absorbing biographer.

In collecting the letters for this volume we want to thank especially E. L. Inabinet, Director of the South Caroliniana Library of the University of South Carolina, who over the years has acquired for his library many of the letters here published. In addition, we are grateful to him and his staff for making available to us the resources of his library. We also want to express our special thanks to Katharine Hantz, formerly on the staff of the University of Arkansas Library, in which much of the research for our annotation was done, for the help she gave us in obtaining interlibrary loans of books, periodicals, and microfilms otherwise inaccessible to us. To Virginia Rugheimer, former Librarian of the Charleston Library Society, we are also most grateful for making available to us the resources of that library. James B. Meriwether, McClintock Professor of Southern Letters at the University of South Carolina and former Director of the Southern Studies Program there, has kindly brought to our attention a number of Simms' letters we would otherwise not have discovered, and he and his assistants have generously helped us with material necessary for our annotations. John C. Guilds, Professor of English and Dean of the J. William Fulbright College of Arts and Sciences at the University of Arkansas, has been of assistance in letting us know of letters he has found while doing research towards a biography of Simms. E. Lee Shepard, Editor of the *Virginia Magazine of History and Biography,* has gone out of his way to answer various inquiries about Simms' contemporary Virginians.

We want particularly to express our gratitude to Ben D. Kimpel, Professor of English at the University of Arkansas, for his aid in deciphering Simms' handwriting, his advice on many matters, and his willingness to proofread much of the work. To Juliet Eaves we are grateful for many things, but chiefly for her encouragement and her help in proofreading.

Many people have given us aid in searching for Simms' letters and in providing us with information needed for our annotations. The following list of names is, we know, an inadequate expression of our gratitude: Harriet E. Amos, Assistant Archivist, Emory University Library; Bette M. Barker, Archivist, Archives and History Bureau of the New Jersey State Library; James J. Barnes, Professor of History, Wabash College; the late E. Milby Burton, former director of The Charleston Museum; Paul I. Chestnut, Manuscript Department, Duke University Library; Richard M. Cox, Curator of Manuscripts, Maryland Historical Society Library; Anthony Cucchiara, Long Island Historical Society; Thomas L. Gaffney, Curator of Manuscripts, Maine Historical Society; Anne M. Gordon, Librarian, Long Island Historical Society; Robert L. Harned, Reference Librarian, Charles Patterson Van Pelt Library, University of Pennsylvania; W. Edwin Hemphill, Editor of *The Papers of John C. Calhoun;* Herbert Hucks, Jr., Archivist, Wofford College; James E. Kibler, Jr., Professor of English, University of Georgia; Margaret Lawrence, Bamberg, South Carolina; Charles E. Lee, Director, South Carolina Department of Archives and History; Harriott Cheves Leland, Archivist, Middleton Place Foundation; Kenneth A. Lohf, Librarian for Rare Books and Manuscripts, Columbia University Library; Douglas MacDonald, Manuscript Assistant of Special Collections, Mugar Memorial Library, Boston University; Kenneth H. MacFarland, Librarian Emeritus, Albany Institute of History and Art; Thomas L. McHaney, Professor of English, Georgia State University; David Moltke-Hansen, South Carolina Historical Society; Rayburn S. Moore, Professor of English, University of Georgia; the late Edd Winfield Park, Professor of English, University of Georgia; Edward Rainey, Grand Secretary of The Grand Lodge of the Most Ancient and Honorable Society of Free and Accepted Masons for the State of New Jersey; Jean S. A. Robertson, Reference Librarian, University of Glasgow Library; Anthony A. Roth, Historical Society of Pennsylvania Library; David J. Rutledge, Greenville, South Carolina; R. Baird Shuman, Professor of Education, Duke University; Susan B. Tate, Assistant Special Collections Librarian Emeritus, University of Georgia Libraries; Robert E. Tucker, Jr., Georgia Historical Society; the late Arlin Turner, Professor of English, Duke University; Mary Ann Wimsatt, Professor of English, Southwest Texas State University; and John R. Woodard, Director of the Baptist Historical Collection, Wake Forest University.

We want to thank the following people, institutions, and libraries for permission to print manuscripts in their collections: Universiteits-Bibliotheek, Amsterdam; the Boston College Library; the

Trustees of the Boston Public Library; the Department of Special Collections, Mugar Memorial Library, Boston University; the Bowdoin College Library; the Department of Manuscripts, the British Library; the Charleston Library Society; the Chicago Historical Society; the Cincinnati Historical Society; the Public Library of Cincinnati and Hamilton County, Ohio; the Connecticut Historical Society; the Dartmouth College Library; the Duke University Library; the Collection of the George Peabody Department, Enoch Pratt Free Library; the James Duncan Phillips Library, Essex Institute, Salem, Massachusetts; the University of Georgia Libraries; the late Katherine Dearing Goodwin, Athens, Georgia; Marjorie Griffin, Los Angeles, California; the Houghton Library, Harvard University; the Henry E. Huntington Library, San Marino, California; the Indiana Historical Society Library; the Iowa State Department of History and Archives; the George Steele Seymour Collection, Knox College Archives, Galesburg, Illinois; the Lehigh University Library; the Library of Congress; the Maine Historical Society; the Marietta College Library; the Maryland Historical Society; the William L. Clements Library, University of Michigan; the Minnesota Historical Society; the Pierpont Morgan Library; the National Archives; the Trustees of the National Library of Scotland; the New-York Historical Society; the Henry W. and Albert A. Berg Collection, the New York Public Library, Astor, Lenox and Tilden Foundations; the Manuscripts and Archives Division, the New York Public Library, Astor, Lenox and Tilden Foundations; the University of North Carolina Library; the Historical Society of Pennsylvania; the Rare Book Department, Free Library of Philadelphia; the Princeton University Library; the Putnam Museum, Davenport, Iowa; the Redwood Library and Athenæum, Newport, Rhode Island; Charles H. Ryland, Warsaw, Virginia; the Scripps College Library; Edwin T. Sims; the South Carolina Historical Society; the South Caroliniana Library, University of South Carolina; the Edgar Allan Poe Collection, Humanities Research Center, University of Texas at Austin; the Watkinson Library, Trinity College, Hartford, Connecticut; the Tulane University Library; the Virginia Historical Society; the Clifton Waller Barrett Library, University of Virginia Library; the Manuscripts Department, University of Virginia Library; the Earl Gregg Swem Library, The College of William and Mary; Yale University Library; and Wake Forest University Library. We also want to thank the many librarians of other libraries who answered negatively our inquiries about Simms' letters.

MARY C. SIMMS OLIPHANT
T. C. DUNCAN EAVES

POSTSCRIPT

I want to express my appreciation to the Board of Trustees and to the President of the University of Arkansas for granting me Off-Campus Duty during the Fall Semester of 1975 so that I could work uninterruptedly collecting and editing the letters in this volume.

T. C. D. E.

CONTENTS

DEPOSITORIES OR OWNERS OF MANUSCRIPTS

AU	Department of Manuscripts, Universiteits-Bibliotheek, Amsterdam
BL	British Library
BPL	Boston Public Library
BoC	Boston College Library
BoU	Department of Special Collections, Mugar Memorial Library, Boston University
BowC	Bowdoin College Library
CHCPL	Public Library of Cincinnati and Hamilton County, Cincinnati, Ohio
CHR	Charles H. Ryland, Warsaw, Virginia
CHS	Connecticut Historical Society
CLS	Charleston Library Society
ChHS	Chicago Historical Society
CiHS	Cincinnati Historical Society
D	Duke University Library
D:JSS	Joseph Starke Sims Papers in the Harry L. and Mary K. Dalton Collection, Duke University Library
DC	Dartmouth College Library
EI	Autograph Collection, James Duncan Phillips Library, Essex Institute, Salem, Massachusetts
ETS	Edwin T. Sims
GU	University of Georgia Libraries
H	Houghton Library, Harvard University
HEH	The Henry E. Huntington Library, San Marino, California
IHS:MC	Mitten Collection, Indiana Historical Society Library
IoSDHA	Iowa State Department of History and Archives,
KC	George Steele Seymour Collection, Knox College Archives, Galesburg, Illinois
KDG	Katherine Dearing Goodwin
LC:KF	Kenrick Fisher Papers, Manuscript Division, Library of Congress
LU	Lehigh University Library
M	The Pierpont Morgan Library
MC	Charles Goddard Slack Collection, Marietta College Library
MG	Marjorie Griffin, Los Angeles, California
MPF	Middleton Place Foundation, Charleston, South Carolina
MU:WLC:BC	The Bradford Club Papers, William L. Clements Library, University of Michigan
MdHS:MR	Mayer-Roszel Papers, Maryland Historical Society
MeHS:F	John S. H. Fogg Autograph Collection, Maine Historical Society
MiHS	Allyn K. Ford Collection, Minnesota Historical Society
NA	National Archives, Washington, D.C.
NCU:BD	Botany Department Collection, University of North Carolina at Chapel Hill
NLS	National Library of Scotland
NYHS:VC	Verplanck Collection, New-York Historical Society

NYPL:A	Anthony Collection, Manuscripts and Archives Division, The New York Public Library, Astor, Lenox and Tilden Foundations
NYPL:B	Henry W. and Albert A. Berg Collection, The New York Public Library, Astor, Lenox, and Tilden Foundations
NYPL:MJ	Merle Johnson Collection, Manuscripts and Archives Division, The New York Public Library, Astor, Lenox and Tilden Foundations
P	Princeton University Library
P:A	Atkinson Autograph Collection, Princeton University Library
PFL	Rare Book Department, Free Library of Philadelphia
PHS	Historical Society of Pennsylvania
PM	Putnam Museum, Davenport, Iowa
RLA	Redwood Library and Athenæum, Newport, Rhode Island
SC	Scripps College Library
SCHS	South Carolina Historical Society
SCL	South Caroliniana Library, University of South Carolina
T:GWC	William Gilmore Simms Letters, George Washington Cable Collection, Special Collections Division, Tulane University Library
TC	Watkinson Library, Trinity College, Hartford, Connecticut
TU:EAP	Edgar Allan Poe Collection, Humanities Research Center, University of Texas
VHS	Virginia Historical Society
VU:CWB	The Clifton Waller Barrett Library, University of Virginia Library
VU:MD	Manuscripts Department, University of Virginia Library
WM:RMH	Robert Morton Hughes Papers, Earl Gregg Swem Library, The College of William and Mary
Y:ACG	A. C. Goodyear Collection, Yale University Library
Y:P	Park Family Papers, Yale University Library

LIST OF LETTERS

In the following list of letters for this volume of the letters of William Gilmore Simms the address as Simms wrote it follows the name of the addressee. Under the address is the postmark, followed by the price of sending the letter. If no address is given, the cover has not survived; if no postmark is given, the cover lacks one. Depositories or owners of the manuscripts of Simms' letters are indicated in the last column. If we have not located the original of a letter, that space is left blank and the source of our text is given in a footnote to that letter.

No.	*Date*	*Addressee*	*Owner or Depository*
		1834	
24a	June 14	PROSPER MONTGOMERY WETMORE | City.	SCL
		1835	
31a	September 10	JOHN P. BEILE | N. York.	NYPL:MJ
31b	September 29	DANIEL KIMBALL WHITAKER | Charleston South | Carolina | Politeness | Mr. Hotchkiss.	SCL
		1838	
62a	January 15	HUGH SWINTON LEGARÉ | (U. S. Congress) | Washington | D. C.	MeHS:F
63a	January 29	HUGH SWINTON LEGARÉ	SCL
65b	April?	EDWARD L. CAREY | Philadelphia | Pa. | By | Mr. McCarter.	PHS
68a	July 1	EDWARD L. CAREY	PHS
69a	September 25	EDWARD L. CAREY | Philadelphia, | Pa. *Postmark*: New-York | Sep 25 | 13	PHS
69b	October 1?	PARK BENJAMIN	VU:CWB
70b	December 20	EDWARD L. CAREY | Philadelphia | *Postmark* : Midway So Ca | Dem 22 | 25	PHS
		1839	
71c	c. February 7	EDWARD L. CAREY	PHS
71d	February 14	EDWARD L. CAREY	PHS
71e	March	EDWARD L. CAREY	PHS
75a	June 21	CAREY AND HART	PHS
77aa	September 13	CAREY AND HART	PHS
77d	November 10	CAREY AND HART	PHS

No.	*Date*	*Addressee*	*Owner or Depository*
		1840	
94a	November 25	CAREY AND Hart | (Publishers) | Philadelphia *Postmark*: Midway S C | Nov 26 | 25	PHS
		1841	
97(1a)	January 15	GEORGE ROBERTS	BoC
101a	February 21	EDITORS OF THE CHARLESTON *MERCURY*	
110a	June 8	SARAH LAWRENCE DREW GRIFFIN | Macon, | Geo. *Postmark*: Charleston S. C. | Jun 9 | Mail	MG
113a	August 10	GEORGE ROBERTS	NYPL:B
116a	September 8	SARAH LAWRENCE DREW GRIFFIN | (Ed. Ladies Family Compa.) | Macon, | Geo. *Postmark*: Charleston S. C. | Sep 10 | 18	MG
119(1a)	September 27	SARAH LAWRENCE DREW GRIFFIN	MG
119b	September 29	SARAH LAWRENCE DREW GRIFFIN	MG
120a	October 14	SARAH LAWRENCE DREW GRIFFIN	MG
122b	November 3	SARAH LAWRENCE DREW GRIFFIN and BENJAMIN F. GRIFFIN | Macon, | Geo. *Postmark*: Midway S C | Nov 3 | 25	MG
125a	December 23	PATRICK HENRY WINSTON	
		1842	
126a	January 10	ISRAEL KEECH TEFFT | Savannah | Geo. *Postmark*: Midway S C | Jany 11 | 18	SCL
128b	March 9	ISRAEL KEECH TEFFT	SCL
128c	March 12	ISRAEL KEECH TEFFT	SCL
135a	June 7	RUFUS WILMOT GRISWOLD	Y:P
139a	July 15	MITCHELL KING	SCL
139b	July 24	BENJAMIN F. GRIFFIN	MG
140b	August 8	JOHN NEAL	H
140c	August 11	RICHARD HENRY WILDE | Augusta, | Geo. *Postmark*: Charleston S. C. | Aug 12 | 12	GU
141a	August 18	SIDNEY BABCOCK | (Publisher) | New Haven, | Conn. *Postmark*: Charleston S.C. | Aug 18 | 25	VU:CWB
147a	December 26	RICHARD HENRY WILDE | Augusta | Geo. | With | a Bundle.	PM
		1843	
148a	1843?	ISRAEL KEECH TEFFT	SCL
149(1a)	January 10	MITCHELL KING | Charleston	CHCPL
149b	February 23	CAREY AND HART	PFL

No.	*Date*	*Addressee*	*Owner or Depository*
315a	July 20	RUFUS WILMOT GRISWOLD | Philadelphia *Postmark*: New-York | 27 Jul | 5 cts.	H
321a	c. September 2	LOUIS ANTOINE GODEY | Ed 'Ladies Book' | Philadelphia. *Postmark*: Charleston S. C. | Sep 3 | 10	SCL
330a	October 22	ISRAEL KEECH TEFFT | Savannah | Geo. *Postmark*: Charleston S. C. | Oct 22 | 5	AU
336a	November 18	THOMAS WILLIS WHITE	TU:EAP
		1847	
358a	February 20	WILLIAM ALFRED JONES | New-York. *Postmark*: Midway S C | feby 22 | 10	SCL
379a	May 21	WILLIAM HENRY CARPENTER	SCL
379b	May 27	CAREY AND HART | (Publishers) | Phildelphia *Postmark*: New-York | 28 May | 5 Cts.	NYPL:B
		1848	
430a	July 1	JOHN JAY	
453a	November 29	CAREY AND HART | (Publishers) | Philadelphia Pa. *Postmark*: Midway S C | Decr 2 | 10	PHS
		1849	
470a	February 27	BRANTZ MAYER | Baltimore | Md. *Postmark*: Charleston S. C. | Mar 2 | 10 | Paid	MdHS:MR
473b	March 10	BRANTZ MAYER | Baltimore | Md. *Postmark*: Midway S C | Mch 11 | 10	MdHS:MR
475a	March 17	CHARLES ÉTIENNE ARTHUR GAYARRÉ | New Orleans, | La. *Postmark*: Charleston S. C. | Mar 23 | 10 | Paid	T:GWC
476 (1a)	c. March 29	BRANTZ MAYER | Baltimore, | M'd. *Postmark*: Midway S C | March 30 | 10	MdHS:MR
478a	April 12	WILLIAM BROWN HODGSON	BoC
482a	May 5	MATTHEW FONTAINE MAURY	NA
488a	May 17	CHARLES ÉTIENNE ARTHUR GAYARRÉ | (Secy of State) | New Orleans | La. *Postmark*: Midway S C | May 18 | 10	T:GWC
491b	June 28	CAREY AND HART | (Publishers) | Philadelphia *Postmark*: Charleston S. C. | Jun 28 | 10	PHS
493a	July 6	THOMAS CAUTE REYNOLDS	VU:CWB
495a	July 13	BRANTZ MAYER	MdHS:MR
495b	July 13	CHARLES ÉTIENNE ARTHUR GAYARRÉ	T:GWC
497a	July 23	NATHANIEL BEVERLEY TUCKER	WM:RMH

No.	Date	Addressee	Owner or Depository
512b	November 6	BRANTZ MAYER | Baltimore, | Maryland. *Postmark*: Midway S C | Nov 9 | 10	MdHS:MR
514a	December 6	ABRAHAM HART	SCL
		1850	
519a	January?	ABRAHAM HART	PHS
528a	March 25	JOSEPH STARKE SIMS | Pacolet Mills P. O. | South Carolina *Postmark*: Midway S C | Mch 26 | 5	ETS
529a	April 3	GEORGE REX GRAHAM | 134 Chesnut St. | Philadelphia | Pa. *Postmark*: Midway S C | Apl 5 | 10	SCL
534a	April 15	WILLIAM JAMES RIVERS | Charleston | So Caro. *Postmark*: 2	SCL
539a	May 31	WILLIAM JOHN GRAYSON | Washington | D. C. | Favored by | Mr Richards	NYPL:A
		1851	
564a	January 30	JOHN NEAL	H
577a	April 8	ABRAHAM HART | (Carey & Hart) | Philadelphia | Pa. *Postmark*: Midway So Ca | April 10 | 10	PHS
580a	May 7	ABRAHAM HART | (Carey & Hart) | Philadelphia *Postmark*: Midway | May 8 | 10	PHS
596a	September 27	ABRAHAM HART | (Carey & Hart) | Philadelphia *Postmark*: Charleston S. C. | Sep 28 | [*Three-cents stamp*]	PHS
600a	November 1	ABRAHAM HART	PHS
601a	December 3	HENRY CAREY BAIRD | (Publisher) Philadelphia. | Pa. *Postmark*: Charleston S. C. | Dec 3 | 10	PHS
		1852	
603a	January 5	GEORGE SEABROOK BRYAN | Charleston | S. C. *Postmark*: Charleston S. C. | 1	D
603b	January 5	ABRAHAM HART | (Carey & Hart) | Philadelphia. *Postmark*: Charleston S. C. | Jan 7 | 5 cts	PHS
618a	March 6	ISRAEL KEECH TEFFT	SC
618b	March 13	BRANTZ MAYER	MdHS:MR
618c	March	BRANTZ MAYER	MdHS:MR
625a	May 10	BRANTZ MAYER | Baltimore. | M'd. *Postmark*: Midway S C | May 11 | [*Three-cents stamp*]	MdHS:MR

No.	Date	Addressee	Owner or Depository
626a	May 29	CHARLES E. TEFFT	TC
626b	June 23	GEORGE PALMER PUTNAM	VU:CWB
626c	July 1	GEORGE PALMER PUTNAM	SCL
630a	July 15	GEORGE PALMER PUTNAM	VU:CWB
630b	July 28	HENRY WILLIAM RAVENEL	NCU:BD
631a	July 31	BRANTZ MAYER	MdHS:MR
635a	August 13	BRANTZ MAYER	MdHS:MR
648a	November 5	BRANTZ MAYER	MdHS:MR
		1853	
655a	January 5	BRANTZ MAYER	MdHS:MR
663a	May 29	HENRY CAREY BAIRD	PHS
663b	June 10	HENRY PANTON	SCL
669a	July 25	JAMES THOMAS FIELDS	SCL
670a	August 16	JAMES THOMAS FIELDS | Boston. | To introduce | Mr. Paul H. Hayne	SCL
676a	September 29	BRANTZ MAYER	MdHS:MR
687a	December 17	BRANTZ MAYER	MdHS:MR
		1854	
691a	January 12	JAMES CHESNUT, JR.	SCL
692a	January 13	JOHN REUBEN THOMPSON	SCL
694a	January 27	JAMES CHESNUT, JR.	VU:CWB
696a	February 8	BRANTZ MAYER	MdHS:MR
705a	March 17	EDWARD DROMGOOLE | (Atty at Law) | Summit P. O. | Northampton County | North Carolina. *Postmark*: Midway S C | Mch 19 | [*stamp removed*]	SCL
707a	April 3	ROBERT S. CHILTON	VU:CWB
709a	April 28	N. B. MORSE, JR. | Brooklyn | New York.	ChHS
719a	June 26	E. M. WOOD	VU:CWB
735a	October 13	HOWARD PUTNAM ROSS | Albany, | New York *Postmark*: Charleston S. C. | Oct 15 | 5 cts	SCL
738a	November 20	HENRY CAREY BAIRD	PHS
740a	November 27	BRANTZ MAYER	MdHS:MR
746a	December 18	CHARLES ÉTIENNE ARTHUR GAYARRÉ	T:GWC
		1855	
752a	January 8	HENRY CAREY BAIRD	VU:CWB
764a	March 25	RICHARD H. SEE	VU:MD
781a	August 20	WILLIAM MAY WIGHTMAN | (Wofford College) | Spartanburg.	SCHS
793a	December 3	ABRAHAM H. SEE	SCL
		1856	
802a	January 27	JOSEPH WESLEY HARPER	M

No.	Date	Addressee	Owner or Depository
803a	February 12	JAMES CHESNUT, JR.	VU:CWB
811a	June 25	WILLIAM CAREY RICHARDS	P
816a	September 6	JOSEPH WESLEY HARPER	M
824a	November 4	SIGOURNEY WEBSTER FAY	BoU
825a	November 8	WILLIAM CULLEN BRYANT	SCL
829a	November 21	SIGOURNEY WEBSTER FAY	BoU
829b	November 21	[CORRESPONDENT UNKNOWN]	MC
829c	November 21	[CORRESPONDENT UNKNOWN]	SCL
831a	November 24	OCTAVIA WALTON LE VERT	SCL
831b	November 26	M. C. BELKNAP	SCL
		1857	
841a	March 15	OCTAVIA WALTON LE VERT	SCL
842 (1a)	March 31	GEORGE PAYNE RAINSFORD JAMES	SCL
844a	April 18	CHARLES ÉTIENNE ARTHUR GAYARRÉ	T:GWC
846a	May 7	CHARLES ÉTIENNE ARTHUR GAYARRÉ	T:GWC
846b	May 9	JUSTUS STARR REDFIELD	SCL
848a	June 16	CHARLES ÉTIENNE ARTHUR GAYARRÉ	T:GWC
849b	July 26	JOSEPH WESLEY HARPER, JR.	KC
849c	July 31	JAMES THOMAS FIELDS	BPL
851a	October 30	C. BENJAMIN RICHARDSON	SCL
852a	December 5	NATHANIEL PAINE	VU:CWB
853a	December 13	DAVID H. BARNES	SCL
856a	December 29	WILLIAM G. WHITE	VU:CWB
		1858	
856b	January 1	D. APPLETON AND COMPANY	EI
878a	May 8	THOMAS ADDISON RICHARDS	SCL
881a	June 9	CHARLES H. GORDON	VU:CWB
889a	July 17?	JAMES THOMAS FIELDS	SCL
895a	August 11	NATHAN COVINGTON BROOKS	BoC
895b	August	D. APPLETON AND COMPANY	VU:CWB
		1859	
911a	January 31	BRANTZ MAYER	MdHS:MR
916a	February 25	ALEXANDER DALLAS BACHE	M:HS
916b	February 26	WILLIAM FULLER	SCL
920a	March 15	A. J. SMITH	P:A
933a	June 13	WILLIAM JAMES RIVERS	SCL
943a	August 18	WILLIAM JAMES RIVERS	SCL
946a	September 12	WILLIAM JAMES RIVERS	SCL
949a	October 10	WILLIAMS MIDDLETON	MPF
949b	November 2	WILLIAMS MIDDLETON	MPF
949c	November 2	EDWARD HERRICK, JR.	BoC
		1860	
973a	March 22	AUGUSTUS BALDWIN LONGSTREET	
973b	March 22	WILLIAM FULLER	SCL

No.	Date	Addressee	Owner or Depository
976a	April 18	ROBERT E. EARLE	GU
999a	c. November 1	WILLIAM FULLER	SCL
1003a	November 9	GEORGE WILLIAM BAGBY	VHS
1026a	December 13	BENSON JOHN LOSSING	Y:ACG
1027a	December 17	GEORGE WILLIAM BAGBY	VHS
1029a	December 19	SIMON GRATZ	PHS
1029b	December 19	THOMAS HICKS WYNNE	HEH
		1861	
1060b	October 21	ANNA WASHINGTON GOVAN STEELE FULLER	SCL
		1862	
1067a	January 16	JOHN REUBEN THOMPSON	SCL
1068a	February 25	GEORGE WILLIAM BAGBY	VHS
1068b	March 24	GEORGE WILLIAM BAGBY	VHS
1071a	April 10	GEORGE WILLIAM BAGBY	VHS
1071b	May 5	RICHARD YEADON | *Private.* | (Courier Office) | Charleston, | S. C. *Postmark*: Midway S C | May 8 | [*five-cents stamp*]	CHS
1071c	May 31	WILLIAM JAMES RIVERS | (College) | Columbia, | South Carolina *Postmark*: Midway S C | May 3 | [*stamp removed*]	SCL
		1864	
1104a	September 5	PAUL HAMILTON HAYNE	NLS
1110a	November 22	THEOPHILUS HUNTER HILL | Raleigh,—| N. C. *Postmark*: Midway S C | Nov 24 | Paid 10	D
		1865	
1112a	January 5	WILLIAM GREGG | Graniteville | S. C. *Postmark*: Midy S C | Jan 8 | Paid 10	BowC
1137a	October 5	[CORRESPONDENT UNKNOWN]	SCL
1141a	December 17	ORVILLE JAMES VICTOR	SCL
1141b	December 18	JAMES A. H. BELL	SCL
1142a	December 28	E. J. MATHEWS	SCL
		1866	
1190a	August 15	GEORGE W. ELLIS	
1200a	October 5	ORVILLE T. SMITH	VU:CWB
		1867	
1221a	February 1	HENRY BARTON DAWSON	RLA
1229a	March 1	[CORRESPONDENT UNKNOWN]	VU:CWB
1238a	March 21	PAUL HAMILTON HAYNE	SCL
1247a	May 1	CHARLES WARREN STODDARD	VU:CWB

INTRODUCTION

In the years that have followed the 1956 publication of Volume V of *The Letters of William Gilmore Simms,* various friends and acquaintances have brought to our attention letters by Simms acquired by libraries or discovered during the cataloguing of manuscript collections already owned. A number of these seemed to us of sufficient importance to warrant a new survey of holdings of libraries and private collections in the hope that enough uncollected letters could be found for a supplementary sixth volume of the *Letters.* This extensive survey was made during the fall and winter of 1975, and we have been fortunate in discovering over two hundred letters not included in our first five volumes. These cover the years 1834 through 1870, the year of Simms' death—in fact, the last definitely dated letter in this volume is, so far as we now know, the last letter Simms wrote. Taken as a whole, they add considerably to our knowledge of Simms and of his times and are of great value in any final assessment of Simms the man and the writer. Some offer further proof of what was already known or suspected about Simms from his published letters; others contain new information about Simms and his works, his opinions on society, on literature, and on politics, his assessment of himself as a man and as a writer and of the position of an author in the South (especially in South Carolina), and his aspirations for himself, for his fellow writers, and for his native state and his country. These letters will undoubtedly be used, as those already published have been widely used, by writers on Simms and on the social, political, and literary history of his times.

Over one-fourth of the letters in this volume were written before 1845, a period for which Simms' known extant letters were fewer in number than for the later periods of his life. A good many of these are addressed to publishers or to editors of periodicals. Notable among them are the large group of letters to his publisher Carey and Hart, of Philadelphia, and the somewhat smaller, but equally important group to Sarah Lawrence Drew Griffin, who was struggling to establish and keep going a literary magazine in Macon,

Georgia. The problems of a southern writer with a northern publisher become abundantly clear with the fear of manuscripts going astray and, when actually lost, whole chapters of a book having to be rewritten; the decisions on when to publish a book, under what title, and in what form; and proof failing to reach the author in time for correction. In the letters to Mrs. Griffin we get a picture of Simms giving advice on starting and maintaining a periodical in the South, an almost impossible task. Simms warned that there will be a scarcity of manuscripts, subscribers will be difficult to obtain and more difficult to keep, and the magazine will inevitably fail, as almost all southern periodicals have failed, largely because the people of the South have little "intellectual appetite."

Except for an occasional flicker of optimism, this last theme is one frequently touched upon in the letters in this volume. In undertaking the editorship of the *Magnolia*, Simms wrote to Richard Henry Wilde on August 11, 1842: "You will do me the favor to believe that in consenting to conduct a periodical, I am not governed by pecuniary considerations. I do not expect to *make* but to *lose* money by the process. But I feel every day, more & more, the humiliating relation in which the South stands to the North, and the gross injustice which naturally results from such relation. To change this in some [degre]e is my object, and for which I make some sacrifices." And in the hope that Charles Étienne Arthur Gayarré would write for his *Southern Quarterly Review*, he wrote to him on May 17, 1849: "You will readily concur with me upon the necessity of securing for the South an organ of opinion. Until this is done, we can never have a literature, & scarcely a character." His *Magnolia* and his *Southern and Western Monthly Magazine and Review* had already joined those southern periodicals that had sunk "into that gloomy receptacle of the 'lost and abused things of earth'" (a prediction he had made for southern periodicals in his letter to Philip Coleman Pendleton of December 1, 1840). The *Southern Quarterly Review* was shortly to follow, and in 1857 Simms wrote in a review of William James Rivers's *A Sketch of the History of South Carolina to the Close of the Proprietary Government by the Revolution of 1719* that it is the duty of southerners "to find fitting recompense for those who write your histories, and, at great self-sacrifice, without the motive of emolument, assist your reputations, interest and renown, in the great arena of nations. . . . After a hundred years of politics, we are scarcely assured of one day of political existence. In truth, our capacity to live, as a free people, in the possession of our rights, has become a most perplexing problem; and we are constrained to think, that all this is due to the one melancholy fact, that, while we have *encouraged all sorts of politicians,* we have, as studiously, *discouraged all sorts of literature.* No writer of the South has ever earned *one* dollar by all his labors in behalf of the South." And he adds that if we fail "in the great *mental* struggle," we will perish "in every other field of conflict." "In truth, we are to remember that literature is a new thing in the South, and especially in South Carolina. . . . It never had—never was suffered to have—an existence." Simms' considered opinion of the attitude of the South, and especially of South Carolina, towards literature and towards authors, in particular himself, is nowhere more clearly stated than in his letter to Rivers of June 13, 1859, in which he pointedly refers to this review of Rivers's book. One must of course remember that Simms was at times captious and imperious and when beset with disappointment apt to lash out against his world—and also apt then to reverse himself. His letters, with their copious annotations, furnish a record of the many honors he received. They record also such appreciation as the successful efforts of his South Carolina friends to raise funds in 1862 to rebuild his plantation home, accidentally burned.

In spite of Simms' melancholy view of the difficulties of the literary man in the South, he constantly strove to create, almost single-handedly, a literature for the South, and in the letters written before 1845 we see him not only writing novels, tales, poems, reviews, essays, and a history of South Carolina, but also attempting to keep the *Magnolia* alive. By the end of 1844 he had started to launch his *Southern and Western Monthly Magazine and Review* (more thoroughly documented in the letters in Volume II than here), and before long he was to take over the editorship of the *Southern Quarterly Review.* Many of the letters written during the years 1849–1854 are concerned with his attempt (often vain) to obtain contributions for his *Review* when the publishers were able to pay little for articles and welcomed amateur authors who did not have to be paid. A long series of letters to Brantz Mayer points up Simms' difficulties, as do occasional letters to James Chesnut, Jr., Charles Étienne Arthur Gayarré, Matthew Fontaine Maury, and others. In the letters of the 1850s we also see Simms writing for periodicals other than the *Review*, reviewing books for Charleston newspapers (which helped to fill his library shelves if not his purse), and writing novels and revising for Redfield's edition those already written. Anonymous publication of his novels still appealed to Simms. On January 5, 1852, he wrote to Abraham Hart that "in our country, the better course is to be anonymous as often and as long as possible. Our people, in their passion for change & novelty (even more great than that of the Athenians) soon tire of familiar names, and a reputation is seldom long the guarantee for circulation."

A number of the letters written in 1856 concern Simms' northern lecture tour, arranged by Justus Starr Redfield and doubtless designed in part to promote his edition of Simms' novels. One letter to Octavia Walton Le Vert of November 24, 1856, which deals in part with this ill-fated tour, cancelled shortly after it began, contains Simms' advice on where to publish: "I learn with great surprise that you propose to publish it [her *Souvenirs of Travel*] in Mobile. This, according to my experience, will seriously prejudice your claims & impair the success of your performance. If you are not too deeply committed to any local publisher, I beg leave most earnestly, to counsel you to get it issued either in New York, Boston or Philadelphia. There, they are professed publishers, with all the mechanism for giving you large circulation." His recent, humiliating rebuff by his New York audience had not kept him from recognizing that it was only in the North that an author could publish with any hope of real success.

A letter to Benson John Lossing written on the eve of the war, on December 13, 1860, shows Simms' concern for his northern friend were he to visit South Carolina to do research at that time: "No personal character however high, no interposition of friends, however influential, though they might save you from personal danger, could serve you to elude suspicion, or to prevent annoyance. . . . Such is the exasperation of our *people* at large that they are no longer controllable by their politicians." For the war years themselves the letters are few in number (as indeed they are in Volume IV), but several letters to George William Bagby, editor of the *Southern Literary Messenger*, and letters to John Reuben Thompson, Richard Yeadon, and a few others add to our knowledge of Simms' reaction to this trying time.

Simms was still fighting his own battle for southern literature. He sent John Reuben Thompson poems for his proposed collection of "patriotic poetry inspired by the Independence of Dixie," and on January 16, 1862, told him of his own grand project: "My plan is to commence the publication of a 'Library of the Confederate States', publishing a volume monthly, and, *seriatim*, representing the states severally. Thus I propose a collection of the writings of old Beverley Tucker, of Virginia, of Hammond, of S. C. &c. . . . New works to be interspersed as prepared, and a wholesome variety to be sought in History, Biography, Statesmanship, Poetry & Fiction. I see that you have publishers in Richmond, disposed to make a beginning. Consult with them on the subject, & you & I may, perhaps better than any body else, put the machine in motion." The "machine" never moved, but when Columbia was burned by Sherman's army in 1865 Simms had in the press of Evans and Cogswell of that city his own "Southern Mother Goose." It is perhaps, then, not surprising to find him in a letter to Theophilus Hunter Hill of November 22, 1864, devoting considerable space to a criticism of Hill's poem "Narcissus" and at the same time giving a clear expression of his poetic creed.

The letters written after the war show, as do those in the earlier volumes, Simms renewing his old northern friendships, making trips to the North, and attempting to repair his broken fortunes through the frantic use of his pen. They help to complete the picture of the strength Simms showed as a financially ruined man, broken in health and sick at heart, yet still determined to do what he could for himself and for his family and friends. Simms was, as always, eager to help younger writers, and in his review of John Esten Cooke's *Wearing of the Gray*, quoted in part in a footnote to a letter to Cooke of June 4, 1867, he gives excellent advice to the novelist who hopes his characters will become living people.

Numerous sketches written by Simms' friends record his genial nature, his storytelling charm, his personal magnetism, and his generous, kindly spirit. A picture of a less socially charming but more fundamentally serious side of his nature is given in an early letter to Mrs. Griffin, of June 8, 1841: "I am a very unconventional sort of person; very ardent in my temperament, very earnest in my object; express myself usually in the first words that come uppermost; write usually as I talk; and as the world goes, am accounted a somewhat rude, blunt man. An unamiable character, enough, but one which, perhaps, is not without its virtues, which, in my case, I must leave to the charity of my friends to find out for themselves." The letters included in this and the earlier volumes now enable us to assess the truth of this self-portrait. Whether a twentieth-century reader is called upon to exercise his "charity" is, of course, an individual matter.

Except as indicated below, the texts of Simms' letters are printed verbatim—misspellings, variations in spelling, and faulty punctuation being retained. Throughout his life, as Simms often tells his correspondents, he was a hasty writer, and though his handwriting becomes more difficult to decipher in his later years, certain problems in transcription occur in letters written at all periods of his life. Simms' punctuation is occasionally ambiguous in that it is difficult to distinguish between a comma and a period; in such cases our choice has been determined by Simms' usual practice or the practice of his day. In capitalization, Simms is sometimes inconsistent, and we have retained his clear inconsistencies. But his capital and lower-case "c's," "l's," "e's," "a's," and "v's" are often so similarly written (even within the same letter) that we have had to decide whether in each instance he intended a capital of lower-case letter—we hope that our interpretations are logical for Simms. Very occasionally, when Simms' misspelling is obviously the result of extreme haste—for example, "Woodland" and "Alaabama"—we have corrected it and in a footnote indicated what he actually wrote. In a few letters we have supplied necessary punctuation (usually a period or a quotation mark) and words necessary to the sense and enclosed them in square brackets. Square brackets are also used to enclose words or parts of words lost through damage to the manuscript, but a footnote explains that here the manuscript is torn. Raised letters have been lowered.

In annotating the letters in this volume we have followed the general principles outlined by us in the Preface to Volume II of the *Letters*. Our aim has been twofold: to throw as much light as we can on the matter of the letters themselves and to connect them with the letters already published in our first five volumes. Identifications and explanations necessary for each letter are made in the customary manner. When fuller information is to be found elsewhere in the letters, cross-references are made to those letters by date and by number. When the information is in another footnote, reference is made to the number of the footnote and the date and number of the letter. A reference to "introductory sketch" is to one of the short biographies included in "Simms' Circle" or "The Family Circle," pages xc–cl of Volume I. Upon occasion some of our footnotes explain matters left unexplained or only partly explained in letters printed in earlier volumes (this is especially true for those in Volume I), and we have in these cases referred to the earlier letters. In a few instances we have corrected errors in the annotations to the letters in Volumes I–V. The reader of *The Letters of William Gilmore Simms*, therefore, would be wise to read this volume along with the first five volumes.

We have followed throughout the style in footnoting used in Volumes II through V. A "see" reference enclosed by parentheses indicates that the reference deals *only* with the matter immediately preceding the parentheses—perhaps only the name of a person, perhaps the contents of an entire sentence. A "see" reference that stands alone as an independent sentence indicates that the reference deals with *all* the preceding information of the footnote. In making reference to published books, in order to make as clear as possible the particular imprint concerned, we have given bibliographical data exactly as they appear on the title pages. Thus, in one footnote, "Carey and Hart" and "Carey & Hart" may be given. The inconsistency is that of the publisher, not that of the editors of Simms' letters.

Appendix II to Volume V of the *Letters* contains letters that came to our attention after the volumes in which they chronologically belong were printed. The numbers we gave those letters indicate their correct position in the chronological arrangement: in other words, letter 21a should follow letter 21, letter 588a should follow letter 588, and so forth. The letters in this volume are similarly numbered in order to indicate their correct position in the chronological arrangement: letter 24a should follow letter 24; letter 65b should follow letter 65a (printed in Appendix II to Volume V); letter 77aa should come between letters 77a and 77b (both printed in Appendix II to Volume V), and so forth. In a few cases we were faced with the problem of numbering a letter that falls between a letter printed in one of the earlier volumes and one included in Appendix II to Volume V; such letters are numbered "(1a)." When in footnotes we refer to letters in Appendix II to Volume V, we have italicized the number of the letter so that the reader will look for it there rather than in this volume.

The Letters
of
William Gilmore Simms

1834-1870

SUPPLEMENT

1834–1844

24a : To Prosper Montgomery Wetmore[1]

N. Y. Saturday Mg. June 14. [1834][2]

dear Col.

I have, at length, determined upon a visit to Washington, and shall be pleased to have letters from you to some of the distinguees—some of those mighty men in whom office lies, and from whom sinecurists have wherewithal to hope and dream. Today I go on 'a party of pleasure' to visit the Passaic, and shall not therefore have an opportunity until tomorrow of seeing you. But tomorrow afternoon, all things agreeing, I shall do myself the pleasure of a stroll up to 508 Broadway, with the hope of a dish of tea from the hands of wife W.[3] All this, however, under the supposition that you are not otherwise disposed of then. Forgive the scrawl, but my pen has but a single nib, and is a gift—so the adage saves it. With all respect, for all—

I am yrs ever sincerely

W. Gilmore Simms

P. M. Wetmore, Esq.

I propose to go on Monday Mg.

24a

[1]Wetmore, New York City businessman and minor poet, was at this time a colonel in the New York State Militia. See introductory sketch.

[2]Simms dated this letter "Saturday Mg. June 13." Simms' first visit to New York City was in 1832, but during the years 1832–1869 when June 13 fell on Saturday (1835, 1840, 1846, 1857, 1863, and 1868) he was not in New York City. The handwriting of the letter is early, and since Simms was not in New York City in June of 1832, 1835, 1836, 1837, 1838, 1839, 1840, 1841, 1842, 1843, or 1844, the letter must have been written in 1833 or 1834. We do not know where he was in June 1833, but on June 12, 1834, he wrote from New York City to James Lawson in Washington (24) that he planned to see him there the following week. His remark in this letter to Wetmore that he proposes to go to Washington on Monday morning, is almost certain proof that the letter should be dated June 14, 1834.

[3]The former Lucy Ann Ogsbury.

31a : To John P. Beile[1]

N. York Sep. 10 [1835][2]

dear John

Enclosed you have two letters, all that I can write at this moment, which you will do me the favour to deliver. I have also left the trunk at the Harpers[3] which you were good enough to promise to take on with you. You will please take care of it until I reach Charleston, and should that never be the case, pray hand it over to Mr. C. R. Carroll for my little daughter.[4] God bless, and be with you, my friend & a pleasant voyage.

Ever regardful,
Yours

Simms

J. P. B.

31a

[1]Beile, who died in 1840, was a bookseller at 296 King Street, Charleston.

[2]This letter could have been written in any year between 1832, when Simms first visited New York City, through 1836, the year before his marriage to Chevillette Eliza Roach—if he had been married when he wrote the letter, he would surely have asked Beile to turn the trunk over to his wife. The date "(1835)" is written on the letter, possibly by Beile, and we have arbitrarily accepted it.

[3]The firm of J. & J. Harper (later Harper & Brothers) began publishing for Simms in 1832.

[4]After the death of his first wife, Anna Malcolm Giles, on Feb. 19, 1832, Simms and his little daughter, Anna Augusta Singleton, stayed for long periods at Clear Pond, one of the plantations in Barnwell District owned by Charles Rivers Carroll. See introductory sketch of the Carrolls.

31b : To Daniel Kimball Whitaker[1]

[September 29, 1835][2]

dear Sir

Enclosed I send you a review of "The Linwoods" by Mr. Paulding. For this you will doubtless be grateful enough. Pray see to the careful correction of the press, for his hand is a difficult one, for printers as well as other people.[3] Accompanying the Publishers forward you a copy in sheets, of Paulding's ["]Letters from the South."[4] They will be published next week. Put no signature to the review, nor, in any wise give it officially as his, though you may talk it over where you please else

Yrs &c.

Simms

29th. Sep.

D. K. Whittaker Esq

31b

[1]For Whitaker, see note 93, Sept. 20, 1843 (174), and note 168, Aug. 2, 1850 (545). In 1835 he was editor of the *Southern Literary Journal, and Monthly Magazine* (Charleston). Simms was a frequent contributor of poems, tales, articles, and parts of plays during the editorship of Whitaker (1835–1837) and that of Bartholomew Rivers Carroll, Jr. (1838). Some of his contributions are published under his name, others under the pseudonym "Linus," still others under initials, and some anonymously. One suspects that the magazine would have failed for lack of material if Simms had not been so prolific.

[2]The year is established by Simms' references to Paulding's works. See notes 3 and 4, below.

[3]"The Linwoods," a review of Catherine Maria Sedgwick's *The Linwoods; or, "Sixty Years Since" in America*, 2 vols. (New York: Harper & Brothers, 1835), was published in the *Southern Literary Journal*, I (Nov. 1835), 175–176.

[4]Paulding's *Letters from the South, Written during an Excursion in the Summer of 1816*, 2 vols. (New York: James Eastburn & Company, 1817), was republished by Harper & Brothers in 1835 as Vols. IV and V of an edition of Paulding's works. In his short notice of Paulding's *Letters* in the *Southern Literary Journal*, I (Nov. 1835), 207, Whitaker remarks that "we are indebted to the publishers for a copy of this very interesting work, transmitted to us, in sheets, before its publication in New-York."

62a : To Hugh Swinton Legaré[1]

Woodlands, near Midway,
Jan. 15. 1838.

dear Sir

Let me thank you for your attentive consideration, and pray permission once more to trespass upon you. Away from the seaboard, I lack the usual facilities of steamboat conveyance to transmit packages which are of too great size and too little importance to justify the expense of the mails. One of these, to a Philadelphia publisher, I take the liberty to enclose to you, and will be glad if you will cover it with your frank to its place of destination.[2] A free construction of the privileges will give you sufficient sanction for so doing, as I may plead that the contents are strictly *pro bono publico.* I see that the Philistines[†] are upon you. Arguments are wasted upon such people, and they must be met, I take it, with a weapon like Sampson's and their own—the jawbone of the ass. I am glad to see that you have wasted little breath upon them, and I smiled (with you no doubt) when I read the challenge of the venerable Mr. Slade.[3] The game as the French say, is not worth the candle.

62a

[1]Legaré (see introductory sketch) was elected to the U.S. House of Representatives in 1836 and served for one term only.

[2]The "Philadelphia publisher" is Carey and Hart (see letter to Legaré of Jan. 29 [63a]). The package probably contained part of the manuscript of *Richard Hurdis* (see letter to Carey of Apr.? 1838 [65b]).

†[e]t al abolitionists. [Simms' note.]

[3]The *Congressional Globe*, VI, 41, reports that on Dec. 20, 1837, William Slade (1786–1859), Representative from Vermont, spoke at great length on referring "two memorials . . . praying for the abolition of slavery and the slave trade in the District of Columbia to a select committee." When Slade began to take up the subject of slavery in the states, he was interrupted by Legaré, who "hoped the gentleman from Vermont would allow him to make a few remarks before he proceeded further. He sincerely hoped that gentleman would consider well what he was about before he ventured on such ground, and that he would take time to consider what might be its probable consequences. He solemnly entreated him to reflect on the possible results of such a course, which involved the interests of a nation and a continent. He would warn him, not in the language of defiance, which all brave and wise men despised, but he would warn him in the language of a solemn sense of duty, that if there was 'a spirit aroused in the North in relation to this subject,' that spirit would encounter another spirit in the South full as stubborn. He would tell them that, when this question was forced upon the people of the South, they would be ready to take up the gauntlet. He concluded by urging

Perhaps, after all, you will be compelled to propose a restoration of the District of Columbia to the original proprietors—thus removing the only legitimate bone of contention. They may have the stones of the Capitol for hauling. I am almost persuaded—and I believe I speak for many of our old friends,—that it may be the wisest course to submit to Congress the inquiry, as to what proportion of the stock in trade they will give as our going quietly out of the concern. The recommendation of a Commission, seriously to examine into the relative claims to profit and stock, of the slave & non slave holding states, will have an effect upon the latter infinitely beyond any arguments upon the abstract question which the best of us could furnish. As to a dissolution of the Union, I do not much fear it,—and still less should I be apprehensive of its effects upon Southern interests & securities. These states could not be long apart, and mutual necessities which make the inevitable will, and best for us the judgments of the majority would soon bring them together again. The abolitionists are of that green-eyed breed that left England quarreling with their neighbours and with themselves—that quarreled with the Quakers and the witches,—and

---

on the gentleman from Vermont to ponder well on his course before he ventured to proceed." When Slade attempted to continue with the reading of a paper on slavery in Virginia, the southern delegations walked out to meet in the room of the Committee for the District of Columbia.

The Charleston *Courier* of Dec. 25 reports Slade's speech and Legaré's interruption. A letter in the *Courier* of Jan. 1 signed "Barnwell" (Simms?) commends the southerners in Congress for their stand against abolitionists, and on Jan. 4 the *Courier* quotes the Washington correspondent of the Philadelphia *Inquirer* on "the glorious appeal, recently made by our distinguished and eloquent Representative, in Congress, in behalf of the rights of the South and the duration of the Union, against the criminal fanaticism of their abolition foes": "By permission of Mr. Slade, Mr. Legare indulged a copious flood of remarks, mild, warm, yet persuasive, in themselves, and calculated in an eminent degree, to reach the hearts of all. In the name of God Almighty, in the name of our common country, in the united names of Justice and Mercy, in the name of all that is pure above, and rational below, by all that was sacred and holy, by all that is held dear to man, or worthy of the adoration of the angels, he begged, implored, conjured, the gentleman from Vermont, to abandon the speech he had commenced, and then suffer peace to be restored to the councils of our beloved country.

"Such a burst of passion, such a storm of eloquence, never before escaped the lips of mortal man. St. Augustine at Rome, St. Paul in the pulpit, Brutus before the people, or Marc Anthony in the Market place in the city of the Cesars, in their proudest days—never appeared so imposing and attractive as did Mr. Legare to-day, and the eloquence of the man will never be erased from the tablets of my memory."

would quarrel with God Almighty himself, if he was not providential to have resolved never to admit them into near neighbourhood with him.

You must pardon me for trespassing so long; but perhaps, it will not be unimportant to you to be shown how this business moves one—and possibly, many—of your constituents. To me, under my present views of matters & things, it is of little real importance—certainly not of vital importance—if we were to secede from the Union; and the policy might be a good one, if it were only to bring the "blatant beast"[4] to his senses. I think the course of the abolitionists-states, highly favorable to Texas—it will have the effect of forcing her into the Union; though with ten thousand rifles she is scarcely wise in halting where she is.[5] Mexico is still a well fortuned damsel, and like most such, is any thing but invulnerable to proper manhood. Yrs Ever &c

W. Gilmore Simms

63a : To Hugh Swinton Legaré

Woodlands. Jan 29. [1838][1]

My dear Sir

I am truly sorry for having trespassed so unprofitably upon you. I knew not the precise degree of your limitations, and in my simplicity of heart, took it for granted that a Representative was beyond all laws. Let me, as such is not the case, trespass still further upon you, by praying you to pay such expenses as have been incurred,

[4]A monster, "a dreadfull feend, of gods and men ydrad," kept by Detraction and Envy in the *Faerie Queene*, Book V, Canto xii, Stanza 37. See also Book VI, where the Blatant Beast is allegorical of slander.

[5]Texas declared its independence from Mexico on Mar. 2, 1836, and established the Republic of Texas. There was considerable controversy over the annexation of Texas by the United States because of the addition of a large slave-holding state to the Union, but on Dec. 29, 1845, Texas technically became a state and on Feb. 19, 1846, one in fact.

63a

[1]Dated by Simms' remarks concerning "the packet" that he had asked Legaré to frank and send to "a Philadelphia publisher." See letter to Legaré of Jan. 15 (62a).

and holding me your debtor until we meet in Charleston, which, I trust, will be in spring following. You will also oblige me by forwarding the packet, as you propose, by any private hand, to whom you think you may entrust it safely, to the original address in Phila.;—provided such opportunity offers within a week after the recpt of this. Should it not—though the purse weeps—send it on by the Mail. I will instruct Mr. Carey[2] by letter, on the instant, of your possession of the packet & he may provide some mean for getting it. I hope, if we are to have any abolition troubles, that your share may be moderate. With due respect, I am

Yr servt &c.

W. Gilmore Simms

Hon. H. S. Legaré.

65b : To Edward L. Carey

[April? 1838][1]

dear Sir

I sent you from Charleston last week, the two concluding chapters of R. H. I trust before you recieve this, you will have the entire work in possession, and hasten on to the publication. While in Charleston, I entrusted my secret to Mr. McCarter, the Bookseller, in whose integrity I can rely, and he begs that you may send him one hundred copies—I suppose on your usual terms—which I doubt not that he will dispose of readily. He commonly sells from 150 to 200 copies, of all my books.[2] Are there any tidings of better things

[2]Edward L. Carey, partner in the firm of Carey and Hart. See introductory sketch of the Carey brothers.

65b

[1]Dated by Simms' reference to the manuscript of *Richard Hurdis; or, the Avenger of Blood. A Tale of Alabama*, published anonymously in 2 vols. (Philadelphia: E. L. Carey & A. Hart, 1838). See letters to Carey and Hart of Apr.? and May 1, 1838 (*65a* and 66). By the latter date the firm had apparently received all of the manuscript of the novel.

[2]James J. McCarter was the proprietor of a bookstore at 112 Meeting Street. See the Charleston *Directory* for that year.

in the Book Market?—What say the Banks—specie & nonspecie paying.[3] Do they intend to continue costive only to destroy our kindred occupations. Can it be that such are their objects—certainly such are the cruel consequences of their evil doings. I trust you keep well in health & spirits, and, having some hopes yourself, can help me to a new supply.

Ever yours &c

W. Gilmore Simms

E. L. Carey, Esq.

68a : To Edward L. Carey

Charleston, S. Carol. July 1. [1838][1]

My dear Sir,

Mr. McCarter, who will hand you this, is in our secret, and one of the few friends in whom I have confided. I have authorized him to make any contract for me, with any publisher, giving a preference however, to your brother, for the disposition of the Copyright of a new romance which I have in preparation, entitled "the Damsel of Darien". This will be ready in October or before; and it will give me pleasure should Mr. H. C. Carey, not determine upon its purchase, if he could then make his arrangements with you.[2] Mr.

[3]In 1837 the banks, led by the Bank of the United States of Pennsylvania, had stopped payment in specie. In July 1838, Governor Ritner of Pennsylvania by proclamation required all of the banks of his state to resume payment in specie by Aug. 1. By the fall of 1838 resumption was general except in the Southwest. See Edward M. Shepard, *Martin Van Buren* (Boston and New York: Houghton, Mifflin and Company, [1899]), pp. 348–349.

68a

[1]Dated by Simms' remarks about *Richard Hurdis* ("the experiment"), published later that year.

[2]In our introductory sketch of the Carey brothers the information we give about Henry Charles Carey's connection with the booktrade is inaccurate. Carey (1793–1879), son of Matthew Carey (1760–1839), became a junior partner in his father's firm in 1817, and the name of the firm became M. Carey & Son. Later, in 1821, it was changed to M. Carey & Sons after the marriage of Matthew Carey's daughter, Frances Anne, to Isaac Lea, who was taken in as a junior partner. Upon Matthew Carey's retirement in 1822, Henry and his brother-in-law purchased the firm, which for a while was known as H. C. Carey & I. Lea, then as Carey, Lea & Carey a few years after Henry's brother, Edward, entered the firm in 1822. In

Mc.C. will probably give you a large order for R. H. His sales of my books generally, are very large—a circumstance, perhaps, chiefly owing to his personal regard for the author. I trust that R. H. will justify, by its own merits, any exertions which, on other grounds, he may make in its behalf. May we soon hope for the experiment?

Yrs with much Esteem
&c

W. Gilmore Simms

Recieved the History of Brazil—a fine copy and in good order.[3] I trust it is not too extravagant for a poor author.

69a : To Edward L. Carey

Private
New York, 25th. Septr. [1838][1]

Dear Sir

By the 'Mirror' you will see that 'R. H.' has found favor in the sight of that Journal. I presume you have seen the notice of which

1829 Edward withdrew from the firm and entered into partnership with Abraham Hart, and Carey, Lea & Carey became Carey & Lea. In Jan. 1833 William A. Blanchard joined the firm as a partner, and the name was changed to Carey, Lea & Blanchard. Henry retired on Oct. 1, 1838, and the firm then became Lea & Blanchard. For a full account of the firm, see David Kaser, *Messrs. Carey & Lea of Philadelphia: A Study in the History of the Booktrade* (Philadelphia: University of Pennsylvania Press, [1957]).

Henry Carey's firm bought the copyright of Simms' new novel, and *The Damsel of Darien* was finished in June 1839 (see letter to Paulding of June 16 [74]) and published in 2 vols. by Lea and Blanchard later that year.

[3]The only history of Brazil that we can locate published before the date of this letter is *The History of the Brasils from the Original Discovery, in 1500, to the Emigration of the Royal Family of Portugal, in 1807*(London: J. T. Ward & Co., 1808).

69a

[1]Dated by Simms' reference to the notice of *Richard Hurdis* in the *New-York Mirror*, XVI (Sept. 22, 1838), 103. The reviewer finds the novel "powerfully wrought" and "ably written." "It proclaims the catastrophe a little too abruptly— and a similar fault is evident throughout. . . . But the author tells his terrible tale of retribution with a force and correctness of style, a power of description, and an earnestness and directness of manner, which amply redeem the minor defects of his story. . . . The interest is well sustained throughout, and there is a harrowing power in many of the scenes. . . . We shall do injustice to this extraordinary work

I speak. Pray, in the event of your writing me in this place, address to the care of "James Lawson, Esq."[2] that your communications may not trouble any unnecessary hands. Your efforts should be chiefly addressed to the special circulation of 'R. H.' in the South-west. In Alabama, and particularly, Mississippi it strikes me, the circulation of the book will be much greater than you have anticipated. At least we may hope so.

Respectfully
Yr obt Sert

W. Gilmore Simms

E. L. Carey Esq

69b : To Park Benjamin[1]

Monday Mg. [October 1? 1838][2]

My dear Sir

I cover to you herewith a sheet of the verses, the only one yet given me by the Printers. Pray let me 'mind you—without desiring to be thought pertinacious—of the promise you made me to gather

---

if we attempt to give any idea of its merits by a quotation. It should be read and judged as a whole."

[2]Lawson, one of Simms' very closest friends, was at this time vice-president of the Washington Marine Insurance Company. See introductory sketch of the Lawsons.

69b

[1]Benjamin (see note 4, Jan. 7, 1843 [149]) was at this time editor of the *American Monthly Magazine*.

[2]The year is established by Simms' reference to "a sheet of the verses, the only one yet given me by the Printers," and to his request for "copies of the Am. Mon. Magazine" (see notes 3 and 4, below). Since Simms is living in "lodgings," he obviously is in New York City, where he undoubtedly had gone to oversee the printing of *Southern Passages and Pictures* (New York: George Adlard, 1839) and *Carl Werner, an Imaginative Story; with Other Tales of Imagination*, 2 vols. (New York: George Adlard, 1839), both published late in 1838 and reviewed in the Dec. 22 issue of the *New-York Mirror* (see note 11, Mar. 30, 1839 [72]). Apparently Simms was not planning a trip to New York City when he wrote Lawson c. Sept. 2 (69), but he did go and had evidently only recently arrived when he wrote to Carey on Sept. 25 (69a). He had to return to Charleston early in Oct. because of the death of his infant daughter, Virginia Singleton, on Oct. 10 (see letter to Lawson of Nov. 5 [70]). We have therefore dated the letter Oct. 1, a Monday, though Oct. 8 is just as probable a date, and Sept. 24 is possible.

up copies of the Am. Mon. Magazine, in order to complete my set.[3] Let me have at the same time the nos. of the Review, not including the first which I already have.[4] If you send these to Mr. Adlard,[5] he will do me the favor to send them to my lodgings—

Respectfully—
Yr obt servt &c

W. Gilmore Simms

Park Benjamin Esq.

70b : To Edward L. Carey

Woodlands,[1] near Midway Dec 20 [1838][2]

My dear Sir

I have put up for you something like ten chapters of the novel which is to succeed R. H. by the same author. The title, you will see, is somewhat altered from what was intended. I call it "Harry Vernon, a Tale of Mississippi",—but there will probably be a second title, which I have not yet determined upon, which may possibly include the other.[3] You will have to send me proofs as before, but these may be taken in galley, and a whole sheet at a time might contain at least 24 or 30 pages. I should like the work printed in the size & style of the novel of mine called 'Mellichampe',[4] unless

[3]Simms wrote to Lawson on Jan. 16, 1838 (63), that he lacked Vol. V of the *American Monthly Magazine* (really N. S., I, for Mar.-Aug, 1835).

[4]The *New York Review* began publication in Mar. 1837 under the editorship of Caleb Sprague Henry (1804–1884). George Dearborn, publisher of the *American Monthly Magazine*, was also publisher of the *Review* through the issue of July 1838. Presumably Benjamin was to get copies of numbers of both magazines from the publisher.

[5]George Adlard, publisher of *Southern Passages and Pictures* and *Carl Werner*, and his family became friends of Simms and his family and after the Civil War visited Woodlands. See letter to Hayne of Mar. 6, 1869 (1348).

70b

[1]Simms wrote *Woodland.*

[2]Dated by Simms' remarks about the manuscript of *Border Beagles; a Tale of Mississippi*, "By the author of 'Richard Hurdis,'" 2 vols. (Philadelphia: Carey and Hart, 1840). See letters to Carey and Hart of 1839.

[3]Harry Vernon is the hero of *Border Beagles.*

[4]*Mellichampe. A Legend of the Santee*, 2 vols. (New York: Harper & Brothers, 1836).

your second edition of 'R. H.'[5] is so nearly like that, as to make the difference of little importance; and, if so, I should prefer that you should make "H. V." identical in appearance with 'RH.' In sending me the proofs omit the title, or send some catchword at the head in place of it, so as to decieve any who may casually set eyes on the sheets.[6] Send duplicate sheets in successive mails, that, if one be lost, the other may take its place. This work will probably make 220 pages per vol. of the size of 'Mellichampe'. Pray send me two copies of the new edition of R. H. Let them be put up carefully & sent to the care of J. P. Beile—to whom I send this week the bundle of M.S. for you. Say to me in your next, at what time Miss Leslie will desire her contribution for "the Gift".[7]

Yrs Ever &c

Simms

E L. Carey Esq.

71c : To Edward L. Carey

[c. February 7, 1839][1]

dear Sir

The accompanying packet contains two stories submitted to Miss Leslie, from which she will make her choice, as my contribution

---

[5]The second edition of *Richard Hurdis* is dated 1838. We have been unable to determine the exact date of publication.

[6]The secret of the authorship of *Richard Hurdis* was so well kept that apparently Simms' friend Bartholomew Rivers Carroll, Jr. (see introductory sketch of the Carrolls), did not know it. Carroll published a long, devastating review of the novel in his *Southern Literary Journal*, N. S., IV (Dec. 1838), 332–349, in which he remarks, "The work, as a whole, is certainly to be condemned in unsparing terms. . . . We like better the vein of our own novelist, Simms, who to a few faults, unites many excellencies."

[7]Eliza Leslie (see note 27, Nov. 5, 1834 [26]), Henry Charles Carey's sister-in-law, edited *The Gift* for Carey and Hart. The annual was published for the years 1836, 1837, 1839, 1840, 1842, 1843, 1844, and 1845. Simms offered Miss Leslie the choice of two stories for *The Gift . . . for 1840*, "The Lazy Crow" and "The Arm-Chair of Tustenuggee"; she chose the former (see following letters to Carey).

71c

[1]Dated by Simms' letter to Carey of Feb. 14, 1839 (71d), in which he writes that "last week I sent you two stories for the 'Gift'" ("The Lazy Crow" and "The Arm-Chair of Tustenuggee").

to the "Gift" for the ensuing year. When she has made her selection you will do me the favor to cover the article which she declines, in a close packet, and address it immediately to "Mr James Lawson, Vice President of the Washington Marine Insurance Company, New York", and forward it to him by a private and safe opportunity. He will be prepared to appropriate it. How would you like for the 'Gift' some half dozen pages 'by the Author of *RH.*'[2] Perhaps, it would be of benefit to all parties. You are, I doubt not, in reciept by this time of the MS. of the book.[3] When you last wrote it had scarcely time to reach you. With best respects

Yrs ever

W. Gilmore Simms

E. L. Carey Esq

71d : To Edward L. Carey

Feby. 14. 1839

My dear Sir

Along with this I send you a batch of proofs which reached me last night. If your Printer continues to pour them upon me so fast, I fear I shall fall behind hand; and with this fear, I shall even now have to set to work, to make up my lee way. Other & pressing tasks have compelled me to throw aside my 'Vernon', though I shall be able to send you M. S. by the very first safe hand. The style of the page suits me very well. It is much superior to that of the first ed. of R. H. (By the way, do send me to Beile's care two copies of the second edition.) Since you resolve that 'Harry V.' should not be the name, let it be called "The Yazoo Borderers"—a Tale of Mississippi. Last week I sent you two stories for the "Gift"—or rather, one of the two, giving to Miss L. the privilege of taking which she pleases;

[2]Nothing "by the author of 'Richard Hurdis' "as published in *The Gift* for any year.

[3]*Border Beagles.*

and both if she pleases.[1] That which she does not wish, you will do me the favor to send by a safe opportunity, to the address of Mr. James Lawson, Vice Presd. of the Washington Marine Ins. Compy. of New York. It is intended for a similar publication to yours, and he will have instructions what to do with it.[2]—Yours Ever

W. Gilmore Simms

E. L. Carey Esq.

71e : To Edward L. Carey

Woodlands, near Midway
March [1839][1]

My dear Sir

Within one hour after the reciept of your letter of the 9th. I returned the sheet contg. pfs. from 97 to 108 to the Post Office. Pray let me have the proofs of all the matter sent. There has been a miscarriage of five chapters, a portion of which I shall have to

---

71d

[1]The two stories were "The Lazy Crow. A Story of the Cornfield" and "The Arm-Chair of Tustenuggee. A Tradition of the Catawba." Miss Leslie chose the former, published in *The Gift . . . for 1840*, pp. 41–72. The same volume contains Simms' "Ellen Ramsay," pp. 222–228.

We erred in assigning Simms' letter to Carey and Hart dated Feb. 1 in which he says he is enclosing "a note for Miss Leslie accompanying a story for the next vol of the Gift" to the year 1839 (*71b*). It probably was written in 1836 and the story, therefore, was "Jocassée," published in *The Gift . . . for 1837*, pp. 56–82.

[2]In Mar. 1838 Simms wrote to Carey (71e) that he had "not heard from you or Miss Leslie which of the Tales she has chosen," and on Mar. 30 he wrote to Lawson (72) that he had written to "a friend in Phila. to forward you a story to be offered to [Monson] Bancroft for the Magnolia." On June 1 he wrote to Carey (*73a*) that his "friend in New York has not received the M. S. story which you tell me was sent by Miss Leslie," and on June 18 he asked Lawson (75) whether he had "recieved a small packet from Carey & Hart or Miss Leslie, containing a story ['of American diablerie'] of some fifty pages. I instructed them to send one to you, which I wrote you to give to Bancroft." Evidently by the time Lawson received the story Bancroft had decided not to issue *The Magnolia* for 1840. On July 7 and again on July 20 Simms asked Lawson (76 and 77) to have the Harpers return the manuscript to him. "The Arm-Chair of Tustenuggee" was published in *Godey's Lady's Book*, XX (May 1840), 193–201.

71e

[1]Dated by Simms' remarks about the loss of part of the manuscript of *Border Beagles*. See letters to Carey of June 1 (*73a*) and to Carey and Hart of Oct. 28 (*77c*).

rewrite, and this I can only do well by a perfect knowledge of the contents of chap. 10. This will be productive of a degree of delay which may increase your printers impatience and rouse his choler, but you must pacify him by assurances of a great deal more work from the Alabama Author—an assurance which, I trust, for the prosperity of all parties, will be realized. When we get started again there shall be no more delay. Indeed, but for some unlooked for toils at home, the preparation of my romance for Lea & Blanchard,[2] and the belief that you would neither commence so soon upon the work nor proceed so rapidly, I should have provided you with a plentiful supply. It may be that in a month or two, I will require you to break ground for another, new, anonymous author, in an entirely new field.[3] But this anon. Touching the title you must be the best judge. Make it what you please. It struck me, that "Border Beagles, a Tale of the Yazoo Frontier" would be a good one, but— 'A Tale of Mississippi' will, perhaps, be as significant & no less popular. Choose you between 'em. How goes on the sale of R. H. Second Edition? Did you send me the copies I asked for. I percieve that the Southwestern journals are clamorous in applause, and this

[2]*The Damsel of Darien.*

[3]Evidently Simms already had in mind *As Good as a Comedy: Or, the Tennesseean's Story*, published anonymously by A. Hart, Philadelphia, in 1852. In his letter to Lawson of June 27, 1845 (261), he mentions it as "a thing of 150 pages to be written."

should lead to good profits.[4] I have not heard from you or Miss Leslie which of the Tales she has chosen.[5]

Yours Ever &c

Simms

E L. Carey Esq.

I find an awkward error at p. 69, Chap. 5 of the proofs which I have, which as it stands uncorrected in my duplicates, may have been suffered to remain uncorrected in that retd. to you. *Selon les*

---

[4]Since Simms usually calls newspapers "newspapers" or "papers" and occasionally refers to periodicals as "journals," we assume that he here means "periodicals." At this date, however, there was only one periodical published in the Southwest, the *Southron* (Tuscaloosa, Ala.), edited by Alexander Beaufort Meek (see the "Prospectus" of the *Southron* in the Tuscaloosa *Independent Monitor* for Dec. 1, 1838, which states that there are no periodicals published in Alabama, Mississippi, Louisiana, and Tennessee). *Richard Hurdis* is reviewed, probably by Meek (see introductory sketch), in the *Southron*, I (Jan. 1839), 52–62. The writer of this long, enthusiastic review begins with praise of the novel's "intrinsic merits, as a romance of great spirit and ability—of thrilling incident and glowing passion." He remarks on the anonymity of the author: "That he is a Southron however, is evident from the inscription 'to the Hon. John A. Grimball of Mississippi, by a friend and *countryman*,' and by the sectional spirit, the antipathy to the Yankees,—breathing throughout the book. Beyond this, concerning the authorship all is conjecture and doubt." "These circumstances,—the anonymousness, not the least,—have served to render this Tale of Alabama, unusually popular in the South-West. Elsewhere it has obtained great popularity, from its intrinsic worth. . . . He [the author] has written a bold and original romance,—in a new field, and in some respects, after a new fashion,—which will stand the scrutiny of criticism, as well as entertain the superficial reader. This we say though we think the book, in addition to many good qualities,—many excellencies,—has many faults, and is deficient in some of the most important properties of a good novel." Among these faults are "its moral tone and temper" ("the portraiture of turbulent passions, and horrid and unnatural deeds," which caters to "a morbid and brutal taste, and should not be pandered to, by any writer"), the failure of the author "in the delineation of female character" ("except for Picket[t]'s wife, and . . . the idiot, Jane, . . . we defy any reader to designate any difference [among the others], if we except the mere *physique*, of one having blue eyes, and another dark ones, and their hair not being of the same color"), a deficiency of "humor and wit," and several historical inaccuracies (for example, "the size and condition of Tuscaloosa, at the time of the story"—"it was the seat of government of Alabama, and had five, instead of one tavern"). If all these faults are avoided in future works, the author "will become,—what we have no doubt he is capable of becoming,—in many respects, decidedly the first of American fictitious writers." It was Meek who, almost four years later, at a public dinner in honor of Simms challenged him as the author of the "Hurdis Novels"—Simms then first publicly confessed his authorship (see note 5, Dec. 26, 1842 [147a]).

[5]"The Lazy Crow" or "The Arm-Chair of Tustenuggee." See note 1, Feb. 14, 1839 (71d).

regles is printed *des* for *les*.—Should it be uncorrected you will have to make one of your Clerks correct it with his pen. There are two or three errors in R. H. which I should like to note in this work—Jane Hurdis is printed for Jane Picket, and Alabama for Tombicbee.[6]

75a : To Carey and Hart

June 21. [1839][1]

Mess'rs Carey & Hart,

Gentlemen.

The copy of Vertot's Knights of Malta may be sent me.[2] If I remember rightly, I commissioned Mr. C. to procure it for me. The duplicate sigs of B. B. did not reach me till yesterday. Another small packet of M.S. has been forwarded, which I trust will reach you, with all succeeding ones, soon & safely. Our next publication shall be arranged, I trust, more satisfactorily to all parties. Would you like to undertake a History of South Carolina, in a single volume 12 mo., or two slender volumes—and on what terms? I should design the single volume for the use of schools. The work might be put forth in two vols. well leaded,—then compressed into

[6]In his "Advertisement" to *Border Beagles* Simms writes: "In the first edition of 'Richard Hurdis,' first volume, page 210, the 'Alabama' is erroneously printed for the 'Tombecbe river.' The same error is repeated at page 162, of the second edition. In the same volume, first edition, page 177, 'Jane Hurdis,' is improperly printed for 'Jane Pickett.' This error is corrected in the second edition. In the present work, *des* règles' occurs for 'les règles' at page 69, vol. i.; and there will be found, scattered through the work, numerous small mistakes of like character, which the reader, while he corrects them, is at liberty to ascribe to the ignorance, the inexperience, or the carelessness of all concerned. An author, removed a thousand miles from his printer and the public, is little likely to heed their clamours about inaccuracies, which the same circumstance makes him peculiarly liable to commit." He continues: "The reader is requested to be indulgent to the inaccuracies of the press, some of which, in 'Richard Hurdis,' were of an annoying and awkward kind; all of them, perhaps, are attributable rather to the writer than to the printer."

75a

[1]Dated by Simms' remarks concerning *Border Beagles*. See his other letters to Carey and to Carey and Hart of this year.

[2]The only translation we can locate of the Abbé René Aubert de Vertot d'Aubœuf's *Histoire des chevaliers hospitaliers de. S. Jean de Jérusalem, appellez depuis les chevaliers de Rhodes, et aujourd'hui les chevaliers de Malte* (1726) is that published under the title of *The History of the Knights of Malta*, 2 vols. (London: G. Strahan and others, 1728).

one. A small edition of the first might find purchasers among general readers, and the other, I doubt not, would prove very profitable in the end.[3] Yrs Ever

W. Gilmore Simms

Mess'rs E. L. Carey & A. Hart.

77aa : To Carey and Hart

Charleston, S. Caro. Sep 13. [1839][1]

Mess'rs Carey & Hart

I regret that Mr. Fogartie,[2] the young man who represents Mr. Beile here in his absence, and to whom the M.S. of Border Beagles has been confided, has not been able to procure an opportunity for its transmission lately. He has had two or three packets in his hands for some time past, and I have just seen him to urge him to avail himself of the first chance that offers. My own sickness, and that of my family,[3] has somewhat interfered with my progress, but, with the exception of a single chapter or two, the work is finished. I trust you will soon receive it all. Are you ready, at once, to undertake another by the same author?[4]

Yrs Ever

W. Gilmore Simms

---

[3]On July 7 Simms wrote to Lawson (76) that he was "now writing a History of S. Carolina, in one vol." *The History of South Carolina, from Its First European Discovery to Its Erection into a Republic: With a Supplementary Chronicle of Events to the Present Time* was published by S. Babcock & Co., Charleston, in 1840.

77aa

[1]Dated by Simms' remarks about *Border Beagles.* See his other letters to Carey and to Carey and Hart of this year.

[2]Probably Samuel Fogartie, an accountant. See note 2, Oct. 28, 1839 (*77c*).

[3]In his letter to Tefft of Aug. 23 (*77a*) Simms calls himself "an invalid." He also complains of "suffering from indispositions of various kinds" in his letter to Lawson of Dec. 27 (78). His wife may have been ill before or after the birth of their daughter Mary Derrille on Sept. 6.

[4]Carey and Hart did not publish another work "by the author of 'Richard Hurdis,' " but in 1842 Lea and Blanchard, Philadelphia, published *Beauchampe, or the Kentucky Tragedy. A Tale of Passion*, 2 vols., as "By the author of 'Richard Hurdis,' 'Border Beagles,' etc."

77d : To Carey and Hart

Midway, Nov. 10 [1839][1]

Mess'rs Carey & Hart

Gentlemen,

Your letter, advising me that the conclusion of "B. B." has not been recieved is a source of positive affliction. I have written to Mr. Beile, by whose Clerk, the M.S.S. were entrusted to some private hand, with a request that he would urge the inquiry to the utmost and instantly, in the hope that the faithless carrier may be discovered. Truly, this poor book has been excessively unfortunate, and the final rewards should be excessively profitable to compensate you for the delay & me for the loss & labor. If in ten days I can get no tidings of the missing copy, I shall go to work to reproduce it—a labor which you may readily concieve to be of the most irksome description, not to speak of the great loss of time which it must occasion to one who has his hands already well filled with other matters. Oblige me, by making my profound regrets to the printer for his annoyances, which it gives me pain to believe can scarcely be less than my own. My best respects to Mr. E. L. C. with congratulations on his restoration to health & home.[2] Yr obt Servt & frd

W. Gilmore Simms

P.S. Address me at "Woodlands, near Midway."

77d

[1]Dated by Simms' remarks about the loss of the manuscript of the conclusion of *Border Beagles*. See letter to Carey and Hart of Oct. 28 (*77c*).

[2]Edward L. Carey had made a trip to Europe. See letter to Carey and Hart of Oct. 28 (*77c*).

94a : To Carey and Hart

Woodlands, Nov 25. [1840][1]

Messrs Carey & Hart

Gentm.

I am glad, that, with returning courage,—probably in consequence of Harrison's election—you have resolved on publishing 'the Gift' once more. I shall endeavor to meet your request in regard to the article[2] and sincerely trust that as your Whiggery has so greatly triumphed, you will regard the interests of literature with more complacency. You have so long considered Van Burenism as the ugly obstacle in the way of public prosperity—the *only* ugly one—that unless you make every thing now wear the *couleur de rose,* you will be liable to be considered false prophets every where. Does not this terror affright you? It should. You are now bound to put forth and publish with Steam Engine Rapidity—to give all your authors constant employment, and to pay them in the best currency that your contemporary & neighbour, Nick Biddle, can devise, *pro bono publico.* Have you thought on these matters. Are you willing to go to press?[3] Because,—I am still,

Yr Ob. Sert. & frd

W. Gilmore Simms

94a

[1]Dated by Simms' reference to William Henry Harrison's election as president of the United States (1840).

[2]In *The Gift . . . for 1842* Simms published "'Murder Will Out.' A Genuine Ghost Story of the Old School," pp. 262–304.

[3]In his campaign against Martin Van Buren, Harrison was supported by the whole Whig Party and by the banks, particularly the Bank of the United States of Pennsylvania. Nicholas Biddle (1786–1844) was president of the Bank of the United States from 1822 until the expiration of its charter in Mar. 1836. At that time it was rechartered in Pennsylvania as the Bank of the United States of Pennsylvania. Biddle continued as president until his resignation in Mar. 1839. Simms, who was a Democrat, was obviously opposed to both Harrison and the Bank.

97(1a) : To George Roberts[1]

P. O.
Woodlands, near Midway
So. Carolina.
Jany 15.
/41

Dear Sir.

Your letter dated the 7th reached me only this day. My professional engagements leave me little time, as my pecuniary necessities leave me little ability, to give my labours gratuitously. I regret this privation quite as much as any of my neighbours, and in proof of this I occasionally display my readiness to oblige, by doing something hurriedly, tho' I greatly fear, at the expense of my reputation, for this or that literary Editor, who like yourself, solicits my contributions. I send you a small piece of verse which may fill, and I hope not unworthily a corner of your journal.[2] I had the pleasure of receiving a copy of your 'Notion' the contents of which were read with pleasure, which, I have no doubt, its succeeding numbers will continue to afford. I shall be happy to receive them.

With our respect
I am Dr Sir. Yr obt Sert.

W Gilmore Simms

Geo Roberts Esq.

97(1a)

[1]Publisher of the *Boston Notion*, one of the "mammoth" weeklies of the time, and of *Roberts' Semi-Monthly Magazine.*

[2]"Stanzas to a Lady Who Asked Why My Verses Were Always Sad," *Roberts' Semi-Monthly Magazine*, I (Feb. 15, 1841), 93. The poem was also published in the *Boston Notion*, II (Apr. 10, 1841), 1. For Simms' later contributions to *Roberts' Semi-Monthly Magazine* and the *Boston Notion*, see note 56, Apr. 8, 1841 (106), and note 3, Mar. 21, 1841 (*104a*).

101a : To the Editors of the Charleston *Mercury*[1]

[February 21, 1841]

To the Editors of the Mercury—

Your kind and indulgent criticism upon "The Kinsmen," contained in your journal of last Saturday, is such as I could have no cause of quarrel with, even if the *amour propre* in my case were more active than it is. But, suffer me to suggest, as a more generous, and in fact, more just, mode of accounting for some of the blunders now charged upon the author, the fact, that the proof sheets were not submitted to him, and no opportunity was allowed him for their revision, prior to the publication of the work. Publishers, it must be remembered, are a very arbitrary sort of people, and have their own ways and times of doing business; with which an author is not often permitted to have any concern. The novel which should have been published in December last, was delayed in consequence of the temporary miscarriage of the MS—a portion of which, in the meantime, most probably made the tour of Canada. The publishers deemed it necessary, in order to the completion of their previous arrangements, to issue the work as soon after the MS. had been received, as possible; and the advantage of reading the proof sheets in person—so important at all times to an author, were lost to him in the present instance. The volumes will be found, accordingly, clouded with errors, many of which are scarcely less monstrous than the one which you have particularly designated and dwelt upon. Oblige me, by supposing that the author, in describing the catastrophe at the close of the first volume, in the passage at arms between the brothers, instead of the word "*heart*" wrote the word "*breast*,"—by which simple substitution, the difficulty ceases, and that he never contemplated—even in the case of an outlaw so obnoxious as the Chief of the Black Riders, to precipitate the

101a

[1]In publishing this letter in the *Mercury* of Feb. 24, 1841, the editors comment: "We know not if the following communication was intended for the public eye by the respected writer—but we will so consider it, as its publication will tend to do him justice, and can do him no harm." We want to thank Professor James E. Kibler, Jr., of the University of Georgia for bringing this letter to our attention.

denouement by a single moment of time. For the correction of the remaining errors, wherein they conflict with the sense, the reader must be left to his own sagacity. It will not require the exercise of much, if, in addition to his thinking, he will employ the smallest grain of charitable allowance.[2] I might, *en passant,*[3] suggest a few considerations in answer to one objection to a part of the design contained in your notice of the work—but this is scarcely necessary, and might be construed to trench somewhat on the proprieties of my position.[4] Believe me, gentlemen, to be perfectly conscious of the kind and generous spirit in which your opinions have been expressed.[5] Hurried, and not in health

I am, respectfully as ever
Your obt. servant and
friend,

W. GILMORE SIMMS.

Woodlands,[6] Feb. 21.

---

[2]The reviewer of *The Kinsmen: Or the Black Riders of the Congaree. A Tale*, 2 vols. (Philadelphia: Lea and Blanchard, 1841), in the *Mercury* of Feb. 20 calls the work Simms' "best novel." He continues: "The interest is admirably sustained throughout, the descriptions happy, and without that *appearance* of elaboration, which often detracted from the merit of pictures in his former novels, and the narrative is very spirited. It is not without faults, and some grave ones. The diffuse and miscellaneous dialogue between the brothers, while engaged in a deadly hand to hand conflict with daggers, could hardly have been more unnatural, if one of them had chosen that occasion for delivering a lecture on Political Economy: and the result of the fight is miraculous! The curtain falls at the close of the first volume, with a dagger *buried in the heart* of one of the combatants [Edward Conway]. We set him down dead, of course. But in the second volume he is alive, and even recovered, to plot and bustle and fight on to the end. We suspect from this oversight and from sundry verbal errata, such as the 'vexed *Bernadotte*' for 'Bermoothes,' that the book was gotten up in a hurry."

[3]The *Mercury* prints *en pessant.*

[4]The reviewer suggests: "The first sketch of the tale probably closed with the death of the mortally stabbed outlaw, whom on second thought, our author determined to carry through the adventures of his second volume, but forgot to *un*kill him. The alteration of a single word would have been sufficient to render him available, and the oversight, though funny enough, weighs nothing against the skill of the writer."

[5]In printing Simms' letter the editors of the *Mercury* accept Simms' explanation of "breast" for "heart" and remark that "the publishers owe him a second edition as an amende for their ill faith to his manuscript."

[6]The *Mercury* prints *Woodland.*

110a : To Sarah Lawrence Drew Griffin[1]

Charleston, S. C. June 8. [1841][2]

My dear Madame

Your last favor has been lying by me unanswered because of my sheer physical inability to bring myself to the labors of the desk. My little family, myself not exempt, have all been suffering from sickness, not the less annoying because it was not actually dangerous. Even now I am suffering from disordered digestion the certain consequence of our warm climate & my sedentary pursuits. I trust this statement of facts will do away with any impression of neglect which may have been induced by my delay to answer.

I gather from something in the tone of your last letter that I must have said some thing in one of mine which was obnoxious to misconstruction.[3] Let me in this place assure you of my innocence

---

110a

[1]Mrs. Griffin (1812–1872) and her husband, Benjamin F. Griffin (1808–1887), both natives of New England, settled in Macon, Ga., in 1835. She was the author of a number of schoolbooks designed for use in the South (see note 13, Sept. 8, 1841 [116a]), published by her husband, who also wrote schoolbooks addressed to a southern audience. In 1856 the Griffins moved to Brunswick, Ga., and four years later to Manhattan, Kans. This letter and the following letters to the Griffins are concerned largely with her periodical, the *Family Companion and Ladies Mirror* (Macon, Ga.). The first issue of this periodical is dated Oct. 15, 1841, the last Feb. 1843.

All of the letters to the Griffins included in this volume of Simms' letters are printed in Robert A. Rees's and Marjorie Griffin's "William Gilmore Simms and *The Family Companion*," *Studies in Bibliography*, XXIV (1971), 109–129. Our texts are from photographic copies of the originals in the possession of Marjorie Griffin, who has kindly given us permission to include the letters in our volume.

[2]Dated by Simms' remarks about the illness of his family and of himself (see letters to Lawson of May 29 and to Roberts of June 2, 1841 [109 and 110]), about his pledge for "two large works to be finished this summer" (see note 6, below), and about his notice of the "Prospectus" of the *Family Companion* (see note 4, below).

[3]We have not located these letters. But judging from Simms' following remarks in this letter, one can assume he repeated to Mrs. Griffin the same ideas on southern periodicals he had at some length expressed in his letter to Philip C. Pendleton, published in the *Magnolia*, III (Jan. 1841), 1–6 (reprinted as letter 95 in *The Letters of William Gilmore Simms*): southern periodicals will inevitably fail because of the scarcity of good articles, the falling off of subscribers, and the pressure of pecuniary difficulties. "The hope of success for your periodical must be built upon something more than an array of formidable names. Is it upon the increasing intellectual appetite among our people? I wish I could believe it. . . . But, I cannot help but doubt;—and when I sit down to write for a Southern

of intention if such is the case. I am a very unconventional sort of person; very ardent in my temperament, very earnest in my object; express myself usually in the first words that come uppermost; write usually as I talk; and as the world goes, am accounted a somewhat rude, blunt man. An unamiable character, enough, but one which, perhaps, is not without its virtues, which, in my case, I must leave to the charity of my friends to find out for themselves. Do me the kindness, my dear madam, to take for granted that I have every disposition to promote your wishes, and to do justice to your claims, as well as Lady as Litterateur. Do not be angry at my inadvertencies; believe only that an habitually earnest—perhaps, dictatorial habit of speech, has beguiled me into a too great plainness of utterance, in which I betray my own bluntness of character, without meaning to offend the sensibilities of yours. I trust I am forgiven for all my unwitting offences.

In giving utterance to my opinions on Magazines, & Southern Literature, I was prompted by a desire to comply with your request. It is not improbable that I exaggerate the difficulties in your way. I trust sincerely you will find it so. But in thinking as I do, I was bound to speak sincerely. The easiest task in the world, is to answer as the world would wish it be answered. My choice is not the easiest, and my opinions, therefore, are not likely to be often the most popular. If in the case of young beginners, however, they produce an extra degree of caution, and lessen to a certain extent, that wild and sanguine confidence, which in our country ruins so many thousand, my purpose will be answered, and I shall be satisfied. I have no doubt that you know better than I do, the sort of materiel which will better please the great body of readers—nay, with some qualification, I am willing to agree with you; but it does not need that we should attempt a discussion which involves so many controversial points. Enough that I wish you god speed, and will try to do what I can to promote your successes.—The notice of the 'Com-

---

periodical . . . I do so under the enfeebling conviction that my labors and those of the editor are taken in vain;—that the work will be little read, seldom paid for, and will finally, and after no very long period of spasmodic struggle, sink into that gloomy receptacle of the 'lost and abused things of earth,' which, I suspect, by this time possesses its very sufficient share of Southern periodical literature."

panion' which I sent you, contained in the Charleston Courier was only in part written by myself. The portions so eulogistic of the novel, were interpolated by the Editor, who is a very warm friend of mine, and, I believe, conscientiously thinks of the work all that he said. I need not again assure you,—in spite of your very flattering remarks in opposition—that, on this subject, I cannot help differing *in toto* from both of you. I wish it were what you believe it, as well for your sakes as for mine. I regret the mistake about the subject of the plate, but it will not be injurious, and is not of vital moment.[4] Am I to understand that the sketches are from your pencil? Are you able to exclaim with the Italian—"*Anch' io son pittore!*" If so, I should like you to send me some of the illustrative sketches you have made, for though no *manipulator,* I am yet, professedly, a wonderful dealer in grouping & landscape.

I enclose you a batch of sonnets, which I really think among the best of these things which I have ever done.[5] I am very much afraid that I shall be able to do nothing in season of the sort you wish. My engagements with my publishers are very pressing. I am pledged

---

[4]In his notice of the "Prospectus" of the *Family Companion* in the *Courier* of May 27 Simms remarks that Mrs. Griffin, "it is understood, is highly accomplished, well read, endowed with no small critical sagacity, and possessed of a nice discriminating taste, which will be sufficient to guaranty to her lady patrons a *melange* of equal interest and delicacy." Richard Yeadon (see introductory sketch), editor of the *Courier*, praises Simms' *Partisan* in the following passage: "It [the periodical] will contain fine steel engravings from original drawings, illustrative of Southern events, romance and scenery. The first of these, now in preparation for the first number of the work, will be the illustration of a battle piece from SIMMS' elegant and striking novel of the 'Partisan'—an appropriate homage to Southern literature." The first number of the *Family Companion* has as a frontispiece an engraving entitled "The Murder of Sergeant Clough, by the Maniac Frampton" (see note 8, Sept. 8, 1841 [116a]), but this was not the scene from *The Partisan* which Mrs. Griffin had wanted illustrated. In her "Editorial Department" (p. 64) she comments: "Our plate for this number is not what we intended it should be. The volume and page of the Partisan was designated from which the artist was to make the sketch, but from some inadvertance, the wrong *volume* was taken, which changed the entire character of the plate." Apparently the scene Mrs. Griffin wanted is that of Major Singleton addressing his troops prior to their ambush of Amos Gaskens and his Tories (II, Chap. xiii)—a scene certainly more suitable, if less graphic, for a "Companion fit for the holiest place in the world, the Family Circle" (see note 7, Sept. 8, 1841 [116a]). But if the *Courier* is correct, Mrs. Griffin had chosen the ambush itself (II, Chap. xv).

[5]"Heart Fancies: A Series of Sonnets." See note 9, Sept. 8, 1841 (116a).

for two large works to be finished this summer;[6] and to coerce the imagination is to destroy it. The task of inventing against the desire is unfavorable to the author and would be productive of discreditable performances. If I feel the impulse I will obey it and you shall have the fruits. But my daily tasks must now be resumed; and I have written so many small stories that I should really be at a loss for a topic. If the scheme, the groundwork, the agents were suggested to me,—if I had any clue to them, there would perhaps be little difficulty. Recollect, even Shakspeare, with all his invention, stole all his plots—his stories ready made to his hands. I fancied, when I sent you Oakatibbe, that I was actually sendg. you one of my best labors—not as a story perhaps, but as comprising a very bold, original philosophical argument, on a subject, of all others, the most vital to the interests and feelings of the South. The grave questions with regard to the Indian & negro races, I sought to discuss in a style equally fanciful & philosophic, and I am pleased to think that there is a gradual & not slow rising of the public mind in our country to the comprehension of these subjects.[7] You are right in the determination to pursue your way as Editress, alone. I did not suppose that Neal was associated with you. I only thought that you might be blinded to his rashness by his real ability—that you might not know his proverbial indiscretion of character.[8] I am pleased to percieve the solemnity with which you address yourself to your task. Without a stern resoluteness nothing of any value has ever yet been done. That you will do well, & prosper, I not only sincerely wish, but sincerely believe—always with the one reservation, however, against any hopes of extravagant success in the South, unless you do what has never yet [been] done by Southern Editors—secure a

---

[6]By Aug. 16 *Confession; or, the Blind Heart*, 2 vols. (Philadelphia: Lea and Blanchard, 1841), was finished and Simms was already at work on *Beauchampe*. See letter to Lawson of that date (115).

[7]"Oakatibbe, or the Chocktaw Sampson; an Indian Sketch" was published in the second and third numbers of the *Family Companion* (see note 16, Sept. 8, 1841 [116a]). Simms had written the tale (originally called "Slim Sampson") for the *Magnolia* (see letter to Lawson of Feb. 24, 1841 [102]). An earlier version had been published in the *Southern Literary Gazette*, I (Sept. 1828), 142–149.

[8]John Neal (see note 170, Dec. 13, 1843 [186]), Simms' acquaintance and correspondent, was notorious for his erratic and quarrelsome nature. He was a frequent contributor to the *Family Companion*.

large, various host of able contributors, depend upon no amateur literature, let your work contend on equal grounds, so far as type, paper, press work & illustration are concerned, with Northern contemporaries, get good agents, and keep your collector (who shall be honest at the same time) constantly at his tasks. Do not fear, now that your hand is in. Remember what Spenser writes over all the doors but one—"Be bold, be bold, be bold!" Over only one door he writes—"Be not too bold."[9] Touching the articles on Southern Literature, I must say but one word at present. I must wait a little while before I can answer you.[10] I will send the volume of Poems[11] to Mr. Hart.[12] In conclusion, while I still say you have undertaken a very serious labor, one that requires great faith, constancy and diligence, I see nothing which should make you faint or fear. There is nothing in your tasks which a noble woman, energetic, believing, having a deep strong heart, a fervent soul and a good mind, may not compass. You will, I think, if anybody. Respectfully and faithfully, Yr friend

W. G. Simms.

113a : To George Roberts

Charleston, S. C. Augt. 10—[1841][1]

dear Sir

I furnished a Prose Story and a Sketch in verse for the forthcoming annual of Mr. Williams, of your city, who, after keeping them all

---

[9]*Faerie Queene*, Book III, Canto xi, Stanza 54.

[10]Probably Mrs. Griffin had asked Simms to contribute articles on "Southern Literature." Evidently he never found time to enliven the pages of the *Family Companion* with thoughts on this interesting subject. The article entitled "Southern Literature" in the "Editorial Department" of the *Family Companion*, II (June 1842), [180]–181, was written by Mrs. Griffin (see note 6, July 24, 1842 [139a]).

[11]*Southern Passages and Pictures*. See following letters to the Griffins.

[12]Samuel Hart, Sr., bought the bookstore of John P. Beile. See letter to Carey and Hart of Aug. 2, 1841 (113).

113a

[1]After Simms' date someone (probably Roberts) has written "1841"; on the back of the letter (in the same handwriting) is written "W. Gilmore Simms Aug. 10. 1841." The year is substantiated by Simms' reference to Rufus Wilmot Griswold (see note 3, below).

summer, now writes me that they are too long for his work.[2] Will these articles suit you? I suppose the story would make some thirty five pages of the usual novel size. The poem, which I took pains with, contains something between 2 and 300 lines. The story is called "Annihilation." I fancy it is quite as good as most of the stories I have written. The poem I value among the best of the kind which I have yet done. It is called "The Traveller's Rest." Pray let me hear from you at once on the subject, as, wanting money, I must make an early disposition of them elswhere should they not suit you, or should your offer not suit me.[3] I wrote copiously sometime ago to Mr. Griswold, but am not apprised of the rect. of my letter.[4] Your paper has not reached me for some weeks—the mage. not for a month. Very respectfully

Yr ob Serv

W. G. Simms

Geo. Roberts, Esq.

---

[2]David H. Williams was publisher of *The Token.* The editors of the annual for 1842 were Williams and George Stillman Hillard.

[3]Either Roberts did not want the tale or the poem for the *Boston Notion* or *Roberts' Semi-Monthly Magazine*, or he did not offer to pay Simms what he wanted for them. They were published in the *Magnolia*, N. S., I (Nov. 1842), 288–298, 385–388. In his letter to Lawson of Oct. 13 (120) Simms writes that Roberts and Griswold "have not treated me well."

[4]Rufus Wilmot Griswold (see introductory sketch) became editor of the *Boston Notion* with the issue of May 6; he severed his connection with Roberts early in Aug. (see Joy Bayless, *Rufus Wilmot Griswold: Poe's Literary Executor* [Nashville, Tenn.: Vanderbilt University Press, 1943], pp. 36, 41). Simms' letter to Griswold written "sometime ago" is doubtless his letter of June 20 (*111a*), containing autobiographical information for the sketch of Simms in Griswold's *The Poets and Poetry of America* (Philadelphia: Carey and Hart, 1842). Lawson wrote the account of Simms for this volume (see letters to Lawson of Oct. 13 and Oct. 16 [120 and 122]).

116a : To Sarah Lawrence Drew Griffin

Charleston, Sep. 8. [1841][1]

My dear Madam

Your first number was recieved yesterday, & I must confess quite surpasses my expectations. You have done wonders. In fineness of paper, neatness of appearance, general propriety and completeness, your work will bear free comparison with the best of our periodicals. Your letter press too is very good. John Neal's verses are rather less mad than usual & contain some forcible & fine lines.[2] Those by Wilde, though not equal to some other of his pieces, are graceful & sensible.[3] The paper on Classical Literature, by our young countryman Holmes, shows reading and is very well expressed. Perhaps it shows too much reading. The notes are quite unnecessary & cumber the narrative, besides giving an air of pedantry to the paper which lessens the reader's interest as well in the writer as in the subject. If they are to be put in, I would recommend that you throw them at the foot of the columns, and not suffer them to be massed like so many unmeaning hyeroglyphics, to themselves.[4] The article on Education, though very sensible & showing thought is too long.[5] The commonplaces of this subject should be rejected in such essays. Of the tales I cannot well judge having only glanced at a few

---

116a

[1]Dated by Simms' discussion of the first number of the *Family Companion and Ladies' Mirror*, dated Oct. 15, 1841. The Charleston *Courier* of Sept. 29 remarks that "we have received the specimen number" of the magazine.

[2]"One Day in the History of the World," pp. 10–13.

[3]"Lines Written for Viscountess ————'s Album," p. 34. Simms later met Richard Henry Wilde (see introductory sketch) and corresponded with him.

[4]"Outlines of an Essay, on the Causes Which Contributed to Produce the Peculiar Excellence of Ancient Literature" (signed "G. F. H."), pp. 56–59. When the continuation of the essay was published in the issue of Nov. 15, pp. 112–120, Mrs. Griffin took Simms' advice and omitted the notes, remarking in her "Editorial Department," p. 128, that she was "obliged" to do so. George Frederick Holmes (see introductory sketch) became Simms' close friend and correspondent.

[5]"Education," pp. 51–55, by John Darby (1804–1877), at this time professor of chemistry and philosophy at the Georgia Female College.

paragraphs.[6] Your own Editorials (Qu?) betray unnecessary timidity.[7] I suspect you feel alarmed, but you really need not. You give an ample quantity of matter, and in this have the advantage of several of your competitors. I do not think that your artists have been quite successful with the plate. The choice of the subject was very unfortunate. The scene itself, now that my taste is more mature, should never have been written.[8] At all events it is one of those scenes of which the artist could make little or nothing. You recollect, also, that I warned you that the Partisan I considered the most faulty and the least successful of any of my books. You were pleased to think differently, but without impressing me with your own more favorable estimate. How you can give a plate at all, is another subject of wonder.—I intended that my sonnets should be published as a series. I wrote you or meant to write you, that I should regularly give you a contribution of *verse* for each number. Let me beg that you will put the remaining sonnets in a batch together—unless they usurp a place that might be better occupied.[9]—I note your offer for prizes. Perhaps, it would be advisable

---

[6]The first number contains the following tales: "The Ins and the Outs, or the Last of the Bamboozled" ("By a Disappointed Man" [John Neal]), "The Governess" (by Mrs. Emma C. Embury), "The Elopement" (by "M. G. M."), the first part of "The Deed of Gift, a Domestic Tale" (by Samuel Woodworth), and the first part of "Vaudrey, a Tale of the Tierra de Guerra" (unsigned), pp. 13–23, 30–34, 36–42, 44–46, 48–51.

[7] In her "Editorial Department," pp. 63–64, Mrs. Griffin discusses the aims of the *Family Companion*: "To cater for every department of the family—afford a guide in the management of its various concerns, and prepare the sprightly tale to while away the leisure hour, require talents as varied as the subjects themselves. . . . While by our tales and essays we would enliven the fancy, cultivate the taste, and establish correct moral principles, we would cultivate the higher intellectual powers by essays of a more labored character, for the subjects of which the vast fields of Science afford ample materials." She pledges that "all which appears in our pages, shall be pure, elevated, and refined; and we shall labor most industriously to make our publication worthy the name it bears—a Companion fit for that holiest place in the world, the Family Circle—a Mirror from whose reflections images may be formed, which will be models worthy of being copied into the life, actions, and sentiments of the Ladies who may peruse its pages."

[8]The frontispiece to the first number is an engraving ("Painted & Engraved by Jordan & Halpin, N. Y.") entitled "The Murder of Sergeant Clough, by the Maniac Frampton," from *The Partisan*, Chap. 9. This is not the scene from *The Partisan* which Mrs. Griffin wanted illustrated (see note 4, June 8, 1841 [110a]).

[9]Under the heading "Heart Fancies: A Series of Sonnets, by the Author of 'Atalantis,' 'The Yemassee,' &c." is printed one sonnet: "I. Invocation," p. 9. In the number for Jan. 15, 1842 (I, 200–201), Mrs. Griffin under the same heading

to define to your readers what you require for a prose tale, of what length &c.[10] A small prize for the best essay of two or three pages might also be of good results. Of course you have the privilege of publishing such as you please of the unsuccessful articles. Mr. Hart has a subscriber for you, for whom you must send a copy. He, Mr. H., suggests that you should send a *show* copy of the work to him. He is an excellent man and will make a good agent.

I do not know what your calculations are. I trust you may not decieve yourself. I suppose you see the Magnolia.[11] I think it not possible that such a work can be successful. It wants *variety*. Yours has enough; but subscriptions in the South are bad things, and correspondents not to be relied on. Your chance is better as your book is larger, better looking, and promises to compete *on equal grounds with the Northern journals of the same* class. In the number of pages you beat both the N. Y. Companion & Godey's Lady's Book.[12] I have just bought one of your first books for children. I think it very good. It is not improbable that your Class Books for the South will take the lead of all others.—[13]

At this moment I am a laborer at the mill. I have some literary engagements with Northern publishers which scarcely leave me time for sleep. I have written you this scrawl, with tremulous fingers, after penning 20 pages foolscap. In the early part of the season

---

reprinted Simms' "Invocation" and followed it with seven other sonnets: "Contemplation," "Autumn Twilight," "Beauty Visions," "Minstrel Yearnings," "Continued," "The Peace of the Woods," and "The Rivulet."

[10]In her "Editorial Department," p. 64, Mrs. Griffin writes, "We would call the attention of writers to our advertisement for prize pieces.—See cover." In the only copy to which we have had access (that in the Emory University Library) the cover is not preserved. In her "Editorial Department" in the number for Jan. 15, 1841 (I, 256), she offers $200 for the best tale and $50 for the best poem submitted for publication in the *Family Companion*; she specifies no length, "as merit alone will be considered in the decision."

[11]At this time Philip Coleman Pendleton was editor and publisher of the *Magnolia* (Savannah, Ga.). See note 79, Dec. 1, 1840 (95).

[12]Simms was a contributor to the *Ladies' Companion* (New York) and *Godey's Lady's Book* (Philadelphia).

[13]Mrs. Griffin was the author of *The Southern Primary Reader*, *The Southern Second Class Book*, and *The Southern Third Class Book*, all published by her husband. See Bertram Holland Flanders, *Early Georgia Magazines* (Athens: The University of Georgia Press, 1941), p. 62.

sickness, night-watching & finally death in my family,[14] kept me from performing my tasks. It will be November before I am free.[15] This will excuse me to you for not having complied with your request for a story. By the way, when you set up my Indian Sketch, perhaps it will be safer to send me a proof.[16] Send me 2.—by different mails; so that, should one fail the other may be sure. In conclusion, let me say, again—you have done wonders. Your work does equal credit to the taste of the publisher and the talents of the Editor. I have little or no fault to find. What I have, is already expressed. I put up a copy of my poems[17] for you some months ago, but it remains still with Hart waiting for an opportunity to be sent. Can you suggest one? With sincere wishes for your success. I am very respectfully

Yr obt servt.

W. G. Simms

Mrs. S. L. Griffin.

119(1a) : To Sarah Lawrence Drew Griffin

Charleston Sep. 27. [1841][1]

Mrs. S. L. Griffin.
My dear Madam.

If I might presume so far, I should concur entirely with your husband in assuming that you do want nothing but practice and

[14]Simms' daughter Agnes, born on May 28, 1841, died in July. See letter to Lawson of Aug. 2 (112).

[15]On Sept. 10 Simms wrote to Lawson (117): "I am very much behind hand [with *Beauchampe*]. It was to have been prepared by August. . . . I average from 15 to 20 pages per diem—write like steam, recklessly, perhaps thoughlessly—can give you no idea of the work. Scarcely have any myself. . . . It is now while I write 2 P. M. and I have written 17 pages since breakfast." On Oct. 15 he wrote to Lawson (121): "I am almost done my 'Beauchampe'. I *see* the end."

[16]"Oakatibbe, or the Chocktaw Sampson; an Indian Sketch," *Family Companion*, I (Nov. 14 and Dec. 15, 1841), 76–82, 163–169.

[17]*Southern Passages and Pictures.* See letter to Mrs. Griffin of June 8, 1841 (110a).

119(1a)

[1]Dated by Simms' discussion of the first number of the *Family Companion.* See letter to Mrs. Griffin of Sept. 8 (116a).

very little more of that, to edit your Companion with satisfactory success. At all events do not weaken yourself by a premature distrust of your own ability. One thing alone should make you confident. *There is precious little ability in any editorial department, in any of the established monthlies.* What is the Messenger's, the Knickerbocker's, which are considered among the best? The one is a blank, the other is a petit maître[2] in the literary lounge of a monstrous petty circle.[3] In the competition, at least, which you are to meet, there is nothing to alarm you. But I trust you will work out your editorials without regard to the doings of your bretheren. The standards of composition should be intrinsic. The ideal of one's own mind should be the highest & the best.

I should prefer that the sonnets should go together. They were meant as a sort of family group.[4] I am very sorry that Oakatibbe does not please you, the more particularly as just now I am over head & ears in labor and can do nothing out of the traces. You are aware that the story was meant to be subservient to the argument. Perhaps a brief note to this effect would be of service.[5] At all events you promised me a proof of it. Do let me have two impressions *sent by different mails*—so that if one sh'd fail, we should still be tolerably sure of the other. Touching the price of these contributions I can say nothing. I leave this matter entirely to yourself for the present. I should be better pleased that you should determine their value for yourself. This will depend on the degree of patronage you recieve. At all events I am willing that it should be so, in respect to

[2]Simms wrote *petit mastier*, but since no such word as *mastier* exists in either French or English, we have emended *petit mastier* to *petit maître* (a fop).

[3]At this time the *Southern Literary Messenger* was edited by Thomas Willis White and Matthew Fontaine Maury, the *Knickerbocker* (with which Simms was not on good terms) by Lewis Gaylord Clark and Willis Gaylord Clark.

[4]See note 9, Sept. 8, 1841 (116a).

[5]In writing about "Oakatibbe" in the "Editorial Department" of the number for Nov. 15 (I, 128), Mrs. Griffin uses Simms' own words in his letter to her of June 8 (110a): "This article is to be regarded, not so much for its interest as a story, but as comprising a very bold, original philosophical argument on a subject, of all others, the most vital to the interests and feelings of the South—the grave questions with regard to the Indian and Negro races—in a style equally fanciful and philosophic. The gradual and not slow rising of the public mind to the comprehension of and interest in these subjects, seems to require an occasional article of the kind."

the sonnets & Oakatibbe. We can have a more decided understanding in the event of further contributions.[6]

I do not know that I shall be free to do anything for a month, unless it be to correct some occasional copies of verse, which are already by me. Pledges of performance made a year ago, and interrupted by the sickness & death in my family, are now pressing upon me. I write daily, on an average from 15 to 22 pages of foolscap. Hard work this, & grievously against the spirit. I trust to be free by November & to continue tolerably free during the winter. The paper of Mr. Curtis on Sacred Poetry is very well written.[7] The Ins & Outs very spirited—very well done. Perhaps a little over done—but still lively & stirring. Who is the author?—I cannot guess.[8]

I repeat that your book is singularly creditable,—not as a first number merely. I do not doubt that you will succeed in making a deserving & valuable miscellany—of your recompense I say nothing. Time will show. You give perhaps too much matter, but you know best.—I regret to hear that you have been sick, but the bracing airs of October are already with us, and you cannot help but do well now. You have my sincere wishes for your restoration to health, with the success of your literary & all other pursuits.

Very respectfully
Yr obt serv &c

W. G. Simms

P. S. You request a *very spirited* article for no. 3? When will that number appear? I know not what leisure will be left me, and can therefore promise nothing. But one thing I may say—I regard the writing of small stories as a grievous task. These things are done by every body. I have become so arbitrary in these matters, that I write only in obedience to my humours. I prefer a spirited essay or Re-

---

[6]No further contributions by Simms were published in the *Family Companion.*

[7]Rev. Dr. Thomas Curtis, "The Poetry of the Bible," pp. 2–9. Curtis's article is continued through seven successive issues of the periodical. Curtis (1787–1859), a native of England, came to the United States in 1829. For many years he was pastor of the Wentworth Street Baptist Church in Charleston.

[8]"The Ins and the Outs, or the Last of the Bamboozled," published as "By a Disappointed Man," pp. 13–23, was written by John Neal.

view—perhaps a sketch mingling philosophy & humour,—as for example, my article in Godey's Lady's Book for Sep.—"The Philosophy of the Omnibus."[9] The toil of inventing a tale of 20 pages is almost as great as that of inventing it for 2 vols. I do not think you will ever want for stories. Our magazine writers are spinning them day & night. They are the staple. You will rather want the graver weights by which they are to be balanced—kept down—kept from being too etherial & flying away with the 'Companion.' You must give me the privilege, accorded me elswhere, of writing according to the movements of my own mind. I shall then write more confidently, and I trust more successfully.

Yr obt Serv.

W. G. S.

119b : To Sarah Lawrence Drew Griffin

[September 29, 1841][1]

My dear Madame.

My new work is not yet published, though I suppose it will be very shortly.[2] I have not a sheet or passage of it in my possession, and by the time you could recieve them from Phila. I suspect the whole work would be in the hands of the public. I should have no sort of reluctance to provide you with the sheets were I able. I send by Mr. Hart's bundle to Mr. Griffin a copy of my Poems.[3] I am in possession of a few copies which I should like to dispose of, as I happened to be originally interested in their sale. Do you suppose that Macon would furnish a market to a small extent. Pray, oblige

---

[9]See note 282, Aug. 7, 1845 (269).

119b

[1]Dated by Simms' reference to the notice of the *Family Companion* in the Charleston *Courier* "of this day." The notice (probably by Simms) says that "we have received the specimen number," lists contributors and some contributions, and is mildly complimentary: "From the specimen before us we are certain that this work will deserve, and we hope it will command success."

[2]*Confession.*

[3]*Southern Passages and Pictures.*

me by making this inquiry of your husband to whom they may be sent if the prospect of selling them shall seem fair to him. For my own part I have no faith in our taste for any of the Fine Arts. I send you, by this mail, a copy of the Charleston Courier of this day which contains a notice of the "Companion". Our papers are chiefly business sheets, do not deal much in literary criticism and perhaps exercise a very small influence over the opinions of our people. You are already in possession of my opinions on the subject of periodical literature and its chances of success in the South.[4] Your state betrays a more active character, and a more ambitious spirit, in literary matters, than any of its Southern sisters, and this may tend to falsify my predictions and disperse my fears. At all events whatever I may do incidentally in promoting the success of your journal, shall be done. But individually I go but seldom into society, and my time is really so much tasked, that I am prevented doing what I would, for yourself & other literary friends, in the shape of an occasional notice in the public prints. I trust shortly to be relieved from this pressure; when, if a kind word from me will be of service, your work shall have it.—The writer of the Pacolette papers is not a Mr. Porter, but "Col. Henry of Spartanburg."[5] I really forget his Christian name & address, but will endeavour to procure & send them to you. Possibly, a communication addressed simply as above will find him out. You should secure the contributions of Dr. Wm. H. Simmons of St. Augustine, a gentleman who writes a very excellent article in prose & verse, though a very villainous scrawl. Your printer will be very apt to regard it as Tony Lumpkin regarded the pothooks of his cousin.[6] He is the author of an account of the Seminole Indians, and of "Onea" one of the most beautiful fragments of Southern poetry which I can now lay my hands on. He

[4]This letter, which we have not located, is referred to by Simms in his letter to Mrs. Griffin of June 8, 1841 (110a).

[5]James Edward Henry (see note 227, Aug. 21, 1847 [400]) was at this time publishing his "Tales of the Packolette" (or "The Tales of Packolette Hall") in the *Magnolia*. To the *Family Companion* he contributed "A Saturday Night's Stroll through the Market," II (Apr. 1842), 30–33.

[6]"A damn'd cramp piece of penmanship as ever I saw in my life. I can read your print-hand very well. But here there are such handles, and shanks, and dashes, that one can scarce tell the head from the tail." Goldsmith, *She Stoops to Conquer*, Act IV.

may also have in his possession some of the inedited MS.S. of his brother who is now Treasurer of the Republic of Texas—Mr. James W. Simmons, the author of "The Exile's Return" and sundry other *volumes* of prose & verse. No doubt you would be able to secure a valuable contributor in W. H. S. and he might prompt his brother ultimately to give you a series of Texan sketches, to which task he is very competent.[7] My History of South Carolina, has now been published about a year. It is very generally adopted in our schools and will probably become in time the Class Book throughout the state. I am now meditating a second & stereotype edition, and would be glad to supply Mr. Griffin with any number for his series on very favorable terms. For the Copyright of the work my price is $3.000.[8] I had commenced taking notes for a History of Georgia, on a similar plan, but laid it aside under the pressure of other labors. I will probably finish it this winter, and should be pleased to find a Purchaser for it in Mr. Griffin. It would not be so copious a work as that of South Carolina. Should Mr. G. be so pleased I should like to treat with him for two abridged Histories of Carolina & Georgia. These, however, it appears to me should be seperate.[9] We in South Carolina are under the impression that there is some little jealousies towards us, in some sections of your state, which operate unfavorably to both countries. It is one important work before you as Editress to smoothe down these ruffling prejudices, and inspire the people of both regions with a sense of the necessity of harmonious action as the only means of securing a common fame and

---

[7]We are unable to attribute to William Hayne Simmons or James Wright Simmons (see introductory sketch of the Simmons brothers) any thing published in the *Family Companion*. William Hayne Simmons' *Notices of East Florida, with an Account of the Seminole Nation of Indians* was printed for the author by A. E. Miller, Charleston, in 1822. "Canto the First" of his *Onea; an Indian Tale* was printed in Charleston by T. B. Stephens in 1820; a corrected and enlarged edition of the poem was published in Philadelphia by J. B. Lippincott & Co. in 1857. James Wright Simmons was the author of *The Exile's Return: A Tale, in Three Cantos: With Other Pieces* (Charleston: Published by the Author, 1819), *The Maniac's Confession, a Fragmentary Tale* (Philadelphia: M. Thomas, 1821), and other works.

[8]The second edition of *The History of South Carolina* was published by S. Babcock & Co., Charleston, in 1842. Simms' question in his letter to Lawson of Jan. 8, 1841 (96), "Did you see the Harpers on the subject of my history" indicates that he had hoped that Harper and Brothers might publish a stereotype edition.

[9]Simms abandoned his plan for a history of Georgia. See letter to the Grifffins of Nov. 3, 1841 (122b).

a prolonged existence. To recur—I should be pleased to have proposals from Mr. G. for either or both of these Histories.—I shall be very well pleased to recieve the series of your Publications.[10] I have two daughters, the one 12, the other 2 years old,[11] to whom they will be valuable.—

With much respect,
I am, Madam,
Yr very obliged &
Obt Servant

W. G. Simms

P. S. I can provide Mr. Griffin with a few copies of three of my works, which I suspect have never been offered for sale in Macon—viz.

Carl Werner & Other Tales, 2 vols.
Southern Passages & Pictures 1— and
Atalantis— (pamphlet)[12]

The sale of these would promote my interests in some small degree.

Respectfully

W. G. S.

Mrs. S. L. Griffin.

120a : To Sarah Lawrence Drew Griffin

Charleston, Oct. 14. [1841][1]

My dear Madame,

Do send your work to "James Lawson, Esq. New York,["] and credit him with his subscription for one year, which amt. you will please charge to me. Mr. Lawson, by the way, is a Gentleman of

---

[10]See letter to Mrs. Griffin of Sept. 8, 1841 (116a).
[11]Augusta and Mary Derrille.
[12]*Atalantis, a Story of the Sea: In Three Parts* (New York: J. & J. Harper, 1832).
120a
[1]Dated by Simms' order for a subscription of the *Family Companion* for James Lawson. See letter to Lawson of Oct. 15, 1841 (121).

Letters who writes both prose & verse with ability, and you would find him a valuable acquisition could you secure his assistance. He writes for the Knickerbocker & the South. Lit Messenger, and was the author of the Biography of Bryant & Review of his writings in the latter work sometime last year.[2] May I hope to hear from Mr. G. shortly on the subjects of my last letter. I should like to treat with him for an edition of 1500 copies of a School History of Georgia. On the first Novr. my address will be "Midway, Barnwell District, South Carolina."—I send you a vol. of Poems in a bundle which Hart puts up for you today.[3]

Very Respectfully

W. G. Simms

Mrs. S. L. Griffin.
Did you get the Charleston paper I sent you.[4]

122b : To Sarah Lawrence Drew Griffin and Benjamin F. Griffin

Woodlands. near Midway P. O.
South Carolina Nov. 3. [1841][1]

Mrs. S L. Griffin
My dear Madam.

You see by this I have changed my abode for the season. Jack Frost gives us *carte blanche* (almost literally) and we are once more among the "woods and braes of bonny"[2] Edisto. Perhaps, this change has somewhat delayed the progress of your proofsheet;[3] the first part of which only reached me last evening. I have corrected it and

[2]"Moral and Mental Portraits. William Cullen Bryant," VI (Jan. 1840), 106–114.
[3]Probably *Southern Passages and Pictures*, promised in his letter to Mrs. Griffin of Sept. 8 (116a).
[4]The *Courier* of Sept. 29. See letter to Mrs. Griffin of that date (119b).

122b
[1]Dated by Simms' proposal for a stereotype edition of his *History of South Carolina*. See letter to Mrs. Griffin of Sept. 29 (119b).
[2]Simms uses the language of Burns, but the phrase does not appear in any of his poems.
[3]Of "Oakitibbe."

return it by this day's mail. You refer to some portions of your last which I left unanswered. The omission was surely accidental. Indisposition & the singular pressure of my literary tasks, may have rendered me more than usually obtuse and unobserving. May I trespass upon you so far as to request that you will readvise me of any topic which I have failed to notice,—as just now, amidst the confusion by which I am surrounded, it will not be easy for me to lay hands upon the letter to which you allude. Your last letter dated Oct. 2. did not reach me till Nov. It is endorsed, as brought by private hand, but at the same time postmarked at Macon, Oct 20. (?) Did I mention to you that one or two of your previous letters, sent by private hand, were postmarked to me, a month after, from N. York? I see favorable notices of your work in several of the Northern papers.[4] I have no sort of doubt that you will make a work highly deserving of both praise & profit. May they always go together. I give the rest of my letter to Mr. Griffin.

Very respectfully,
Yr obt Servt.

W. G. Simms

Mr. B. F. Griffin,
Sir

My suggestion on the subject of my History of South Carolina was in anticipation of a new stereotype edition of that work which I am about to prepare. Since writing to you on the subject I have opened a sort of treaty with Mr. Hart, Bookseller of Charleston, who, being in the city, in the way of trade, appears better calculated than myself to attend to the publication of such a work. I have requested him to treat with you on the subject.—I have ordered that a certain small supply of copies of Carl Werner, Southern Passages, Atalantis, and the Defence of Slavery,[5] should be sent to you on sale. The remaining copies are few, and I have counselled

[4]We have not located these notices.
[5]*Slavery in America, Being a Brief Review of Miss Martineau on That Subject* (Richmond: Thomas W. White, 1838).

them not to burden your shelves unnecessarily. Please advise me what number of these works you may recieve.—We very much want a Southern Publishing House in our country, and a Publisher of any courage & tact must do well. Our public ought to be provided with educational books at home, which should do justice to the fame of our people, and conserve the character of our Institutions. They are, I think, fast becoming aware of this necessity, but the cursed *Parley Books,* which are vile & injurious humbugs, should be written down.[6] I am not wedded to the Northern Publishers, and should freely give my strength & succor to any enterprising gentleman at home who would launch fairly into the stream. I spoke a few days ago in Charleston to Mr. Tefft of Savannah,[7] and suggested the propriety of getting up a series of Southern biography, after the manner of Sparks'.[8] I suggested to him that the state might be brought to co-operate in this object, in the creation of County School libraries, as is now done in N. Y. Mass. N. J &c. &c. If the Histl. Society of Savannah would take it up, & your legislature would second the plan, I suspect that not only North & South Caro, but that Virginia & Alabama,[9] Mississippi & Louisiana, would follow suit. A moderate appropriation, from each of these states for a certain number of copies would make a permanent foundation. I should be willing and partially prepared to begin with a life of Marion, one of Sumter, one of Greene, &c.[10] This would be a good subject for the editorial pen of Mrs. Griffin. The Histy of Georgia I have determined to decline, as I find Dr. Stevens busy upon a

[6]Under the pseudonym of "Peter Parley," Samuel Griswold Goodrich (1793–1860), of Connecticut, wrote a number of very popular books for children.

[7]Israel Keech Tefft (see introductory sketch) became one of Simms' closest friends.

[8]Jared Sparks (1789–1866) edited *The Library of American Biography*, 25 vols. (Boston: Hilliard, Gray and Co.; London: R. J. Kennett, 1834–1848).

[9]Simms wrote *Virginia & Alaabama.*

[10]Simms wrote *The Life of Francis Marion* (New York: Henry G. Langley, 1844) and *The Life of Nathanael Greene, Major-General in the Army of the Revolution* (New York: George F. Cooledge & Brother, [1849]). He did not write a biography of Gen. Thomas Sumter (1734–1832).

similar work.[11] I have not rec'd. the copy of your Botany which you speak of in your letter.[12] Very respectfully Yr obt Serv.

W. G. Simms

Carl Werner retails in Charleston for $2.00. South Passages for $1.00. Atalantis 50/100 and the Defence of Slavery for 50/100. I suppose they should command the same prices in Macon,

125a : To Patrick Henry Winston[1]

Woodlands S. Carolina Dec. 23d
1841

P. H. Winston Esqr.
Sir:—

It gives me great pleasure to recieve and to comply with the complimentary request of the Philomathesian Society of Wake Forest College of which you are the organ.

I shall have much pride in acknowledging and remembering the honorary distinction which this institution confers upon me. You do not mistake my feelings in regard to the literature of our common country & the anxiety which I feel doubly, as a man of letters and a patriot in seeing a proper impulse given & especially to that of the South.

---

[11]William Bacon Stevens (see introductory sketch) published Vol. I of *A History of Georgia* in 1847, Vol. II in 1859. On surrendering his project Simms wrote to Stevens on Dec. 30, 1841 (126), that he "had done but a week's work" on his history.

[12]John Darby's *A Manual of Botany, Adapted to the Productions of the Southern States* (Macon: B. F. Griffin, 1841). It ran through many editions and was a popular textbook for schools in the South.

125a

[1]We have not located the original of Simms' letter. Our text is from a copy in the "Philomathesian Literary Society Letter Book, 1835–1849," in the Z. Smith Reynolds Library, Wake Forest University. Winston was corresponding secretary of the society and had written to Simms on Dec. 15 asking "the honor of enrolling" his name on the society's "catalogue of Honorary Members" (original in the Charles Carroll Simms Collection, South Caroliniana Library). Winston (1820–1886) was later a planter in Bertie County, N.C., a member of the N.C. General Assembly (1850–1854), financial agent between North Carolina and the Confederate States of America (1863), and president of the Council of State (1864).

Such Societies as these which you represent are the most able agents that I know in the promotion of the holy cause of letters, and that you will do great good in your generation and after it, is as much my confident faith as hope.

Accept sir for yourself & society my honest and warm wishes that you may succeed happily in all the good works you undertake.

Yours respectfully,
Your obt. servt. & friend

W. Gilmore Simms.

126a : To Israel Keech Tefft

Woodlands, Jan 10. [1842][1]

My dear Sir

Am I to understand that it is permitted me to defer my Lecture before your Society, according to an intimation contained in my last letter? I should much prefer to visit you in March, or, at least, to have until the 20th or 25th of that month allowed me. I might put myself in sufficient readiness by the 25th. of February & *would*, if it be insisted on; but so much labor presses on me just now that I am for securing every possible chance of respite.[2] Added to my

126a

[1]Dated by Simms' remarks that his "friends & neighbours . . . have forced me into nomination for the Legislature—my first candidacy" (see letter to Stevens of Dec. 30, 1841 [126], and following letters). Simms withdrew from the race in May (see letters to Hammond of Apr. 30 and June 17 [131 and 137]).

[2]On Dec. 21, 1841, Tefft, Solomon Cohen, and Robert Milledge Charlton, a committee of the Georgia Historical Society, wrote to Simms informing him that he had been elected one of the lecturers before the society and asking that the lecture be delivered before Mar. 1 (original in the Charles Carroll Simms Collection, South Caroliniana Library). Simms accepted the invitation around Dec. 30 (see letter to Stevens of that date [126]). He delivered two lectures, on Mar. 8 and Mar. 10, on "The Epochs and Events of American History, as Suited to the Purposes of Art in Fiction" (see letter to Tefft of Feb 26 [*128a*]). Three extracts from these lectures were published in the *Magnolia*: "Hernando de Soto; a Study for the Poet," "Pocahontas; a Study for the Historical Painter," and "The Settlements of Coligny," IV (May 1842), 286–288, 305–306; N. S., I (July 1842), 29–31. Parts of the lectures were later published in Simms' *Southern and Western Monthly Magazine and Review*, I (Mar., Apr., and June 1845), 182–191, 257–261, 385–392; II (July, Aug., and Sept. 1845), 10–16, 87–94, 145–154. This material

other & usual toils, my friends & neighbours, knowing me to be a sturdy loco foco, & giving me credit for being more, have forced me into nomination for the Legislature—my first candidacy—and this implies a necessity, it seems, of showing myself at musters, barbacues, sale days, sessions & other gatherings of the people. This will consume some profitable time & all that you can secure me will be valuable. Recieve my sincere thanks for your courtesy & the kind invitation it conveys,—of which I shall be most happy to avail myself. I wish you well over your journey & safe home with your assets—no unmeaning wish in these days when money is so scarce and the morality of the highways so very questionable.

Very faithfully Your
friend &c

W. Gilmore Simms

I. K. Tefft, Esq.

128b : To Israel Keech Tefft

Wednesday Mg. [March 9, 1842][1]

That noggin last night! Let it be no more called punch, but Judy. Never was thing more feminine—nay, it was positively old womanish. At least, it maintains a sort of tingling to this moment in my ears. Judy be the name, hereafter, of all such night caps. But, I must keep quiet for the Dinner with the Dr.[2]—At present, head & stomach, equally, revolt at the idea of compounds, such as good Hosts fancy under the name of creature Comforts. Did you think to throw the letters in the P. O?

Simms.

I. K. Tefft.

---

was revised and published as "The Epochs and Events of American History, as Suited to the Purposes of Art in Fiction" in *Views and Reviews in American Literature, History and Fiction*, First Series (New York: Wiley and Putnam, 1845), pp. 20–101.

128b

[1]Since Simms lectured before the Georgia Historical Society on Tuesday, Mar. 8, 1842, this letter dated "Wednesday Mg." should undoubtedly be assigned to the same year.

[2]Probably William Bacon Stevens, who by profession was a physician.

128c : To Israel Keech Tefft

Saturday MG [March 12, 1842][1]

Mon Ami.

Do get me copies of the paper for this morning, and that of Thursday last. I am anxious that my wife should see what the solemn-bearded authorities of Savannah say in my honor. I am one of those good husbands, you see, who refer for the final favour to the Domestic Divinities. Madame is no ways literary, but it makes her little heart jump to hear that I have pleased those who are; and *entre nous,* —when all is said & done, I prefer rather to please that little, unliterary heart, than the grave philosophical heads of all the whole world of criticism. But this confession must not reach either of these two parties. It might make the little heart too vain and proud, and the big heads angry. So mum!—

Yours Ever &c

W. Gilmore Simms

Mons. Tefft.

128c

[1]Dated by Simms' request for "copies of the paper for this morning, and that of Thursday last" in which his lectures (see letter to Tefft of Mar. 9 [128b]) are reviewed. The lectures are favorably reviewed at length in the Savannah *Georgian* of Mar. 10 (Thursday), Mar. 12 (Saturday), and Mar. 14 (Monday).

Simms refused payment for his lectures (see letter to Tefft of Mar. 12 [129]). He must have left Savannah on Mar. 13 or 14, since on Mar. 15 Tefft, as corresponding secretary of the society, wrote a formal letter addressed to Simms at Woodlands in which he quotes the resolution of the society at its meeting on Mar. 14: "Resolved that the Society feel under peculiar obligations to the disinterested kindness of William Gilmore Simms Esq: one of its honorary members, in contributing so largely to the gratification and instruction of our fellow citizens and the Society, by his two able and interesting lectures delivered on the evenings of the 8th. and 10th instant" (original in the Charles Carroll Simms Collection, South Caroliniana Library).

135a : To Rufus Wilmot Griswold

Charleston, June 7. [1842][1]

dear Sir

I see by the papers that you have become Editor of Graham's Magazine. By the accompanying circular, you will see that I also am among the prophets.[2] It will give me pleasure to exchange with you, magazines & courtesies. Shall it be so? I have just glanced over your 'Poets'. It is decidedly the best collection ever made. The plate is not so well done, but the work is beautifully got up in every respect.[3] Personally I have no complaint. I could have wished however that you had been less costive with some & a little more so with others,—but it is difficult to satisfy every body. Very Respectfully

Yr ob. Serv &c

W. G. Simms

R. W. Griswold, Esq.

135a

[1]Dated by Simms' remark that Griswold has become editor of *Graham's Lady's and Gentleman's Magazine*. Griswold became associated with *Graham's* in May 1842. His work as editor began with the July number and ended with the Oct. 1843 number. See Bayless, *Rufus Wilmot Griswold*, pp. 54–55.

[2]Simms became editor of the *Magnolia; or Southern Monthly* with the July 1842 number. In moving the magazine from Savannah to Charleston he altered the title to the *Magnolia; or, Southern Apalachian. A Literary Magazine and Monthly Review.* (see note 41, June 4, 1842 [135]). In her "Editorial Department" Mrs. Griffin writes in the *Family Companion*, II (Sept. 1842), 374: "This Southern work in changing hands, has almost entirely changed its character. It can no longer be called a periodical of light literature, occupied as it is with weighty material. It now bids fair to become one of the standard works of the country, if continued with the sound sense, vigor, and industry which have characterized the numbers already issued. We are pleased also to see by an announcement in a Portland paper, that the pen of the gifted John Neal, one of our own favorite contributors, has been engaged for the Magnolia. We are the more pleased at this, as it shows that the narrow policy of employing *only Southern* writers has been abandoned, and more just views taken of the means best adapted to foster a taste for literature among the people, which must be done ere the South can lay claim to a literature of its own. Our own efforts have been directed to this end, and with the co-operation of our older and now abler brother, the Magnolia, we trust the South will not remain long under the reproach of being a people who neither read nor write. Long life to the Magnolia, and all other enterprises calculated to cherish and sustain Southern literature."

The "Literary Circular" of the *Magnolia* (not preserved with this letter) is reproduced in Vol. I of *The Letters of William Gilmore Simms*, facing p. 329.

[3]In his review of Griswold's *The Poets and Poetry of America* (Philadelphia: Carey

139a : To Mitchell King[1]

[July 15, 1842][2]

Dear Sir

If you can conveniently lay hands upon the vol. which contains the "Alfred" of Mr. Hasell, you will very much oblige me by letting me have its use for some two weeks.[3] I will do myself the honor of making an early afternoon call.

Very faithfully
Yr frd & servt.

W. Gilmore Simms

M. King. Esq. Friday Aftn.

139b : To Benjamin F. Griffin

Charleston, July 24 [1842][1]

My dear Sir.

In making out my account and drawing upon you, I entirely forgot to give you credit for the subscription of Mr. Lawson (not

---

and Hart, 1842) in the *Magnolia*, N. S., I (Aug. 1842), 117–122, Simms repeats these sentiments: "Briefly . . . this certainly is the most complete collection of American poets, that has ever been made. . . . We cannot entirely approve of the plate of portraits—that of Halleck is good, that of Longfellow tolerably so, while that of Bryant, seems a very wretched carricature." But he censures Griswold for omitting "certain Southern writers" and for his partiality to the northern poets. The frontispiece to the volume is an engraving of a bust of Richard Henry Dana and of portraits of Bryant, Halleck, Longfellow, and Charles Sprague.

139a

[1]King was one of the leading lawyers of Charleston. See note 183, June 26, 1858 (885).

[2]Someone (probably King) wrote at the bottom of the sheet "15 July 1842." Since this date was a Friday, we have accepted it.

[3]Simms was collecting material for *The Charleston Book: A Miscellany in Prose and Verse* (Charleston: Samuel Hart, Sen., 1845). The "Prospectus" is dated July 15, 1841 (see letter to Lawson of Aug. 16, 1841 [115]); the volume was copyrighted July 23, 1844, and the "Advertisement" in the volume is dated Oct. 1, 1844 (p. iv). A brief review of the work appears in the New York *Morning News* of Nov. 14, 1844. For Hasell's "Alfred," see letter to King of June 17, 1843 (163a).

139b

[1]Dated by Simms' remarks about his "Notice" of Mrs. Griffin's "School Books." In the *Magnolia*, N. S., I (July 1842), 58–60, Simms published an article entitled

Hall) of New York. But I will send an article to Mrs. Griffin which will square our obligations. I deducted one half of the difference of exchange, however, amounting to something like six dollars.[2] I had directed an exchange with the Companion before recieving your letter, and, by this time, I suppose that Mrs. G. must be in reciept of the July number of the Magnolia. A notice of her School Books was prepared but excluded from our July number by the press of matter which had been lying some time on hand. I am in hopes that Mr. Burges[3] will treat with you for the Companion. Say to Mrs. G. that I should really be well pleased to have her a resident of Charleston.[4] I do not see that the injustice of her contemporaries is any evil, since it will have the effect of stimulating her exertions to disprove their disparagements, and baffle their hostility. If wrong indues her with the proper strength and courage it will prove a blessing rather than an injury. As for the Knickerbocker[5] & some

---

"Southern Education—Books," in which he discusses for the most part the books which S. Babcock and Co. had published. In the Aug. number, p. 126, he published a short note entitled "Griffin's School Books," in which he commends Mrs. Griffin's *Southern Primary Reader, Southern Second Class Book*, and *Southern Third Class Book* "to the examination of Southern teachers generally." He remarks that it is "absolutely important in the South" to have this class of writings prepared by southerners.

[2]Griffin tried to collect the money for Lawson's subscription from Lawson. Simms wrote Lawson to pay him nothing: "The scamp owes me five times the money & was told to charge me with your subt. I have this day written him to the same effect" (see letters to Lawson of Oct. 16 [177 and 178]). Simms seems to have collected nothing from Griffin for his contributions to the *Family Companion*, since on Nov. 9, 1843, he wrote to Lawson (183): "Of course pay nothing to Griffin. I have heard nothing from him since giving him his answer."

[3]James S. Burges of the firm of Burges and James, publisher of the *Magnolia*. Robert James was his partner.

[4]Early in 1842 Griffin, needing help for himself and for his wife, negotiated with William Tappan Thompson (1812–1882) to merge his *Augusta Mirror* with the *Family Companion* under the latter title. Thompson became Mrs. Griffin's coeditor with the issue for Mar. 15, 1842, but left the periodical after the June 1842 number (for the quarrel that ended this partnership, see Flanders, *Early Georgia Magazines*, pp. 64–65). The Griffins apparently were discouraged about the future of the magazine. In a letter to John Neal dated Aug. 3, 1842 (original in the Houghton Library, Harvard University), Mrs. Griffin writes that she wishes someone would buy the *Companion*—"not . . . a bad speculation, for we have nearly a thousand subscribers. . . . If Mr. G. could dispose of the C. for $2500 I think he would do it and removing to Charleston go into the publishing line altogether. He is strongly inclined that way."

[5]In her letter to Neal of Aug. 3, Mrs. Griffin writes that she thinks the *Knickerbocker* has "very much deteriorated." "As for the gossip I had as lief take a jest

of its kindred works, as I happen to know them well, I know how to despise them. I am glad that Mrs. G. is sufficiently *bold* to see the truth, even through that thick veil of veneration, which, in the South, our people are too apt to cast over the real character of what is distant. Here, we venerate any thing that is not known. By a joint & corresponsive action, we may soon strip these miserable jays of their borrowed plumage.—[6]

---

book and join the jokes with twaddle and read it as to read said gossip—weak as skimmed milk. He [Lewis Gaylord Clark] has not inherited his brother's [Willis Gaylord Clark's] mantle. He is no gentleman. He is *low.*"

[6]In an editorial entitled "Southern Literature" published in the June 1842 number of the *Family Companion*, II, [180]–181, Mrs. Griffin writes: "Neither of the above words are of new coinage; though it is only of late years that they seem to have had any significant meaning, in the relative position in which they are placed at the head of this article. Scarce a lustrum has elapsed since they were regarded as unmeaning sounds; and one might search the magazines from beginning to end and find no such term. But of late a meaning has been attached to it of dire import, and it is not unfrequently that we see 'southern literature' condemned as a heresy which is destined to work incalculable injury to the cause of letters, and to retard the diffusion of literary taste among the people: it is made synonymous with sectional literature, and held to be strictly antagonistical to the vaunted 'National Republic of Letters.' A portion of the press, in certain quarters, endeavor to attach to it all the pernicious consequences of sectional feeling and prejudice, which in their wide-spreading, all-embracing policy is so strongly to be deprecated and avoided in our land of republican principles. Another portion of the literary press, more politic, but less candid, affect not yet to have made the discovery, and carefully avoid the slightest notice of any other literature than that which emanates from the 'great republic of letters,' *i. e.*, from their own particular clique." She considers the objects of both portions of the press the same: "one would prejudice the unreflecting by the parade of patriotic sentiments and false doctrines; the other would seek to hold its place by affecting a contemptuous disregard for all literary enterprises which may presume to contend with them for a share of public patronage. Having long enjoyed the undivided support of all sections, and becoming pampered and inordinately vain, they regard themselves as above competition, and seek, by unblushing effrontery and the employment of all manner of *ad captandum* devices, to supersede all others, whatever their claims or merit." Though Mrs. Griffin disclaims advocacy of "sectional prejudice," she does "approve of sectional literature." "We believe the soul of any literature is its local inspiration—its sectionality. . . . we cannot but esteem literature as enhanced by its local character. . . . We believe the South is destined to take the lead in the formation of what may be properly termed, a national literature. . . . We glory in the thought that we have the germ—and a vigorous one it is, too—of a domestic literature, and that the spirit is abroad in the land that will sustain it. . . . We would not be thought to entertain sectional prejudices, such as are attributed to all who manifest any degree of respect for the genius and talent of our own section. We harbor no such prejudices. We have the highest appreciation of talent wherever it is found. None can feel a greater deference for the literature of the north than ourselves, and in the degree that it is purely northern, in tone and spirit, untainted by foreign bias, do we esteem it worthy our admiration. We desire to see northerners

On the subject of the work "Beauchampe" I should much prefer just now to say nothing. It & its companions are imputed to me, and in such cases I neither deny nor admit. It will give me no sort of concern whether they impute it to me or not, in whatever terms;—my rule is simply, not, myself, to give them any authority, which they might use, for doing either. Mrs. G— will not only easily understand me, but my reasons, in this matter. Say to her that the Magnolia shall always be sent her—that I have an unfeigned respect for her talents & congratulate her sincerely on what she has done, & upon her increasing courage. Her article on Campbell was well done.[7] I shall be really happy to know her better.—I fancy that you & Pendleton had best say nothing to each other. You seem both too bitter & too hostile to concur in any arrangement. Mr. Burges is a man of plain business habits—much moderation & good sense—very strict in what he undertakes & very cautious in all money matters. He tells me that your charge for your list is an extravagant one.[8] On this subject, as I really know nothing, I pretend to no opinion. With best respects to your lady & good wishes.

I am, (hastily)
Your obt. serv &c

W. G. Simms

Mr. B. F. Griffin

---

write like northern men and Americans, and southrons write like southern men and Americans. But d[o] let them all write—men and women too—and not one set up to speak for the other. Let them write, write, write, and speak, speak, speak—but let us all be heard in our own way, and we may be assured, the world in general, and the 'Republic of Letters' in particular, will be none the worse off for it; provided always that we write and speak as Christians and men of sense should write and speak."

[7]"The Pilgrim of Glencoe" (a review of Thomas Campbell's poem) in the *Family Companion*, II (May 1842), [120]–123.

[8]See note 4, above.

140b : To John Neal

Charleston Augt. 8. [1842][1]

Dear Sir

You are a man after my own heart. I like plain speaking. You shall have the highest price that our Publishers pay to any body, viz. Two dollars a page, and large pages they are,—but I am well assured that the single consideration of the pecuniary recompense is not yours. I shall be pleased to advise you of any improvement in the resources of the work which shall enable it to offer more. We should be pleased to recieve from you a paper for each no.—not exceeding five pages, if possible.[2] I need not say to you what sort of stuff we desire. You have had a long magazine experience—sufficiently long to enable you to determine what is best for our pages. It may seem anomalous, but you will understand me, when I say, that one of the reasons why the South has had so little periodical literature, is in consequence of the high standards upon which her educated men insist. They are too fastidious in their tastes to recieve pleasure from ordinary sources, and the ignorant, knowing their opinions, adopt them though with no such good reason. Yours &c. W. G. Simms

140c : To Richard Henry Wilde[1]

Charleston, Augt 11. [1842][2]

My dear Sir

Your mode of self estimate is quite foreign to the practice of the day. But one may safely disparage himself, to whom his neighbours

---

140b

[1]In Neal's "Letter Book" in the Houghton Library, Harvard University, this letter is arranged with the 1842 letters. It is obviously an answer to Neal's reply to Simms' letter of July 27 (*140A*), requesting contributions to the *Magnolia*.

[2]Neal published two pieces of prose in the *Magnolia:* "Other Days; or Disinterred Opinions" and "The Lottery Ticket," N. S., II (Jan. and June 1843), 41–47, 364–367.

140c

[1]This letter is printed by James E. Kibler, Jr., in "A New Letter of Simms to Richard Henry Wilde: On the Advancement of Sectional Literature," *American Literature*, XLIV (1973), 667–670.

everywhere are ready & willing to do justice. Permit me to say that my opinions were sincere, and their expression has not been confined to your own ears, nor to the present day.

Should I, at any time, be passing through Augusta, I shall have equal pride and pleasure in availing myself of your friendly invitation. To know you, in pro: per:, will even tempt me to go out of my way. I had the pleasure of seeing & hearing you, I think, in 1832,—at Washington, but I did not make your acquaintance. I beg that you will not scruple to seek me out, when you come to Carolina.[3] I shall always be rejoiced to see you. When in the city (Charleston) by applying at the Bookstore of Hart, he will send a guide with you to my wigwam, which is rather an obscure one in the suburbs; and, during the winter, I am mostly to be found at the plantation of my wife's father[4] in Barnwell District, on the Rail Road Line, and within a mile of the Midway Station, some 62 miles from Augusta. It might be, at a moment of greater ennui than usual, that a run down to our place would put you in better humour with the great outer, and the little inner world of man; and by giving me an intimation, a few days, or even a day before hand of your contemplated benevolence, I should take the carriage to meet you at Midway. Though we are in opposite political houses,[5] yet our stock of poetical talk will supply topics sufficiently numerous to exclude discussion by a most natural process; and that you are a Southern man & poet, justifies me in taking for granted that you are sufficiently sectional to enable us to get up a little exclusively home party in Letters. You readily understand the distinction between a determined advocacy of Southern mind, its claims, rights & pretensions, and that hostility to Northern mind, which is impertinently alleged against me, by those who desire to shift their own responsibility to the shoulders of their little neighbourhoods.

---

[2]Dated by Simms' remark that he has consented "to conduct a periodical." He had become editor of the *Magnolia* with the number for July 1842.

[3]In 1832 Wilde was a member from Georgia of the U.S. House of Representatives. His home was Augusta until late 1843 or early 1844, when he moved to New Orleans. See Edward L. Tucker, *Richard Henry Wilde: His Life and Selected Poems* (Athens: University of Georgia Press, [1966]), pp. 33, 68.

[4]Nash Roach. See introductory sketch of the Simms family circle.

[5]Wilde was a Whig.

You will do me the favor to believe that in consenting to conduct a periodical, I am not governed by pecuniary considerations. I do not expect to *make* but to *lose* money by the process. But I feel every day, more & more, the humiliating relation in which the South stands to the North, and the gross injustice which naturally results from such relation. To change this in some [degre]e[6] is my object, and for which I make some sacrifices. Of course, I insist upon my pay,—but I am very far from esteeming this compensation.—But a long letter, unless from a Politician, is, I take for granted, scarcely agreeable to a Politician. Believe me, even while editing maga, I regard myself as more genially engaged than you. You will call this self complacence, but—what do you think of the news from North Carolina?[7] Does it not persuade you of the better policy of giving us some fine sketches from Italian Life, scenery character, &c. by which you will be enabled to escape from the cloudy atmosphere of party, into one more blue & serene.[8] Faithfully, Yr friend &c

W. G. Simms

P.S. You were an absentee from the beginning & during the greater part of my brief literary career. I have not all the poetical works which I have put forth during that period; but I send you one of them,—the crude performance of nineteen.[9] You will find in a volume called "Southern Passages & Pictures", a better sample of my muse,—if the subject be worth regard.

Again, Very respectfully
Yr obt Servt

W. G. Simms

Hon. R. H. Wilde.

---

[6]The MS. is torn.

[7]The Charleston *Courier* of Aug. 11 prints under the heading of "Correspondence" a letter from Goldsboro, N.C., dated Aug. 9, reporting on the election held on Aug. 4: "The vote for Governor will be much closer than for the last eight years. [Louis D.] HENRY runs well up with his ticket, and the Democrats gain every where." See also the *Courier* of Aug. 8 and Aug. 10.

[8]Wilde had reluctantly become a candidate for election to the U.S. House of Representatives. See Tucker, pp. 65–66.

[9]Either *Lyrical and Other Poems* (Charleston: Ellis & Neufille, 1827) or *Early Lays* (Charleston.: A. E. Miller, 1827).

141a : To Sidney Babcock[1]

Charleston, Aug. 18. [1842][2]

dear Sir

I have this day put into the hands of Mr. Fogartie, your Brother's representative, the concluding portions of the Geography of South Carolina, a work of great labor, which has cost me much time & industry. I shall expect you to send me proofs of it, duplicated as before, by different mails, so that in the failure of one, we shall still have another to rely on. On the subject of payments, I propose that you should accept my draft, at one month, in favor of your brother for Fifty dollars; the remaining Fifty to be paid on the first day of March, (1843) Eighteen Hundred & forty three. I propose to take the first instalment of fifty dollars,[3] in goods, out of your Brother's store, and will pledge myself that such shall be the case. I fancy these terms will suit you. I shall expect some ten or fifteen copies of the Geography, for my own private distribution. These

141a

[1]Babcock (1796–1884), the son of John Babcock (1764–1843) of New Haven, Conn., joined his father's publishing firm in 1815. In 1825 the firm of John Babcock & Son was dissolved "in consequence of John Babcock's declining business." Under the terms of the dissolution the business was to be carried on by Sidney, Henry L., and William R. Babcock under the name of Babcock and Company. In 1818 William Rogers Babcock (1800–1859) came to Charleston to open a bookshop and stationery store on behalf of himself and his older brother Sidney. In 1829 the shop was moved from Church Street to King Street. In the 1840s Sidney and William dissolved their partnership, and William took on Samuel Fogartie, an employee of the Charleston house, as his partner. William retired from business in 1859, Sidney in 1880. William became a friend of Simms, and S. Babcock & Co., Charleston, published the first and second editions of Simms' *History of South Carolina* in 1840 and 1842. Like the *History*, many of the Babcock publications were children's books. Notable among them were numerous textbooks (some of which Simms may have contributed to) aimed specifically at southern children. We are indebted to David Moltke-Hansen for this information, which corrects the information we gave on the Babcocks in note 5, Mar. 2, 1840 (80*a*).

[2]Dated by Simms' remarks about *The Geography of South Carolina: Being a Companion to the History of That State* (Charleston: Babcock & Co., 1843).

[3]Simms first wrote *I shall want no* [*money*?] and then struck through the words.

shall be given so as to promote rather than impair your sales. Pray, let me hear from you, on the reciept of this letter.

Very respectfully, Yr servt

Wm. Gilmore Simms

Mr Sidney Babcock.

147a : To Richard Henry Wilde

Woodlands, Decr. 26. [1842][1]

My dear Sir

I felt quite vexed with myself, on leaving you the other night, at having neglected to remind you of the copies of verse, which you were pleased to promise me for publication. These, if I remember, were two pieces, an exquisite little song, and a translation from Michel Angelo,—a brief dialogue between himself & Country. Do not, I pray you, consider me too inveterately editorial, in bringing this kind promise to your recollection; but it is a point of honor, in the Editorial bosom, not to forego its hold upon a good thing, when it fortunately happens upon it.[2] I send you, herewith, a copy of the Tales of which I spoke to you.[3] Some of them are crude & puerile,—the fruits of my first beginnings. But the imaginative things will, I trust, give you pleasure. I had the satisfaction to find my little family in good condition. A merry Christmas, & Happy New Year to yours. Pray, present me kindly to Mr & Mrs J. Wilde

147a

[1]Dated by Simms' remarks about the poems that Wilde had promised to give him for the *Magnolia*. Wilde evidently sent them soon after he received Simms' letter. See note 2, below.

[2]"Odi D'un Nom [Uom] Che Muore" and "Madrigal on Florence, under the Tyranny of Duke Alexander De' Medici, in the Form of a Dialogue," *Magnolia*, N. S., II (Feb. and Mar. 1843), 117, 153. Simms also prints the Italian for the second of these, and notes say that the poems are "from a Volume of MS. Poems, entitled 'Specimens of Italian Lyrics.' "

[3]*Carl Werner, an Imaginative Story; with Other Tales of Imagination.* Wilde was "greatly pleased" with the tales. See note 5, July 20, 1843 (*169a*).

& Miss Wilde,[4] to whom & yourself I owe one of the pleasantest days which I have spent in the year.[5]

Very faithfully, Yours,

W. Gilmore Simms

Hon. R. H. Wilde.

---

[4]After his return from Italy in 1841 Wilde, his two sons (William Cumming Wilde and John Patterson Wilde), and his sister Catherine lived in Augusta with his brother, John Walker Wilde, and his wife, Emily (see Tucker, *Richard Henry Wilde*, p. 61). In annotating Simms' letter to Wilde of July 20, 1843 (*169a*), we incorrectly identify "Mr. J. W. & Lady" as Wilde's son and his wife.

[5]In his letter to Wilde of Aug. 11, 1842 (140c), Simms had promised Wilde to avail himself "of your friendly invitation" to visit him: "To know you, in pro: per:, will even tempt me to go out of my way." Around Dec. 1, 1842 (see letter to Lawson of Nov. 17 [146]), Simms left for Tuscaloosa, Ala., where on Dec. 13 he delivered before the Erosophic Society of the University of Alabama an oration later published under the title of *The Social Principle: The True Source of National Permanence* (Tuscaloosa: Published by the Society, 1843). Evidently on his return to Woodlands he stopped off at Augusta to meet Wilde. It was probably at this time that Simms "had the pleasure of hearing portions" of Wilde's never–finished life of Dante "read, by the accomplished writer himself" (*Southern and Western Monthly Magazine and Review*, II [Aug. 1845], 144).

The Tuscaloosa Lyceum also invited Simms to lecture before its members during his visit to Alabama (see letter to Simms dated Sept. 14, 1842, and signed by A. B. Meek, Robert T. Clyde, and D. H. Robinson, original in the Southern Historical Collection, University of North Carolina). The Tuscaloosa *Independent Monitor* (edited by Stephen F. Miller) of Dec. 14, 21, and 28 gives a rather full account of Simms' visit to Tuscaloosa. Simms arrived in the city on Dec. 8 and was the guest of Benjamin Faneuil Porter (see note 134, July 14, 1849 [496]). The *Independent Monitor* calls Simms' oration "one of the most eloquent and polished Discourses ever listened to in the South-West" and remarks that through it Simms "gained fresh laurels to his brightly encircled brow." On Dec. 14, at the twelfth annual commencement of the University, the Board of Trustees conferred on Simms the degree of LL.D. On the evenings of Dec. 15 and 16 he lectured before the members of the Tuscaloosa Lyceum "and a crowded audience, at the Methodist Church, on the subject of 'American History, and the uses for which it is employed by Art in Fiction.'" The *Independent Monitor* remarks that "much of the intelligence of the State was present, in the members of the Legislature, and there was no dissenting voice as to the ability of the performance." And there were "other demonstrations of regard, in which the bestowers were more honored than the recipient . . . a man of genius, pure taste and high cultivation, to which may be joined exalted personal character." One of these "demonstrations" is reported at length by the *Independent Monitor.* On the evening of Dec. 17 Simms was honored with a public dinner at which Porter officiated as president. The third toast was "Our distinguished Guest": "The Historian, the Novelist, and the Poet. By the purity and beauty of his writings, he has shed honor upon our country's literature; and proven to the world that the land of his birth can assume the same high place in Letters which she has ever held in the Field and the Forum." After "the enthusiastic applause . . . had subsided," Simms "rose, and in a style peculiarly his own, enriched with all the graces of literature, loftiness of sentiment and

148a : To Israel Keech Tefft

[1843?][1]

dear Tefft.

I send you some more antiques, among which I trust that your keen eyes will discern a gem or two. There is a letter

---

originality of combination, addressed the company about three quarters of an hour." Before the ninth regular toast was announced, Alexander Beaufort Meek "addressed the company, and referred to the various conjectures which had been afloat in the public mind, as to the authorship of the Hurdis Novels, some of the scenes of which were located in our city. He had never heard the writer acknowledged, but he had good reasons to believe that he was within the vicinity of the table. Then pointing to Mr SIMMS, he adopted the language of another, and said, 'Thou art the man.' " The toast to "The Author of Richard Hurdis" was then given: "Though like the Knight of the sable plume, he fights under strange colors and his vizor down, yet we recognize in his the same strong arm which has won noble laurels in other fields of southern literature." After "the bursts of applause" had ceased, "Mr SIMMS found himself at the confessional; and after entertaining the company with some happy remarks, he threw himself on their indulgence, while he admitted that the secrecy with which he wrote and published had not protected him from the well founded suspicion which had just been uttered. He was the author of Richard Hurdis, the materials for which work he collected when travelling in Alabama twenty years ago." The tenth scheduled toast, to "Woman" ("The soul of society—the inspiration of the Poet. In every festival our warmest thoughts are turned to her"), was followed by "other addresses . . . and many volunteer toasts." "Mr SIMMS also made a few additional remarks, which he concluded by making a compliment to *Alexander B. Meek*—the warm and generous friend, and manly writer. May the State honor him whose genius has honored her." The company separated "at a late hour," and on the following day Simms left for South Carolina. The *Independent Monitor* also reports that "during the ten days Mr S. remained in the city . . . his drawing room was thronged with visitors, all anxious to improve his acquaintance, and to testify their respect." Since the only other Tuscaloosa newspaper we know of for this period (the *Flag of the Union*) contains no reference to Simms, it must have been the *Independent Monitor* of Dec. 28 which Simms sent to Lawson on Jan. 7, 1843 (149), with the comment that it "gives a very meager account of the dinner." One wonders what Simms wished the newspaper had included in its copious report. Apparently the lectures Simms delivered before the Tuscaloosa Lyceum were the same as those he had earlier delivered before the Georgia Historical Society (see note 2, Jan. 10, 1842 [126a]).

148a

[1]Simms' close friendship with Tefft seems to have begun during his visit to Savannah in Mar. 1842 (see letter to Tefft of Jan. 10, 1842 [126a], and following letters). By 1843 Simms was sending him autographs for his collection (see letter to Tefft of c. Apr. 3, 1843 [158]). Since two (and perhaps all) of the autographs mentioned in this note were originally part of the collection of Laurens MSS. that Simms had acquired at some time before 1845 (see letter to Duyckinck of Feb. 11, 1845 [233], and notes 3 and 4, below), it is probable that Simms went through

from Thos. Day, author of Sanford & Merton,[2]
" Lady Penn,[3]
" Dr. Price[4]
" L'd Sandwich[5]
Sydney[6]
Craven[7] &c.

Yours truly

Simms.

---

this collection shortly after he became intimate with Tefft and sent him autographs from it which he thought would not damage the historical value of the collection as a whole. We have, therefore, dated this note 1843?, though, of course, it could have been written at any time between Mar. 1842 and the date of Tefft's death (1860). Neither the handwriting nor the paper casts any light on the date.

[2]Lot 1961 in the *Catalogue of the Entire Collection of Autographs of the Late Mr. I. K. Tefft, of Savannah, Ga. . . . The Whole to Be Sold by Auction, without Reserve, at the Trade Sale Rooms, 498 Broadway, New York. Leavitt, Strebeigh & Co., Auctioneers, on Monday, March 4th, and Following Days . . .* (New York: Leavitt, Strebeigh & Co., 1867), p. 183, is "Day, Thomas . . . A. L. S., 4to, 1783. 2 Portraits." Day (1748–1789) is remembered for *The History of Sandford and Merton* (London, 1783–1789), a novel which for a number of decades was forced upon children by moralistic adults.

[3]Among the autographs listed as lot 1037 in ibid., p. 107, is "A. L. S., 4to. pp. 2, of Lady Juliana Penn, addressed to Henry Laurens, requesting his protection for her son, whom she wishes to send to America with him, '*and be presented by you to those who ought to be, and I trust will prove, his friends.*' Dated 'Spring Garden, London, Nov., 1782.' " Lady Juliana (b. 1729), daughter of Thomas Fermor, 1st Earl of Pomfret, was the wife of Thomas Penn (1702–1775), second son of William Penn and one of the hereditary proprietors of the province of Pennsylvania.

[4]Among the autographs listed as lot 2459 in ibid., p. 238, is "Price, Dr. Richard . . . Note in 3d person, to Mr. Laurens, with a request to forward a package to Dr. Franklin, 4to, pp. 1, 1782." Price (1723–1791) was a nonconformist minister who wrote on morals, economics, and politics. He was an opponent of Britain's war with the American colonies.

[5]Among the autographs listed as lot 2547 in ibid., p. 251, is "Sandwich, frank." Undoubtedly this is an autograph of John Montagu, 4th Earl of Sandwich (1718–1792), the corrupt first lord of the Admiralty during Lord North's administration. He is perhaps just as well known today as one of the "monks" of Medmenham Abbey.

[6]Among the autographs listed as lot 2547 in ibid., p. 251, is "Sydney, 2 franks." Thomas Townshend (1733–1800), a leader of the opposition to Lord North's administration, was created Viscount Sydney on Mar. 6, 1783. He held various important posts in the government during the 1780s.

[7]Among the autographs listed as lot 1904 in ibid., p. 176, is "Craven, *Lord*, note in 3d person, 1782." William Craven, 6th Baron Craven of Hampsted Marshall (1738–1791), unlike Sandwich and Sydney, was not prominent in public affairs.

149 (1a) : To Mitchell King

Charleston Jan. 10. [1843][1]

My dear Judge

Suffer me to remind you that you promised me a small contribution in prose & verse, for the projected miscellany called the Charleston Book, which the publishers contemplate putting to press by the summer.[2] If sent to my address, care of Saml. Hart, Sen. Bookseller, by the first of March, it will be in season.—Meanwhile, may I beg of you the use, for a brief period, of the Magazine Vol. which contains the poem of Alfred. You will add to this favor by furnishing me with the complete name of the author—Hasell,—I believe,[3]—and with any information, touching any other author of that period whose remains you may deem worthy of preservation.

Very faithfully,
I am, Sir,
Your obt servt.

W. Gilmore Simms

Hon. Mitchell King.

149b : To Carey and Hart

Feb. 23. [1843][1]

Mess'rs Carey & Hart
Gentlemen.

I have succeeded in preparing you a story called "Barnacle Sam or the Extempore Judgment, a Tale of the Edisto;" which I will send

149(1a)

[1]Since King was recorder of the City of Charleston and judge of the city court during the first part of 1843 (see his obituary in the Charleston *Courier* of Nov. 15, 1862), we have assigned this letter to that year.

[2]Only one work by King was published in *The Charleston Book*—a poem entitled "The Resolve." See letter to King of June 17, 1843 (163a).

[3]For Hasell's "Alfred," see letter to King of June 17, 1843 (163a).

149b

[1]Dated by Simms' letter to Carey and Hart of Mar. 28, 1843 (156b), saying that he is sending "'The Two Camps . . .',—a story for the Gift" and requesting Carey

you by first safe private hand. I am on the lookout now for an opportunity.—

I have recd. Pericles & Aspasia, with Napier,[2] and thank you for your attentions. Did I not write you for certain old books, among them the Life of Kenelm Digby & his writings?[3]

Yours faithfully

W. G. Simms

---

and Hart to "get a purchaser for the other story." Though this "other story" is not named, Simms' letter to Carey and Hart of July 7, 1843 (167), and his letter to Carey of Jan. 31, 1844 (190), make it clear that it was sold to Griswold for *Graham's* sometime during 1843 and was supposed to have been published in the Jan. 1844 number of the periodical. Nothing by Simms was published in *Graham's* during 1844, but under the title "The Boatman's Revenge," "Barnacle Sam" was published in the Mar. 1845 number of the magazine (XXVI, 109–120). As "Sergeant Barnacle; or, the Raftsman of the Edisto," it was republished in *The Wigwam and the Cabin*, 2d ser. (New York: Wiley and Putnam, 1845), pp. 44–78.

[2]Walter Savage Landor, *Pericles and Aspasia*, 2 vols. (Philadelphia: E. L. Carey & A. Hart, 1839), and Sir William Francis Patrick Napier, *History of the War in the Peninsula and in the South of France, from the Year 1807 to the Year 1814* (Philadelphia: Carey and Hart, 1842).

[3]Probably *Private Memoirs of Sir Kenelm Digby, Gentleman of the Bedchamber to King Charles the First. Written by Himself. Now First Published from the Original Manuscript, with an Introductory Memoir* (by Sir Nicholas Harris Nicolas) (London: Saunders & Otley, 1827). In 1837 Simms had written three acts of a tragedy based on the life of "the unfortunate Venetia Digby, wife of Sir Kenelm," but wanted the opinion of Edwin Forrest (for whom the play was designed) before continuing, and Forrest apparently either never gave one or reacted unfavorably (see letters to Lawson of Mar. 31, July 20, Aug. 3, Aug. 7, Aug. 20, Sept. 10, Sept. 19, and Nov. 4, 1837, and c. Sept. 2, 1838 [46, 51, 53, 54, 55, 57, 58, 59, and 69]). Simms' request for this book suggests that he was contemplating taking up his pen again and finishing his play. Sir Kenelm Digby (1603–1665) fell in love with Venetia Stanley, a woman of extraordinary beauty and considerable intellectual attainments, to whom he bound himself with the strongest vows. His mother opposed the match, and he was induced to go abroad in 1620. At Angers, where he had gone to escape the plague in Paris, the queen-mother, Marie de Medicis, attempted to seduce him, and in order to preserve his virtue he spread the report of his death and fled by sea to Italy. He returned to England in 1623, heard and believed the rumors (apparently in part true) of the less-than-modest behavior of Venetia, who thought that her betrothed had died. Meeting her by chance, he again fell hopelessly in love, and they were secretly married in 1625. Upon the death of Venetia in 1633 there were reports that he had killed her by insisting she drink viper-wine to preserve her rare beauty. His grief was profound. Such doubtless was the main plot of Simms' unfinished tragedy.

154a : To Israel Keech Tefft

Charleston, March 15. [1843][1]

My dear Tefft

Mr. Solomons who is the Bearer of this, is the agent for the Apollo Society, an institution the character of which he will explain to you, cheap, admirable of plan & highly attractive.[2] Pray push it in your city.—I have an autograph for you, or two—probably will visit you next month, & bring with me Wm. Cullen Bryant & Lady.[3] What say you?—Why do I not hear from you. My best respects at home.

Yours faithfully

W. Gilmore Simms

156b : To Carey and Hart

Charleston, March 28. [1843][1]

Mess'rs Carey & Hart
Gentlemen

I have this day put into the hands of Mr. Saml. Hart, Bookseller of this place, "The Two Camps, a Legend of the Old North State",—

154a

[1]Dated by Simms' reference to the Bryants' visit to South Carolina. See his other letters of this month.

[2]In a notice of the *Transactions of the Apollo Association for the Promotion of the Fine Arts in the United States* (New York, 1842) the *Knickerbocker*, XXI (Apr. 1843), 388, remarks that "for the small sum of *five dollars* a membership [in the Association] is secured, and a chance of obtaining by lot some one of the many fine paintings, from eminent artists, which are constantly made the property of the Association; to say nothing of an annual engraving, in the first style of the art, of one of the best paintings submitted to the Society." The name of the association was soon changed to the American Art-Union, of which Simms' friend Prosper Montgomery Wetmore was the first president.

[3]See introductory sketch.

156b

[1]Dated by Simms' reference to the visit of William Cullen Bryant and his wife to Woodlands. See Simms' other letters written in Mar. 1843.

a story for the Gift, to be sent by the first safe opportunity.[2] I trust it will prove equally readable & unexceptionable. As soon as you get a purchaser for the other story, pray advise me,[3] for authorship as you know, among us, always a needy business, is particularly so at this juncture. Are we to have any change. I have noted the following works in your Quarterly Advertiser which I should like you to send me, viz.

Hoole's Tasso's Jerusalem Delivered 2 vols. 8vo bd – $5.00[4]

Lingard's Histy of England (Paris Ed— 8 vols 10.00[5]

We never get your books for the Magnolia, though our circulation and authority now is very far greater than any Southern newspaper.—My best respects to Carey. I have, as a visitor, at the plantation, W. C. Bryant & Lady, where the latter, who came as an invalid, has very much improved.[6]

Yours

W. G. Simms

159 (1a) : To Carey and Hart

Charleston, April 8. [1843][1]

Mess'rs Carey & Hart
Gentlemen

"The Two Camps" a story for the Gift was forwarded to your address a week ago by S. Hart, of this city. I trust that ere this

[2]"The Two Camps. A Legend of the Old North State" was published in *The Gift* . . .[*for*] MDCCCXLIV, pp. 149–181.

[3]Evidently Miss Leslie found "Barnacle Sam," a tale of seduction, suicide, and murder, "exceptionable" as a story for the delicate readers of *The Gift.* See letter to Carey and Hart of Feb. 23, 1843 (149b).

[4]John Hoole's translation of Tasso's *Jerusalem Delivered* was first published in London in 2 vols. in 1763. We do not know what edition Simms is here ordering.

[5]John Lingard, *A History of England, from the First Invasion by the Romans*, 5th ed., 8 vols. (Paris: Baudry's European Library, 1840).

[6]According to Simms' children, on this visit Mrs. Bryant deeply offended Simms' housemaids by turning up their skirts to see for herself the quality of their underwear as evidence of the treatment of slaves in the South.

159(1a)

[1]Dated by Simms' remark about "The Two Camps." See letter to Carey and Hart of Mar. 28 (156b).

reaches you you will have recd. it.—I will thank you to send me a copy of Wilson's Noctes,[2] in the same neat style of binding, in which you have issued Macauley's, Talfourds[3] &c.—a half binding, calf, I believe. Send me also in the same style, the 4th. Vol. of Macauley.[4] I have all the rest.

Yours truly

W. G. Simms

P. S. I am very anxious to put forth a volume or two of Tales, a neat 12 mo.—as Border Stories of the South & West. I have one or two that have never been printed & several that have & which are among my best writings. What would be the chance of an edition in two volumes, at 75/100 or $1.00?—And how would you like to try one—my profits to depend upon yours?[5]

---

[2]John Wilson, *The Noctes Ambrosianæ of "Blackwood"* (Philadelphia: Carey and Hart, 1843). When Simms was planning his *Southern and Western Monthly Magazine and Review*, he thought of including a department modeled on Wilson's *Noctes* (see letter to Holmes of Dec. 30, 1844 [224], and note 47, Jan. 18, 1845 [228]).

[3]Sir Thomas Noon Talfourd, *Critical and Miscellaneous Writings* (Philadelphia: Carey and Hart, 1842).

[4]Carey and Hart began publishing an edition of Thomas Babington Macaulay's *Critical and Miscellaneous Writings* in 1842. A fifth volume was published in 1844. The firm also published (in 1843) a one-volume edition, which Simms in his *Magnolia*, N. S., II (June 1843), 397, describes as a "new and *cheap* edition," but because of the paper and type he recommends the purchase of "the *dear* edition in four stout duodecimo's."

[5]Carey and Hart evidently declined, since on June 12, 1843, Simms wrote to Lawson (163) asking him to propose the volume to Harper & Brothers. He there mentions "most" of the proposed contents: "Ellen Halsey, or my Wife against my Will; 2. Castle Dismal, or the Bachelor's Christmas, 3. Barnacle Sam, or the Edisto Raftsman. 4. The Last Wager, or the Gamester of the Mississippi, 5. Murder will out; a Ghost story; The Arm Chair of Tustenuggee, a Legend of the Catawba. 7. The Lazy Crow, a Story of the Cornfield, &c." "Ellen Halsey" was later published in book form as *Helen Halsey: Or, the Swamp State of Conelachita. A Tale of the Borders* (New York: Burgess, Stringer & Co., 1845). Six chapters of "Castle Dismal; or the Bachelor's Christmas; a Nouvellette" were published in the *Magnolia*, IV (Jan., Feb., Mar., Apr., and June 1842), 27–32, 97–109, 183–186, 240–247, 371–376. Why he discontinued its publication, we do not know, but the work was later published in book form as *Castle Dismal: Or, the Bachelor's Christmas. A Domestic Tale* (New York: Burgess, Stringer & Co., 1844). For "Barnacle Sam," see note 1, Feb. 23, 1843 (149b). "The Last Wager, or, the Gamester of the Mississippi, A Frontier Story" was published in *The Gift . . . [for] MDCCCXLIII*," pp. 275–327. For " 'Murder Will Out,' " see note 2, Nov. 25, 1840 (94a). For "The Arm-Chair of Tustenuggee," see note 2, Feb. 14, 1839 (71d). For "The Two

163a : To Mitchell King

June 17. [1843][1]

My dear Judge

I trust you have been enabled to prepare the little paper which I begged at your hands for the forthcoming issue of the "Charleston Book." If not will you endeavour to have it ready for me by the 1st. proxo. You know what I want—something in prose, unique, sketchy, picturesque. Our southern writers have been almost too uniformly too grave, if not severe in their writings for our purpose. The paper should not exceed three or four printed 12 mo. pages. Your poem I will select from the mag. vol. in your collection, which I once more beg that you will send me. I wish that vol. which contains the poem of Alfred by Hasell.[2]

Yrs faithfully &c

W. G. Simms

Hon. M. King.

Camps," see note 2, Mar. 28, 1843 (156b). All of these tales except *Helen Halsey* and *Castle Dismal* were later included in *The Wigwam and the Cabin*, First and Second Series (New York: Wiley and Putnam, 1845).

163a

[1]Dated by Simms' remarks about the "mag. vol." which he had been trying to borrow from King for almost a year (see letters to King of July 15, 1842, and Jan. 10, 1843 [139a and 149 (1a)]). He had the volume before Aug. 1843, when in his review of Griswold's *The Poets and Poetry of America* in the *Magnolia*, N. S., I, 117–118, he quotes from it in discussing Griswold's omission of Hasell from his book.

[2]Simms wanted the two volumes of the *Monthly Review and Literary Miscellany of the United States* (the title of the second volume is the *Monthly Register, Magazine, and Review of the United States*), published in Charleston during 1806–1807. Stephen Cullen Carpenter edited the first volume; with the second volume John Bristed became coeditor and, upon Carpenter's resignation in May 1807, sole editor. "Alfred: An Historical Poem. Delivered at the Public Commencement at Yale-College, in New-Haven, September 11, 1799," by William Sorenzo Hasell (1780–1815), of Charleston, was published in the *Monthly Review and Literary Miscellany*, I (Oct., Nov., and Dec. 1806), 311–312, 358–360, 391–392; II (Feb. 1807), 145–147. King's "The Resolve" (signed "The Wanderer" and dated "Charleston, 1806") was published in the same magazine, I (Oct. 1806), 332–344. "Alfred" and "The Resolve" are included in *The Charleston Book*, pp. 50–61, 77–88. Before its publication in Carpenter's magazine "Alfred" had been published separately: *Alfred: An Historical Poem, Delivered at the Public Commencement at Yale College, in New-Haven, September 11, 1799. Written by a Carolinian of Eighteen, a Student in the Said College* (Charleston: Printed by T. C. Cox, 1800).

171a : To John Caldwell Calhoun[1]

[August, 1843][2]

Hon. J. C. Calhoun
dear Sir

The writer of the above letter, Mr. J. Kenrick Fisher is an amiable gentleman and an excellent artist, who is now engaged enthusi-

---

171a

[1]See introductory sketch. We want to thank W. Edwin Hemphill, editor of *The Papers of John C. Calhoun*, for bringing this letter to our attention. Since the letter is in the Albert Kenrick Fisher Papers, Library of Congress, it apparently was not sent to Calhoun.

[2]This letter is written on the bottom of the third sheet of the following letter:

New-York, August 1843.

Hon. John C. Calhoun.

Sir: I am desirous to render such aid as I can to the cause of Commercial Freedom; and, as one means, to procure, for publication and wide circulation, a statement of what should be the ultimate policy of this nation and all nations, in reference to tariff imposts, and other checks upon trade. Such a statement would be most sure of a general and attentive reading, if it should come from a man already well known to the public; and if that man were so situated that his views might be regarded as a probable indication of the future policy of this country, its publication would produce considerable influence on the public feeling and the legislation in other countries. I believe you to be the man from whom such an outline, given as a personal opinion, would come with the best effect—if your views accord with the laws which nature has predetermined: and my object in addressing you now, is to beg you to inform me whether you would approve a total abolition of the tariff;—for, to speak with the candor due to yourself and all others concerned, I should be painfully disapponted to learn that you are not ready, at any time, to abolish this mode of taxation, even without waiting for any other mode, save that indicated by the Constitution: but if you would sketch out a general policy, based on unqualified freedom of trade; and state what you deem the just claims of existing interests as to the *time* to be allowed for the transition; and also what means should be taken to induce other nations to adopt a reciprocal course; I should believe that I might render good service, by asking some of the friends of free trade to join in requesting your views, and in making arrangements to publish them in the way most likely to secure to them the attention of American citizens, and of the friends of free trade in other countries.

I would ask for your views on this course to be pursued, if, contrary to the belief of free traders, it should prove disadvantageous to us to admit goods free, while other nations do not reciprocate; because there are many, in both parties, who believe that *reciprocal* free trade would be best for all; and who would join in the free trade movement if they thought that all fair means would be used to make other nations follow, with respect to us, any such liberal movement which we might make. Of course, it should not be proposed as a condition; but only as an opinion as to what is *the true policy*—which we are not to contrive, but to discover.

astically in concocting a scheme by which foreign art will be made familiar to our people.[3] I am not so sure that it will lie within your usual custom to respond to his application,—but this is a matter which, of course, will wholly lie within your own judgment. Enough for me that I can assure you of the good faith with which his application has been made. He fancies that the slight but grateful acquaintance with which I have been honored by you will persuade you to regard his letter in an inoffensive light. With very great, respect, I am Sir, your obt. & obliged Servant—

W. Gilmore Simms

of South Carolina

I would also ask how far—to what amount per year—we ought to make sacrifices for the general good of the world. The idea that each nation is to act for its own advantage exclusively, not regarding the influence of its example, is frequently inculcated by political teachers; but I apprehend that a loss, for a short time, of a few millions per year, should not deter us from being the first to adopt what we believe to be the true policy.

I have read the speech to which you referred the Committee of the Indiana Convention; which, though it fully answers the inquiries of that Committee, does not enable me to judge whether you would favor the views I wish to advance.

Your obedient servant,

J. Kenrick Fisher.

246 East Broadway, New-York.

The fact that Simms attempted to get Calhoun to pay attention to Fisher's letter perhaps indicates that he approved of his views.

[3]John Kenrick Fisher (b. 1807), portrait and historical painter, studied in England and exhibited at the Royal Academy and other London galleries during 1830–1832. In 1837 and early 1838 he worked in Charleston, and Simms could have met him there. In 1843 he was living in New York City. We do not know what "scheme" he was "concocting . . . by which foreign art will be made familiar to our people."

172a : To Sarah Josepha Buell Hale[1]

Tremont House,
Tuesday Mg. Aug 29 [1843][2]

My dear Madam

I should have been pleased to have presented in person the enclosed letter from our mutual friend, Mrs Gilman, but that I have been unable to learn your address. I need not add how happy I shall be to make your acquaintance.

Very truly & respectfully
Yr obt Serv.

W. Gilmore Simms

Mrs. Hale.

172b : To Cornelius Conway Felton[1]

Tremont House
Thursday Mg. [August 31, 1843][2]

Dear Sir

I very much regret that my previous engagements (which however willing, I am unable to alter) will prevent me having the pleasure of seeing you today. I must reserve this pleasure for another season,

172a

[1]Mrs. Hale (see note 190, Oct. 15, 1849 [509]) was one of the editors of *Godey's Lady's Book*.

[2]Dated by Caroline Howard Gilman's letter of introduction (dated July 22, 1843), which is preserved with this letter. For Mrs. Gilman, see introductory sketch of the Gilmans.

172b

[1]Felton (1807–1862), classical scholar and educator, was born in Newbury, Mass., and was graduated from Harvard College in 1827. In 1829 he was appointed tutor in Latin at Harvard and in 1830 tutor in Greek. In 1832 he became professor of Greek, and two years later he received the Eliot Professorship of Greek Literature, which he held until his election as president of Harvard College in 1860.

[2]Dated by Simms' remark that he leaves "for New York this afternoon." In his letter to Lawson of Aug. 28, 1843 (172), he writes that he plans to leave Boston on "Thursday next."

as I leave Boston for New York this afternoon. I have taken leave to cover a note for M. Perdicaris.[3]

Very truly & respectfully
Yr obt ser.

W. Gilmore Simms

Professor Felton.

174 (1a) : To Matthew St. Clair Clarke[1]

Charleston. Sep. 21. [1843][2]

M. St Clair Clarke, Esq.
Sir

Under the instructions of Mr. Peter Force, I take the liberty to send to your address, for him, a copy of the History of South Carolina, and of the Geography of the same state, which you will please place in his hands. With great respect

I am Sir
Yr obt Servant

W. Gilmore Simms

---

[3]Probably Gregory A. Perdicaris, who later wrote *The Greece of the Greeks*, 2 vols. (New York: Paine and Burgess, 1846).

174(1a)

[1]Until his death in 1851 Clarke, who was in 1843 clerk of the U.S. House of Representatives, was associated with Peter Force (see note 310, Oct. 12, 1845 [276]) in the compilation and publication of *American Archives* (Washington, D.C., 1837–1853). On Mar. 2, 1833, Congress passed an act authorizing the secretary of state to make a contract with Clarke and Force for the publication of this work (see *The Public Statutes at Large of the United States of America*, IV [Boston: Charles C. Little and James Brown, 1846], pp. 654–655).

[2]Someone (possibly Force) has dated this letter and the two following letters to Force "1843" (174 [2a] and 175a). The date seems probable because of Simms' reference to the third volume of Force's *Tracts* in his letter to Force of Oct. 9 (175a).

174 (2a) : To Peter Force

Charleston, S. C.
Sep. 22. [1843][1]

P. Force, Esq

Washington.
Dear Sir

By this day's mail I address to M. St. Clair Clarke, for you, a copy of my Histy of South Carolina, and of my Geography of the same state. I trust that they will reach you safely. My anxiety to be put in possession of your collection of Tracts[2] emboldens me to remind you of the kind promise which you made me recently that I should have them.

Very truly Sir,
Your obt. Servt

W. Gilmore Simms

175a : To Peter Force

Charleston, Oct 9. [1843][1]

My dear Sir:

I thank you for the 2 vols of Tracts which reached me safely & seasonably. I shall look for the third with anxiety and recieve it gratefully.[2]—It will give me great pleasure to reciprocate these courtesies with you. I believe I gave you to understand that I am groping for materials for a Life of Marion & Sumter.[3] Whatever I put forth

174 (2a)

[1]For the date, see note 1, letter to Clarke of Sept. 21, 1843 (174 [1a]).

[2]See note 2, Oct. 9, 1843 (175a).

175a

[1]For the date, see note 1, letter to Clarke of Sept. 21, 1843 (174 [1a]).

[2]*Tracts and Other Papers Relating Principally to the Origin, Settlement, and Progress of the Colonies in North America, from the Discovery of the Country to the Year 1776* (Washington: Printed by Peter Force) was published in 4 vols. (1836, 1838, 1844, 1846).

[3]*The Life of Francis Marion* was published by Henry G. Langley, New York, in 1844. Simms did not publish a life of Thomas Sumter.

in this way I shall send you promptly. Accompanying I send you some trifles not of an historical character, but they may please you in an idle moment,[4] as the result of the idle moments of

Your Very obt. &c

W. Gilmore Simms

Peter Force, Esq.

199b : To Sidney Babcock

Woodlands, 20th. April [1844][1]

S. Babcock, Esq.
Dear Sir—

Modifying your proposition in one point only, I make it mine as follows:

1.	You pay for the Questions, already due, for the Geography[2]——— ———	$12.00
2	You pay for those wanted for the History	12.00
3	You honor my draft in favor of Babcock & Co of Charleston August 1st. 1844	76.00
3	You honor my dft May 1.!! 1845	100.00
4	" " " " Sept 1. 1845	100.00
		$300.00

You see that I take your offer only requiring the draft in favor of your brother to be paid four months sooner. Let me add that *I can get the cash for the whole amount*, at any moment, for the same

[4]Probably *Donna Florida. A Tale* (Charleston: Burges and James, 1843) was one of these "trifles."

199b

[1]Dated by Simms' remark that his draft should be honored by Aug. 1, 1844.

[2]At the end of Simms' *Geography of South Carolina* is a section entitled "Questions on the Geography of South Carolina," pp. 17[7]–192.

privilege from another publishing house. But as long as we can agree, you have undoubtedly a right to the preference.

Yours truly

W. G. Simms

P. S. Pray let me hear from you shortly.

202b : To Sidney Babcock

Charleston, June 16. [1844][1]

My dear Sir

I have not thought it worth while to say any thing in answer to your last letter stating your determination to accept my terms for the new edition of the History of South Carolina. But, upon reflection, it seems to me quite as well that I should do so. A simple recapitulation for the help of mutual recollection, will suffice. You are then to have the right of publishing three thousand (3000) copies of my history of South Carolina, forming the third edition of that work, on the following conditions: You are

1st.	To cancel a charge against me for Questions to my Geography—of	$12.00
2d.	To provide similar questions to my Hy.	12.00
3"	" Honor my draft in favor of S. B & Co. Augt. 1. 1844 ———	76.00
4th.	" Honor my dft on May 1. 1845 ———	100.00
5"	" " " " " Sept. 1. 1845	100.00
		$300.00

202b

[1]Dated by Simms' remarks about his agreement with Babcock. See letter to Babcock of Apr. 20, 1844 (199b).

I have no doubt that we shall find the arrangement mutually advantageous.[2]

Very truly &c

W. Gilmore Simms

S. Babcock, Esq.

202c : To Brantz Mayer[1]

Charleston, S. C. June 16. [1844][2]

Sir

I am honored by the election of the Maryland Historical Society to a place among its members. Do me the kindness to convey to that body my high sense of the compliment conferred upon me. It will give me pleasure, as soon as an opportunity offers, to send you, for the Library of the Society, a copy of my History of South Carolina.[3] For yourself, be pleased, Sir, to recieve my acknowledgments.

I am, Sir, very much
Your obliged & obt
servt.

W. Gilmore Simms

Brantz Mayer Esq.
Cor. Sec. Md Hist. Socy.

---

[2]This edition was not published. A "New and Revised Edition" (the third) was published by Russell & Jones, Charleston, in 1860.

202c

[1]Mayer (see note 299, Aug. 20, 1845 [273]), lawyer and author, was corresponding secretary of the Maryland Historical Society from its founding in 1844 until 1847.

[2]Dated by Simms' election as an honorary member of the Maryland Historical Society on June 6, 1844. The other honorary members elected at the same time were John Quincy Adams, Lewis Cass, James Fenimore Cooper, Washington Irving, Robert Walsh, Joel Roberts Poinsett, John Macpherson Berrien, and Alexander Hill Everett. See Vol. I of the "Minutes of the Council" (Maryland Historical Society Archives MS. 2008). We want to thank Richard J. Cox, Curator of Manuscripts, Maryland Historical Society, for this information.

[3]The Maryland Historical Society Library contains a copy of Simms' *History of South Carolina* (1840).

1845–1849

230a : To Brantz Mayer

Woodlands, Jan 25 [1845][1]

Brantz Mayer, Esq.
dear Sir

I have delayed writing you until I could recieve some tidings of the diplomas meant for Mr. Poinsett and myself. My opportunities for sending to Mr P have been frequent of late, but the instruments have not yet reached me. In a late visit to Charleston, however, I recieved some inkling of their whereabouts, and am, I trust, in train for getting them in possession. Should it occur to you hereafter to honor me with any packets beyond the scope of the ordinary mail, by addressing them to the care of "Saml. Hart, Sen. Bookseller" they will most probably reach me in season.—I sent you, not long since, a copy of the Geological report of S. C.[2] I trust it has been recieved. We find it impossible to say by whom the copy of my History of S. C. meant for your Society & addressed to you was dispatched. I will endeavour at an early opportunity to see that you are supplied with the work.

With great respect, I am
Sir, Very truly Yours

W. Gilmore Simms

230a

[1]Dated by Simms' remark concerning the "diplomas" meant for himself and Joel Roberts Poinsett (see introductory sketch). At the meeting of the Council of the Maryland Historical Society on June 6, 1844, at which Simms and Poinsett were elected honorary members (see note 2, June 16, 1844 [202c]), it was reported that the diploma for honorary members had been prepared and a specimen "beautifully designed and executed" was exhibited to the members (see Vol. I of the "Minutes of the Council" [Maryland Historical Society Archives MS. 2008]).

[2]Michael Tuomey, *Report of the Geological and Agricultural Survey of the State of South Carolina* (Columbia, S.C.: Printed by A. S. Johnston, 1844).

240a : To Joel Tyler Headley[1]

[February 28? 1845][2]

It will always give me pleasure to hear from you, whether you consider me or my magazine. Our friends Duyckinck & Mathews are scarcely such constant correspondents as I could wish. The former began tolerably well, but he has somehow fallen off. As for the latter, I fear his Big Able has disabled him, and his Little Manhattan has whittled him off *infinitesimally.*[3] Give him the benefit of this scandalous conjecture that he may be awakened to a just sense of his (supposed) demerits.—Mrs. Simms is obliged by your recollection & begs me to say so. For myself, please believe me

Very faithfully
Yours &c.

W. Gilmore Simms.

255a : To Joseph Starke Sims[1]

Charleston, June 10. [1845][2]

J. S. Sims Esq
dear Sir

I thank you for your letter, and for the warm kindness with which you speak of my labors in the cause of Southern letters. It is Cowper,

---

240a

[1]See introductory sketch.

[2]This letter is an answer to Headley's letter to Simms dated Feb. 21, 1845 (original in the New-York Historical Society Library), quoted in part in note 58, Jan. 19, 1845 (229). Simms' letter is postmarked "March 1."

[3]In the first number of Simms' *Southern and Western Monthly Magazine and Review* (Jan. 1845) Headley published "An Incident of Waterloo," Evert Augustus Duyckinck (see introductory sketch) "Time's Wallet. I. The Hystorie of Hamblet," pp. 54–60, 61–66. Cornelius Mathews (see introductory sketch) at this time was at work on *Big Abel and the Little Manhattan* (New York: Wiley and Putnam, 1845).

255a

[1]Sims (1802–1875), born in Union District, S.C., was graduated from the South Carolina College in 1819. He was a lawyer and planter in Union, twice represented Union in the S.C. House of Representatives, and was a member of the Secession Convention in 1860. He is probably the same as the "J. S. Simms" to whom Simms wrote on Apr. 22, 1850 (535*a*).

[2]Dated by Simms' enclosure of the prospectus of the *Southern and Western Monthly Magazine and Review*, dated Dec. 1, 1844.

I think, who somewhere tells us that pay or praise is necessary to the man of letters;[3] and some of them cannot well do without both. Such is the mental appetite & such the physical necessity. To me, it is particularly fortunate that some of the former should be given now and then, as I have not often been favored with the latter. The rewards of literature in this country, particularly in the South, are the saddest absurdities. For my part, I have been all my life drawing water[4] in a sieve, & have had few other consolations than are to be found in the secret assurance, that I shall not always labor without some sort of recompense. That of fame comes slowly it is true, but it is one of those rewards that a man may wait for, through his children, even to the third and fourth generation. To win the tones of friendly & favoring voices, such as yours, while one is yet struggling in the field of combat, is an earnest of hope, calculated greatly to strengthen his confidence in the awards of the future. I have no reason to suspect you of flattery, whether I regard your character and position and duly estimate my own. Why should you or any man "flatter so poor a man as Brutus?"[5] On the contrary, praise "from mouths of wisest censure"[6] is quite too agreeable, not to be taken in its most literal signification.—Your conjecture, touching the authorship of the article on Boone proves your critical sagacity. The paper was mine; though I very frequently prefer the anonymous to any open blazon of my performances. The article was compiled from various sources, and these may not always have been the best authorities. It is fortunate that the point of difference between my statement and that of Moseley is a minor one. Small as it is, however, I shall find a place for it in the magazine in the course of the forthcoming number. I shall also take the liberty of putting on record what you say of James Moseley. These veterans deserve some recognition.[7]—I cover to you a prospectus for which

[3]We have not located this sentiment in Cowper's poetry. The remark could be in one of his letters, but it does not sound like one Cowper would have made.

[4]Simms wrote *I have been all my life been drawing water.*

[5]Not identified.

[6]Simms misquotes *Othello*, II, iii, 193.

[7]"Daniel Boon; the First Hunter of Kentucky" was published in the *Southern and Western Monthly Magazine and Review*, I (Apr. 1845), 225–242. In it Simms describes Boone as "a tall man of powerful frame." Sims in his note published under the title of "Daniel Boone.—James Moseley," ibid., II (Aug. 1845), 131–132

you may find friends in your neighbourhood. If you can do this without going too much out of your way, you will promote the cause of letters among us. I am writing *con amore*. The work does not & never will pay me. But it is a work that is wanted.—I shall be happy to hear from you whenever it is convenient, and should I ever stray into Union will certainly seek you out, and share your hospitality.

Very faithfully &c
Yours

W Gilmore Simms

285a : To William Campbell Preston[1]

H: Repr. Decr. 11. [1845][2]

Dear Sir

Let me remind you of the request I made you, to procure, if possible, that young Govan should be permitted to return with me to his Uncle's family for a couple of weeks.[3] I propose to leave

(which in note 242, June 25, 1845 [260], we incorrectly assign to Simms), writes of Moseley: "An old man, truthful honest and highly esteemed by all around him," named James Moseley, claimed to have known Boone well and to have frequently slept in his cabin and been the companion of his wanderings. He came from the Yadkin to the Pacolet and lived in Boone's neighborhood on the former river. He described Boone in the fullness of his vigor as weighing about one hundred and fifty pounds and not above five feet, eight or nine inches in height, "marked by a lively, sparkling blue eye," "very active," "athletic," and "well-made."

285a

[1]At this time Preston (see introductory sketch) was president of the South Carolina College.

[2]Simms was a member of the S.C. House of Representatives during 1844–1846. His reference to Dec. "16th. (Tuesday)" establishes the year.

[3]Daniel Chevillette Govan (1829–1911), was the son of Andrew Robison Govan (see note 83, Aug. 16, 1841 [115]), only brother of Nash Roach's late wife, Eliza. The University of South Carolina Archives show that he was admitted to the South Carolina College as a freshman on Oct. 6, 1845, and left the College in 1847. A brother, William Hemphill Govan, entered the South Carolina College in 1848 and was graduated in 1850. We are indebted to Libby Alford, Research Asssistant to Professor James Meriwether of the University of South Carolina, for this information.

Daniel Govan moved from Mississippi to Arkansas and was a brigadier-general in the Civil War. After the war he lived in Mississippi, the state of Washington, and Tennessee.

Columbia on the 16th. (Tuesday) and would like to take Govan with me. The object of the rule of The Trustees being to keep the young men from the excesses and temptations of Christmas, (I assume this) you may safely answer for his behaviour during his stay with us. If you can serve me in this particular you will very much oblige me.

Respectfully &
faithfully
yours &c

W. Gilmore Simms

Hon W. C. Preston

292a : To William Alfred Jones[1]

Woodlands, Jan 25. [1846][2]

Wm. A. Jones, Esq
Dear Sir

I have suffered your kind and complimentary letter, sent through our friend Duyckinck two months ago, to remain unseasonably long unnoticed. But my apology is one which you will readily comprehend & recieve. When it came to hand, I had just taken my seat in our Legislature, and had my hands too full of public affairs to think of private.[3] When I returned home, the professional and domestic duties, provided me a world of drudgery to go through, and keep me still as busy as single mortal should be at any time. But I must make my acknowledgments for your courtesy, though I do so in a somewhat unsatisfactory manner.—For a month or so back, up to the present time, the Temperance Society in Charleston, has been hammering at your heretical essay in most belligerent

292a

[1]See introductory sketch.

[2]Dated by Simms' remarks about the controversy caused by Jones' "The Temperance Question." See note 4, below.

[3]Simms was elected a member of the S.C. House of Representatives in 1844 and served for one term.

style of debate. It is probably quite as well that your ears were not privy to your castigation. Whether you felt them tingle where you are, or not, is a matter for your own memory & conscience. I did not hear any of the discussion, but learn that they rowed my correspondent up *salt* river,—I suppose in the hope that he would *keep* there. A correspondent of one of the Charleston newspapers, has quite cleverly discussed you, and handled your weak points with considerable skill of weapon. I will try & send you one or more of the papers.[4]—I am truly glad that my 'Views' please you.[5] One thing,[6] I fancy may be said of them—they are the honest expressions of one who tries, if he has not altogether learned, to think from & for himself.—When I go to the city, I will contrive to send you all the wanting numbers of my Magazine. Its connection with the Messenger, puts the critical dept. of both works under my control, *if I please to exercise my privilege.* As yet I have done nothing for the Messenger, being quite too busy in my own affairs.[7]—I am now busy on the Life of Capt. John Smith—the famous Capt. of Virginia. It will make a vol. like that of Marion,—and I think quite an interesting one.[8]—When are we to have your essays?[9] Positively our American publishers treat our American authors after a rascally fashion. We must wait upon the ragtag & bobtail of Europe, and—but indignation is only wasted.—When I write Jones—you shall have a copy.[10] I am now waiting for material. Of Smith, I shall see

---

[4]Jones' "The Temperance Question" was published in the *Southern and Western Monthly Magazine and Review*, II (Nov. 1845), 305–313. Simms thought the article "clumsily & carelessly written, & by no means profound"; he omitted a passage on the Methodists and accompanied the paper with some remarks of his own (see letter to Duyckinck of Aug. 8, 1845 [270]). Articles entitled "The Temperance Question," signed "Claude" and attacking Jones' essay, were published in the Charleston *Courier* of Jan. 14, Jan. 21, and Jan. 23.

[5]The First Series of Simms' *Views and Reviews in American Literature, History and Fiction* was published around May 1, 1846, the Second Series in July 1847. See note 284, Aug. 7, 1845 (269).

[6]Simms wrote *think*.

[7]At the end of 1845 Simms' *Southern and Western* was merged with the *Southern Literary Messenger.* See letter to Lawson of Oct. 27, 1845 (279).

[8]*The Life of Captain John Smith. The Founder of Virginia* (New York: Geo. F. Cooledge & Brother, n.d.). Though copyrighted 1846, the volume was not published until Mar. 1847. See note 4, Jan. 2, 1847 (350).

[9]*Literary Studies, a Collection of Miscellaneous Essays.* See note 1, Feb. 20, 1847 (358a).

[10]Simms was planning a biography, apparently never written, of John Paul Jones.

that you are not neglected. I shall send you shortly a little vol of Sonnets—a *brochure* not meant for publication, of which only a few copies are struck off for private circulation.[11]—I hope to see more of you when I visit the North next summer,—& meanwhile shall be glad to hear from you & of your health & prosperity.

Very much Yours &c

W. Gilmore Simms

296a : TO RUFUS WILMOT GRISWOLD

Woodlands, Feb 10. [1846][1]

Rev. R. W. Griswold
Dear Sir

I sent the carriage for you on Monday last to Midway, but was quite disappointed to see it return empty. I must now beg that, if you do me the honor of a visit, you defer it until the last of next week, as, on Thursday next,[2] I am compelled to set out on a trip to Savannah river. After my return, it will give me a great deal of pleasure, as I have already signified, to recieve you at Woodlands.—If you have made no inquiries yet touching the publication of an illustrated volume of Poems, or of the vol. of which I spoke to you, made up of Legends of Apalachia, will you take early occasion to do so?[3] You know so much more of the business of publishing than

---

See letter to Holmes of Nov. 6, 1844 (213), and note 62, Jan. 19, 1845 (229).

[11]*Grouped Thoughts and Scattered Fancies. A Collection of Sonnets* (Richmond, Va.: Printed by Wm. Macfarlane, Messenger Office, 1845).

296a

[1]Dated by Simms' plans for Griswold to visit him at Woodlands. In Dec. 1845 Griswold arrived in Charleston to visit his wife (the former Charlotte Myers) and her family and remained there about five months (see Bayless, *Rufus Wilmot Griswold*, pp. 109–112). On Jan. 1 Simms wrote to him repeating his invitation to visit Woodlands (289). On Feb. 9 he wrote to Duyckinck (296), "Griswold . . . appointed to visit me at the plantation but failed to come."

[2]Feb. 12.

[3]Since Simms' *Areytos: Or, Songs of the South* (Charleston: John Russell, 1846) was already "in press" by Mar. 17 (see letter to Lawson of that date [301]), the "illustrated volume of Poems" here proposed would be another, which was not published. "Lays of Apalachia" was not published (see letters to Lawson of Feb. 3 [295] and to Duyckinck of Feb. 20 [297]).

myself, & know so much better who are the right persons to apply to, that I prefer your offices to my own endeavor, removed as I am, just now, from the scene of operations.—Let me hear from you at your best convenience, & believe me Very respectfully

& truly, Yr obt Servt &c

W. Gilmore Simms

308a : To Wiley and Putnam[1]

Charleston, May 31. 1846

Mess'rs Wiley & Putnam
Gentln.

I have taken the liberty of drawing upon you for One Hundred Dollars, in two drafts of fifty dollars each; one in favor of Mr. Saml. Hart Sen, and the other in favor of Mr. John Russell,[2] both of this place & both booksellers. I trust that you will find it convenient to honor these drafts though the balance, as per statement, in my favor on the 1st. Jany. last, fell something short of this amount. Yours truly &c.

W Gilmore Simms

315a : To Rufus Wilmot Griswold

New York, July 20 [1846][1]

My dear Sir

I thank you very much for your attention to the matter with Hart, and hope I gave you no very troublesome task. Of course we

---

308a

[1]The firm of Wiley and Putnam (John Wiley and George Palmer Putnam), of New York City, published Simms' *Wigwam and the Cabin* in 1845. In May 1846 the firm published the First Series of Simms' *Views and Reviews in American Literature, History and Fiction.*

[2]See introductory sketch.

315a

[1]Dated by Simms' remarks about "the letter & book." See letter to Duyckinck of Aug. 9, 1846 (319).

shall have to bide our time.[2]—Duyckinck happened to come in the moment after I got your letter, but neither he nor I had heard from you before, nor of the vol. of Poets.[3] Where they be,—the letter & book,—we know not. How does your work advance?[4] We shall both be very glad to see you here, where there is much hope of a good business campaign in the publishing world. It is not feared that the Whig cry of 'Wolf' will reproduce the ancient panic.

Yours respectfully &c

W. Gilmore Simms.

Rev. R. W. Griswold

321a : To Louis Antoine Godey[1]

[c. September 2, 1846][2]

My dear Godey

I am not solicitous about the small matter to which you refer me on the sheet which you return, & have made the alteration as you desire. You are properly prudent in your management. I can not just now say what the residue will make, since subjects such as this are apt to grow under one's hands. But let me know how many pages will suffice for each number. How far, for example, will the Chap. go which I sent you.[3] Don't forget that you have some sonnets

[2]Probably Griswold had approached Abraham Hart on the subject of publishing Simms' proposed "illustrated volume of Poems," which Simms himself later unsuccessfully attempted to convince Hart he should publish. See letters to Griswold of Feb. 10 and to Carey and Hart of Oct. 26 and Dec. 13, 1847 (296a, 409, and 416).

[3]*The Poets and Poetry of England, in the Nineteenth Century* (Philadelphia: Carey & Hart, 1844). See letter to Duyckinck of Aug. 9, 1846 (319).

[4]Griswold was working on his *Prose Writers of America* (Philadelphia: Carey and Hart, 1847).

321a

[1]See introductory sketch.

[2]This letter is postmarked "Sep 3." The year is established by Simms' remarks concerning his contributions to *Godey's Lady's Book.* See notes 3 and 4, below.

[3]"Maize in Milk. A Christmas Story of the South," a novelette, was published in *Godey's Lady's Book,* XXXIV (Feb., Mar., Apr., and May 1847), 62–67, 146–152, 199–204, 249–258.

of mine in hand, some of which I think particularly good.[4] I thank you for your attention to the music &c. I sent you a notice which I made of one of your late nos.

Yours truly

W. Gilmore Simms

330a : To Israel Keech Tefft

Charleston, Oct 22. [1846][1]

My dear Tefft

I am in reciept of the very interesting copy of Bayard from the Library of Mr. Smets, of which you may assure him I shall be particularly careful. It may be that I shall be slow in returning it, as I do not now hope to have my own work finished till the spring.[2] But, in the meantime, I shall keep it safely. I thank you, and dear little Mama,[3] for your kindly sympathies. We have been grievously made to suffer in our young, and have now but three left out of seven, and one of these an infant.[4] But, it will be well for us, if in the language of one of our old Poets,—God,—

'To save the parents takes the child.'

I trust you flourish and keep young. You deserve to do so. And you

[4]"Heart Fancies.—A Series of Sonnets" ("First Love," "Profitless Fidelity," "Tears," "Meteor at Sea," and "The Three Graves") was published in ibid., XXXIV (Mar. 1847), 156; "Despondency and Self-Reproach. A Group of Sonnets" ("Oh, friend, but thou art come to see me die!" "Hadst thou come sooner! But 'tis not too late . . .," "Ah! *thou* didst use to steer her chartfully . . .") in ibid., XXXV (Oct. 1847), 168.

330a

[1]Dated by Simms' remarks about Caruthers and Jackson. See below.

[2]For Alexander Augustus Smets (1795–1862), owner of a varied and extensive library, see note 102, June 9, 1868 (1305). In the "Advertisement" of *The Life of the Chevalier Bayard* (New York: Harper & Brothers, 1847), p. [v], Simms thanks Smets for the use of the "rare and quaint old volume" Symphorien Champier's *Les Gestes encelble la vie du preulx chevalier Bauard* . . . (Lyons: Villiers, 1525), one of the main sources for his book.

[3]Mrs. Tefft, the former Penelope Waite.

[4]Valeria Govan Simms died on Sept. 20; Mary Lawson Simms was born on Sept. 13. Simms' other children alive at this time were William Gilmore Simms, Jr., and Anna Augusta Singleton Simms (his daughter by his first wife). In addition to Valeria, Simms had lost three other daughters: Virginia Singleton Simms (d. 1838), Agnes Simms (d. 1841), and Mary Derrille Simms (d. 1842).

have lost Caruthers. Poor fellow What was his disease.[5] I take for granted and trust, that Charlton, Elliott [6] and all other friends are well. How was it that Jackson suffered his Regt. to become so insubordinate.[7] And how comes it farther that you suffered Cohen to be so consumedly beaten.[8] Very much Yours &c

W. Gilmore Simms

Tell Mama she must not be surprised if I look in upon her this winter.

---

[5]William Alexander Caruthers (b. 1800), a native of Virginia, was a physician in Savannah. He was the author of *The Kentuckian in New-York* (1834), *The Cavaliers of Virginia* (1834–1835), and *The Knights of the Golden Horse-Shoe* (originally published serially in the *Magnolia* in 1841). He died in Marietta, Ga., on Aug. 29.

[6]Robert Milledge Charlton (see note 178, Sept. 1854 [733]) and Stephen Elliott, Jr. (see introductory sketch).

[7]Henry Rootes Jackson (see note 108, June 16, 1854 [719]) was colonel of the First Regiment of Georgia Volunteers. Men of two of his companies, the Irish Jasper Greens of Savannah and the Kennesaw Rangers (also called "Invincibles") of Cobb County, had an altercation in which a Col. Baker and several of his men of the Fourth Regiment of Illinois Volunteers became involved. At least one man (Sgt. Whalen of the Jasper Greens) was killed and several others wounded. For an account of this confused incident (about which there were conflicting reports in the newspapers), see Wilbur G. Kurtz, Jr., "The First Regiment of Georgia Volunteers in the Mexican War," *Georgia Historical Quarterly*, XXVII (1943), 314–317. We want to thank Robert E. Tucker, Jr. Georgia Historical Society, for bringing this article to our attention.

[8]The Charleston *Mercury* of Oct. 7 reports from the Savannah *Republican* of Oct. 5 the results of the election for a member of Congress to represent the First Congressional District: "T.[homas] B.[utler] King, (Whig) 606 / Sol[omon] Cohen, 395 / Blank, 3." Cohen (1802–1875), a lawyer in Georgetown, S.C., moved to Savannah in 1838 and represented Chatham County in the Georgia legislature. He was U.S. postmaster in Savannah (1853–1861) and continued as postmaster under the Confederate government. In 1866 he was elected to the U.S. Congress from the First Congressional District but was not admitted. Cohen was a member of the committee of the Georgia Historical Society which asked Simms to lecture before the society in 1842 (see note 2, Jan. 10, 1842 [126a]). We want to thank Robert E. Tucker, Jr., for sending us biographical information about Cohen.

336a : To Thomas Willis White[1]

Woodlands. Nov. 18. [1846][2]

Dear Sir

I propose to send you in season for the January number, a paper on *Rudolph alias Ney*, which will make 8 or 10 pages. I could wish that my review of Street should appear as soon as possible. It will grow stale—and he has had an intimation of it as forthcoming.[3] Perhaps a greater attention to your critical department would be of service.—You are perhaps prudent as regards giving publicity to your desire to dispose of a portion of your work. But what if I hint to Judge Porter[4] to apply to you, as deeming it possible you would admit him to a participation of interest with you?—Can you procure for me a copy of the Correspondence of Mrs Myers, & of her address to the public. I hear of these things, but do not see them. Is there any doubt of her guilt?[5]

Yours truly &c

W. G. Simms.

336a

[1]White was at this time editor of the *Southern Literary Messenger.* See note 38, July 20, 1839 (77).

[2]Dated by Simms' reference to his article "Michael Ney, Otherwise Michael Rudolph," published in the *Messenger*, XIII (Jan. 1847), 17–23.

[3]On July 31 and Aug. 26, 1846 (315 and 321), Simms had written Alfred Billings Street (see introductory sketch) that he was reviewing his *Poems* for the *Messenger.* The review, entitled "Street's Poems," was published in the Dec. 1846 number (XII, 711–720).

[4]Benjamin Faneuil Porter, at this time living in Alabama. See note 134, July 14, 1849 (496).

[5]On Sept. 28, 1846, William R. Myers, aided by his brother, Col. Samuel S. Myers, and William S. Burr, shot Dudley Marvin Hoyt in his bedroom at Richmond. Hoyt died on Oct. 9. All three men were arrested and during their examination before the Hustings Court gave as their defense that Hoyt had seduced Myers' wife, Virginia Pollard Myers. They were discharged without trial "with rounds of applause from the crowded courtroom." At least two pamphlets concerning the murder were published: *An Authenticated Report of the Trial of Myers and Others, for the Murder of Dudley Marvin Hoyt. With the Able and Eloquent Speeches of Counsel, and "the Letters", in Full, with Explanatory Notes Which Furnish a Clear and Complete History of the Case. Drawn Up by the Editor of the Richmond Southern Standard* (New York: Richards and Company, [1846]) and *The Letters and Correspondence of Mrs. Virginia Myers, (Which Have Never Before Been Published or Even Read in Court,) to Dudley Marvin Hoyt, Who Was Murdered at Richmond . . . by Wm. R. Myers, and Two Others. Together with a Denial of the Truth of Mrs.*

358a : To William Alfred Jones

Woodlands, Feb 20. 1847

dear Sir

Permit me to enclose you a brief notice which expressed, through one of our city papers, my feeling with regard to your pleasant volume of Essays.[1] These are highly creditable specimens of your studies & your thinkings, and betray equal research & discrimination. There are two things to which serious objections might be made,—the occasional roughness and *slipshoddiness* of your style, and the fact that your too great devotion to the essayical form of writing has not only caused you erroneously to measure other writings by this standard, but has evidently led you to appreciate it quite too highly. That you should do so, the bent of your own genius & taste being considered, is natural enough, but you owe it both to yourself & to your neighbours, to remove from sight the selfish impulse, whenever you sit in judgment upon those who toil in far different departments.—I write hastily & under indisposition,[2]

Myers' Letter of Explanation of November Last, from Alta Vista. Likewise Added a Short Biography of D. M. Hoyt, by a Relative of the Deceased (Philadelphia, Jan. 1847). We have not had access to a copy of the first of these. The second speaks of the "unavoidable delay" in "the publication of this pamphlet" and states that "it is put forth for the purpose of denying the foul charge of Dudley Marvin Hoyt having basely seduced Mrs. Virginia Myers." The pamphlet contains over fifty letters purported to have been written by Mrs. Myers to Hoyt. The following quotation, typical of these letters, indicates that Mrs. Myers, if not actually the seducer herself, was certainly an eager participant in the affair: "Oh! dearest, promise me you will ever be my guardian angel. While I have thy precious heart, there is no sorrow too great for me, for when I feel as if I should sink under so many griefs [she frequently complains of her husband's mistreatment of her], I have only to think of thy love, and it supports me through every trial. Oh! beloved one, I have given into your keeping all my happiness, I have confided to you this poor broken heart of mine. I have told you how it clings to your embrace, how it loves you. I pray you, dearest, keep it, 'tis yours; and, lacerated, torn, though it be, it still beats for you with undying, eternal love. I entreat of you, my idol, my worshiped one, never to leave me desolate, for think, without thee, what would become of me? Alas! the thought kills me." (p. 23)

358a

[1]Simms reviewed Jones' *Literary Studies, a Collection of Miscellaneous Essays* (New York: E. Walker, 1847) in the *Southern Patriot* of Feb. 16. See note 56, Feb. 25, 1847 (360).

[2]Simms himself appears not to have been ill, but he was very much worried about the health of his wife. On Feb. 15 he had written to Lawson (358): "It is probable that I shall take my family into the backcountry for the improvement

and beg that you will give me credit for a long letter, in which I have discoursed equally as a critic & a friend. It will always give me great pleasure to hear from you, and of your successes.

Very truly Yours &c.

W. Gilmore Simms

379a : To William Henry Carpenter[1]

New York, May 21. [1847][2]

dear Sir

Saddled with a good lady & her children twain just as I was leaving Charleston for N. Y., and somewhat delayed by the weather *en route*, I found it quite impossible to pause in Balto. in my transit, though really desirous of doing so. I will make a serious effort to give you a day on my return, which I calculate will be towards the close of June.[3] Meanwhile, I trust it is not impossible for you to ramble off in this region. You might be just as well employed here as at home, at all events so far as relates to the acquisition of

---

of my wife's health. Seriously, I am greatly concerned at her condition. An invalid for months & reduced to a mere skeleton, she was just beginning to improve a little in strength and appetite, but very slowly, when she was seized with an epidemical cold or influenza which has fastened upon her head, and has been distressing her for a week past with intense pains, soreness in her head & bones, and a troublesome cough. My life is past in constant drudgery & unremitted anxieties, & I feel myself growing old with fearful rapidity." See also letters to Lawson of c. Feb. 20 (359) and to Duyckinck of Feb. 25 (360).

379a

[1]This letter is printed by R. Baird Shuman in "William Gilmore Simms to W. H. Carpenter: A New Item," *Manuscripts*, XIV (Spring 1962), 17–19. Our text is from the original, now in the South Caroliniana Library. For Carpenter, the Baltimore novelist, historian, and editor, see note 133, Apr. 24, 1847 (374).

[2]Dated by Simms' excuse for not stopping off at Baltimore on his way to New York City. On Apr. 24 he had written to Carpenter (374) that he planned to do so, and on May 8 he wrote from Philadelphia to Lawson (376): "Tell your wife that I was saddled with another man's woman, on leaving Charleston, who was old, ugly, had two children & twenty trunks, boxes, bundles, baskets &c, to take charge of. . . ."

[3]Simms did not visit Baltimore on his return to Charleston. On July 3 he wrote to Carey and Hart (387): "I am on the wing for the South, and shall leave for Charleston, by the Steamer this afternoon."

material for your journal;[4]—and it is not impossible that I might suggest topics for handling, suitable to your tastes & objects, such as you have so kindly counselled for mine. Your hints shall be carefully considered, and I shall look to the subjects indicated with curious inquiry.—My Life of Bayard is about to go to press. I shall probably be in the hands of the devil in a day or two. I shall instruct my publishers to place a copy of the work at your disposal, when it is ready for the reader.[5] Present me to Mr. Kennedy,[6] and keep me favorably in your remembrance, refreshing mine by a letter when most convenient.

Very faithfully
Yours &c

W. Gilmore Simms

W. H. Carpenter, Esq.

379b : To Carey and Hart

New York: May 27 [1847][1]

Gentlemen

I wrote to Mr. Griswold, some ten days ago, to say that I had finished the biographical sketch of Greene, and to ask how I should convey it to you free of expense & in safety. It is probable that my letter has not reached him, or that he is out of town; and I now submit the question to you, remembering that you were anxious to

[4]Carpenter was coeditor (with William Tappan Thompson) of the *Western Continent* (Baltimore).

[5]The *Literary World,* I (July 31, 1847), 616, announces that Simms' *The Life of the Chevalier Bayard* "is rapidly passing through the press," and the same periodical, II (Dec. 11, 1847), 459–460, quotes excerpts from the biography and describes it as "now in press." It is reviewed in ibid., III (Jan. 29, 1848), 628–631 (see note 24, Feb. 11, 1848 [421]).

[6]John Pendleton Kennedy (see introductory sketch), whom Simms had met in 1840. See note 3, June 23, 1852 (626a).

379b

[1]Dated by Simms' remarks about his "biographical sketch of [Nathanael] Greene" and "Maize in Milk." See notes 2 and 4, below.

get your work out with all possible rapidity.[2]—I published in the magazine of our friend Godey, a Christmas Story of the South, which it has been suggested to me would form a very good little Christmas publication *a la Dickens*, and with the aid of two or three or more illustrations by Darley[3] would probably command the popular favor. Miss Leslie is said (by Godey) to have thought well of the story, to which some descriptive additions might be made, if the present matter is not enough. Will it suit to look at the thing in question—Godey will place it in your hands,—or take Miss Leslie's opinion as to the chances of its success in the form which I suggest.[4]—Will Mr Baird[5] be pleased to remember the books he was to send me, which did not reach me at the hotel in Phil.

Very truly Yours &c

W. Gilmore Simms

Mess'rs Carey & Hart

P. S. The Christmas Story in question is called "Maize-in-Milk"—&c. It appears in four parts, in as many numbers of Godeys Book, each part making about half a dozen of his pages. 24 of his pages may, with the aid of large type & a sea of margin, be made to cover 100 in a duodecimo. To this some 20 or 30 more pages might be added.

---

[2]Actually Simms had written to Griswold c. May 18 (377) that he had "done a portion of the paper on Greene, and will have all ready in a few days." For Simms' contribution to Griswold's *Washington and the Generals of the American Revolution*, 2 vols. (Philadelphia: Carey & Hart, 1847), see letter to Carey and Hart of Aug. 9, 1847 (399).

[3]Felix Octavius Carr Darley (1822–1888), the popular illustrator of this time.

[4]"Maize in Milk" was not issued as a separate publication. It was later included in *Marie De Berniere: A Tale of the Crescent City* (Philadelphia: Lippincott, Grambo, and Co., 1853), pp. 320–422.

[5]Henry Carey Baird (1825–1912), a nephew of Edward L. Carey, entered his uncle's firm in 1841. Carey died in 1845, and when the firm of Carey and Hart was dissolved in 1849, Baird established his own firm while Abraham Hart continued the old under his own name.

430a : To John Jay[1]

Charleston, July 1. [1848][2]

John Jay Esqr.
Dear Sir

I hasten to say, in answer to your note, that I will at once proceed to obtain signatures to the Memorial—I think with you, that the prospect is just now better than ever for procuring the passage of an act with regard to Int. Copyright. When my list is filled, I shall at once forward it to some Members of the Committee of Congress. A pleasant summer excursion; it is indeed men *travel* now—no longer *travail* to make the trip to Europe.[3]

Yours Very truly &c

W. Gilmore Simms.

453a : To Carey and Hart

Woodlands Nov. 29. [1848][1]

Mess'rs Carey & Hart.
Gentlemen.

I do not percieve that you are doing much in the way of publication, and being anxious to beguile you into more activity, I beg

---

430a

[1]Jay (1817–1894), the grandson of Chief Justice John Jay, was an author, lawyer, and diplomat. He was admitted to the bar in New York City in 1839 and practiced law there for about twenty years. During 1847 and 1848 Jay took a strong interest in an Anglo-American copyright agreement, went to Washington and interviewed various congressmen, and in March 1848 sent a memorial to Representative Thomas Butler King of Georgia. A select committee with King as chairman was appointed, and Jay wrote various authors, including Simms, urging them to petition King's select committee. No action was taken by Congress. For an account of Jay's efforts, see James J. Barnes, *Authors, Publishers and Politicians: The Quest for an Anglo-American Copyright Agreement 1815–1854* (Columbus: Ohio State University Press, 1974), pp. 86–94. Simms' letter to Jay was copied by Maunsell Bradhurst Field (1822–1875) and included with copies of other letters to Jay in his letter to Jay of July 11, 1848 (original in the Jay Family Papers, Columbia University Libraries). We have not located the original of Simms' letter.

[2]See note 1, above.

[3]Jay had sailed for Liverpool around May 11.

453a

[1]Since Simms was trying to complete his "Huguenots in Florida" (*The Lily and*

leave to propose to you a work, semi historical, upon which I have been for some time engaged, & which needs but a few weeks of being finished. It is entitled

"The Lily and the Wampum,
a narrative of the
Colonies of Coligny
in Florida."

It is in two volumes of probably 300 or 320 pages each, contains the history of a most exciting and interesting endeavour of the French to colonize Florida, with Huguenots, all enveloped in an atmosphere of fiction. I am prepared to share with you the profits, or to make any reasonable arrangement for the publication.—What tidings of the anonymous volume, and when do you propose to publish.[2] Let me hear from you at your first convenience.

Yours very faithfully

W. Gilmore Simms

470a : TO BRANTZ MAYER

Woodlands, 27 Feb. 1849

Brantz Mayer Esq
dear Sir

I am glad to have your promise for the article in season for the April issue. I shall keep a space for it. I trust that you will be able to continue your favors, & doubt not that the increasing resources of the Review will justify the publisher in making the compensation

the Totem) in Aug. 1848 (see letters to Lawson of Aug. 27 and to Hammond of Aug. 29 [441 and 442]), this letter in which he says the work, here called "The Lily and the Wampum," "needs but a few weeks of being finished" should be dated 1848. He had the work in mind as early as 1845 (see note 180, Sept. 11, 1850 [549]), but his reference in this letter to "the anonymous volume" (*As Good as a Comedy*), referred to by Simms in his letters to Carey and Hart of c. Sept. 6 ("the work of which you wot") and Dec. 13 ("the volume . . . which . . . shall be ready for you in the spring"), 1847 (403 and 416), is further evidence of the date. Abraham Hart did not publish *The Lily and the Totem*; it was published by Baker and Scribner, New York, in 1850.

[2]*As Good as a Comedy* was not published by Hart until Mar. 1852. See note 79, Mar. 28, 1851 (575).

adequate to the claims of contributors. Yours, let me assure you, will be always highly appreciated by myself.[1]—Will you do me the favor to instruct your publishers to send me a copy of your writings on Mexico. I purchased sometime ago, two numbers of your work on the ancient & modern history of that country, but either you discontinued that form of publication, or the issues never reached our city, as I have since been able to procure none of them.[2] I shall always be glad to hear from you and feel the kindness and compliment conveyed in your note. Be pleased to believe me Very truly

Your friend & obt Servt

W. Gilmore Simms

473b : To Brantz Mayer

Woodlands S. C. March 10 [1849][1]

Hon. Brantz Mayer
Dear Sir.

I am in reciept of your article in relation to the origin of the War with Mexico, which shall have a place in our next issue. The Publisher, Mr. Burges writes me from Charleston, that your draft shall be duly honored. Permit me to hope that you will continue your favors to the Review in spite of the inadequate compensation, assured that with its improving fortunes (which necessarily depend upon the value of its papers) the remuneration will be increased. Though not myself personally interested in the *business* of the Review, you will recieve my assurance that with the improvement of its means shall be the increase of its pay to contributors. I have

470a

[1]Simms succeeded John Milton Clapp (1810–1857) as editor of the *Southern Quarterly Review* with the number for Apr. 1849. Burges and James had published the periodical during Clapp's editorship, but with Simms' first number James S. Burges became sole publisher (see note 56, Mar. 15, 1849 [474]). To this number Mayer contributed "Origin of the War with Mexico" (signed "B. M."), XV, 83–113.

[2]*Mexico as It Was and as It Is* (New York: J. Winchester, 1844). A third edition, revised and corrected, was published by W. Taylor and Co., Baltimore, in 1846.

473b

[1]Beneath Simms' date Mayer wrote, "Answd. 23d March 1849."

myself agreed for the present, in the day of its exigency, to work for little pay, yet no one feels more imperatively than I do, the policy & the necessity of paying contributors handsomely. Let me hear from you at your leisure, and hold me Very faithfully Yours &c

W. Gilmore Simms.

475a : To Charles Étienne Arthur Gayarré[1]

Woodlands S. C. March 17. 1849

Charles Gayarré Esq.
dear Sir:

Though personally unknown to you, I assume that the subject upon which I approach you will justify my freedom in doing so. Having lately been persuaded to accept the seat of Editor of the Southern Quarterly Review, I am naturally anxious to strengthen myself by a goodly array of able contributors. It is with this desire that I address myself to you. I need not insist upon the value of such a periodical, particularly to a sparsely settled people like ours— so wanting in the facilities of information, and so particularly deficient in elevated organs of literary opinion. We need equally such a review for the purpose of instruction & defence. To render it properly useful, it requires that we should bring together as many of the endowed gentlemen of the South, as duly feel our deficiencies, and desire to cure them. Suffer me to include you in this category, and to hope that you will find pleasure in making the Review the medium of your future communion with the public. Very respectfully & truly,

Yr obt Servt.

W. Gilmore Simms.

475a
[1]At this time Gayarré (see introductory sketch) was secretary of state for Louisiana.

476 (1a) : To Brantz Mayer

[c. March 29, 1849][1]

dear Sir

I am not the less sincere and earnest because my present labors require me to be brief. Believe me I feel quite grateful for the friendly interest you express for the Review, and the friendly regard for myself.[2] I shall endeavor to requite your sympathies.—My purpose in writing now is less to make this assurance than to beg that you will send me early copies, when published, of the works which you have on hand. Should you have a friend capable, in whose judgments and justice you have perfect confidence, I should prefer to have reviews from his hands.[3] But at all events, send me the volumes. Believe me, Very truly

Yr obliged frd & Servt.

W. Gilmore Simms

P.S. Has not your Maryland Hist. Society been publishing a vol. of Collections recently? I should be sorry not to recieve them.[4]—I percieve that a late History of Maryland has been put forth by a publisher in your city.[5] Is it a work of any value or character. I have Bozman's[6] only, which needs improvement & extension. This might be a subject for you?

W. G. S.

---

476 (1a)

[1]This letter is postmarked "March 30." The year is established by Simms' reference to a new history of Maryland. See note 5, below.

[2]We have been unable to locate Mayer's letter to Simms of Mar. 23 (see note 1, Mar. 10 [473b]).

[3]Mayer later got his friend James Morrison Harris to write a review of his *Mexico, Astec, Spanish and Republican.* See letter to Mayer of Mar. 1852 (618c).

[4]The Maryland Historical Society began publishing papers shortly after it was founded in 1844. The most recent publication was James Wynne's *Memoir of Major Samuel Ringgold, United States Army . . .* (Baltimore: John Murphy, 1847).

[5]James McSherry, *History of Maryland; from Its First Settlement in 1634, to the Year 1848* (Baltimore: John Murphy, 1849).

[6]John Leeds Bozman, *The History of Maryland, from Its First Settlement, in 1633, to the Restoration, in 1660, with a Copious Introduction, and Notes and Illustrations*, 2 vols. (Baltimore: J. Lucas & E. K. Deaver, 1837).

478a : To William Brown Hodgson[1]

Woodlands April 12. 1849

Hon. Wm. B. Hodgson.
dear Sir:

You are already aware that your request has been complied with in relation to the application for the name of the author of the article on the Turkish Language. Mr. Miles (the author) advises me that he has written to you in person. Let me hope that the affinity of tastes & studies between you, will result in an intimacy which shall be equally grateful and instructive to both parties.[2]—Let me add to this wish another of more selfish character—that Mr. Hodgson will be pleased to find in the Southern Quarterly Review, which is now under my conduct, an appropriate organ for the utterance of his occasional studies and opinions to the public.[3] With this hope, permit me to subscribe myself his respectful & most obt servt. &c

W. Gilmore Simms

482a : To Matthew Fontaine Maury[1]

Woodlands S. C. May 5. [1849][2]

M. F. Maury Esq.
dear Sir:

There needs no apology for desiring and demanding compensation for your contributions. The vulgar adage is suggestive of a just

478a

[1]For Hodgson, author, diplomat, and linguist, see note 100, May 9, 1849 (487).

[2]James Warley Miles (see introductory sketch of the Miles brothers) published "The Turkish Language" (signed "J. W. M.") in the *Southern Quarterly Review*, XIII (Jan. 1848), 54–78. Hodgson was greatly impressed (see Simms' letter to him of May 9, 1849 [487]).

[3]We are unable to attribute to Hodgson any article published in the *Southern Quarterly Review* during Simms' editorship.

482a

[1]Maury (1806–1873), naval officer, oceanographer, and the author of many books and articles, was in 1842 made superintendent of the Depot of Charts and Instruments at Washington. He later was a commander in the Confederate States Navy.

[2]Maury's reply to this letter, dated May 12, 1849, is printed in Nathan Reingold's

principle—the laborer is worthy of his hire. If I could have my way, our Review should publish nothing which was not paid for, and liberally. But you probably, quite as well as myself, know the usual history of the needy condition of southern periodicals, circulating through sparsely settled community, and established mostly by persons without means. I am authorized by our Publisher to say that he will pay at the rate of *one dollar* per page of printed matter. This insignificant & inadequate compensation, he tells me, is what is paid by the North American. At all events, it is all (he professes) which he can pay at present. Should you send an article for the October number of the Review, at this rate, it will be acceptable. The contents of our July number are prepared already. Yet I should greatly relish the paper on the Gulf of Mexico.[3] With great respect & very truly.

Yours &c

W. Gilmore Simms.

Science in Nineteenth-Century America: A Documentary History (London: Macmillan, 1966), pp. 147–148.

[3]Maury wrote Simms that he had sent his article to Francis Bowen, editor of the *North American Review*, provided he would publish it in the July number: "I impressed this upon him by telling him I attached more importance to its timely appearance than to pay, and that if he would not publish in July I would prefer to let some other journal have it, gratis. . . . I am rather sorry that Bowen agreed to pay for it, because I wrote it with your Journal and Southern readers in my mind. And I offered it to B. to preserve the peace between conscience and inclination, for I felt that I ought to try for pay and having tried and failed conscience could have been quiet. I heard the Southern Quarterly had been in tight places before, and did not much expect that it would be in a condition to pay." Evidently the contents of the July number of the *North American Review* were, like those of the *Southern Quarterly Review*, already prepared and Bowen returned the manuscript to Maury. "The Panama Rail-Way and the Gulf of Mexico" was published in the *Southern Literary Messenger*, XV (Aug. 1849), [441]–457.

488a : To Charles Étienne Arthur Gayarré

Woodlands S. C. May 17. [1849][1]

Hon. Charles Gayarré
Dear Sir:

I have suffered your obliging favor to remain for some time unanswered, hoping that I might, in the meantime, be enabled to acknowledge the copies of the valuable works you were pleased to address to my use.[2] But Mr. De Bow[3] not arriving (as far as I can learn) in our latitude, and being anxious to suggest to you a subject for Review which seems to lie particularly in your path, I determined to wait no longer before answering you. I am anxious to procure for the Southern Review, elaborate notices of the several distinguished cities of our Southern States, including New Orleans, Mobile, Charleston, Savannah &c—their early history, their vicissitudes, their chief men and chief performances, all strung together upon some one leading idea which would enable the writer to generalize largely, and thus absorb much matter in little space, and at the same time, where the subject happened to grow concentrative, and full of interest, to descend to details, and thus give a dramatic interest to the history. In considerable degree you have pursued this plan in your Romance of Louisiana.[4] An article of 40 printed pages might answer for such an article, and *two* of your M.S. letter sheet pages would probably make *one* in print. In following out such a plan, beginning with the first settlement, you can digressively afford brief biographical sketches of particular persons who have distinguished themselves in the colony; and, where the matter is copious & interesting at the same time, you might specially reserve it for a chapter to itself; or the several governments might each have a chapter, thus carrying the subject through several articles, which

488a

[1]Dated by Simms' reference to "the peculiar afflictions of your great city." See note 6, below.

[2]Possibly the books mentioned in Simms' letter to Gayarré of July 13, 1849 (495b).

[3]For James Dunwoody Brownson De Bow, see note 42, Feb. 17, 1852 (613).

[4]*Romance of the History of Louisiana. A Series of Lectures* (New York: D. Appleton & Company; Philadelphia: G. S. Appleton, 1848).

might subsequently be embodied in a volume. I throw out this topic for your consideration, in the hope that you will find the leisure to bestow some of your literary regards on the Southern Quarterly.[5] You will readily concur with me upon the necessity of securing for the South an organ of opinion. Until this is done, we can never have a literature, & scarcely a character. I am happy to assure you that in writing to the distinguished men of the South throughout the country, I have every where their voices in concurrence, & have secured many contributors in most of the Southern States, from among their most able men. Our pages are now full for July, and the work has gone to press. We shall publish again in Oct. & again in Jany. For either of these I shall be glad to hear from you.— We deeply sympathize with the peculiar afflictions of your great city.[6] I sincerely hope that you may soon find relief, and that the virtues of your good may avert the wrath of Providence.

With great respect, I am
Sir
Yr obliged & obt Servt.
&c

W. Gilmore Simms

---

[5]Gayarré did not write on this topic.

[6]The late Arlin Turner, Professor of English at Duke University, kindly sent us the following information on Sauvé's Crevasse: "On May 3 the levee broke seventeen miles above the city of New Orleans, at Sauvé's plantation; on May 6 the *Picayune* could repeat comic sayings, such as that of a man in Jefferson parish who said he was going to rig out a boat, take his compass, set out from the second story of his house, and land at the newspaper office in Camp Street. On May 8 the water was still rising; the editor was grimly serious. There was a proposal to cut through Metairie Ridge and let the water into Pontchartrain. On May 10 it was feared that even the First Municipality would be inundated. The water rose for another ten days or longer; the crevasse was not closed until June 20; meanwhile a ship had been filled with rock and sunk in it, to no avail. In the city 220 inhabited blocks were flooded." The Charleston newspapers for this period report the latest news of the crevasse.

491b : To Carey and Hart

Charleston, June 28. 1849.

Mess'rs Carey & Hart
Gentlemen

I have had your directions touching the subscription of the Camden Literary Society, to the South. Quart. Review, duly attended to. The work for the present year will be dispatched. I have had the sub. charged to myself, and enclose the Reciept to you. *You*, therefore, will credit *me* with the amount. Are you publishing any thing? Your works do not reach me, which I regret, on my own account quite as much as yours. My plan is to have short notices in the Review in connection with the acknowledgment of new publications—an opinion being adjusted in a brief & quotable paragraph, of one or more sentences. I am, besides, looked to by one of our daily presses here for the current report on new books.[1] Some of these I have already sent you, and I have a little parcel made up for you (of your own books) to be sent you hereafter. Does the trade improve, or are you in a surly temper. Would you not venture now upon a new copyright publication?—I must not forget to mention that I have ordered the Review to your address, in the hope that it will secure me your favors. If you send any thing, address it to me individually. It will then be more like to reach me safely.

Very truly Yours &c

W. Gilmore Simms

491b
[1]Probably the *Mercury*.

CARL A. RUDISILL LIBRARY
LENOIR RHYNE COLLEGE

493a : To Thomas Caute Reynolds[1]

Charleston July 6. 1849.

Hon. T. C. Reynolds.
dear Sir

It will give me great pleasure to recieve from your brother the Review of *El Buscapié,* of which you speak.[2] His contributions, as well as your own, I trust to make always welcome to the pages of 'our Review'. If sent to the Publisher, J. S. Burges, Charleston, by the 15th. August, and not too long, I should find a place for it, I believe, in our October issue. If sooner the better. Our July number has been published, & is no doubt already in your hands. I trust that you are again quietly settled down at your old pursuits. With much respect, but in some haste, I am

Very truly Yours &c

W. Gilmore Simms

495a : To Brantz Mayer

Charleston S. C. July 13. [1849][1]

Hon. B. Mayer.[2]
dear Sir.

Indisposition alone has prevented me from answering your letter in regard to your late contribution for the South. Quarterly. But I have been by no means regardless of your interests. As soon as I recieved your communication, I covered it to Mr. Burges, the

493a

[1]See introductory sketch of the Reynolds brothers. At the top of this letter Reynolds wrote: "Received at Richmond July 9th. 1849."

[2]James Lawrence Reynolds (see introductory sketch of the Reynolds brothers) published an article entitled "El Buscapié" (signed "J. L. R.") in the *Southern Quarterly Review*, XVI (Oct. 1849), 205–223.

495a

[1]Dated by Simms' remarks concerning payment for Mayer's contribution to the *Southern Quarterly Review*, his article entitled "Origin of the War with Mexico." See letters to Mayer of Feb. 27 and Mar. 10 (470a and 473b).

[2]Simms wrote *Mayr.*

Publisher requesting him to attend to it, and provide me with the necessary reply or make it himself. I must premise that Mr. B. is an invalid, whose life is of doubtful tenure, very feeble, and that he is unequal to much excitement or many exertions.[3] He has but lately returned from a trip to the South & West, where he has been endeavoring to put his claims, which are large, in proper train for collection. He is pretty embarrassed, though, I believe that, in the end he will satisfy all creditors. Certainly, I think, that those who contribute to his pages, now, though there may be some delay in case of payment, will most surely get it in the sequel. I beg leave to add that in taking charge of the Review, I confined my agreement solely to the Editorial part of the task, & have no sort of connection with the monetary matters. He begs me to say that he expects to remit you before long the amt. for your contribution, and regrets that he should have been compelled to disappoint you. He pleads in excuse for having done so that your draft found him equally unadvised & unprepared—that his rule is not to pay for contributions before their publication, and though not unwilling, where the means of payt. are obvious, to depart from this rule, the period of your demand was quite unfavorable to his doing so,—his funds having been exhausted by other claimants already recognized, and his collections needing further time before his resources could be resupplied. He repeats the assurance that in a little time, he will provide for your demand.—For myself, permit me to regret the mischance, though I hold myself usually aloof from all this sort of business. I will cheerfully jog the publisher's memory, however, in your case, only entreating you to not to confound his shortcomings with my offences, which are quite enough for my anxieties.—I greatly wonder & regret that my History of South Carolina has not reached the Maryland Hist. Society.[4] I cover, this very day, a second copy for that Society, to your address, and will have it dispatched by the earliest opportunity.

Yours very truly &c

W. Gilmore Simms

[3]Burges died in Feb. 1850. See letter to Tucker of Feb. 26, 1850 (526).
[4]See letters to Mayer of June 16, 1844, and Jan, 25, 1845 (202c and 230a).

495b : To Charles Étienne Arthur Gayarré

Charleston July 13. [1849][1]

Hon Charles Gayarré
dear Sir:

Sympathizing very sincerely with you in regard to the onerous duties of the political contest which keeps you from more agreeable toils, I still congratulate myself with the hope that you will be able soon to appropriate the necessary leisure on the semi-historical & social subject of which we have spoken. I write now rather with the view to saying that I have just put up to be sent you by the earliest vessel a copy of my Histy of South Carolina, which I trust you will find not utterly unworthy of a place in your library. You will find in it proofs, at all events, that I am a genuine Southron if not an historian. With best wishes, believe me Very truly

Your friend &c

W. Gilmore Simms.

P. S. I must not forget to acknowledge the reciept of your excellent history[2] & very agreeable Sketches from History.[3]

495b

[1]Simms' reference to "the onerous duties of the political contest" suggests 1853 as the date of this letter: in that year Gayarré was defeated, probably by fraudulent votes, as an independent candidate for the U.S. House of Representatives. But Simms' expressed desire for Gayarré soon to have "the necessary leisure" to devote to "the semi-historical & social subject of which we have spoken" seems clearly a reference to the article that Simms in his letter of May 17, 1849 (488a), asked Gayarré to write for the *Southern Quarterly Review.* The "political contest," then, would be the election of 1849, in which Gayarré as secretary of state of Louisiana would necessarily be involved.

[2]*Romance of the History of Louisiana.*

[3]Not identified.

497a : TO NATHANIEL BEVERLEY TUCKER[1]

Charleston, July 23. [1849][2]

dear Sir:

Can you not throw off for our October pages a brief and lively article upon some familiar topic. I could wish that it would not exceed 10 pages, and that the vein should be playful or satirical. I do not know how you relish the practice in either of these veins, but I fancy that your success in them should lend you to their frequent exercise. Our October contents are generally of a grave character, and of too great length. My contributors are not yet reduced to proper training.—I was fortunate in finding the copies of the Reviews, meant for Europe, still in the hands of the Publisher, so that the correction of the errors pointed out was still in our power.—I still fail to find an opportunity to forward you the packet of my wares designed for your use. Let me repeat the inquiry, previously made, whether you have any person, friend or agent, in Balto. to whose care I might consign it.[3] I write in haste, but with best regards and Very faithfully

Your frd & servt

W. Gilmore Simms

P. S. Have you read the 'Kavanagh' of Mr. Longfellow. That bloodless stuff seems sufficiently flat & feeble for the purposes of a

---

497a

[1]See introductory sketch.

[2]Dated by Simms' remarks concerning the corrections Tucker wanted made in his "Macaulay's History of England," *Southern Quarterly Review*, XV (July 1849), 374–410, before the copies of the *Review* were sent to Europe. See letter to Tucker of July 14 (497).

[3]Simms had been sending or planning to send Tucker as many of his published volumes as he "could lay hands on." See letters to Tucker of Apr. 23, May 6, May 29, June 1, and July 13, 1849 (480, 483, 489, 490, and 495).

critic who would make himself merry over a victim whom it would not be necessary, perhaps, to show up, but for the impertinent & stupid laudits of its friends.[4]

512b : To Brantz Mayer

Woodlands Nov. 6. 1849

Hon. Brantz Mayer
dear Sir

I do not know whether in the variety of my avocations, particularly the toils of a transfer to my country from my city residence, I have not quite overlooked your letter of the 4th Oct. It was not my desire to do so, and if such has been the case, that you have remained to this moment unanswered, I must earnestly entreat your forgiveness. When you wrote Mr. Burges was absent in the interior, travelling for his health. He returned to the city when I was leaving it; but assured me he would be able to honor your draft when due. I trust that he has done so; but have not seen him since. He is still in the interior, I believe, travelling equally for health and business. The truth is, I regard him as a dying man—irrecoverably consumptive. He has been greatly distressed, and has been so much the subject of my commisseration that I have foreborne greatly to

[4]The *Southern Quarterly Review*, XVI (Oct. 1849), 245–246, contains a review (probably by Simms) of *Kavanagh, a Tale* (Boston: Ticknor, Reed, and Fields, 1849). The reviewer comments: "It is of the same slender staple [as Longfellow's 'previous prose writings']—with few thoughts, few incidents—unimportant action and a rather cold interest; but marked by his usual felicity and smoothness of style, the play of a gentle fancy, and a pleasant sentiment. Kavanagh must depend for its attractions on their agencies wholly. It is a bald village story, in which love appears somewhat of the school girl fashion and philosophy,—which seemed to have fed on bread and butter all its life. . . . But we should be doing injustice to Mr. Longfellow not to admit the beauty and felicity of many of his passages. Some of the apothegms are marked by a delightful fancy, and much of his criticisms, on literature and society in America, is just and forcible. It is his invention that lacks. Nothing can be more bald than Kavanagh as a story; and for its design as little may be said. The author seems to have begun his book without fairly grasping his purpose. His moral is at once slight and commonplace."

urge my own claims, which have been quite as little regarded as those of any other person.[1] He tells me still that he will soon be able to put himself *rectus in curia,* and I repeat his words to you. But, as he has disappointed you, me and others, I dare not farther to solicit your favors, which I could only do in the perfect conviction that you would be paid for them promptly. The present auspices of the work are good—the subscribers increase, and public opinion seems to speak decidedly in its favor. Under these circumstances it must, I fancy, be in a condition soon to satisfy all claimants, and prosper to the satisfaction of all its friends.

You are pleased to proffer yourself to do for me any passing service at the North. A history of Maryland was published in yr. city not long ago. I should be glad if you would intimate to the Publisher of that work, that it would be proper only to place a copy of it in the hands of the Editor of the Southern Quarterly, and give him my address, care of the Publisher in Charleston.[2] Your own publications have never reached me, and I should be pleased to acknowledge their reciept in our pages.[3] I cover to you a trifle by this mail.[4]

Yours faithfully &c

W. Gilmore Simms.

P.S. A passing hint to all your publishers in Balto., of the policy of sending their publications to the Review, will perhaps have its effect such is the feeling now in the South, and increasing rapidly every day, that the imprimateur of a Southern periodical will be felt necessary to the sale or recognition of every northern book.

512b

[1]In his letter to Holmes of Apr. 13, 1850 (533), Simms writes: "Mr. Burges has paid the last debt—that of nature—the only one I fear that he can pay. The estate is pronounced insolvent. He owed me 8 or 900 dollars."

[2]James McSherry's *History of Maryland; from Its First Settlement in 1634, to the Year 1848*, published by John Murphy in 1849.

[3]Mayer had recently published *History of the War between Mexico and the United States, with a Preliminary View of Its Origin* (New York and London: Wiley and Putnam, 1848).

[4]*The Cassique of Accabee. A Tale. With Other Poems* (Charleston: J. Russell, 1849) was published in Sept. (see letter to Duyckinck of Sept. 19 (507).

514a : To Abraham Hart

Woodlands S. C. Decr. 6. [1849][1]

A. Hart, Esq.
dear Sir:

Looking over a late Catalogue of your books, I find a few which I should like to have, if you are willing to put them on account of the anonymous MS. in your possession. The following is a list:

1	Berrington's Lit. Hist. Middle Ages[2]—		.87
2.	Five old plays by Collier[3]		2.25
3	Dodsley's Coll. of Poems	6 vols[4]—	3.00
4	Ellis's Fabliaux	2 " [5]	4.50
5	Fosbroke's Brit. Monachism[6]—		3.75
6	Izard's Official Correspondence[7]—		1.00

514a

[1]The dating of this letter poses a problem. Until Henry Carey Baird left the firm of Carey and Hart and established his own firm during the latter half of 1849, Simms always addressed letters to the firm to "Carey & Hart." It was written, therefore, in 1849 or later. The "anonymous MS." mentioned in this letter is the manuscript of *As Good as a Comedy*, which had been in the hands of the firm since 1848 (see letter to Carey and Hart of Nov. 29 [453a]). By Mar. 1851 Hart had made arrangements with Simms to republish *Katharine Walton* (see letter to Hart of Mar. 28 [575]), first published in *Godey's Lady's Book* during Feb.–June 1850 (see note 191, Oct. 15, 1849 [509]), and it is not unlikely that negotiations for this publication were in progress during the latter half of 1850. Since Simms does not mention *Katharine Walton* along with the "anonymous MS.," we have decided that 1849 rather than 1850 (the two possible dates for the letter) is the more probable date.

[2]Joseph Berington, *A Literary History of the Middle Ages* (London: J. Mawman, 1814). Another edition was published by David Bogue, London, in 1846.

[3]John Payne Collier, *Five Old Plays, Forming a Supplement to the Collections of Dodsley and Others* (London: W. Pickering, 1833).

[4]Robert Dodsley, *A Collection of Poems . . . by Several Hands*, 6 vols. (London: R. Dodsley, 1748–1758). There were many later editions, and additional volumes were added to the *Collection*.

[5]George Ellis wrote the preface, notes, and an appendix to *Fabliaux or Tales, Abridged from French Manuscripts of the XIIth and XIIIth Centuries, by* M. [Pierre Jean Baptiste] *Le Grand* [d'Aussy], *Selected and Translated into English Verse by the Late Gregory Lewis Way, Esq.*, 2 vols. (London: Printed by W. Bulmer and Co., Sold by R. Faulder, 1796–1800).

[6]Thomas Dudley Fosbroke, *British Monachism; or, Manners and Customs of the Monks and Nuns of England* (London: J. Nichols and Son, 1802). Other editions were published in 1817, 1843, and 1848.

[7]*Correspondence of Mr. Ralph Izard, of South Carolina, from the Year 1774 to 1804; with a Short Memoir* (New York: C. S. Francis & Co., 1844).

7	Prov. Gov. Pennsylvania	3 vols[8]—	3.50
8	Plowden's Ireland	5 vols[9]—	4.50
9	Rose's Amadis de Gaul[10]		2.00
10	Raynals Indies &c.	6 vols[11]—	7.50
11	Southern's Plays &c	3 " [12]	6.00
12	Thatcher's Mil. Journal.[13]		2.00
13	Theatre of the Greeks[14]		3.50
14	Winterbotham's U. States	4 vols[15]	2.25
			46.62
15	Molina's Chili	2 vols[16]———	3.00
16	Thomas's Reminiscences	2 vols[17]	1.50
			$51.12

[8]*Minutes of the Provincial Council of Pennsylvania from the Organization to the Termination of the Proprietary Government*, 3 vols. (Harrisburg: Published by the State, 1838–1840).

[9]Francis Peter Plowden, *An Historical Review of the State of Ireland, from the Invasion of That Country under Henry II. to Its Union with Great Britain on the First of January 1801*, 5 vols. (Philadelphia: William F. M'Laughlin and Bartholomew Graves, 1805–1806).

[10]William Stewart Rose's translation of *Amadis de Gaul; a Poem in Three Books* was first published by T. Cadell and W. Davies, London, in 1803.

[11]Guillaume Thomas François Raynal, *A Philosophical and Political History of the Settlements and Trade of the Europeans in the East and West Indies*, tr. John Obadiah Justamond, 2d ed., 6 vols. (London: A. Strahan, 1798). There were earlier and later editions, some in four and others in eight volumes.

[12]*Plays Written by Thomas Southerne, Esq. Now First Collected*, 3 vols. (London: T. Evans, 1774).

[13]James Thacher, *A Military Journal during the American Revolutionary War, from 1775 to 1783, Describing Interesting Events and Transactions of This Period, with Numerous Historical Facts and Anecdotes, from the Original Manuscript* (Boston: Richardson and Lord, 1823).

[14]*Theatre of the Greeks, Containing, in a Compendious Form, a Great Body of Information Relative to the Rise, Progress, and Exhibition of the Drama, Together with an Account of Dramatic Writers from Thespis to Neander* (Cambridge: Grant, 1825).

[15]William Winterbotham, *An Historical, Geographical, Commercial and Philosophical View of the American United States, and of the European Settlements in America and the West-Indies*, 4 vols. (London: Printed for the Editor, J. Ridgway, 1795).

[16]Juan Ignacio Molina, *The Geographical, Natural and Civil History of Chile*, tr. R. Alsop, 2 vols. (Middletown, Conn.: I. Riley, 1808).

[17]Ebenezer Smith Thomas, *Reminiscences of the Last Sixty-Five Years, Commencing with the Battle of Lexington. Also, Sketches of His Own Life and Times*, 2 vols. (Hartford: The Author, 1840).

This will leave a balance due me on account of $49. If you send address them to the care of J. Russell.[18] May I soon hope to see the M.S. in type? Put it forth in new style & thus give it a fair chance.

Yours truly &c W. Gilmore Simms

---

[18]Check marks by Berington, Plowden, Southerne, Thacher, and Thomas probably mean that these books were sent to Simms.

1850–1857

519a : To Abraham Hart

[January, 1850?][1]

A. Hart Esq. Publisher
Philadelphia—
dear Sir

The Hon. Henry R. Jackson, of Georgia, whom I regard as having written some of the best fugitive poetry ever published in this country, is desirous of collecting and binding together his stray performances. His volume will make 100 pages or thereabouts, and he is not unwilling to incur a portion of the cost of publication. I have mentioned a dollar a page (duodecimo—edition of 500 copies) as the probable cost in print, and if I understand him rightly he is not unwilling to pay one moiety of the expense. May I entreat of you to entertain his proposition with as much favor as you may deem consistent with your own safety.[2] He is a gentleman whom personally, no less than for his talents, I very much esteem.

Yours very truly &c

W. Gilmore Simms

519a

[1]This letter was written after Henry Rootes Jackson's appointment as judge of the Superior Court of the Eastern District of Georgia in 1849. Since his volume of poems was published in 1850 (see note 2, below), Simms' letter was probably written early in 1850.

[2]Jackson's *Tallulah, and Other Poems* (Savannah: John M. Cooper, 1850) is reviewed by Simms in the *Southern Quarterly Review*, N. S., III (Jan. 1851), 257–262. Simms finds some faults and many virtues, remarking that "with a sweet and lively fancy, chaste and spirited, our author unites correct and appropriate thought, a pure moral, and a faculty for song, which, with proper training, will hardly shrink from comparison with the best of our lyrists."

528a : To Joseph Stark Sims

Woodlands S. C. March 25. [1850][1]

J. S. Sims, Esq.
dear Sir:

I have just been put in possession of a note of yours addressed to Mr. Littlejohn[2] touching your non-reciept of the Southern Quarterly Review. I have found pleasure in giving the proper instructions so that your wishes in regard to the work shall be complied with. We have succeeded in securing as publishers a firm of known ability & enterprise, by which the certainty, punctuality & neatness of the work will be permanently ensured. May I entreat of you to use your influence among your neighbours & friends in increasing our Subscription List. It is in the deficiency of patronage that our periodicals fail, or falter; and just now, such an organ of opinion as the Review is absolutely necessary. We have been quite too heedless of the power of such an agent.

Yours very truly &c

W. Gilmore Simms

529a : To George Rex Graham[1]

Woodlands S. C. April 3. 1850

Geo. R. Graham, Esq.
dear Sir:

I congratulate you on your resumption of the management of your magazine.[2] It will always give me pleasure to communicate for

---

528a

[1]Dated by Simms' remarks about the new publishers of the *Southern Quarterly Review*. James S. Burges, who died in Feb. 1850, was succeeded as publisher by Joseph Walker and William Carey Richards ("Walker and Richards"). See note 67, Feb. 26, 1850 (526), and note 98, Apr. 13, 1850 (533).

[2]Not identified.

529a

[1]See note 257, Oct. 19, 1847 (405).

[2]Because of financial difficulties Graham had been forced to assign *Graham's American Monthly Magazine of Literature and Art* to Samuel D. Patterson and Company in Aug. 1848, though he remained the editor. In Mar. 1850 he bought back the magazine.

your pages as before. In respect to the "Bride of the Battle," I have certainly no objection to your use of it, provided Mr. Godey has not made any other disposition of it. When informed of the failure of the Mage. I gave him instructions & an order to procure it, and he advised me of a *quasi* sale of it to one of your neighbours.[3] *If this be not done,* I shall be glad that it should be transferred to you and shall write him to this effect; but you must permit me to request the cash for it, as it has been already furnished for some time & I am grievously in want of money, being just now *minus* some *nine* hundred dollars through the failure of one of my publishers.[4] In the case of Godey, the cash is always paid me on delivery of the MS. and this is surely the right principle. I have now three applications for similar tales for which the cash is tendered.[5]—I have on hand a story which will make some four or five parts in your magazine of 8 or 10 pages each. It is entitled "Marie De Bernieré, or the Mask—a Tale of the Crescent City[")—it is social and psychological in character. A small portion of the first part was furnished to and published in a magazine entitled "the Metropolitian" issued by Mr Israel Post. The work failed, I believe, with the first number, and I never got paid for what was furnished.[6] This part I have rewritten and the name of the story has been changed. It has probably been seen by very few persons. For the reason that it has been published already i.e. a very small portion of the *first* part, not more than ⅛th of the whole, I am willing to furnish the story at Twenty five dollars each part. If you wish it, let me know; but you will allow

[3]Evidently Simms feared that *Graham's* was failing or at least that Samuel D. Patterson and Company would not pay him for "The Bride of the Battle. A Southern Novelet," eventually published in *Graham's*, XXXVII (July, Aug., and Sept. 1850), 23–29, 84–91, 163–169 (see letter to Godey of c. Mar. 15, 1850 [527]). Perhaps it was *Sartain's Union Magazine of Literature and Art* (Philadelphia) to which Godey almost sold Simms' story.

[4]James S. Burges. See letter to Holmes of Apr. 13, 1850 (533).

[5]We are unable to determine which magazines had asked Simms for tales.

[6]The *American Metropolitan Magazine*, edited by William Landon and published by Israel Post, ran for only two numbers (Jan. and Feb. 1849). The first installment of Simms' "The Egyptian Masque; a Tale of the Crescent City" appears in the Feb. issue, I, 69–73. The tale was later published as "Marie De Berniere; a Tale of the Crescent City" in *Arthur's Home Gazette*, II (Feb. 14, Feb. 21, Feb. 29, Mar. 6, Mar. 13, Mar. 20, and Mar. 27, 1852). See note 172, Nov. 20, 1848 (451).

me to request that the numbers shall be paid for severally as recieved. To conclude, whatever Mr. Godey may determine upon I cheerfully accede to. Address me for the present at "Woodlands, Midway P. O. South Carolina."

Very respectfully &c

W. Gilmore Simms.

534a : TO WILLIAM JAMES RIVERS[1]

Woodlands, S. C. April 15 [1850][2]

W. J. Rivers, Esq.
dear Sir:

I should greatly like an article from your pen for our July issue of the Southern Quarterly Review. Choose your own subject, and handle it, in your own way, in an article not to exceed, if possible 25 pages. I would rather that you should not take up any subject of Carolina history, inasmuch as I shall make your little pamphlet the text of a paper of my own, which was prepared for the forthcoming number of the Review, but excluded by the contributions of others. Let me entreat you to this field of exercise. It will give you a larger circle of readers than would the publication of an independent pamphlet. *Pamphlets never sell,* and when the subject is *local,* are, *in Charleston,* particularly avoided. In the Review, your audience is the whole South.[3] Let me hear from you shortly & believe me

Very truly Yours &c

W. Gilmore Simms

534a

[1]Rivers (see note 168, Aug. 2, 1850 [545]) was at this time head of a private classical school in Charleston.

[2]Dated by Simms' reference to his article on Rivers' *Topics in the History of South-Carolina* (Charleston: Walker & James, 1850), published as "Topics in the History of South-Carolina" in the *Southern Quarterly Review*, N. S., II (Sept. 1850), 66–84.

[3]Rivers contributed "Manual of Ancient Geography and History" to the *Southern Quarterly Review*, N. S., I (July 1850), 499–503.

539a : To William John Grayson[1]

Charleston, May 31. [1850][2]

Hon. W. J. Grayson.
dear Sir:

This will be handed you by Mr. W. C. Richards, one of the new publishers of the Southern Quarterly.[3] He is seeking friends & patrons of the Review in Washington. A word from you may greatly promote his objects. He is a young gentleman of worth & intelligence, particularly endowed with that energy & those business habits, which the work has hitherto so much needed. I need not say more to you. "A word to the wise &c."

Yours very truly

W. Gilmore Simms

564a : To John Neal

Woodlands S. C. Jan 30. [1851][1]

To

John Neal.
dear Sir:

The sun of the season with you. It was on the eve of leaving home that I sent you some of my metrical trifles. I have just returned to find your letter, and thank you for its good wishes. In a few days I hope to send you a Poem called the City of the Silent, which I lately delivered at the Consecration of a Public Cemetery near

539a

[1]At this time Grayson (see introductory sketch) was a member from South Carolina of the U.S. House of Representatives.

[2]Dated by Simms' remarks about William Carey Richards. See note 3, below.

[3]After the death of James S. Burges the firm of Walker and Richards (Joseph Walker and William Carey Richards) became the publisher of the *Southern Quarterly Review.* For Richards, see introductory sketch of the Richards family.

564a

[1]Dated by Simms' reference to his "lately delivered" *The City of the Silent. A Poem . . . Delivered at the Consecration of Magnolia Cemetery. November 19, 1850* (Charleston: Walker & James, 1850).

Charleston. If you will mention the names of the things which you have recieved from me, it is probable that I can supply you with others not already sent; as in a recent visit to Charleston I was fortunate in picking up a few copies of some matters that are almost out of print. Of my prose writings I have scarcely any duplicates, and they are matters scarcely to be sent by mail. Give you God speed in your publication.[2]

Yours very truly &c

W. Gilmore Simms

577a : To Abraham Hart

Woodlands April 8. [1851][1]

A. Hart, Esq.
dear Sir:

I believe I forgot to say that in neither of the works you have of mine will it be necessary that I should have proofs sent me. The MS.S. are quite intelligible & may be revised by any careful printer. I may suggest, however, that it may be prudent that the two books should be confided to different printers, or they may discover the identity of scribblement & scribbler. Your package by the Albatross

---

[2]Neal had announced in the press that he had in preparation "A History of American Literature" in two volumes. In a notice of this never-completed work in the New York *Daily Tribune* of Sept. 4, 1850, Neal asks his "literary brethren throughout the land . . . to furnish him with copies of such works as they have not lost all their interest in, by express or otherwise, directed to him in Portland, Me." Probably he had written to Simms for copies of his works.

577a

[1]Dated by Simms' remarks about "the two books" which Hart is preparing to publish: *Katharine Walton: Or, the Rebel of Dorchester. An Historical Romance of the Revolution in Carolina* (Philadelphia: A. Hart, late Carey and Hart, 1851), which had appeared serially in *Godey's Lady's Book* during 1850 (see note 191, Oct. 15, 1849 [509]), and *As Good as a Comedy.* See letter to Hart of Mar. 28, 1851 (575).

not yet recieved.[2] Please, hereafter, address to the care of J. Russell.[3] Mr. Godey will probably hand you a package for me to be sent with your next favor through J. Russell.

Very truly Yours &c

W. Gilmore Simms

580a : To Abraham Hart

Woodlands May 7. 1851

A. Hart, Esq.
dear Sir:

I think it well to suggest to you when our novel[1] is published, to send promptly a considerable supply to South Carolina—Charleston in particular—where the scene is mostly laid. There will be a good deal of curiousity there to see it. I should also advise that a good supply be sent to Augusta, Georgia, where I am told, my personal popularity has been greatly increased of late, in consequence of a very successful lecture which I delivered in that place in January last.[2]—I have had for some time on hand an Historical Romance, founded upon the expedition of DeSoto for the Conquest of Florida. It is a tale of War and Intense Passion, which, I fancy, if wrought out as I design it, would prove the most interesting of all my romances. Please let me know if you would like to engage in its publication for next fall. It is about one third written, and has been for some time lying by me; but if encouraged, I should

---

[2]Probably a copy of Marie Anne Adélaïde Lenormand's *Historical and Secret Memoirs of the Empress Josephine, First Wife of Napoleon Bonaparte*, 2 vols. (Philadelphia: Carey & Hart, 1848), which Simms had requested in his letter to Hart of Mar. 28 (575) and which he again requests in his letter to Hart of Nov. 1 (600a).

[3]John Russell, Charleston bookseller and publisher. See introductory sketch.

580a

[1]*Katharine Walton.*

[2]On Jan. 6 Simms had lectured on "Poetry and the Practical." In his letter to Simms of Jan. 21, James Henry Hammond (see introductory sketch) wrote, "I have never known any speech to produce such a sensation in Augusta. . . ." See note 4, Jan. 30 (564).

resume the story & press it forward to conclusion.[3] You can answer this at your leisure. I propose to visit Philadelphia in July or August.[4]

Yours very truly—

W. Gilmore Simms.

596a : To Abraham Hart

Private
Charleston, Sep. 27. [1851][1]

A. Hart, Esq.
dear Sir.

I regretted that I could not see you in Phil., and failed to have a long chat with you in N. Y. Let me, in few words, convey to you something that I wished to say. I have more than half written, a novel entitled "Fair, Fat & Forty; or the Sword and the Distaff." It was begun, as a nouvellette for Mr. Arthur,[2] but has run out to a reasonable sized novel. It takes up the scene and action at the close of the revolutionary war in S. C., showing the fortunes, in love, of an old soldier, with broken fortunes, whose military occupation, like that of Othello, is gone. Shall I send it you when finished, which will probably be in January?[3]—I will thank you to

---

[3]*Vasconselos a Romance of the New World*, earlier offered to *Godey's Lady's Book* (see letter to Mrs. Hale of Oct. 15, 1849 [509]), was rejected by Hart. Under the pseudonym "Frank Cooper" it was published by Redfield, New York, in Dec. 1853 (see letter to Hammond of Oct. 4, 1853 [677]).

[4]For Simms' itinerary of his trip to the North in Aug. and Sept., see note 187, Aug. 13 (596).

596a

[1]Dated by Simms' remarks about *Katharine Walton* and *As Good as a Comedy*. See Simms' other letters to Hart of this year.

[2]Timothy Shay Arthur (see note 291, Nov. 30, 1860 [1017]) was editor of *Arthur's Home Gazette* (Philadelphia), a weekly.

[3]*The Sword and the Distaff; or, "Fair, Fat and Forty," a Story of the South, at the Close of the Revolution* was first published in semimonthly supplements to the *Southern Literary Gazette* (Charleston) during 1852. It was also issued by Walker, Richards and Co., publisher of the *Gazette*, in book form, dated 1852. See note 130, July 7, 1852 (628).

send me half a dozen copies of K. W., which, they tell me, sells very well here. I would not, were I you, include the anonymous book among the humourous series,[4] but send it forth in the form of a regular novel, like K. W.—The new novel which I propose to you, I would publish with my name. But you will let me hear also in respect to the romance which I told you of, and which, as in the case of Richard Hurdis, I would put forth as from a new hand.[5] Write me at your leisure and believe me Very truly Yours &c

W. Gilmore Simms.

600a : To Abraham Hart

Charleston. Nov. 1. 1851.

A Hart Esq.

(Publisher)
dear Sir:

I have just put up a bundle of parts of Thiers' Consulate & Empire and of Montholon's Napoleon, to be sent you as soon as Russell can find a place in the steamer,—perhaps, next week. In sending these, my object is to obtain both of these works, *Bound,* as far as they go, & of uniform style. The numbers sent me were irregular, some on fair & some brown paper, and several wanting. Of Montholon I got but two or three,—just enough for provocation. Your representative last summer was pleased to assure me that you would receive these & let me have others *half bound.* Send me accordingly Thiers, Montholon & in addition Madm. Normand, and charge me for the binding.[1] Have you a good edition of Goethe in *the*

[4]As *Good as a Comedy* was published as part of the "Library of Humorous American Works."

[5]*Vasconselos* was published as by "Frank Cooper."

600a

[1]Adolphe Thiers, *History of the Consulate and the Empire of France under Napoleon* (Philadelphia: A. Hart, late Carey & Hart, 1850); Charles Jean Tristran, Marquis de Montholon, *History of the Captivity of Napoleon at St. Helena* (Philadelphia: Carey and Hart, 1847); Marie Anne Adélaïde Lenormand, *Historical and Secret Memoirs of the Empress Josephine, First Wife of Napoleon Bonaparte*, 2 vols. (Philadelphia: Carey & Hart, 1848). All were first issued in parts.

original & in what style. So also Burger[2] in the *original,* and advise me. K. W. I am told, continues to sell here. In fact it is the most *symmetrical* & *truthful* of all my Revolutionary novels. You shall have the other book in season.[3]

Yours faithfully

W. Gilmore Simms

P.S. I began on this sheet without observing its condition.[4]

601a : To Henry Carey Baird

Charleston, Decr. 3. [1851][1]

My dear Master Harry.

I enclose you an autograph letter of DeKalb. It is among the most rare of all the Generals of the Revolution. But how is it that my requests are so slighted? You send me no books. I trust that, as one good turn deserves another, you will supply the South. Quarterly with your publications while I remain Editor. In particular, send me such of the poets as you have published.[2] There are some which you have put forth, in fine editions, which I cordially covet.

Yours truly

W. Gilmore Simms

[2]Gottfried August Bürger (1747–1794), German poet popular with the Romantics.
[3]*Vasconselos.* See letters to Hart of May 7 and Sept. 27 (580a and 596a).
[4]The sheet is slightly soiled.

601a

[1]Dated by Simms' sending Baird an autograph letter of "Baron de Kalb." See letter to Baird of Jan. 29, 1852 (608).
[2]Baird sent Simms *The Poetical Works of Thomas Gray.* See letter to Baird of Jan. 13, 1852 (604).

603a : To George Seabrook Bryan[1]

Jany. 5. [1852][2]

dear Bryan.

Your notice of Kennedy is in hand & shall appear in our January issue, which has (in this respect) fortunately, been delayed. The proofs shall be sent you. Recieve my thanks, with the blessings of the New Year, on you & yours.

Very truly &c

W Gilmore Simms

Geo. S. Bryan, Esq.

603b : To Abraham Hart

Charleston. Jany 5. [1852][1]

A. Hart, Esq.
dear Sir:

Before recieving your letter I was distressed at hearing of your loss by fire. I trust that you were quite insured & that you will suffer no serious detriment or loss. I have recieved the Books. Is Thiers' Consulate complete.—In respect to the anonymous book, I could wish still that it should be anonymously published. I do not see that the title should be changed as originally sent you. It is an experiment in a path which I never pursued before, and I am disposed to think that, in our country, the better course is to be anonymous as often and as long as possible. Our people, in their passion for change & novelty (even more great than that of the Athenians) soon tire

603a

[1]For Bryan, a Charleston lawyer and later judge of the United States Court for the District of South Carolina, see note 122, May 1, 1850 (536).

[2]Dated by Simms' remark about the forthcoming publication of Bryan's "Kennedy's Swallow Barn" (signed "G. S. B."), *Southern Quarterly Review*, N. S., V (Jan. 1852), 71–86.

603b

[1]Dated by Simms' references to the "anonymous book" (*As Good As a Comedy*) and to *Katharine Walton* (published in 1851).

of familiar names, and a reputation is seldom long the guarantee for circulation.—I fear that the profits must be small upon so small an edition of Kath. Walton at so small a price. Make it as much as you please & can, for the sake of the poor devil author to whose stock of responsibilities, his wife has just made a new contribution.[2]—I fear your Christmas has been too *warm* a one: let me sincerely hope for you a Happy and a still more prosperous *New Year*

Yours truly

W. Gilmore Simms

618a : To Israel Keech Tefft

Charleston 6th. March 1852.

My dear Tefft.

God willing, I propose on Saturday next, the 13th. inst., with my daughter,[1] to pay you & your city a visit: nothing but a serious and unexpected evil shall prevent us. I shall not be able to remain with you more than a day or two, arriving on Saturday & leaving on Monday; but Miss S. will no doubt be pleased to trespass for ten days, or a couple of weeks, upon the hospitality of Mama.[2] My labours at this season are so exacting as to render it impossible for me to suffer my own desires to linger with you to prevail. I am busy with the Review, to be issued on the 1st. April, and which is only half prepared. But I need not make excuses to you. You will, I know, understand without my assurance, the pleasure of which I deprive myself in making my holiday so short in Savannah. Enough. In writing now, my only purpose is to apprise you of our coming. My wife & the rest of my family are still at the plantation. The former would be quite happy to accompany me if she could.

Yours very truly

W. Gilmore Simms

---

[2]Sydney Roach Simms was born on Nov. 9. See note 224, Oct. 31, 1851 (600).

618a

[1]Augusta.

[2]Mrs. Tefft, the former Penelope Waite.

618b : To Brantz Mayer

Charleston S. C. March 13. [1852][1]

Hon. Brantz Mayer.
dear Sir:

We now never hear from you. Why is this? We shall still be pleased to have an occasional paper from your pen for the Southern Quarterly. I regret, however, that our Publishers still avow the necessity of *costiveness*, and declare their inability to pay more than "a Mexican" per page.[2] I am aware that this is no consideration to you, but for myself I am pleased to say that your contributions are a consideration to us. May we not hope to hear from you even on the poor terms of our publishers?

Yours Very truly

W. Gilmore Simms

618c : To Brantz Mayer

Woodlands, March [1852][1]

Hon Brantz Mayer.
My dear Sir:

I am an invalid, and in retirement at the plantation for a season, compelled to rusticate from overwork. I can only scribble you a paragraph to say that the promised article will no doubt prove very acceptable. I am sufficiently conscious of your general merits as a writer & historian to be prepared to admit the just assertion of your claims, & the guaranty which you give, of the capacity of your

618b

[1]Of the years that Simms was editor of the *Southern Quarterly Review*, 1852 is the only one in which he was in Charleston on Mar. 13. On that date he planned to visit Tefft in Savannah (see letter to Tefft of Mar. 6 [618a]). He could have written Mayer in the morning before leaving, or perhaps he did not make the trip on the day planned. It is also possible that "March 13" is an error for "March 12."

[2]Simms repeats this phrase in his letter to Mayer of Mar. 1852 (618c).

618c

[1]Dated by Simms' reference to his notice of Mayer's "*brochure*, anent Cresap." See note 3, below.

reviewer, assures me that the article is one that I may safely promise to publish.[2]—You will find in the Review a favorable notice of your *brochure,* anent Cresap &c.[3]—We are pretty much agreed as to the historical value of tradition in modern history. I could expose a thousand falsehoods in our credible books, but *cui bono?*—I regret that our publishers still plead poverty as a reason for not paying more liberally for contributions. I would have it otherwise, if it were possible; but cannot. Let me beg that when you perforce prepare an article, that you will give our pages the preference at all events, even at the poor pay of a *Mexican* per page.

Very truly Yours &c—

W. Gilmore Simms.

The sooner we recieve the article & books the better.

---

[2]Mayer's *Mexico, Astec, Spanish and Republican: A Historical, Geographical, Political, Statistical and Social Account of That Country from the Period of the Invasion by the Spaniards to the Present Time . . . ,* 2 vols. (Hartford: S. Drake and Company, 1852), is reviewed by Mayer's friend James Morrison Harris (1817–1898), a prominent lawyer of Baltimore and later a member of the U.S. House of Representatives (1855–1861), under the title of "Brantz Mayer's Mexico" in the *Southern Quarterly Review,* N. S., VI (July 1852), 117–141.

[3]In his notice of *Tah-Gah-Jute; or, Logan and Captain Michael Cresap; a Discourse by Brantz Mayer; Delivered in Baltimore, before the Maryland Historical Society, on Its Sixth Anniversary, 9 May, 1851* (Baltimore: Printed by J. Murphy & Co., 1851) in the *Southern Quarterly Review,* N. S., IV (Oct. 1851), 543–544, Simms writes: "Mr. Mayer has argued the case [for Captain Michael Cresap] with great fullness, has arrayed all the evidence before the reader, and establishes triumphantly the innocence of the worthy pioneer, whose memory has so long remained dishonored under the false an unmeaning imputations of a drunken and lying Indian [the Shawnee Chief, Logan], whose wild eloquence was fortunate in having an editor in so accomplished a writer, and we may add, artist, as Thomas Jefferson." In his *Notes on the State of Virginia* Jefferson reprinted the eloquent speech of Tah-gah-jute or James Logan (c. 1725–1780), a Mingo leader, accusing Michael Cresap (1742–1775) of the slaughter of certain members of his family in the Yellow Creek Massacre of Apr. 1774, which occasioned the outbreak of Dunmore's War. In a brief introduction Jefferson described Cresap as an "infamous" murderer of the Indians.

625a : To Brantz Mayer

Charleston May 10. [1852][1]

Hon. Brantz Mayer.
My dear Sir.

I thank you very much for your volumes, which I shall read with peculiar interest, not less on their account than your own. Pray remember in future that the obligation is large enough, in the acquisition of your writings, without needing that you should pay the express for transmitting them. Please believe me to be very grateful for your kindness.—We are also in reciept of the article reviewing the volumes from the pen of your friend, Mr. J. Morrison Harris. It is well written,—perhaps a little too floridly—and is already given out to the printers. It will appear as Article vi in our July issue.—Your paper on American Agriculture should have appeared long ago, but that by some wretched carelessness of the printers, it was mislaid. It has only recently turned up. You are aware that our Review is strongly anti-protective. This rendered it necessary that I should not seem to sanction what might favor the policy of the protectionists. But, as you percieve, I confined myself simply to entering a *caveat* here & there, and did not go into the discussion, which has been gone over with us *ad nauseam.*[2]—The sheets shall be sent you as you request. I shall be happy to hear from you at all times & thank you for the pamphlets.[3]

Yours, very faithfully &c

W. Gilmore Simms

625a

[1]Dated by Simms' remarks about Harris's "Brantz Mayer's Mexico." See note 2, Mar. 1852 (618c).

[2]In publishing Mayer's "American Agriculture" in the *Southern Quarterly Review*, N. S., V (Apr. 1852), [273]–301, Simms added a number of his own notes pointing out what he considered the fallacies in Mayer's argument for a protective tariff.

[3]Possibly Osmond Tiffany's *A Sketch of the Life and Services of Gen. Otho Holland Williams, Read before the Maryland Historical Society . . . March 6, 1851* (Baltimore: Printed by J. Murphy & Co., 1851) and Mayer's *Calvert and Penn*, which are noticed along with Sebastian Ferris Streeter's *Maryland, Two Hundred Years Ago: A Discourse . . . Delivered . . . before the Maryland Historical Society . . . May 20, 1852* (Baltimore: J. D. Toy, 1852) in the *Southern Quarterly Review* for Apr. 1853. See note 2, July 31, 1852 (631a).

626a : To Charles E. Tefft[1]

Office South. Quart. Review.
Charleston, May 29. 1852.

C. E. Tefft Esq.
My dear Charles.

I am not willing that you should evade the preparation of a paper on the History of Georgia. It is no reason that a work should not be reviewed because it is incomplete or inferior; nay, that such are its characteristics suggests the very best reason for showing them up. Neither White, nor Stevens, nor Arthur, nor McCall, could make a *good history,* and it is not necessary to decide upon the degree of comparison among them. All, together, might afford the text for a *good article,* and I should like to see you begin a bolder career than you have usually pursued, by an ambitious effort in this department. Try it, if you can.[2] You have not copied the marked passages for me from Washington? If yea, forward them when you can, by steamer; but if not, do not give yourself any trouble about them as they can be done without. We have just removed from the plantation to the city, and I am yet in the thick of packages & unpackings. I very much regret that you do not report more favorably of Papa. Say to him that I am now preparing a running commentary on DeKalb for our July issue,[3] and when finished, I

626a

[1]Tefft (1824–1853) was the youngest son of Israel Keech Tefft. See note 141, Dec. 17, 1853 (686).

[2]Tefft did not write this article on George White's *Statistics of the State of Georgia: Including an Account of Its Natural, Civil, and Ecclesiastical History; Together with a Particular Description of Each County, Notices of the Manners and Customs of Its Aboriginal Tribes, and a Correct Map of the State* (Savannah: W. T. Williams, 1849), Vol. I of William Bacon Stevens's *A History of Georgia from Its First Discovery by Europeans to the Adoption of the Present Constitution in MDCCXCVIII* (New York: D. Appleton and Co., 1847), Timothy Shay Arthur's and William Henry Carpenter's *The History of Georgia, from Its Earliest Settlement to the Present Time* (Philadelphia: Lippincott, Grambo & Co., 1852), and Hugh McCall's *The History of Georgia, Containing Brief Sketches of the Most Remarkable Events, up to the Present Day*, 2 vols. (Savannah: Seymour & Williams, 1811–1816).

[3]"The Baron DeKalb," *Southern Quarterly Review*, N. S., VI (July 1852), 141–203.

will detach for him one of D.K's original letters. My daughter[4] joins me in affectionate regards to him, Mama & yourself. She entertains very grateful reminiscences of her visit to Savannah.

Yours very truly but in
great haste

W. Gilmore Simms

626b : To George Palmer Putnam[1]

Office South. Quarterly Review.
Charleston June 23. 1852.

Geo. P. Putnam, Esq.
Dear Sir:

Mr. Richards [2] has not yet returned to the city. As soon as he does so, I will confer with him & contribute all I can to your objects. But, though really disposed to do honor to my friend Kennedy, whom I regard *as a gentleman* as well as an author,—characters not always associated in our country, I fear I cannot venture to do so. Just now I am not only something of an invalid, but I have my hands quite too full of work to hope to do justice either to myself or friend, by any new duties of the sort which you propose. In fact, I could no more tell you what sort of a house K. lives in than I could fly. He lives well, I know, and did live at Ellicott's Mills when I last had the pleasure of visiting him, but that is some years ago, and the impression, except the general one, is all effaced from my memory. Kennedy himself is an amiable, observant gentleman, as perhaps you know;—a good talker, with a decided vein of humour, nice in sensibility though a politician, & usually just in his judgments, though, as I think, somewhat erring in his politics.[3] Write

---

[4]Augusta.

626b

[1]For Putnam, the New York publisher, see note 244, June 25, 1845 (260).

[2]William Carey Richards.

[3]Simms met John Pendleton Kennedy in 1840. On June 28 of that year Kennedy wrote from Ellicott's Mills to his "dear Puss" (his wife, Elizabeth Gray Kennedy), at Saratoga Springs: "Who do you think dined here to day?—Guy Rivers. He brought a letter to me from Charleston which he enclosed to me through the P.

to Brantz Mayer, or Reverdy Johnson[4] for a biographical sketch,—or Hon. C. J. M. Gwinn,[5] or S. T. Wallis.[6] Either of them, I fancy would be quite willing and fully able to serve you in every substantial particular.[7]—I have not troubled you with any of my own literary projects, since I saw that you were in a crowd that would contrive to keep your hands full for a busy season. Whether all of these would contribute to fill your pockets, was a more doubtful matter, but I have several times thought of an experiment which we might make in the publication of my novels of the South during the Revolution—some 5 in number—all of which have been successful & highly popular books,—for some of which, in particular, now out of print, there is a growing demand particularly in the South. My notion was to try an experiment with these 5 vols., forming a class—the Romance of the Revolution in the South—which, if successful would justify a second experiment in my Border Stories—

O on Wednesday [June 24]. . . . So at a venture I wrote to him asking him to dinner out here on Sunday. Somewhat unexpectedly he came,—having been, in the interval, at Washington. . . . He is tall, well made, not handsome in feature, amazingly pedantic, Sir Oracle in conceit, a thorough Loco, and shortsighted in every sense [Kennedy's note: "wears glasses"]. He talked literary—but fortunately I had not read or believed I had not, any of the books he wanted me to criticize, and so shuffled off every imputation of scholarship he was pleased to presume in my favour. I abused Bryant to him for being *political,* and spoke of his editing a party newspaper as altogether derogatory to his fame. I was not overnice in my phrase in this matter—and after all, discovered that my new friend himself—who, by the by, claims to be a poet—was also, or had been, a party hack editor. I cant say I took *very violently* to him. . . . I think the tribe, *author,* is not altogether the best of the Twelve of Israel. . . . These soldiers of the quill, I fear, do not often leave me greatly prepossessed with my comradeship. They get no memorabilia or Kennedianas out of me, and, of course, put me down as stupid." (Original in the collection of the George Peabody Department, Enoch Pratt Free Library, Baltimore, Md.)

[4]Johnson (1796–1876), a prominent Baltimore lawyer, was elected to the U.S. Senate in 1840, but resigned to become attorney general under President Taylor. Like Kennedy, he was an ardent Whig. He later allied himself with the Democrats and in 1868 was appointed minister to Great Britain.

[5]For Charles John Morris Gwinn, see note 80, Apr. 27, 1849 (481).

[6]Severn Teackle Wallis (1816–1894), of Baltimore, was one of the leading Maryland lawyers. He was the author of addresses, verses, and criticism and was one of the founders of the Maryland Historical Society.

[7]Putnam was attempting to get various people to contribute to *Homes of American Authors* (New York: G. P. Putnam & Co., 1853). An unsigned account of Kennedy appears on pp. [341]–346. A picture of Ellicott's Mills, drawn by David Hunter Strother (see note 11, Jan. 16, 1862 [1067a]) and engraved by William Lilly Ormsby (1809–1883), accompanies the sketch.

constituting, The Border Romance of the South—some half dozen vols. more. I have some preliminary matters to adjust, before the thing can be done, but shall be obliged to, if, at your leisure, you can give me your opinion of it.[8]

Yours very truly

W. Gilmore Simms

626c : To George Palmer Putnam

Charleston July 1. 1852.

My dear Sir:

I waited the return of Mr. Richards before fully replying to your letter. He has just got home, and professes to have understood you very imperfectly as to the design of your publication, for which you desire some notes respecting myself and my whereabouts. Please let me know what you want and to what extent—in other words what space will you accord to the subject. If a personal or biographical or literary sketch, with description of abode—in short any thing in relation to what I may becomingly give information, I will cheerfully do so. Mr. T. Addison Richards, while on a visit to us last winter made a pencil sketch of my residence in Carolina. This, I suppose, he will gladly put at your service.[1] He is also, perhaps, better prepared than his brother to do any letter press which you may need. The latter always has his hands full. In making such sketches successful a great deal depends upon the capacity of the writer to enter into the moral nature of the subject. The younger Mr. R. has probably more *insight* than the elder. He is, in fact, under the most unobtrusive features in the world, a remarkably

[8]Putnam did not republish any of these novels.

626c

[1]An engraving of Woodlands by Samuel Valentine Hunt (1803–1893) from the sketch by Thomas Addison Richards (see introductory sketch of the Richards family) accompanies the account of Simms and Woodlands in *Homes of American Authors* (see note 154, Aug. 10, 1852 [634]). It is reproduced in Vol. I of *The Letters of William Gilmore Simms*, facing p. 168.

clever young man. Let me hear from you as to what I am required to contribute and I shall be as prompt as many toils, and some physical infirmities will allow, in making my response.—I said something in my previous letter touching a scheme of publication turning in my head, in which I was disposed to wish that you would co-operate. When Carey & Hart put forth their two volumes of American Biography under the title of Washington & the Generals of the Revolution, I was employed to contribute a body of Southern Biography. My articles included Lives of Sumter, Moultrie, Greene, Gadsden, Huger, Kosciusko, Lee,[2] and others. To these I am prepared to add sketches of John Rutledge, Baron de Kalb [3] and some few others military & civil, and to make up a couple of volumes of my own. In some of these, as in the case of De Kalb I publish correspondence original & hitherto unknown & inedited. Altogether, I should suppose the collection, to which I should affix my name, would be particularly attractive in the South and of general interest throughout the country. Would such a projêt suit you.[4]—I have also prepared a volume of somewhat novel character, no less than a descriptive & legendary poem—especially descriptive of the rare, little known & rarely beautiful scenery of our mountain country. The subject, manner and material are all novel. The poem extends to 2500 lines octosyllabic, and would be enriched with copious notes, original and borrowed from such quaint, pleasant old authors as Adair, Bartram &c.[5] It would make a handsome volume for illustration & with only a couple of good engravings would probably prove attractive as an annual, at a moderate price. As I concieve myself to have been quite successful in the verse, as well as the plan, I should really anticipate considerable success &

---

[2]Thomas Sumter (1734–1832), William Moultrie (1730–1805), Nathanael Greene (1742–1786), Christopher Gadsden (1724–1805), Isaac Huger (1743–1797), Thadeusz Andrzej Bonawentura Kościuszko (1746–1817), and Charles Lee (1731–1782).

[3]John Rutledge (1739–1800) and Johann Kalb (1721–1780), known as "Baron de Kalb."

[4]This work was not published.

[5]James Adair, *The History of the American Indians . . .* (London: E. and C. Dilly, 1775) and William Bartram, *Travels through North and South Carolina, Georgia, East & West Florida . . .* (Philadelphia: Printed by James & Johnson, 1791).

circulation for it.[6]—Another matter: Can you procure for me any back numbers which I may lack, of the Shakspeare & Percy Society publications?[7]

Please answer me at your earliest convenience in regard to these several topics & hold me, meanwhile,

Very truly Yours &c

W. Gilmore Simms.

Send me a copy of Hood's Whimsicalities which I did not recieve.[8]

630a : To George Palmer Putnam

Charleston, S. C. July 15. 1852.

Geo. P. Putnam, Esq.
dear Sir:

I have furnished Mr. W. C. Richards with all the necessary notes from which he may elaborate the sketch of Woodlands, leaving it to himself to say what he pleases of my personal self, with which portion of his work I can, of course, have nothing to do. His brother could have done it quite as well, but he tells me that the latter is now on a tour in your interior. There is a Mr. D. H. Jacques, of N. Y. now editing a child's magazine in your city, who is very clever and who could furnish you some notes of me, my personal habits &c. if applied to. He is a very modest, worthy & intelligent person whom you might find it advantageous sometimes to employ.[1] I have

[6]Simms took the manuscript of this unpublished poem, "The Mountain Tramp. Tselica; a Legend of the French Broad," to New York City in Sept. 1852, and later asked Evert Augustus Duyckinck (see introductory sketch) for his "notion as to the propriety of publishing with copious descriptive, legendary, historical & other notes . . . with illustrated title & vignettes from Darley." See letters to Duyckinck of Feb. 16, 1850 (525), and Nov. 10, 1852 (649).

[7]Simms had earlier asked Frederick Saunders for these. See letter to Saunders of Apr. 4, 1852 (619).

[8]See note 3, July 15, 1852 (630a).

630a

[1]We have been unable to discover what "child's magazine" Daniel Harrison Jacques (see note 199, Oct. 16, 1860 [995]), was editing.

sent you a review of my poetical writings, written by the Rev. Professor Miles of this city, which is carefully & spiritedly done, from which you might gather some particulars.[2] The want of time, is an embarrassing circumstance in the way of such a performance. Of the publication projects we may talk hereafter. I can very well understand how the success of much of our present publication should be doubtful. But!—I have not recd. from you the Cooper tribute, nor the "Roughings", nor the "Whimsicalities."[3]

Yours in haste but truly

W. Gilmore Simms

630b : To Henry William Ravenel[1]

Office South. Q. Review.
Monday Mg. July 28. 1852

H. W. Ravenel Esq.
dear Sir:

I have been encouraged by our mutual friend Dr. F. P. Porcher,[2] to hope that you would continue your contributions, so happily begun, to the South. Quarterly Review, and in the special department which you are so successfully appropriating to yourself. May I hope that you will be persuaded to make the Review a frequent medium for communicating with our Southern public? Through

---

[2]For James Warley Miles' review of Simms' *Poems*, see note 152, June 9, 1851 (588).

[3]In the *Southern Quarterly Review*, N. S., VI (Oct. 1852), 543, 537, 540, Simms notices the following books published by Putnam: *Memorial of James Fenimore Cooper*, Susannah Strickland Moodie's *Roughing It in the Bush; or, Life in Canada*, 2 vols., and Thomas Hood's *Whims and Oddities, in Prose and Verse*, all issued in 1852. A second notice of the first appears in ibid., N. S., VII (Jan. 1853), 251–252.

630b

[1]Ravenel (1814–1887) was an authority on fungi.

[2]Francis Peyre Porcher (see introductory sketch) was a Charleston physician and close friend of Ravenel, who aided him with his *Resources of the Southern Fields and Forests, Medical, Economical, and Agricultural. Being Also a Medical Botany of the Confederate States; with Practical Information on the Useful Properties of the Trees, Plants, and Shrubs* (Charleston: Evans & Cogswell, 1863).

such a medium, you publish free of cost; and the publishers are prepared to furnish you with fifty or a hundred extra copies of your communications in pamphlet form, by way of *quid.* It would give me great pleasure, I assure you to welcome your favors, as often as you should be pleased to accord them.[3]

Very respectfully & truly
Yr. obt. & obliged sert.

W. Gilmore Simms
Ed. S. Q. Review.

631a : To Brantz Mayer

Office South. Quart. Review.
Charleston, July 31. 1852.

Hon. Brantz Mayer.
Dear Sir:

I have ordered the extra copies, 25 in number, of the art. on your Mexico, to be addressed to you, at Balto., paying the postage upon them. Some of these copies are designed for Mr. Harris. Will you please divide them with him. We are agreed upon the merits of his art. A more severe taste in the matter of style, would leave us no occasion for complaint. The military articles in the Review, are from the pen of Col. Hammond, of this State, who lately served as President of the Board of Examiners at W. P.[1] I am in reciept

[3]Ravenel's "Cryptogamous Origin of Fevers" was published in the *Southern Quarterly Review*, N. S., I (Apr. 1850), 146–159. No other article in the *Review* can be attributed to him during Simms' editorship.

631a

[1]Marcus Claudius Marcellus Hammond (see introductory sketch of the Hammonds) had published in the *Southern Quarterly Review* the following articles about the Mexican War: "The Battles of the Rio Grande," N. S., II (Nov. 1850), 427–463; "Battle of Buena Vista," N. S., III (Jan. 1851), 146–189; "The Siege of Vera Cruz," N. S., IV (July 1851), 1–40; "Battle of Cerro Gordo," N. S., V (Jan. 1852), 121–153; "The Battle of Contreras," N. S., V (Apr. 1852), 373–426; and "The Battle of Churubusco," N. S., V (July 1852), 78–116. He went on to publish three more: "Battle of El Molino del Rey," N. S., VI (Oct. 1852), 281–315; "Chapultepec and the Garitas of Mexico," N. S., VII (Jan. 1853), 1–52; and "Secondary Combats of the Mexican War," N. S., VIII (July 1853), 92–130. In ibid., N. S., VI (July 1852), 277, Simms notes that when "Colonel . . . Hammond [was] placed on the late board of visitors, at the late examination of the United States Military Academy [at West Point] he was properly honoured with the presidency of the board."

of your discourses on Penn & Calvert, but have not yet had an opportunity to read them.[2] I am sorely drudged. I should like a paper from you for the October number of the Review—for January, at all events, but the publishers will not allow me to offer more than the one dollar per page. Even this, I must tell you, they only pay to a favored few, and this, by the way, is as much as is done by any periodical in the country.[3] I note what you say of Kossuth with great interest. The invitation to him was the *first* blunder begetting all that followed.[4] I wrote to Col. Hammond making the inquiry you suggest. Much hurried and far from well, you will yet believe me very truly & faithfully Yr friend & Servt.

W. Gilmore Simms

---

[2]Simms briefly notices *Calvert and Penn; or the Growth of Civil and Religious Liberty in America, as Disclosed in the Planting of Maryland and Pennsylvania: A Discourse by Brantz Mayer, Delivered in Philadelphia before the Pennsylvania Historical Society, 8 April 1852* (Baltimore: Printed for the Pennsylvania Historical Society, 1852) with Tiffany's *A Sketch of the Life and Services of Gen. Otho Holland Williams* and Streeter's *Maryland, Two Hundred Years Ago* ("historical pamphlets of interest and value . . ., some of the fruits of the public spirit and intelligence of the Maryland Historical Society") in the *Southern Quarterly Review*, N. S., VII (Apr. 1853), 514–515.

[3]We cannot attribute to Mayer any article published in the *Southern Quarterly Review* after this date.

[4]In the latter part of 1851 Lajos [Louis] Kossuth (1802–1894), the Hungarian patriot, then in exile in Turkey, was by a unanimous vote in the Senate offered asylum in the United States. He left Turkey on an American man-of-war and after a visit to England arrived in New York City in early Dec. 1851. He made a procession throughout the United States, and his eloquent oratory urging support for the liberation of Hungary from Austria was met with extraordinary enthusiasm. "Hungarian" (or "Kossuth") bonds were bought by many, and some people apparently wanted the United States to intervene actively in the affairs of Hungary. In the *Southern Quarterly Review*, N. S., VI (July 1852), 221–235, Simms published an article entitled "Kossuth and Intervention," possibly written by Simms himself (see letter to Duyckinck of Apr. 5, 1852 [621]), attacking Kossuth and his "creed": "If the people of the United States permit themselves to be beguiled by the crafty subtleties of foreign or native demagogues, into this course of aggression upon the rights of other nations, by intermeddling with their domestic affairs, under no matter what specious pretext of sympathy or fraternity, the growth, the mighty future wealth and power of our country, will prove a scourge and a curse, not a help and a blessing, as we hope they will, to the feebler nations of the earth. We shall play again the game of universal dominion, and furnish to the world another lesson on the true meaning of the solidarity of the peoples and the disinterested benevolence of aspiring demagogues."

635a : To Brantz Mayer

Office So. Quarterly Review.
Charleston, Augt. 13. 1852.

Hon. Brantz Mayer
dear Sir:

If you will let me have the paper on the Isthmus for the October, and another paper on Pontiac, for the January issue of the Review, I shall be obliged to you. Of course, I shall wish both on the same terms. I should wish also that neither should exceed 30 pages. Of course, a page or two over, or even five would make no difference; but I should prefer them to range at from 25 to 30.[1] You have, I trust, recieved the pamphlet copies of the article on your Mexico. If you can persuade Mr. Harris to an occasional article for us, *as an amateur,* I will esteem it a favor. I say *amateur,* for though I should prefer to pay for every article we publish, yet our Publishers restrain me.[2] In fact our collections are so slow in our sparsely settled country that, with a good subs. list, we are always needy.

Yours very truly

W. Gilmore Simms

648a : To Brantz Mayer

Charleston, Nov. 5. 1852.

Hon. Brantz Mayer.
dear Sir:

I am sorry that our Correspondent should misrepresent you, as he seems to have done. I am sure his purpose was not to do so, and will transmit your letter to him, in order to enable him to shape

---

635a

[1]Apparently Mayer was considering writing articles on Chauncey D. Griswold's *The Isthmus of Panama, and What I Saw There* (New York: Dewitt and Davenport, 1852) and Francis Parkman's *History of the Conspiracy of Pontiac . . .* (Boston: C. C. Little and J. Brown, 1851) for publication in the *Southern Quarterly Review.* No articles on these subjects were published in the *Review.*

[2]We cannot attribute to James Morrison Harris any article published in the *Southern Quarterly Review* during the remainder of Simms' editorship.

an explanation, so as to relieve you from the false attitude in which you are placed. I write only to acknowledge your communication, & to state this determination. Here we are just recovering from the stagnation caused by an epidemic which is retiring from us with due rapidity, having done its work.[1] My hands are full of preparation. I am packing up preparatory to the annual exodus of the family to the plantation, whither we shall probably go sometime next week. When I hear from Col. Hammond, who is the author of the paper which misrepresents you, you shall be advised of what he says. But in all probability, he will write you himself.[2]

Yours truly

W. Gilmore Simms

655a : To Brantz Mayer

Woodlands, Jan 5. 1853.

Hon. Brantz Mayer.
dear Sir.

The smiles of a new year upon your fortunes. You are, I learn, the proprietor of the Baltimore American, a valuable paper, in which, you have an opportunity of exercising an important sway in public opinion, & of doing good service to letters & the laws. Be just & fear not. Be prosperous, also! Let me hope, that your new position will not prevent you from doing for us an occasional

---

648a

[1]For an account of this epidemic, see the unsigned article "Yellow Fever in Charleston in 1852," *Southern Quarterly Review*, N. S., VII (Jan. 1853), 140–178.

[2]In the *Southern Quarterly Review*, N. S., VII (Jan. 1853), 230–231, Simms published a letter from Mayer dated "Baltimore, Nov. 1, 1852," objecting to Hammond's having said in his "Battle of El Molina del Rey," ibid., N. S., VI (Oct. 1852), 292, that Mayer (among others) considered Santa Anna a "*feeble poltroon*" in this battle: "I . . . [never] entertained the idea, or promulgated it, that Santa was a '*feeble poltroon*' in the midst of *any* crisis. . . . [His] genius and courage rose with disaster and failed with prosperity." The same issue, pp. 231–232, contains a letter from Hammond dated "Nov. 7, 1852," apologizing for his remark: Mayer's "complaint is perfectly just," he had prepared his article hastily and had not read Mayer's book, and perhaps "poltroon" is too "harsh"—but certainly Santa Anna was a "*dastard.*"

article. In particular let me remind you of the promised paper, which I should like to have in season for our April number. Our January is in press, but delayed, in consequence of a change in the business of the publishers.[1] I have been taking steps which, I trust, will enable me to compensate adequately our contributors, secure a few able ones additional, & dispense with others. I hope to do this during the present year & put the Review upon a permanent basis, when it is my present purpose to leave it. It consumes too much of my time, as I think unprofitably, & by no means compensates me in a pecuniary way. And I am not able to dispense with the creature comforts. Let me hear from you occasionally, & please send me copies of any of your papers, in which you pour yourself out editorially.

Yours very truly &c

W. Gilmore Simms

663a : To Henry Carey Baird

Charleston, S. C. May 29, 1853.

Dear Master Harry.

Enclosed I send you an autograph letter of Moultrie, with the added signature of Gen. Is. Huger.[1] I shall have others to send you when I look over my papers. None of your books reach me. On recieving your letter I called upon Saml Hart, showed him the passage & date on which you said that books were forwarded to his care. He looked over his books and said that he had recieved nothing from you for months before or since! So I got nothing then,

---

655a

[1]In Oct. 1851 Edwin Heriot bought from Walker and Richards a third interest in the *Southern Quarterly Review*, and the firm of Walker and Richards changed its name to Walker, Richards & Co. (see note 191, Oct. 11, 1851 [597]). Late in 1852 Heriot left the firm, Richards moved to New York City, and Joseph Walker and Thomas A. Burke formed the firm of Walker and Burke and published the *Review* through 1853 (see note 192, Oct. 11, 1851 [597], and note 218, Nov. 24, 1852 [652]).

663a

[1]Gen. William Moultrie and Gen. Isaac Huger.

& nothing since. Did you procure any information touching Arnold's wife &c?[2] Now, will you inquire for me at Blanchard's & Lea's, if they have got setts of the American Quarterly which they will dispose of cheaply?[3] I believe they advertised such sometime ago. I have the two first volumes & would be content to have the rest; but they might not be willing to break a sett. Copies ought to be got for a very moderate sum. Enquire & let me know. I think it likely I shall visit Phila. in July or August, when I hope to see you & your collection.[4]

Yours very truly
&c

W. Gilmore Simms

663b : To Henry Panton[1]

Charleston, June 10. 1853

dear Panton.

Accompanying, you will find the portrait, done by H. B. Bounetheau, from life, and here thought to be singularly faithful—too faithful in fact, since he has even included in it the marks made by the spectacles across the nose, which is thought to be unnecessary to the likeness, & which you will get the engraver to efface. Put on the plate the inscription of the artist, who is, like yourself an amateur, & whom I shall make to know you when he next visits

[2]Simms had asked Baird for information about Margaret Shippen Arnold in his letter of Mar. 4, 1853 (658); he continued to ask him for information in his letters of Sept. 15, 1853 (672), and Oct. 14, 1855 (792). Undoubtedly he wanted it for revision of his play about Benedict Arnold on which he had been working for years and which was eventually published as "Benedict Arnold: The Traitor. A Drama, in an Essay" in the *Magnolia Weekly* during 1863 (see note 21, Jan. 25, 1850 [521]).

[3]The *American Quarterly Review* (Philadelphia) ran from Mar. 1827 through Dec. 1837.

[4]Simms left for New York City around Aug. 1 and returned to Charleston on Sept. 26. See his letters to Lawson of July 16 (669) and Sept. 28 (675).

663b

[1]Panton, brother-in-law of Evert Augustus Duyckinck, was connected with Justus Starr Redfield's publishing house, Redfield.

New York. I enclose you a few strips of my signatures done more decently than usual, from which you may detach an autograph for the same page. I trust you will give us a really good engraving.[2] In the same packet you will find seven chapters of Vasconselos, 28 to 34 inclusive. I shall condense the residue as much as possible, but will not be able to compress within your limits as all that remains will be the action and incidents which are unavoidable from what is already written. You must do the best with it and if two volumes cannot be made (though I do not see how you are to escape it) perhaps it may be well to print the rest without leads—an awkward necessity which I do not like to contemplate. It is greatly to be regretted that we began with leads.[3] An occasional work in 2 vols. may be an occasional temptation, as, in degree, it is a novelty now-a-days. You will also find in the package 64 pages (taking the folios of the old volume) of the revised edition of "The Yemassee". I have laid the sheets all regularly, one after the other, and by using them only as they are wanted, there can be no confusion. In the first portions you will see that my alterations are considerable. They will lessen as we proceed. Russell thinks the Revolutionary novels should be the ones to begin with. I shall get the Partisan ready for you the next, & can correct the press while I am in New York.[4] I hope to be on in July.—The Yemassee is not a long novel, and will, I suppose, furnish a good general average for all my books. I have here the plates of two nouvellettes, Helen Halsey & Castle Dismal—each about the size of Martin Faber,—both as good or better, and both quite popular in their day—and both long out of print. Shall I have them sent on.[5] The plates of Wiley & Putnam's editions

---

[2]The original drawing of Simms by Henry Brintnell Bounetheau (1797–1877), the Charleston miniaturist, is reproduced as the frontispiece to Vol. I of *The Letters of William Gilmore Simms*; it is now owned by Mary Simms Oliphant Furman. Bounetheau's drawing was engraved by W. J. Alais and published as the frontispiece to Vol. I of Simms' *Poems Descriptive Dramatic, Legendary and Contemplative*, 2 vols. (New York: Redfield, 1853). The volumes were also issued with the imprint of John Russell, Charleston, S.C. (see letter to Chesnut of Jan. 12, 1854 [691a]).

[3]Chaps. XXVIII–L (pp. 342–531) are printed without leads.

[4]Redfield's editions of *The Yemassee* and *The Partisan* are dated respectively 1853 and 1854.

[5]Redfield did not publish editions of *Helen Halsey* or *Castle Dismal*. Nor did he publish an edition of *Martin Faber: The Story of a Criminal*, first published by J. & J. Harper, New York, in 1833.

of the Wigwam & Cabin can be procured at a small price? Is it worth while to buy them? Will they correspond with our edition?[6] Think over all these points and advise me that I may duly act upon them. I think it likely I shall be able to take steamer for N. Y. about the 10th. July. If you design any ornament for the back of the Yemassee &c. Indian weapons wrapt round with a rattlesnake skin &c. will do.[7] On the Poems,—my crest is an eye in the shoulder of a wing—*volans video.*[8]—But this matter may be reserved until I see you.

Yours very truly, &c

W. Gilmore Simms

669a : To James Thomas Fields[1]

Charleston, July 25. [1853][2]

dear Sir:

On the 30th. inst. I propose to sail for New York, in and about which city and Philadelphia I propose to be about four weeks.[3] Let me hope that you will seek me out should you happen to come thither during that space. You will hear of me in N. Y. at Putnam's

---

[6]Redfield removed the line under the running title of the plates of the text of *The Wigwam and the Cabin*, altered the two-volume pagination to continuous pagination, and reissued the work with a new title page dated 1856, a new dedication to Nash Roach, and a new table of contents.

[7]A design similar to the one Simms here describes is used on the backstrip of *The Yemassee.*

[8]Redfield did not adopt Simms' suggestion.

669a

[1]For Fields, Boston publisher and author, see note 16, c. Jan. 18, 1854 (693).

[2]Dated by Simms' plan to sail for New York City on July 30 and to visit Philadelphia also on this trip to the North. See letter to Lawson of July 10 (667).

[3]Simms did not visit Philadelphia. See letter to Baird of Sept. 15 (672).

or Redfield's—in Philadelphia from Lippincott, or Butler.[4] In haste but very truly Yours &c

W. Gilmore Simms.

James T. Fields, Esq.

670a : To James Thomas Fields

New York. Augt. 16. [1853][1]

James T. Fields, Esq.
dear Sir:

My young friend, Mr. Paul H. Hayne, of South Carolina, will shortly visit your city, and as he is one of our craft, though a young beginner, a young Poet & the Editor of a Literary Weekly in Charleston, I take for granted that it will be agreeable to you to know each other.[2] You will find Mr. Hayne, one of the most amiable of Gentlemen, intelligent and modest. He is of our best families, & a nephew of the General, Robt. Y. Hayne, well known to you, as honored by his antagonism with Webster, on the famous Foote resolutions.[3]

---

[4]In 1853 Lippincott, Grambo, & Co. issued editions of *The Sword and the Distaff, The Wigwam and the Cabin, Norman Maurice*, and *The Pro-Slavery Argument*, containing (pp. 175–285) Simms' "The Morals of Slavery." In the same year E. H. Butler & Co. published *Egeria: Or, Voices of Thought and Counsel, for the Woods and Wayside*. See note 130, July 7, 1852 (628), and notes 60 and 62, June 20, 1853 (666).

670a

[1]Dated by the visit of Paul Hamilton Hayne (see introductory sketch) to Boston in 1853 to seek a publisher for his poems. Fields' firm, Ticknor and Fields, published Hayne's *Poems* in Nov. 1854 (the volume is dated 1855). See Rayburn S. Moore, *Paul Hamilton Hayne* (New York: Twayne Publishers, Inc., [1972]), pp. 17–18.

[2]Hayne was editor of the *Weekly News*. See note 226, Nov. 24, 1849 (513).

[3]On Dec. 29, 1829, Samuel Augustus Foote of Connecticut submitted in the U.S. Senate a resolution to inquire into the expediency of limiting the sales of the public lands to those then in the market, to suspend the surveys of the public lands, and to abolish the office of surveyor general. The debate against it was opened by Thomas Hart Benton of Missouri and continued by Robert Young Hayne (1791–1839) of South Carolina with Daniel Webster of Massachusetts as his opponent. For almost a fortnight the Senate was crowded with listeners to this celebrated debate, which among other subjects dealt with the tariff, Negro slavery, the merits of South Carolina and Massachusetts in the Revolution, the character of the Constitution, the virtues and vices of nullification, and the rights of the states. Hayne was a major general of the Second Division of the South Carolina Militia.

I am in New York, you see, and if you come thither, you will find me at a friend's, 136 Twelfth Street.[4]

Very truly &c Yours—

W. Gilmore Simms

676a : To Brantz Mayer

Charleston Sept. 29. [1853][1]

Hon. Brantz Mayer
dear Sir:

I have just got back from New York where I regret that I did not meet you. I now write only to answer the business part of your last friendly note. An article on eith[er][2] nay both, of the subjects which you mention, would be very agreeable to us, but I regret to say that our publishers profess themselves unable to accord more than their former price of $1. per page. If you can tolerate this poor compensation—as I confess so totally inadequate—send me *both* articles.[3] We are in hopes shortly to do better with the Review. It is improving & increasing in subscribers, & under a new *regime,* which begins with 1854, I hope to deal more liberally with our friends.

Yours in great haste, but
Very truly

W. Gilmore Simms

---

[4]This was James Lawson's address.

676a

[1]Dated by Simms' remark about "a new *regime*, which begins with 1854." The *Southern Quarterly Review* was purchased by Charles Mortimer, a Virginian, who published the periodical through 1855.

[2]In going from one line to another Simms failed to complete the word.

[3]See letter to Mayer of Aug. 13, 1852 (635a).

687a : To Brantz Mayer

Office "Southern Quarterly Review."

Charleston, S. C., Decr. 17. 1853[1]

Hon. Brantz Mayer
My dear Sir:

The review has passed into the hands of a new publisher who is apparently quite as liberal in his view as he is active in his business. He is pressing & earnest, & the subscribers to the work are rapidly increasing. He authorizes me to offer you $1.50 per page, for such articles as will suit us, and this pay will be increased with the increasing means of the work. May I hope, therefore, to recieve from you on these terms, the two articles which you suggested to me some time ago?[2] It is possible that I shall be in Washington to lecture some time this winter.[3] If so, I shall try to see you when passing through Baltimore.

Yours very truly

W. Gilmore Simms

691a : To James Chesnut, Jr.[1]

Woodlands Jan 12. 1854.

Col. James Chesnut jr.
My dear Chesnut.

Did I not send you a year or two ago, a prospectus of my Poems, and did you procure me the names of any subscribers, good men & true? If I did, did you forward me the list, or dispose of it in any way. Please let me know, as the volumes are now published & ready for distribution.[2]—

687a

[1]"Office 'Southern Quarterly Review.'/Charleston, S. C., 1853" is the printed letterhead.

[2]See letters to Mayer of Aug. 13, 1852, and Sept. 29, 1853 (635a and 676a).

[3]See letter to Mayer of Feb. 8, 1854 (696a).

691a

[1]See introductory sketch of the Chesnuts.

[2]On Feb. 5, 1852 (610), Simms had sent Chesnut a prospectus of his *Poems*

Let me recal to you another matter. In years past you gave me a *quasi* promise to prepare an article for the Southern Quarterly. That work is still prepared to give you a welcoming reception, and I shall be very happy to have something at your hands.[3]—

I trust you prosper as I do *not*. Literature in the South is hardly worse than ditching, I grant you, but it is hardly better.

Very truly Yours &c

W. Gilmore Simms

692a : To John Reuben Thompson[1]

Woodlands, Jan. 13 [1854][2]

My dear Thompson.

Don't talk to me of stories and contributions just now. I have my hands full, with my Lectures, and preparing the contents of the April review, before I can possibly leave home. These things disposed of, I am your man for any thing. I would I had you here now, in my den, to blow a cloud with me and break a bottle: but not to write. The Messenger for January has not yet reached me. Pray send me one here. I am afraid that for Review in Charleston has miscarried. I shall probably pass through Richmond, about the 3d. of February. Shall return from Washington to lecture. May go on to New York first, on a flying visit. Have you recieved copies of The Yemassee & the Poems.[3] My Lectures will run over an hour,

---

Descriptive Dramatic, Legendary and Contemplative, 2 vols. (Charleston, S.C.: John Russell, 1853).

[3]We obviously erred in suggesting that Chesnut might have been the author of two articles in the *Southern Quarterly Review* signed "J. C.": "Authority in Matters of Opinion" and "The Destinies of the South." See note 29, Feb. 5, 1852 (610).

692a

[1]Thompson (see introductory sketch) was editor of the *Southern Literary Messenger* during 1847–1860.

[2]Dated by Simms' reference to his letter to Thompson of Jan. 3, 1854 (690), in which he requests various back issues of the *Southern Literary Messenger*, and by his remarks about his forthcoming lectures (see note 4, below).

[3]*The Yemassee* is reviewed in the *Messenger* for Jan. 1854, *Poems Descriptive Dramatic, Legendary and Contemplative* in the *Messenger* for Mar. 1854. See note 6, Jan. 3, 1854 (690).

say 1 ¼ each. Can you endure it. Let the citizens bring their nightcaps with them.[4] I think I mentioned in my last certain numbers of the Messenger that I needed. Do forward them. I really should be glad to send you a story or two, but it is physically impossible.[5] See what a nervous scrawl I write. I have been at it all day. Hurriedly but truly

Yours &c

Simms

J. R. T.

694a : To James Chesnut, Jr.

Woodlands, S. C. Jan. 27. [1854][1]

My dear Chesnut.

I am too much hurried to do more than thank you for your kind letter, & your attention to the Vols. of Poems. I shall communicate your list of subs. to J Russell, & instruct him to forward the copies to your address. Please add to your kindness, by having them delivered, procuring the *quid,* and transmitting it to Russell. I note

[4]Simms left Charleston on Feb. 1 (see the Charleston *Courier* of Feb. 2) and arrived in Washington on Feb. 3 (see letter to Baird of Feb. 4 [696]). He lectured at Washington on Feb. 9(?), 10, 13, and 15 (see note 1, Feb. 8 [696a]), left for Philadelphia on Feb. 18 or 19, and arrived there the same day (see letter to Baird of Feb. 17 [701]). Mrs. Simms did not want him to go to New York City because of the prevalence of smallpox there, so he remained in Philadelphia until Feb. 27, when he left for Richmond (see letters to Lawson of Feb. 21 [702] and to Thompson of Feb. 24 [703]). He arrived in Richmond on Feb. 28, but had to postpone his first lecture on "Poetry and the Practical" until Mar. 2 because of the loss of his trunk; his second lecture on the same subject was delivered on Mar. 3 (see note 38, Feb. 24 [703]). He lectured at Petersburg on Mar. 6 and 7 (see note 1, Mar. 17 [705a]) and returned to Woodlands on or before Mar. 13 (see letter to Duyckinck of that date [704]).

[5]In the *Messenger* for July and Aug. 1854 (XX, 396–403, 492–503) Simms published "The Legend of the Happy Valley, and the Beautiful Faun," signed "by a Southron." The tale is an expanded version of "Haiglar: A Story of the Catawbas," *The Book of My Lady. A Melange* (Philadelphia: Key & Biddle, 1833), pp. 126–135.

694a

[1]Simms wrote *Feb. 27.* The correct month and year are determined by his remarks about his *Poems* (see letter to Chesnut of Jan. 12 [691a]) and his forthcoming lectures in Washington (see letter to Thompson of Jan. 13 [692a]).

that there are 11 copies. I shall have a dozen sent you, and you will be able probably to get rid of the odd one. We shall be pleased if more are wanted, for in truth, we have to create the taste for Poetry in the South, and the process, unless by subscription, would be a parlous danger. The reason of my hurry is briefly this. I am to deliver four Lectures in Washington early in February, and am busy packing up for the city whither I go on Saturday.[2] It is barely possible that I may take Camden in my way from Washington, and seize you by the fist when you little dream of.[3] Meanwhile prepare me the notes of which you speak for correcting errors of fact & opinion in my History[4] & Biography.[5] I am grateful for all hints and information. Don't forget the *brain*-work in the *brick* work, nor let your *mortar* particles entirely crush your *mental* articles. In plain terms try & prepare a paper for our July or October issue.[6]

Very faithfully Yours &c

W. Gilmore Simms

P.S. I took the liberty of giving your name to a firm in New York [7] which desired to find a Camden Lawyer, in some suspicious case of indebtedness.

696a : To Brantz Mayer

Washington, D. C. Feb. 8. [1854][1]

Hon. Brantz Mayer.
dear Sir.

I am here delivering certain lectures before the Smithsonian, and would like to know if I could glean a few pennies for the performance

[2]Jan. 28.

[3]There is no evidence that Simms did stop by Camden.

[4]*The History of South Carolina.*

[5]We do not know which of his biographies Simms here has in mind.

[6]We are unable to attribute to Chesnut any article published in the *Southern Quarterly Review* during Simms' editorship.

[7]Not identified.

696a

[1]Dated by Simms' reference to his lectures before the Smithsonian Institution. His first two lectures, "Poetry and the Practical," were delivered on Feb. 9(?) and

of like duties in Baltimore. Have you not some Societies there, who accord the quid for such performances. I shall be here till Wednesday of next week, when I propose to take the route north for a week or more; and, *en passant,* I should be pleased to engage for a couple of lectures in the hope of some moderate compensation. Can the thing be contrived? Please advise me if possible, before I leave this place.[2] I have not heard from you, in reply to a couple of letters previously, in which my publisher authorized me to offer you $1.50 per page for contributions.[3]

Yours very truly &c

W. Gilmore Simms

705a : To Edward Dromgoole[1]

Woodlands, Midway P. O. S. C.
March 17. 1854

Edw. Dromgoole, Esq.
dear Sir.

I have had the Southern Quarterly Reviews, the numbers for January & April, forwarded to you at Summit P.O. as you desired.

10. On the evenings of Feb. 13 and 15 he lectured on "The Moral Character of Hamlet." See note 27, Feb. 10, 1854 (698).

[2]Simms did not lecture at Baltimore on this tour. For his itinerary, see note 4, Jan. 13, 1854 (692a).

[3]See letter to Mayer of Dec. 17, 1853 (687a).

705a

[1]This letter is addressed to "Edwd. Dromgoole Esq./(Atty at Law)/Summit P. O./Northampton County/North Carolina." We are unable to locate an Edward Dromgoole residing in Summit at this date; there was, however, an Edward Dromgoole who was a prominent planter at Lawrenceville, Brunswick County, Va., only a short distance from Summit. Paul I. Chestnut of the Manuscript Department, Duke University Library, writes us that this Dromgoole (d. 1895) was graduated from the University of North Carolina in 1845 and that a number of his papers are included in the George C. Dromgoole and Richard B. Robinson Papers now at Duke. The *National Union Catalogue* lists an *Address of E. Dromgoole of Brunswick on Fertilizers, Delivered before the Farmers' Convention, in Petersburg, August 13th, 1872 . . .* (Petersburg: J. B. Ege, 1872). Simms lectured at Petersburg, Va., on Mar. 6 and 7 (see below), and since the Petersburg *Daily South-Side Democrat* of Mar. 7 lists among the arrivals at Jarratt's Hotel on Mar. 6 "E. Dromgoole, Brunswick," there can be little doubt that he met him there—perhaps Dromgoole had gone to Petersburg especially to hear Simms. Dromgoole must have been in Summit on business at the time Simms wrote his letter.

I enclose you the Publishers Reciept for five dollars the subscription for the present year. With the hope that you have reached your home safely, as I mine, and the expressio[n][2] of much pleasure at having made your acquaintance, I am, dear Sir,

Yr obt & obliged Servt.

W. Gilmore Simms.

When we edited Vol. III of Simms' *Letters*, we did not have access to a file of a Petersburg newspaper for 1854 and were, therefore, unable to ascertain the dates and subjects of Simms' lectures there. The Petersburg *Daily South-Side Democrat* of Mar. 6 announces that Simms is to lecture at the Library of the Petersburg Library Association that night and the following night, remarks "that his lectures at the Richmond Athenæum last week, were the finest things ever heard there," and cautions its readers "to go early or a seat will be an impossibility." The same newspaper of Mar. 7 reports: "We had a grand lecture last night. Mr. Simms addressed us on 'Poetry and the Practical,' telling the muck-rakes and Mammon worshippers, that all beautiful things are useful; that there is a standard higher than the stock market and the rates of exchange; that there are temples of pure thought from whose grand arches, and dreamy aisles the money changers should be lashed with scorpion whips as unworthy an entrance. It was a noble sight—a man and and [*sic*] a poet, with a fine commanding person, a thoughtful eye and dominant brow shaking off the trammels of conventionalism, swearing that Baal was no God of his, and that if the Deity was the perfected embodiment of Bank notes, he would be an infidel, *and his audience appreciated it.* A breathless, eager attention pervaded the assemblage; even the cry of fire which burst forth in the middle of the performance fell unheeded on ears which were enchained on lips pleading the cause of the TO KALON." The *Democrat* of Mar. 9 remarks: "Mr. Simms concluded Tuesday night [Mar. 7] his lectures on 'Poetry and the Practical,' and we echo the sentiment of every one of his auditors who were capable of appreciating him when we say that, for originality of thought, felicity of expression, boldness of statement and truthfulness of conception, such a lecture has never been delivered in Petersburg *on any subject.*"

Simms was as impressed by his auditors as they were by him. In the *Southern Quarterly Review*, X (July 1854), 271, he remarks of the Petersburg Library Association: "We can speak of the Library from personal observation, and bear grateful testimony to the courtesy, intelligence, enterprise and honourable ambition of the officers and members of the Institution. A large, growing and well selected library, constantly in use by eager citizens desiring knowledge and curious to study;—crowded lecture rooms, silently watchful of all that falls from the lips of the speaker;—the old and young, male and female, all zealously uniting in the common cause;—all seeking to combine the elegant and the useful in knowledge;—the truthful and the beautiful;—these are the proofs which the people of Petersburg daily give of the utility of their Library Association, and of the wise use which they are making of it."

[2]The MS. is torn.

707a : To Robert S. Chilton[1]

Woodlands, S. C. Midway P. O.
April 3. 1854.

R. S. Chilton, Esq.
dear Sir:

Absence from home has kept me from sight of your letter till the present moment. I have just written to remind Mr. Thompson[2] of his promise, in your behalf, touching the M.S. of Poe; and I trust you will not be disappointed. Mr. T. has the M.S. and has, I am sure, every disposition to comply with your wishes.[3] Until the 15th. May my address will be at this post town (Midway P. O. So. Caro.) After that period, Charleston. I mention this, as the misdirection leads to circuitous routes, and some delays, which, in certain cases might be of mischievous effect.

Very truly Yours &c

W. Gilmore Simms

709a : To N. B. Morse, Jr.[1]

Woodlands, So. Carolina
April 28. 1854.

N. B. Morse, Jr.
Sir.

Your request so modestly urged is cheerfully complied with. I feel it always a pleasure, as a privilege, to promote the wishes of my

---

707a

[1]Chilton, a native of New Jersey, was in the diplomatic service and in 1898 was United States consul at Goderich, Ontario.

[2]John Reuben Thompson.

[3]Chilton was an avid collector of autographs and manuscripts. When his collection was exhibited at the Rowfant Club, Cleveland, Ohio, in 1898, it did not contain a manuscript of Poe. It did contain a manuscript of Simms' "The Lost Pleiad." See *Catalogue of Autographs and Manuscripts Shown by the November Section of the Rowfant Club at the Club House, Prospect Street, Cleveland . . . Saturday Evening, November 26, 1898.*

709a

[1]The cover of this letter gives Morse's address as Brooklyn, N.Y. Anne M. Gordon, Librarian of the Long Island Historical Society, writes us that in Lain's

young friends when they exhibit a desire beyond ordinary aims, and narrowly selfish considerations. My autograph is one that will do no great honor to your collection, but it is that of one whose sympathies always go with the young, as they constitute the proper guardians of the future. With regard,

Your obt servt &c.

W. Gilmore Simms

719a : To E. M. Wood[1]

Charleston S. C. June 26. 1854.

E. M. Wood, Esq.
dear Sir:

It gives me pleasure to comply with your request. Such an application is in proof that an author's labours are not entirely in vain. It encourages him with the idea that his toils have been successful, and offers him proof of the possible award of posterity. I am, accordingly,

Very truly yours &c

W. Gilmore Simms.

Brooklyn Directory for 1854 N. B. Morse, Jr., is listed as an attorney and counsellor-at-law with an office at 9 Court Street and a residence at 71 West Warren Street. We have been unable to discover any further information about him.

719a

[1]The cover of this letter has not survived, and it is, therefore, impossible to determine where Wood lived. Possibly he was Ezra Morgan Wood (1838–1912), who later was a clergyman-poet of Pittsburgh, Pa.

735a : To Howard Putnam Ross[1]

Summerville, So Caro.[2]
Oct. 13. 1854

Sir:

Your letter of 22d Aug. asking for my autograph, has only reached me within the last two days, in consequence of my absence from the state for the last two months.[3] I cheerfully send you my sign manual; but, as for a sentiment, I am in pretty much the condition of the needy knifegrinder, and must answer in his language, with "Story, God bless you, I have none to tell, Sir."[4]

With respects,
Yr obt servt &c.

W. Gilmore Simms

Howard Putnam Ross, Esq.

738a : To Henry Carey Baird

Woodlands Nov. 20 [1854][1]

My dear Harry

I have only within a few days recieved your letter of 23d. ulto. Heaven knows where it has been all this while. Its contents some-

735a

[1]The cover of this letter gives Ross's address as Albany, N.Y. Kenneth H. MacFarland, Librarian Emeritus of the Albany Institute of History and Art, writes us that Ross was the son of William H. and Harriet Putnam Ross. William was in the lumber business by himself and with various partners from 1833 until 1870, when he retired. Howard was in the lumber business as H. P. Ross and Co. from 1858 until 1861, when he became a partner with his father and brother (Edward A.) in the firm of William H. Ross and Sons. He retired in 1875. We have been unable to discover the dates of his birth and death.

[2]Simms had gone to Summerville because of the epidemic of yellow fever in Charleston. See note 1, Nov. 27, 1854 (740a).

[3]Simms had been in New York City. See note 1, Nov. 27, 1854 (740a).

[4]George Canning, "The Friend of Humanity and the Knife-Grinder," line 21.

738a

[1]Dated by Simms' references to the death of Henry Hope Reed (see note 4, below) and to his plan to withdraw from the editorship of the *Southern Quarterly Review*.

what relieved me of the fear that had begun to trouble me, that in your excess of good fortune, becoming a *millionaire* you were disposed to turn a cold shoulder upon all your poor relations,—the authors. I made one or two efforts to find you in New York,—hearing at intervals that glimpses had been caught of you, or the skirts of your coat, as you wheeled from one bookseller's shop into another. But the chase was fruitless. I even sent a couple of missives to you addressed to Phila.—but they obtained no answer. With a sigh I began to feel & fear that you and your sweet little wife[2] had both given me up, as an old fogy, and no longer fashionable, and you can't concieve how desponding the apprehension made me, until, like a pleasant peep of light—a streak of sunshine through the dim sky panes in October—your billet unfolded a promise of better prospects hereafter.—Why didn't you advise me of your proposed excursion to Lake George & Saratoga? I might have found time, and would surely have found gratification in a ramble with you to the Lakes. You could have painted, while I poetized the landscapes. But no! All I could learn certainly of you was that Philadelphia did not contain you, and this was partly the reason why I did not visit that good city this summer—every body being out of town. I would have made an effort, spite of the hard work which pressed upon me, to have run over to the city of Bro. Love for a week, had I been sure of meeting you; but the failure of my letters to produce an answer made me abandon all such idea, particularly as I knew not whether my young friends, the Hammonds, had not taken flight also.[3] I am glad that Harry makes himself agreeable. He is a smart and ingenious young gentleman, with whose parents I am closely intimate, and I have long esteemed him as a youth of great personal worth, and of a mind which only needs cultivation & attrition to produce excellent fruits. I sympathize with you very sincerely for the loss you have sustained—yourself and city—in the amiable & interesting Professor, Henry Reed. The impression which he made upon me was an exceedingly grateful

[2]The former Elizabeth Davis Penington.

[3]James Henry Hammond's sons Harry and Spann were at this time medical students at the University of Pennsylvania. See note 7, Jan. 30, 1851 (564), and note 181, Dec. 30, 1856 (837).

one, and it was my pleasant anticipation that he would always prove one of my social resources when visiting Phila. What a terrible fate, that of the Arctic, and how very easily it seems to me, it might have been averted, and all saved, but for the cowardly selfishness & miserable insubordination on board[4]—You are quite right in holding back from publication. Be prudent. The worse is not yet. The drought of last summer has been a loss to the country, in provision crops alone, of fifty million; and any dimunition of the bread stuff of a country, always makes itself felt first upon the intellectual luxuries, as the most easily dispensed with by the masses. If one could turn in to selling beer & brandy, instead of books, during a time of pressure, it would be always a profitable diversion of capital. I have not yet recieved the Books you mention, but shall be glad to do so. They will probably turn up shortly. I remember Mr. Wood distinctly, & shall be curious to see his history of the American stage, a subject in which I have always taken interest.[5] Hereafter, please direct your books to me *personally*, care of Russell, Courtenay[6] or Hart, as it is quite probable that with the present year I shall withdraw from the Editorship of the Review and use my pen through another literary vehicle. I can't get on comfortably

---

[4]Henry Hope Reed (1808–1854), a native of Philadelphia, was from 1835 until his death professor of rhetoric and English literature at the University of Pennsylvania. He prepared editions of Wordsworth, Gray, and other English poets. Reed was drowned on Sept. 27 when the *Arctic*, a steamer on which he was sailing home from England, struck a French vessel in a fog and sank.

[5]William Burke Wood (1779–1861), actor and manager at various times of several Philadelphia theaters, was the author of *Personal Recollections of the Stage* (Philadelphia: Henry Carey Baird, 1855). In noticing the book in the Charleston *Evening News* of Dec. 14, 1854 (see note 1, Jan. 8, 1855 [752a]), Simms writes of Wood: "We had the pleasure of meeting him only a year ago, with our legs under the mahogany of a friend; and we found him a kindly, courteous gentleman, and an agreeable reminiscent."

[6]Samuel Gilman Courtenay, Charleston bookseller. See note 199, Nov. 10, 1852 (649).

with the present publisher.[7] Present me with affectionate respect to your wife—& to the family of Mr. Pennington,[8] & hold me

Ever truly Yours &c

W. Gilmore Simms

740a : To Brantz Mayer

Woodlands, Nov. 27. 1854.

My dear Mr. Mayer

Your two very grateful letters have only recently reached me, in consequence of a three months vagabondism which has found me every where but at home.[1] As yet I have not the leisure to do them or you or your book justice. The latter I have not yet been able to read, though it reached my address sometime ago. I did not therefore pen the notice to which you refer, though I fancy it proceeded from a young friend of mine.[2] I am still in all the confusion of putting my library & studio in order, for the proper beginning of a severe winter campaign. When I have read Canot, I shall endeavour to do justice to its & your merits through some one of our local literary mediums.[3] It may be that I shall prepare a notice of it in the Review,

---

[7]Charles Mortimer. See note 125, Nov. 30, 1853 (683).

[8]The father of Mrs. Baird, John Penington (1799–1867) was a scholar, biographer, and bookseller. By his wife, Lucetta Davis, he had, in addition to his daughter Elizabeth, another daughter, Mary Lawrence, who married Commodore John Roberts Goldsborough, and a son, Edward. See Frank Willing Leach, "Old Philadelphia Families," *North American* (Philadelphia), Apr. 26, 1908.

740a

[1]Simms left Charleston for New York City around July 30, returned to Charleston in early Oct., and had to go immediately to Summerville because of the yellow fever epidemic. He was back in Charleston in early Nov. and at Woodlands on Nov. 15. See his letters for this period.

[2]We have examined the Charleston newspapers for this period but have been unable to find a review of Mayer's *Captain Canot; or, Twenty Years of an African Slaver; Being an Account of His Career and Adventures on the Coast, in the Interior, on Shipboard, and in the West Indies* (New York: D. Appleton and Company, 1854). The work is referred to in an anonymous article entitled "The Slave Trade" in the Charleston *Mercury* of Oct. 27, 1854. Possibly this is the "notice" to which Mayer had referred. Which of his young friends Simms thought might have written it we do not know.

[3]In his letter signed "Lorris" in the Charleston *Mercury* of Feb. 13, 1855, Simms

though it is highly probable that I shall withdraw from all connection with that work, by the close of the present year. The publisher & myself do not agree sufficiently well to permit me to continue with him, and I shall only do so in the event of his making concessions to which he objects. In brief, he fancies that he has rights, as Publisher, which do not consist with mine as Editor. But I shall write you hereafter. Meanwhile, believe me,

Ever truly Yours, &c.

W. Gilmore Simms

Hon. Brantz Mayer

746a : To Charles Étienne Arthur Gayarré

Midway P. O.
Decr. 18. 1854.

Hon. Ch. Gayarré
My dear Sir:

Having withdrawn from the Southern Review, I am squaring off with publishers and authors, & in a series of letters to two of our

---

reviewed *Captain Canot*: "I take for granted that you have read the very curious and interesting narrative of the *Life of Canot, the Slaver*, from the pen of my excellent friend, Mr. Brantz Mayer,—a gentleman who formerly served as Secretary of Legation in Mexico, when Powhatan Ellis was Minister; and who possessed ten times the capacity of the latter, for occupying the higher and more responsible station. . . . Mr. Mayer made one good use of his Secretaryship, and gave us one of the best Histories of Mexico, ancient and modern, which we can now refer to. . . . He has since done good work for the Maryland Historical Society, in the elucidation of some of our obscurer chronicles. The present work, *The Life of Canot the Slaver*, is, he assures me, a bona fide narrative, drawn from the very life of the hero, who, in his old age, has made a full confession of the sins of his youth. It reads very much like a romance,—is full of startling adventure and strange events and characters; and embodies, besides, much valuable matter, which will be found useful to him who would philosophize upon the history of the slave-trade, and the characterisitics and capacities of the negro race. It contains a large body of evidence in regard to these topics, which deserve heedful consideration. The whole story is full of life, and written, as is usual with Mr. Mayer, in clear, good, manly style, without blur or affectation."

newspapers,[1] I am dismissing such books as have lately reached me. In this performance, you have afforded me the topic for a letter to the Charleston Mercury, a copy of which I enclose.[2] Be pleased to believe that I recal, with great satisfaction, our meeting in New York, & shall always be glad to hear from you, and see you.

Very truly Yours

W. Gilmore Simms

752a : To Henry Carey Baird

[January 8, 1855]

Dear Harry

Accompanying I send you a notice of your publishing self, which, as I have withdrawn from the editorial *fauteuil* of the Review, I have embodied in letter form for one of our newspapers.[1] Hereafter my reports of current literature will take this shape in the newspapers, and except in this way I shall have as little to do with the periodical press as possible. I wrote you some time last month. I

746a

[1]The Charleston *Mercury* and *Evening News.* See letter to Duyckinck of Dec. 20, 1854 (747).

[2]For Simms' "Charles Gayarre's Writings" in the *Mercury* of Dec. 13, see note 292, Dec. 20, 1854 (747), and note 1, June 16, 1857 (848a).

752a

[1]In a letter dated "New York, Dec. 6, 1854," and signed "Querícus," published in the Charleston *Evening News* of Dec. 14, Simms writes of Baird's recent editions of Cowper's *Poetical Works*, Beckford's *Vathek*, Walpole's *Castle of Otranto*, and William Burke Wood's *Personal Recollections of the Stage.* Of Baird himself Simms remarks: "Henry Carey Baird is one of the most promising of our young publishers. He succeeds to the business of his uncle, Edward Carey, who was considered one of the most accomplished, amiable, and interesting of his class. He was a man of fine tastes and agreeable manners; a liberal dealer with authors, and a judicious patron of artists. His death was a loss to the artists and literary men of this country. His nephew, Baird, is naturally emulous of his tastes and reputation. He is amiable and courteous in business, has had the advantages of foreign travel, and is a great admirer of pictures. His publications are usually well selected, and he sends them forth in proper habits."

have now only to add my best wishes for yourself & little family during the year which we have just begun.

Yours truly

W. Gilmore Simms

Woodlands,
Midway P. O.
8 Jan 1855

H. C. B.

764a : To Richard H. See[1]

Woodlands, Midway P. O.
South Carolina, March 25. [1855][2]

Dear Sir.

The blunder of your printer is of a sort which I find constantly occurring among that worthy set of people, who can rarely be persuaded that they cannot teach editors, authors, and all classes of people, the whole art & mystery of all their several professions. The word in question is a beautifully appropriate one which seems happily to illustrate that dreamy and regular movement of the stars, by which it was suggested.[3]—Enclosed you will find an order for the story in the hands of my friend Mr. Duyckinck of New York. It will be easier for you to procure it from that city, than for him to fall upon an agent for its conveyance.[4] In respect to future stories

764a

[1]In 1854 Richard H. See and Co. succeeded George Rex Graham as publisher of *Graham's American Monthly Magazine of Literature and Art.* Sometime during 1855 the firm's name was changed to Abraham H. See.

[2]Dated by Simms' remarks about "the blunder of your printer" and the "enclosed . . . order for the story in the hands of . . . Duyckinck." See notes 3 and 4, below.

[3]In printing "The Triumph of the Moon. A Night Picture" in *Graham's*, XLVI (Apr. 1855), 349–350, the printer emended Simms' "twiring" to "twirling" in "As the twiring beauties/Sped . . ." (11. 21–22). The correct reading appears in the text of the poem when it was printed as "Queen Hecate's Triumph" in *Simms' Poems Areytos or Songs and Ballads of the South with Other Poems* (Charleston, S.C.: Russell & Jones, 1860), pp. 154–157. "Twiring" (now an obsolete word) means "peeping" or "winking."

[4]The "enclosed . . . order," dated Mar. 25, 1855, was sent to Evert Augustus

for your mag. I will give you an answer hereafter. I am just now too busy to frame a letter.

Yours in haste, but
Very respectfully &c

W. Gilmore Simms

781a : To William May Wightman[1]

College Hill.[2]
Friday morning [August 20, 1855][3]

My dear Dr.

When I told you that I had no engagement for Saturday night, I had unaccountably forgotten a pledge that I had made to pay a visit on Saturday to Mrs. Zimmerman at Glenn's Springs—Mr. Z. and Col. Keitt being the bearers of her invitation, & my promise

---

Duyckinck (see introductory sketch) and is printed as letter 764. At the bottom of the sheet is a note dated "Philada. March 28th/55" and signed "Abm. H. See Pub: Graham's Magazine": "By forwarding to us the above named article ["The Pirate's Hoard"], you would much oblige. . . ." Underneath See's note Duyckinck wrote, "Sent Mar 30, 1855 via Redfield." "The Pirate's Hoard," designed for *Putnam's Monthly Magazine* or *Harper's New Monthly Magazine*, was sent to Duyckinck in Dec. 1854, but both *Putnam's* and *Harper's* rejected it (see letters to Duyckinck of Dec. 6 and Dec. 20, 1854, and Feb. 2, 1855 [744, 747, and 755]). Under the title "The Pirates Hoard. A 'Long Shore Legend" it was published in *Graham's*, XLVIII (Jan., Feb., Mar., and Apr. 1856), 54–59, 124–131, 224–229, 344–351.

781a

[1]Wightman (1808–1882), a native of Charleston, S.C., was graduated from the College of Charleston in 1827 and was licensed as a Methodist minister the same year. In 1834 he became financial agent for Randolph-Macon College in Ashland, Va., and served in that office for five years. He then returned to the ministry in South Carolina. In 1854 he became president of Wofford College and in 1859 chancellor of Southern University at Greensboro, Ala. He was elected a bishop of the Methodist Episcopal Church, South, in 1866 and made his home in Charleston until his death.

[2]College Hill was the name given the campus of the Spartanburg Female College, a fifteen-acre tract of land on the summit of a hill overlooking the town of Spartanburg. The Spartanburg Female College was opened by the South Carolina Methodist Conference in Aug. 1855. It was closed in 1873. We want to thank Herbert Hucks, Jr., Archivist of Wofford College, for this information.

[3]Dated by Simms' visit to Spartanburg in Aug. and Sept., where on Aug. 22 he delivered an address on the inauguration of the Spartanburg Female College, published in a pamphlet entitled *Inauguration of the Spartanburg Female College, on the 22d August, 1855, with the Address, on That Occasion, by W. Gilmore Simms,*

being made to them to go with them on Saturday.[4] Under these circumstances of pre-engagement, may I hope that you will excuse me on the day referred to? But as I am really anxious to be with you & enjoy the pleasure of your society, let me say that I shall be here all next week, when I hope that you will be able to command the leisure and make an opportunity, when I can give you an evening. I beg that you will do so, and seasonably designate the day when I shall enjoy this opportunity. Meeting so many old acquaintance, men with whom I have served in the Legislature & elswhere, I am naturally a good deal employed, & could wish that you would fix me by a specific pledge for some evening in advance of other claimants for my time. I am, dear Dr. your

obliged friend & Servt.

W. Gilmore Simms

Rev. Dr. Wightman.

793a : To Abraham H. See

Woodlands, Midway P. O.
South Carolina. Decr. 3. [1855][1]

My dear Sir:

If you have resolved not to take my story of the Pirate's Hoard, at $50, will you do me the favour, *immediately*, to put it up to my

---

Esq. . . . (Spartanburg: Published by the Trustees, 1855). He was still in Spartanburg on Sept. 4., but on Sept. 7 he was in Yorkville (now York), S.C. (see note 166, July 30, 1855 [780]). Since in this letter to Wightman he remarks "that I shall be here all next week," Aug. 27 (Friday) is undoubtedly the date.

[4]John Conrad Zimmerman (1802–1875), a native of Orangeburg County, S.C., was in 1825 married to Selina Wannamaker (1810–1889), of Orangeburg. In 1830 he purchased a farm on the Fair Forest, a few miles from Glenn's Springs, prospered, and in 1845 became sole proprietor of Glenn's Springs, which in his hands became the most popular and fashionable watering place in South Carolina (see Simms' remarks quoted in note 229, Aug. 21, 1847 [400]). He later was one of the most prominent cotton manufacturers in Spartanburg County. For Lawrence Massillon Keitt, in 1855 a member of Congress, see note 162, July 11, 1850 (544), and note 86, Feb. 22, 1858 (868).

793a

[1]Dated by Simms' remarks about "The Pirate's Hoard." See letter to Baird of Dec. 3, 1855 (794).

address, in a sealed packet, and send it to Henry C. Baird, Esq. of your city. I will send you a poetical trifle, in a week or two, for which I shall be pleased to have your work continued to me next year.[2] I believe that I want one or two of your back numbers to complete my set, & shall write to you on the subject whenever I can do so with certainty. I am now at the plantation drinking in as much of the Indian Summer, as will come to me at my desk. I am busy preparing "Eutaw", the sequel to "The Forayers."[3]

Yours truly &c

W. Gilmore Simms

A. H. See, Esq.

802a : To Joseph Wesley Harper[1]

Woodlands, Jan 27. [1856][2]

Dear Captain.

I will do the article for you, according to the plan & terms proposed by Fletcher,[3] & shall have it ready for you some time in March. The material is abundant, &, with the plates, can be rendered very interesting. The plan may be pursued with every city in the union and may be made a highly interesting feature of your work. I throw out this hint to you. A dozen or 15 prints of public buildings might suffice for each. If I go to Savannah, as I expect to do in a month or so, I can inquire after some body who would do that city. If you write to Hon. A. B. Meek,[4] of Mobile, he can

---

[2]During 1856 Simms published only one poem in *Graham's:* "Ballad" ("Beside the sea, beside the sea"), signed "Adrian Beaufain," XLIX (Oct.), 343.

[3]*The Forayers or the Raid of the Dog-Days* was published by Redfied, New York, in 1855; *Eutaw a Sequel to the Forayers, or the Raid of the Dog-Days a Tale of the Revolution* was published by the same firm in 1856.

802a

[1]Joseph Wesley Harper, of the firm of Harper and Brothers, was known as "the Captain." See note 186, Dec. 15, 1848 (455), and note 1, Sept. 24, 1836 (*41a*).

[2]Dated by Simms' remarks concerning his article for *Harper's New Monthly Magazine*—"Charleston, the Palmetto City." See note 1, Sept. 6, 1856 (816a).

[3]Fletcher Harper. See note 46, Mar. 5, 1866 (1150).

[4]Alexander Beaufort Meek.

do for that place a good article. In N. Orleans, you can find many able persons for the task there, &c.

Your friend as ever

W. Gilmore Simms.

If Fletcher has any hints to give, let him give them promptly.

803a : To James Chesnut, Jr.

Woodlands Midway P. O. So. Caro.
Feb. 12. 1856.

My dear Col.

I wrote to you last year, but got no answer, and prefer ascribing this failure to a failure of the mails, rather than to your neglect.[1] I now write, renewing the subject of my former letter. I am invited to Lecture before the Lyceum at Cheraw & have consented to do so. This will carry me into your precincts, & I am anxious to know, if an arrangement can be made which will enable me to Lecture before your people. My terms are fifty dollars for a single Lecture, but $100 for a course of *four.* The usual plan pursued hitherto has been this: the gentry of a town & its precincts, form a committee, invite the Lecturer, raise subscriptions, assume the responsibility & throw the doors open to the community *pro bono publico.* This is the popular, perhaps, the only mode in a country like ours. Now, can this thing be done with Camden. Can you set in motion a circle of intelligent gentlemen who will be at the pains to collect the subscriptions & make the arrangements. I will agree, as it is in some degree *en route,* to give two Lectures for $50, or 5 for $100 at Camden, sometime in March. Of course, I need not to you, dwell upon the necessities of popular education among us, or expatiate upon the utility, of a public Lecturer to a people such as ours. This is the popular mode of education at the North. This,

803a

[1]We have not located Simms' letter.

with periodical literature, is the only agency for interesting a sparsely settled people on general topics.[2] Please write me, & let me know what you think & what you can do, & oblige

Yours Ever truly

W. Gilmore Simms.

811a : To William Carey Richards

Charleston. June 25. 1856.

My dear Sir:

It requires at this moment no small amount of courage & fortitude simply to pen a letter. We are in the enjoyment of the most melting moods of June. The thermometer for the last few days has ranged between 90 & a 100 in otherwise cool places. We stew, fry, roast, broil, bake, burn,—rather than live, eat, sleep, drink, breathe or dream. There is no thinking to be done, and, for the last 10 days, I have scarcely touched pen & paper; and when I fail in this proclivity you may reasonably calculate on the strangest atmosphere changes. Give me credit, accordingly, for the effort to write you now. That I shall be enabled to get through with the performance, is another and a still doubtful matter. But I am anxious to satisfy you, by a sufficiently prompt answer to your last letter, that if you have not recieved those which I assert myself to have written, then the devil or the Post master is in it! Of those of which you speak, I have recieved nothing. Of the birth of your daughter in February I now learn for the first time. I congratulate you on the advent of Mabel, and sincerely trust that she will prove a May belle until the happy period, when some good fellow will be properly authorized to call her *Ma Belle.* Please present to Mrs. R. my congratulations on the auspicious progress of the new comer. Her "Aspiration" by the way, does not yet reach me.[1] But I learn from the newspapers

[2]Simms lectured at Cheraw, Sumter, and Camden, S.C., in late Feb. and early Mar. See letter to Chesnut of Mar. 7, 1856 (804).

811a

[1]Richards married Cornelia Holroyd Bradley, daughter of George and Sarah

with great pleasure that it has gone through its 2nd Edition. I am myself doing nothing—& can do nothing. I have been sick, am bilious & dyspeptic still—need respite, & am overwhelmed with toils. The increasing feebleness of Mr. Roach[2] devolves upon me a large share of the plantation business, and adds to my anxieties as well as toils. What I may be able to achieve during the summer is problematical. If I can succeed in the preparation of 2 or 3 popular lectures it is as much probably as I shall attempt. Will you, by the way, suggest to me some topics, such as you may suppose would be tolerable to Northern ears? Indicate, please, the sort of topics which they most relish—moral, political, social, historical or what?[3]—I rejoice to learn that your church prospers under your hands. I trust that they pay the Preacher decently. I shall be pleased to hear, especially, that this is the case.[4]—Touching Addison, I have to acknowledge a present from him recently (and a letter)—a pretty little bit of landscape which I have assigned to a high place in my city wigwam.[5] I shall write him shortly. Make my best regards to Mrs. B. and the fair Alice—when you see her. I am glad to hear that both keep their health, youth & beauty, and still find & furnish food in books.[6] I have not seen 'Bessie'.[7] Somehow, nowadays, I

Brown Bradley, of Hudson, N.Y. Under the pseudonym of "Mrs. Manners" she had contributed to her husband's *Orion* (1842–1844) and *Schoolfellow* (1849–1857?). Under the same pseudonym she published *Aspiration: An Autobiography of Girlhood* (New York: Sheldon, Lamport and Blakeman, 1855). She was the author of several other books, including a memoir of her sister, *Cousin Alice: A Memoir of Alice B. Haven* (New York: D. Appleton and Company, 1865). A review of *Aspiration* (probably written by Simms) was published in the Charleston *Mercury* of Sept. 3, 1856.

[2]Nash Roach, Simms' father-in-law.

[3]Simms was planning this lecture tour in Apr. 1856. See letter to Mary Lawson of Apr. 17 (805) and following letters.

[4]Richards was associate pastor of the Brown Street Baptist Church in Providence, R.I. See note 20, Jan. 28, 1859 (908).

[5]We do not know the subject or whereabouts of this painting. Perhaps Simms took it to Woodlands and it was destroyed when stragglers from Sherman's army burned the plantation house.

[6]"Alice" was Mrs. Richards's sister, Emily Bradley Neal Haven (1827–1863). Her father died when she was three years old, and she was adopted by her mother's brother, Rev. J. Newton Brown. As "Alice G. Lee" she contributed to *Neal's Saturday Gazette and Lady's Literary Museum*, a Philadelphia weekly, and met the editor, Joseph Clay Neal (1807–1847), whom she married in 1846. After his death she, in partnership with Charles J. Peterson, carried on the periodical. She was admired in Philadelphia literary circles for both her intelligence and her beauty.

see nothing. I fear that I am growing *passie* & passing insensibly, but rapidly, into the foggy regions of fogiedom!—If I visit the North this autumn, on the lecturing expedition, I shall probably take my daughter with me.[8] In that event she will certainly be most happy to accept your invitation. She & my wife send their best regards to Mrs. R. in which you will please believe me to join very heartily. For yourself, pray hold me as ever, Very truly Yours &c

W. Gilmore Simms.

What of Griswold's affair?[9]

816a : To Joseph Wesley Harper

Charleston Sep. 6 1856.

My dear Captain.

By the steamer of today, or next week, you will recieve a roll and a box, which contains my long promised description of Charleston (M.S.) and 23 illustrations, either engravings or daguerretypes. I have been more than a year getting the daguerretypes out of the hands of the artists. You should otherwise have had the matter long before. There are 23 illustrations, or rather 22, though the letterpress calls for 23. One of these, however, may be had in your city. It is the engraved sketch of a building which is known here as "the Charleston Stewarts"—the fashionable retail shop of our city as

---

She was a contributor to various Philadelphia magazines and as "Cousin Alice" published a number of very popular books for children. In 1853 she married Samuel J. Haven, a broker of New York City. She also published books under the names of "Alice B. Neal" and "Alice B. Haven." She is obviously "our fair friend 'Alice'" (whom we were unable to identify) in Simms' letter to Joseph Lemuel Chester of c. July 9, 1849 (494).

"Mrs. B." is probably a sister-in-law of Mrs. Richards and Mrs. Haven, but we are unable to identify her conclusively.

[7]We have been unable to identify this work.

[8]Augusta.

[9]Charlotte Myers Griswold had brought suit in Philadelphia to have her divorce decree from Rufus Wilmot Griswold set aside. The sensational trial opened on Feb. 24, 1856, and Judge Oswald Thompson dismissed the case because the divorce decree had not been entered on the books of the Prothonotory. See Bayless, *Rufus Wilmot Griswold*, p. 251.

Stewarts is of Gotham. For this you will please apply to the engraver, J. Lansing, 42 Cedar St. N. Y. who will provide you with a copy. Ask for Browning and Leman's engraved building. The roll contains engravings of Calhoun Monument, and sundry churches. The box holds the Daguerretypes & M.S. For the Daguerretypes I have had to pay an average price of $5. Some have cost me $6 and $7. others $3 & 4. I trust that the paper will suit you. Of course you are at liberty to abridge, or to alter any thing which you may deem amiss.[1] But I fancy that the publication will be very acceptable here, and will furnish a motive for a series of similar papers, illustrating Baltimore, the monumental city, Philadelphia, the Quaker City, New Orleans, the Crescent City, Savannah, the city of Oglethorpe or Yamacraw, &c. Let me hear from you, & Believe me very truly as ever, Yours &c

W. Gilmore Simms

816a

[1]Simms' "Charleston, the Palmetto City," *Harper's New Monthly Magazine*, XV (June 1857), [1]–22, was evidently revised before publication. There is no mention of "the fashionable retail shop," Browning and Leman, which, according to *The Charleston City and General Business Directory for 1855* (Charleston: David M. Gazlay, 1855), was located at the corner of King and Market Streets. Nor is there a picture of the building. Probably this alteration was made because in 1857 the firm no longer was in existence: the Charleston *Mercury* during the early part of that year carries advertisements for A. F. Browning of the late firm of Browning and Leman at 243 King Street, opposite Hasell, and of Bancroft, Leman and Co. The article carries engravings of a "Bird's-Eye View of the Palmetto City," of eighteen buildings (seven of them churches), of two monuments (a "Monument in Magnolia Cemetery" and the "Calhoun Monument") and of two plans—twenty-three illustrations in all.

824a : To Sigourney Webster Fay[1]

New York: 4th. Nov. [1856][2]

Sigourney W. Fay, Esq.
Dear Sir.

Mr. Redfield hands me your note, representing the Mercantile Library Association, & I hasten to say that my single lectures are on the following subjects:

"South Carolina in the Revolution"[3]

824a

[1]Fay (1836–1908) was born in Boston and died in New York City. He was involved in the dry goods trade for over forty years and was one of the escorts of the first regiment of black troops to march through New York City after the draft riots of 1863. He was a member of the New York City Chamber of Commerce and was on the Board of Directors of the Hanover National Bank and the Citizen's Savings Bank. He was also a charter member of the Union League Club. See his obituary in the New York *Times* of June 2, 1908. We are indebted to Douglas MacDonald, Manuscript Assistant of Special Collections, Muger Memorial Library, Boston University, for this and other information concerning Fay and Simms' plan to lecture in Boston.

[2]Dated by Simms' plan to lecture before the Mercantile Library Association of Boston. Fay, as secretary of the lecture committee, invited Simms to lecture, and Justus Starr Redfield wrote to Fay on Oct. 23: "Your favor of the 20th addressed to W. Gilmore Simms Esq was received this morning. Mr Simms will be most happy to appear as a Lecturer before a Boston audience. He will be at the north all Nov. Dec & Jan—has quite a number of appointments already and on looking over his programme I find it will suit him best to be with you between Dec 19th and Jan 7—if you can arrange it so it will accommodate his other engagements." (Original in the archives of the Mercantile Library Association, Mugar Memorial Library, Boston University.)

The Mercantile Library Association of Boston was established in 1820 as an agent in the self-culture movement, and by the 1840s it had risen to a high place in the intellectual and social life of Boston. The Mercantile Library Association's lecture series featured such distinguished men as Ralph Waldo Emerson, Horace Greeley, Henry Ward Beecher, Oliver Wendell Holmes, and Herman Melville.

[3]On Sept. 20, 1856 (820), Simms wrote to Marcus Claudius Marcellus Hammond: "I do not know what the papers have said of my Lectures or Lecturing, . . . but I am drudging upon my Northern course, & am nearly exhausted. I have just finished one to be delivered in Boston, on 'South Carolina in the Revolution.'—If they will listen to me!" This lecture (printed in *The Letters of William Gilmore Simms*, III, 521–549) is for the most part an answer to that portion of a speech delivered in the Senate on June 28, 1854, by Charles Sumner of Massachusetts, who, provoked by Senator Andrew Pickens Butler's remark that "the independence of America . . . was won by the arms and treasure . . . of slave-holding communities," attempted to prove by copious quotation from contemporaries as well as historians "the small contributions of men and the military weakness of the Southern States, particularly of South Carolina, as compared with the Northern States." Simms' defense of South Carolina's conduct during the

"Ante Columbian Discovery in America."[4]
"Ante Colonial Settlement in the South."[5]
"Choice of a Profession.[6]

I confess that I should prefer using the first of these in your city, but shall cheerfully leave it to you to choose either. The last named is a favorite with me. My other lectures are in sets or courses of 2 or 3—as for example—

1 & 2. Marion, the Carolina Partisan—[7]
1 & 2. The Apalachians—a South. Idyll—[8]
1 & 2. Moral Character of Hamlet—[9]
1, 2 & 3. Poetry & the Practical.[10]

Very truly Yours &c

W. Gilmore Simms.

Revolution (with its hostile remarks about Senator Sumner and Massachusetts) would have angered a Boston audience at any time, but if it had been delivered as planned, seven months after Preston Smith Brooks had caned Senator Sumner on the floor of the Senate, the reaction would doubtless have been far more violent than that of the audience and the press of New York City when it was delivered there on Nov. 19. After the fiasco of Nov. 19 Simms cancelled his tour (see letter to Bancroft, Bryant, and others of Nov. 21, 1856 [827], note 131, Nov. 24, 1856 [830], and letter to James Henry Hammond of Dec. 8, 1856 [833]). For Sumner's speech of June 28, 1854, see his *Works* (Boston: Lee and Shepard, 1874–1883), III, 368–423.

[4]Simms later lectured on "Ante-Columbian Discovery in America" at Greensboro, N.C., in Mar. 1857 (see note 37, Mar. 16, 1857 [842]). Perhaps it was the same lecture as "Ante-Columbian History of America" delivered at Raleigh, N.C., in Feb. 1857 (see note 36, Mar. 16, 1857 [842]) and at Yorkville (now York), S.C., in Oct. 1857 (see note 74, Oct. 27, 1857 [851]).

[5]Simms had lectured on "Ante-Colonial History of the South" at Augusta, Ga., In Apr. 1856 (see note 33, Apr. 18, 1856 [806]); he lectured on "Ante-Colonial History of America" at Norfolk and Petersburg, Va., in Feb. 1857 and on "Ante-Colonial Discovery in America" at Raleigh and Greensboro, N.C., in Mar. 1857 (see notes 33, 34, 36, and 37, Mar. 16, 1857 [842]). Doubtless all of these are variant titles for the same lecture.

[6]Simms first delivered "The Choice of a Profession" before the Chrestomathic Society of the College of Charleston on Feb. 23, 1855 (see note 44, Feb. 21, 1855 [758]).

[7]See note 117, Nov. 3, 1856 (824).

[8]See note 117, Nov. 3, 1856 (824).

[9]See note 3, Jan. 3, 1854 (690), and note 27, Feb. 10, 1854 (698).

[10]See note 4, Jan. 30, 1851 (564), and note 3, Jan. 3, 1854 (690).

825a : To William Cullen Bryant

New York Nov. 8.
1856

Dear Bryant.

I have been absent from N. Y. for some days in Jersey; and will flit on Monday to Buffalo to be absent for a week.[1] I will apprise you of my return when it takes place. Here, I am, as a matter of course, with our old friend Lawson. Now, if you are not willing to see me there, send me word. I trust that you recieved my letter, written some months ago from Carolina, in which I spoke frankly, not only as becomes an old friend, but with the feeling of one who is not willing to lose an old friend![2] Very hurriedly, but truly as Ever, Yours &c.

W. Gilmore Simms

829a : To Sigourney Webster Fay

New York: Nov. 21 [1856][1]

My dear Sir:

I find myself compelled, from a just sense of what is due to your Society, not less than a consideration of what self respect requires, to forego all my lecturing engagements in the Northern States. My subjects, and birthplace, seem to have been so sufficiently provocative in themselves, as to establish prejudices in advance of my appearance, which are utterly hostile to any idea of successful usefulness. I fear,—and feel—that I should bring no profit to your

825a

[1]Simms was going to Buffalo to lecture on "South Carolina in the Revolution" on Nov. 11. See letter to Lawson of Nov. 12 (826).

[2]During his trip to New York City in 1855 Simms had not called on Bryant, and Bryant and his family were apparently offended. Simms attempted an explanation and a friendly reconciliation in his letter to Bryant of Jan. 1, 1856 (798), but evidently Bryant had not answered his letter. Bryant's newspaper, the New York *Evening Post* of Nov. 21, 1856, however, defended both Simms and his lecture on "South Carolina in the Revolution" (see note 141, Dec. 8, 1856 [833]).

829a

[1]Dated by Simms' cancellation of his lecture tour. See his other letters of this date.

Institution, rather hurt than help it, and I prefer to forego all considerations of my own simply, & to withdraw seasonably, so as to afford you a sufficient opportunity to secure a more acceptable substitute.

I am, dear Sir
regretfully but truly &

W. Gilmore Simms

829b : To [Correspondent Unknown][1]

New York: Nov. 21. [1856][2]

dear Sir:

I regret to say that I am forced to decline abruptly any farther continuation of my Lectures in the North. Thus far, my subjects have given such offence, and so much abuse follows my steps as a South Carolinian, that it is very clear I should only hurt, not help, the Institution that calls me to its desk. It is no small self sacrifice that I make in foregoing a tour from which I had promised myself much. But conscientiousness & self respect, equally require that I should make the sacrifice. I write promptly, accordingly, in order that you may have sufficient time to procure a proper substitute.

I am, Sir, very
respectfully
& regretfully, Your
obt Servt.

W. Gilmore Simms

829b

[1]We do not know all the cities in which Simms planned to lecture. Perhaps this letter or the following (829c) was written to someone in Providence, R.I., Hartford, Conn., or Portland, Me.

[2]Dated by Simms' cancellation of his lecture tour. See his other letters of this date.

829c : To [Correspondent Unknown]

New York: Nov. 21. 1856

Dear Sir:

I regret to be compelled to decline the engagement which I made to lecture before you. The hostility which, thus far has followed my footsteps, as a lecturer on Southern topics, satisfies me that my performances would in no ways prove profitable to your institution. The temper of the public mind seems inauspicious just now to one of my temper. I trust there will be no sense of disappointment, and I write promptly, and as soon as my decision is made, in order that you may be able seasonably to supply yourself with a more acceptable substitute. I am, Sir,

Very respectfully
Your obt Servt.

W. Gilmore Simms

831a : To Octavia Walton Le Vert[1]

New York. Nov. 24. [1856][2]

My dear Mrs. Le Vert.

Your graceful & courteous letter has been this moment recd. I write promptly, rather to make my acknowledgments than to respond in the spirit which you and it equally deserve. I am too much oppressed with labour, at this time, to do more than say how glad I am to hear from you, and how grateful for the sweet temper of your epistle. I am preparing to take my way homeward, disappointed in all my lecturing expectations, driven away, in fact, in consequence of the deep & bitter hostility expressed here, in regard to the very subjects of my Lectures, which are chiefly Southern & South Carolinian. I have accordingly abandoned the field, & return to my own poor little Parish.[3] But I will not trouble you with my

831a

[1]Mrs. Le Vert (1810–1877), the daughter of George Walton II and Sally Minge Walker, was born at "Bellevue," near Augusta, Ga. Educated at home, she was a mistress of Greek, Latin, French, Italian, and Spanish. She was equally interested in politics and society, and during a tour of the United States in 1833–1834 she became known as "the belle of the Union." In 1835 her father moved to Mobile, Ala., and in the following year Octavia married Dr. Henry Strachey Le Vert. Her "Mondays" at her home on Government Street were crowded from eleven in the morning until eleven at night. In 1853 Mrs. Le Vert, accompanied by her father, her daughter Octavia, and her servant Betsey, visited England, where almost instantly she was taken into the best society. A few years later she and her husband visited the Continent, and she became acquainted with Napoleon III, various noblemen and noblewomen, a number of the leading artists and writers of the day, and Pius IX. Her salon in Paris was called the "Tower of Babel." Everywhere she was celebrated for her intelligence and beauty—even her feet were admired. It was said of her that "her remarkable experience was to wear the crown of beauty and genius without a thorn." Dr. Le Vert died one year before the close of the Civil War, and after the war Mrs. Le Vert returned to "Bellevue," where she lived until her death. See Mrs. John K. Ottley, "Octavia Walton Le Vert," in *Library of Southern Literature*, ed. Edwin Anderson Alderman, Joel Chandler Harris, and Charles William Kent (Atlanta: Martin & Hoyt Co., 1907–1910), VII, 3221–3225.

[2]Dated by Simms' remarks about the cancellation of his lecture tour. See his other letters written during this month.

[3]Richard Henry Stoddard (1825–1903), the poet and editor, who was living in New York City at the time of Simms' lecture, evidently blamed Simms' failure on lack of tact, discretion, or judgment. On Dec. 15, 1856, Simms' friend Paul Hamilton Hayne wrote to Stoddard: "There is much truth undoubtedly in what you say of Simms. He has no tact—discretion, or judgment[.] But if you knew the circumstances of his career—what, from boyhood he has had to contend against here [Charleston], your surprise at his Conduct would be vastly modified. There

petty cares. I prefer to speak (and I must do so hurriedly) of yourself & your proposed publication. I learn with great surprise that you propose to publish it in Mobile. This, according to my experience, will seriously prejudice your claims & impair the success of your performance. If you are not too deeply committed to any local publisher, I beg leave most earnestly, to counsel you to get it issued either in New York, Boston or Philadelphia. There, they are professed publishers, with all the mechanism for giving you large circulation. I have submitted the matter to my own publisher, Mr. J. S. Redfield, who authorizes me to say that he will gladly become your Publisher, take all the risk upon himself, and pay you 10 per cent on the reciepts. He is a good man, energetic, attentive, courteous, & honorable, and capable, I think, of doing as much for your work, as any publisher in the country. There! That's all![4] And now, my dear Mrs. Le Vert, hold me profoundly sorry that I have to deliver myself to you, in such a bald disjointed epistle. But though out of joint myself, hold me still to be at your feet, with most grateful regard.

Yours faithfully,

W. Gilmore Simms

831b : To M. C. Belknap[1]

New York: Nov. 26. [1856][2]

M. C. Belknap, Esq.
dear Sir:

The circumstance which I most greatly deplore, in withdrawing from my engagements, is the embarrassment which it must cause

---

is great nobility at the bottom of his nature, but the surface is not pre-possessing. "To me he has always been a kind friend—& I regret his failure deeply." See Daniel Morley McKeithan, *A Collection of Hayne Letters* (Austin: University of Texas Press, 1944), p. 22.

[4]Mrs. Le Vert's *Souvenirs of Travel*, 2 vols., carries the following imprint: New York and Mobile: S. H. Goetzel and Company, 1857. Lamartine had suggested that she "write a few souvenirs of European travel," and this work was the result.

831b

[1]Not identified.

[2]Dated by Simms' cancellation of his lecture tour. See his other letters written in Nov.

to the Societies which have honored me with an invitation. I feel greatly chagrined on this score myself, and but for the exceeding self-sacrifice—bad enough as I feel it now—would gladly serve those who still desire to hear me. But, having abandoned *all* my engagements, assured that my topics would be, just now, unseasonably brought before a Northern audience, to depart in a single instance from the rule laid down for myself would involve me in a world of reproaches from all other quarters, besides materially interferring with those business arrangements which my change of purpose rendered it necessary that I should immediately adopt. I have already made my preparations for returning next Saturday[3] to my own humble home in Carolina. Believe me, my dear Sir, that nobody grieves more feelingly than I do over that necessity which it seems to me proper that I should obey; and I would respectfully entreat of you to convey to your Association, the sincere conviction I feel, that, under existing circumstances, I should rather injure than serve the interests of those who desire my Lectures. At another period, perhaps, it may be your pleasure to hear me, as it would be mine, with a different order of compositions, to appear before you. But now, it takes the shape of a duty, equally to your people & myself, that I should not trespass upon them with argument in defence of mine. Very grateful to you, as I am, for the kind language of your letter, I am dear Sir, most regretfully, but most respectfully,

Your obt. Servt.

W. Gilmore Simms

[3]Nov. 30.

841a : To Octavia Walton Le Vert

Woodlands, Midway P. O.
So. Caro. March 15. [1857][1]

Your letter, my dear Mrs. Le Vert found me along the roadside some ten days ago. It had been covered to me by my wife, with sundry others, had followed me to Washington, & took the back track after me, with such eagerness, that it overhauled me in the heart of North Carolina. Of course you winged it especially after *my* heart, or it never could have 'fetched['] so successful a compass, in pursuit. It found me, however, quite ill, suffering severely from catahrrhal affection contracted along the highways, and from which I continue to suffer. I seize upon the earliest possible moment, after reaching home, to reply to its genial contents.[2]—I am quite glad to learn that your 'Souvenirs' are so rapidly approaching completion. Permit me to say that your friends are quite right in counselling you to a *single* volume. Should you find your materials expand more than you calculate, then make 2 slender volumes, under one title, both issued from the press together, rather than two separate works. I should judge, however, that 900 pages of your M.S. would make a good duodecimo, of popular size, of 580 pages, print.—You are quite right in publishing at the North. There are two essentials for successful publishing, both of which we lack in the South—viz: a large city, & a regular publisher. It is because of these wants, especially, that we have so little Southern literature. I have no doubt that Redfield, my publisher, will be glad to entertain the proposals of your agent, & will deal with him as liberally, and, I am sure, as honestly, as any of the trade. I believe I wrote to you to this effect from N. Y. He authorized me, in fact, to do so.—Let me hope, that, no matter what publisher may enjoy the pleasant duty of introducing you formally to our pretty public, your book will prove

---

841a

[1]Dated by Simms' references to his "Northern *progress*" and to his letter to Mrs. Le Vert of Nov. 24, 1856 (831a).

[2]For Simms' itinerary on this lecture tour, see note 1, Jan. 1, 1857 (838).

as welcome to the masses, as you yourself have always been among the 'select, the favored few'. I beg to say that I shall watch eagerly its advent, and doubt not to enjoy its contents quite as greatly as any of the multitude.[3]—Thanks for your sympathy, touching my Northern *progress,*—where I could make no progress. As a gentleman, they left me hardly any choice. I had simply to button my coat, close my portfolio, and quietly withdraw. So Meek is married![4] I trust happily & prosperously. Pray believe me, dear Mrs. L. V. Ever truly Your obliged frd & Servt.

W. Gilmore Simms

842 (1a) : To George Payne Rainsford James[1]

Woodlands, Midway P. O.
So. Caro. March 31. 1857.

My dear James.

I have been home for three weeks, but so sick, so sore, so suffering, and so oppressed with visitors & business that I have not been able to command my mind, for writing to the friends with whom I should be most anxious to commune. Our house is crowded at this moment, and I have stolen a midnight hour for this scribble, while they resign themselves, in the phrase of the Irish damsel, to the arms of Murphy![2] There are half a score of aunts & cousins—my wife's—now with us. My eldest daughter has just returned from Georgia where she has been visiting for six weeks.[3] My eldest son has his Spring vacation & has just come up from Charleston bringing with him a couple of his school companions.[4] There is a young

---

[3]Mrs. Le Vert chose as her publisher Sigmund H. Goetzel, of Mobile, who also had an office in New York City. See note 2, Jan. 10, 1863 (1078).

[4]In 1856 Meek married Emma Donaldson Slatter (d. 1863).

842(1a)

[1]In 1852 James (see introductory sketch) was appointed British Consul at Norfolk, Va. In 1857 he was living in Richmond, and in Sept. 1858 he left Virginia to become British Consul General at Venice.

[2]We have not identified the source of this joke.

[3]Doubtless Augusta had been visiting the Teffts.

[4]William Gilmore Simms, Jr. was attending the Charleston High School (see note 11, Jan. 5, 1857 [839]).

gallant—a physician here[5]—doing his devoirs to one of my wife's cousins, and with half a dozen children besides, the house is in a perpetual turmoil of clatter & chat & bustle & humming.[6] The plantation too is distracting me.—It is the planting season, and we are just finishing some 250 acres of corn planting; next week we commence some 250 acres more of Cotton planting; and I have been getting new seed; and there are cares besides of peas & potatoes; and there are cares of ditching & laying off; and my new garden where every thing begins to blow & bloom, is a pleasurable care. Tell Florence[7] that my strawberries promise like ladies lips, blushingly red, through their white blossoms; and my snap beans and green peas are beginning to assert themselves; and I have set out a wilderness of celery; and today planted a new bed of potatoes; and tomorrow—but sufficient for the day is the planting thereof. Another season, my dear fellow, I hope to have the plantation in prime condition and prosperous as it never was before; and then you will steal away to us in the Spring, and share with us our hog & hominy, and your wife[8] shall gravely sit and prattle with mine, while you, Florence and myself,—the children—will enjoy ourselves in the woods, and conjure up English elves & fairies under Carolina oaks at Woodlands. I shall get some good old Scotch Whiskey for your special behoof; and we will conjure up other images from the bright gay world of old romance to *keep* our young hearts young. So much for the future in the Eye of Hope. May it be so!—Well, I got home sick. Whether it was leaving Florence, and being chilled thereby; or that I went to bed that night too late, and got up too soon—which I certainly did—and caught cold in consequence of one or other, or both—I know not; but I suffered as I have not done at any one time for 25 years. I barely made out to finish my Lecturing engagements at Raleigh & Greensboro, and came home speechless; hoarse with constant cough, sore of throat, of breast, of body, and unable to go to lecture in Charleston.[9] For

[5]Probably John Dickson Bruns. See introductory sketch.
[6]See letters to Mary Lawson of Mar. 16 and May 4 (842 and 845).
[7]James' daughter, Florence Frances. See note 196, July 2, 1858 (886).
[8]Frances Thomas James. See note 196, July 2, 1858 (886).
[9]Simms lectured at Richmond on Feb. 24. He returned home on Mar. 15 or 16. For his itinerary, see note 1, Jan. 1, 1857 (838).

three weeks I have thus suffered & am still not well. But I am better, & begin to be busy. I have yet some Lectures to deliver, but hope to get through shortly, and then to my desk.[10] I have laid the keel of a new novel which my Publisher wishes to launch in Sept.[11] But, *quien sabe?* Please say to Florence that I shall send her, by mail, in a day or two, a copy of my Poems, in 2 vols.[12] They will go to your address. Oblige me by specially asking for them should they fail to reach you speedily after this. She will find them, I trust, frank, manly, honest, in thought and sentiment, after the best English models of a thousand years. They aim at some thing more than mere commonplaces & jingle. Tell her I regard poetry as *wingéd Thought.* This is my brief definition. She will please look to it as such in these volumes, though I may decieve myself in supposing that I have reached the 'specular mount'[13] at which I aimed. Pray say to Master Courtenay[14] that I thank him for his cigars which I did not open on the roadside, but which I have been enjoying at intervals since I reached home. For yourself, my dear fellow, God forgive you, and keep you heedfully in the hollow of his hands.

Yours Ever truly

Simms

---

[10]Simms lectured at Augusta, Ga., in Apr. See letter to Hammond of May 6 (846).

[11]*The Cassique of Kiawah a Colonial Romance*, planned by Simms as early as 1845, was not finished until Apr. 1859. It was published by Redfield, New York, in May 1859. See letters to Duyckinck of June 25, 1845 (260), and Apr. 22, 1859 (926), and note 137, May 23, 1859 (930).

[12]*Poems Descriptive Dramatic, Legendary and Contemplative.*

[13]*Paradise Regained*, IV, 236.

[14]Courtenay Hunter James, James' son. See note 196, July 10, 1858 (887).

844a : To Charles Étienne Arthur Gayarré

Woodlands, Midway P. O.
South Carolina, April 18. [1857][1]

My dear Mr. Gayarré

I see with equal pleasure & surprise, that you have been printing for private distribution, a pamphlet on General Jackson. I feel mortified that you did not include me in your catalogue of recipients. Pray let me reproach you by begging for one.—I last heard of you as taking a wife.[2] Let me hope that you are in the full realization of all the lost bliss of Eden—that you are prosperous & happy.

Yours ever truly

W. Gilmore Simms

846a : To Charles Étienne Arthur Gayarré

Woodlands, Midway P. O.
So. Caro. May 7. 1857

My dear Mr. Gayarré

Thanks for your prompt compliance with my request. I have read your pamphlet with a great deal of satisfaction, especially as old Hickorie was a great favorite of mine. Did you ever read my Ballad of Old Hickorie & the Battle of N. Orleans?[1] You, perhaps, never saw an impromptu of my father, who served with him in the Creek

---

844a

[1]Dated by Simms' request for a copy of Gayarré's *Sketch of General Jackson: By Himself* (New Orleans: Printed for E. C. Wharton, 1857), a pamphlet of twenty-one pages consisting largely of extracts from Jackson's private letters. See letter to Gayarré of May 7, 1857 (846a).

[2]Gayarré married Annie Sullivan Buchanan (d. 1914), of Jackson, Miss.

846a

[1]"The Ballad of Old Hickorie" is included in *Simms's Poems Areytos or Songs and Ballads of the South with Other Poems* (Charleston, S.C.: Russell & Jones, 1860), pp. 42–47; under the title "New-Orleans" it had earlier been published in *Early Lays*, pp. 73–75. "The Ballad of Old Hickorie" was also published (anonymously) in the Charleston *Evening News* of July 27, 1854, with the editorial comment that "it is from the pen of a distinguished Southern Poet, and is, in our opinion, one of the most graphic and vigorous 'Ballads' we have ever read."

& Seminole War. It was written while Jackson was very sick at the Hermitage, his election for U. S. Senate pending in the Tenn. Legis. and a report, meant to defeat his election, was put in circulation of his sudden death. My father extemporized—

"Jackson is dead," cries noisy Fame,
But Truth replies, "That cannot be,
Jackson & Glory are the same,
Both born to Immortality!"[2]

My father once told me, that J—n was more like Washington, according to what he had heard of W. than any man that had ever lived. It is a great misfortune that we have no such man now,—i.e. if there should be any one who desires to preserve the Confederacy at whatever sacrifice to the South. I take for granted that you are not in politics.[3] You talk too happily for that. You are evidently too well pleased with home to be solicitous of the smile of Demos (roars rather) or of the echoes of the Forum. Well, be wise & keep close to the Domestic Gods. The Lares familiaries will sweeten sleep for you, when all the trump of Fame (Qu? Bugle & Beagle blasts of party) would drive all sleep from your eyelids. The politician nowadays hears a perpetual voice crying, as in the case of Macbeth—"Sleep no more to all the House."—"*Demos* doth murder sleep![""][4] Let your wife look to it & keep you at her apron strings. Meanwhile (and then) you can go more deeply into History, & give us one of Florida, which in your hands, would supply every desideratum. Thanks again.

Yours very truly

W. Gilmore Simms

Hon. C. Gayarré.

---

[2]Simms also quotes his father's impromptu lines in his autobiographical letter to Lawson of Dec. 29, 1839 (79). Jackson was elected to the U.S. Senate in 1823.

[3]After his defeat in 1853 as an independent candidate for the U.S. House of Representatives Gayarré took part in the formation of the Know-Nothing Party in Louisiana, but in June 1855 he was excluded from the general council of the party in Philadelphia because of his Roman Catholicism. He thereupon gave up his political aspirations.

[4]Simms paraphrases Macbeth, II, ii, 34–35: "Sleep no more/Macbeth does murther Sleep. . . ."

846b : To Justus Starr Redfield

Woodlands. May 9. [1857][1]

My dear Publisher.

A sudden emergency compels me to draw upon you for three Hundred dollars. My draft, however, is dated May 15. 1857. and this will afford you sufficient notice of its presentation. I am an invalid—have been so, off & on, for more than two months—catarrhal & dysenteric affections. Have done nothing as yet—doing nothing still—can do nothing till I get relieved of my annoyances of body.[2] I have never suffered so much for 30 years.—I trust things are better with you. Present me with best regards to Mrs. R.[3]

Yours truly

W. Gilmore Simms

848a : To Charles Étienne Arthur Gayarré

Charleston, June 16. 1857.

My dear Sir:

Extreme indisposition of a very acute sort, has for the last six weeks almost incapacitated me for any performances involving a reference to pen & paper. This will account to you for my long silence. I cannot find an extra copy of my Ballad of old Hickorie. Should I do so, it shall be sent you, though it is too long for singing, and would suit better the declaimer from the stage. I thank you for your political comedy. But it was not new to me. I had read it, and

---

846b

[1]Dated by Simms' reference to the date of his draft.

[2]Redfield wanted to publish Simms' *The Cassique of Kiawah* in Sept. of this year. See letter to James of Mar. 31, 1857 (842 [1a]).

[3]The former Elizabeth Eaton Jones.

noticed it in print when originally published.[1] It is a highly spirited satire, which I *know* to be *generally* truthful, & I had supposed it to be from the life in your precincts. Had you used the same materials for a social & satirical *novel,* you would have secured it a thousand times better chance for circulation & favour. But I am too much of an invalid for even a letter, and taking it for granted that I would write more at length, if my case permitted, you will believe me however brief my scribble Yours very faithfully

W. Gilmore Simms

Ch Gayarré, Esq.

848a

[1]In "Charles Gayarre's Writings" (signed "Lorris") in the Charleston *Mercury* of Dec. 13, 1854, Simms had written of Gayarré and his *The School for Politics. A Dramatic Novel* (New York: D. Appleton & Co., 1854): "CHARLES GAYARRE . . . was, not long since, defeated, as you may remember, as a candidate for Congress; and published a bitter pamphlet [*Address . . . to the People of the State, on the Late Frauds Perpetrated at the Election Held on the 7th November, 1853, in the City of New Orleans* (New Orleans: Printed by Shuman & Wharton, 1853)], exposing the processes by which the true public sentiment was baffled in the election, in his case, by a degree of barefaced chicanery and corruption, which, according to his showing, was almost unexampled, even in our licentious times; when, to succeed foully for office, is rather supposed to be a creditable proof of political skill and dexterity, than any exhibition of a want of patriotism and morals.

"Recently, Mr. GAYARRE has made his experience of the tricks of politicians, available in a Comedy, just published by the APPLETONS, and called, 'The School for Politics, a Dramatic Novel.' It is a novel, rightly—a social and political novel—in a dramatic form—that is, in dialogue. The story is very lively; the action rapid; the satire very good. The characters, though drawn from the life, are yet not designed to reflect upon particular persons. The subjects will identify them at their own peril, and with due heed to the adage—'*Qui capit ille facit.*' The author writes good humoredly, without bitterness, and, certainly, without betraying any of the mortification of a defeated candidate. His temper, I should say, was one not to cherish malignity; and that, after a first single gush and overflow of feeling, he would dismiss all sense of wrong from his bosom; and that, too, without needing to be assured, that malice is, at once, a bad tenant and a worse housekeeper"

849b : To Joseph Wesley Harper, Jr.[1]

Charleston, July 26. [1857][2]

My dear Master Joseph.

I will keep your offer under consideration, to be acted on when leisure allows, and I am seized with a specially inventive paroxysm. At this moment, I am dreadfully busy. But, let me tell Uncle Fletcher that love stories, to have any originality, are not easily manufactured, and for such big pages as yours, Ten dollars per page would be little enough. If I do any thing specially fresh & good I should insist upon this sum.[3] For mere commonplaces such as too much fill our magazines, six would be quite enough & too much too.[4] If you published an edition of Macaulay's two last vols. in 8 vo. do send me a copy, to match with the two preceding.[5] Best regards to the Bretheren,[6] and my particular respects to your mother, wife and sisters.

Yours very truly

W. Gilmore Simms

J. W. H. Jr.

849b

[1]At this date Harper (see note 15, Jan., 1856 [802]) was in charge of at least some of the correspondence of the firm of Harper and Brothers.

[2]On the back of this letter is written, probably by Harper, "W. Gilmore Simms./ Jy. 26th. 1857."

[3]Fletcher Harper was the creator of *Harper's Weekly*, which began publication on Jan. 3, 1857. We cannot attribute to Simms anything published in the periodical.

[4]Harper and Brothers published a five-volume edition of Macaulay's *History of England* (1849–1861).

[5]Fletcher Harper and his brothers, James (1795–1869), John (1797–1875), and Joseph Wesley (1801–1870).

849c : To James Thomas Fields

Charleston, July 31. [1857][1]

My dear Fields.

Looking over a pile of Critical Notices furnished to the Charleston Mercury, I detached these for you. You will observe that none of your recent publications are included among them, for the reason which I must regretfully state, that I have not for some time been honoured with your favours. Certainly, I have, in this quarter, done your state some service. I had wished especially,—though Scott is now pretty much beyond criticism & above puffery—that I should be favoured with your beautiful edition; and if you have not wilfully designed otherwise, I hope that you will supply me with such recent issues of your house as do not recieve notice among the papers sent.

Yours truly

W. Gilmore Simms

J. T. F.

851a : To C. Benjamin Richardson[1]

Woodlands, Midway P. O.
So. Caro. Oct. 30. 1857.

C. Benj. Richardson Esq.
Dear Sir.

Do me the favour, henceforth, to forward the His. Mag. & the Reg.[2] to the P. O. at Midway. I have left the city for the plantation,

---

849c

[1]Dated by Simms' request for Ticknor and Fields' edition of Scott. Ticknor and Fields' "Household Edition" of the *Waverley Novels*, 50 vols., was published during 1857–1859, but Simms' letter could not have been written in 1858, since in this letter he remarks that he has not recently received any of the firm's publications and on June 18, 1858 (884), he requests books from Fields which he reviewed in July of that year (see letter to Fields of July 17? [889a]).

851a

[1]In Jan. 1857 Richardson founded in Boston the *Historical Magazine, and Notes and Queries Concerning the Antiquities, History and Biography of America.* See note 311, Dec. 21, 1866 (1215).

[2]The *New England Historical and Genealogical Register and Antiquarian Journal* (Boston), founded in Jan. 1847.

where I shall remain till June of next year. I see that you announce on sale the Hist. Mag. of the Maine Hist. Soc.[3] If you will send me a copy of this work, thro' *Russell & Jones*,[4] I will compensate you in future contributions to your Mag. and either copy the papers myself or pay for the copying.[5] You shall have the proper quid.—Had you not better make Russell & Jones your agents in Charleston? I enclose you two or three slight notices which I wrote for the Ch. Mercury. I have endeavoured, with each issue of your work, to draw attention to it. If you had an agency in Charleston, this might be of service. I have not preserved the other notices, tho' these will suffice to show that your work has not been totally overlooked.

Yours in haste,
But truly—&c

W. Gilmore Simms

852a : To Nathaniel Paine[1]

Woodlands So Caro.
Decr. 5. 1857

Nathl. Paine, Esq.
dear Sir:

I have much pleasure in complying with your complimentary request, and am, Sir,

Your obt servt. &c.

W. Gilmore Simms.

---

[3]Thomas L. Gaffney, Curator of Manuscripts of the Maine Historical Society, writes us that Simms probably had in mind *The Collections of the Maine Historical Society*, V (1857). The first volume of *Collections* appeared in 1831, the last in 1906.

[4]James C. Jones (d. 1861) had gone into partnership with John Russell.

[5]For Simms' contributions, see note 311, Dec. 21, 1866 (1215), and note 55, Feb. 12, 1867 (1226).

852a

[1]Though the cover of this letter has not survived, Paine was probably Nathaniel Paine (1832–1917), banker of Worcester, Mass., who early developed "the collecting instinct" and was an ardent collector of stamps, coins, medals, photographs, and autographs. In 1857 he was promoted from assistant cashier to cashier of the

853a : To David H. Barnes[1]

Woodlands. So. Caro.
Decr. 13. 1857

David H. Barnes, Esq.
dear Sir:

I find pleasure in complying with your wishes, & am accordingly

Your obt servt. &c

W. Gilmore Simms

856a : To William G. White[1]

Woodlands, So. Caro.
Decr. 29. 1857.

Wm. G. White, Esq.
Dear Sir:

I find pleasure in complying with your request, and am, Very respectfully,

Your obt. Servt, &c.

W. Gilmore Simms.

City Bank, and in 1898 he was made president. He was a member of the American Antiquarian Society for sixty-six years, for sixty years a member of its council, and for forty-four years its treasurer. He was the author of a number of important papers, including biographical notices of Benson John Lossing and others and catalogues of various collections in the American Antiquarian Society. See his obituary in *Proceedings of the American Antiquarian Society*, N. S., XXVII (1917), 12–16.

853a
[1]Not identified.

856a
[1]Not identified.

1858–1866

856b : To D. Appleton and Company

Woodlands Midway P. O.
So. Caro Jany. 1, 1858.

Gentlemen.

The best auspices of the New Year upon you!—I enclose you a few additional mems. of which you may make use of what you please.[1] I enclose you a list also, of distinguished persons, locally of high repute, of North Carolina; you will please mark with an asterisk (*) such as you have not, and send the mem. back to me. All these notices will be short, & it will be advisable to include most, if not all of these names. I have brought the list down to the letter H.—I expect to visit Charleston in February, & when there will procure the facts in the lives of Grimke, Hayne, Hamilton &c.[2] Do not fail to get Forsyth of Georgia, one of the most accomplished masters of fence, in partisan politics, that this country has ever known.[3] You will please advise me as to the degree in which what I have sent you satisfies. I endeavour to make them as short as possible; but where there is great local popularity, it is perhaps

---

856b

[1]Simms was helping D. Appleton and Company, New York, secure biographical information for *The New American Cyclopædia: A Popular Dictionary of General Knowledge*, ed. Charles Anderson Dana and George Ripley, 16 vols. (1858–1863).

[2]John Faucheraud Grimké (1752–1819), prominent South Carolina lawyer and judge and the author of several books on law; Col. Isaac Hayne (1745–1781), Revolutionary soldier hanged by the British, or Robert Young Hayne (see note 3, Aug. 16, 1853 [670a]); and James Hamilton (1786–1857), a native of Charleston, who was a member of Congress (1822–1829) and governor of South Carolina (1830–1832) and in 1855 moved to Texas.

[3]John Forsyth (1780–1841), a native of Virginia, moved to Georgia at an early age. A graduate of Princeton, he was admitted to the bar in Georgia in 1802. He was at various times a member of Congress, senator from Georgia, and minister to Spain. In 1834 Jackson appointed him secretary of state, and he held this position for the remainder of Jackson's term and through the administration of Van Buren. As an orator, he is said to have had few equals, and his oratorical contest with John Macpherson Berrien at Milledgeville, Ga., in Nov. 1832 on the subject of nullification (approved of by Forsyth) was famous in its day.

only right, as it certainly is most politic, to make the details sufficiently full to content the public mind. I am governed in this matter by these considerations. If you have not already done so secure the help of John R. Thompson of Richmond, Va. with reference to names of that state. John B. Minor,[4] also, (of the same place,) & Edmund Ruffin,[5] will give you help cheerfully, I think; see also Peter Force of Washington, D. C. Write to I K Tefft, of Savannah, & Hon. E. Starnes[6] of Augusta, for information touching Georgia names. To Meek (Alex. B.) of Mobile, & A J Pickett,[7] of Montgomery, for Alabama names; to Gayarre (Ch.) of New Orleans, and Hon. John Perkins,[8] for names of Louisiana. To Dr. J. G. Ramsey,[9] of Tennessee. But, no doubt you have already arranged your sources of information. As I am compelled, from the variety of my labours, to work desultorily, you will please advise me seasonably of what you require & what you would dispense with. I enclose you some notices of your new publications, published editorially in the Ch. Mercury.

Yours truly

W. Gilmore Simms

One of the vols. of the Debates in Congress, for which I wrote to you as never having reached me & which you said you would for-

[4]John Barbee Minor (1813–1895) was professor of law at the University of Virginia and the author of various books on law.

[5]Ruffin (1794–1865), agriculturist and publisher, was so ardent a secessionist that he went to South Carolina and was given the privilege of firing the first gun on Fort Sumter. He later shot himself because he was unwilling to live under the government of the United States.

[6]Ebenezer Starnes (1810–1870) served Georgia as a member of the legislature, attorney general, judge of the Superior Court and associate justice of the Supreme Court. He was the author of several books, including *The Slaveholder Abroad; or, Billy Buck's Visit, with His Master, to England* . . . (Philadelphia: J. B. Lippincott & Co., 1860), a reply to *Uncle Tom's Cabin.*

[7]For Albert James Pickett, see note 1, Apr. 14, 1847 (*369a*).

[8]John Perkins, Jr. (1819–1885), New Orleans lawyer, was a member of Congress (1853–1855) and later served in the Confederate States Senate (1862–1865). Simms dedicated *Eutaw* to him.

[9]James Gattys McGready Ramsey (1797–1884), physician and historian, was the author of *The Annals of Tennessee* . . . (Philadelphia: Lippincott, Grambo & Co., 1853).

ward as soon as the new ed. was struck off, has not reached me yet,[10] and you will see that I have referred in print to some of your holiday publications which were not sent me, or not recieved.[11]

878a : To Thomas Addison Richards

Woodlands, S. C.
May 8. 1858.

T. Addison Richards, Esq.
My dear Pictor.

I have been confidently looking for a visit from you for some time back; for though my family has been compelled, ever since February last, to take up their abode in the city, yet I have been, as I am at present, keeping Bachelor's Hall here, & should have been most happy to give you, & if you pleased your bride,[1] the cordial welcome of that nondescript person. I advised you in one or two letters to which I recieved no answer,[2] to call at our town house, should you reach Charleston, & ascertain whether I was there or here. The changed circumstances of our present & recent mode of life, so

---

[10]In the Charleston *Mercury* of Nov. 10, 1857, Simms published a notice of Vol. IV of Thomas Hart Benton's *Abridgment of the Debates of Congress . . . From Gales and Seaton's Annals of Congress; from Their Register of Debates; and from the Official Reported Debates, by John C. Rives*, 16 vols. (New York: D. Appleton and Company, 1858–1861).

[11]In the *Mercury* of Dec. 17 Simms published a favorable notice of Sarah S. Cornell's *Cornell's Grammar-School Geography: Forming a Part of a Systematic Series of School Geographies, Embracing an Extended Course and Adapted to Pupils of the Higher Classes in Public and Private Schools* (1858); in the *Mercury* of Dec. 21 he published notices of Edith J. May's *Bertram Noel; a Story for Youth* (1859), Maria Jane McIntosh's *Meta Gray; or, What Makes Home Happy* (1859), and Maria Louisa Charlesworth's *The Ministry of Life* (1858). Under the heading "Holiday Publications" in the *Mercury* of Dec. 27 he noticed *The Stratford Gallery; or, the Shakspeare Sisterhood: Comprising Forty-Five Ideal Portraits, Described by Henrietta L. Palmer* . . . (1859), "an exquisite collection," and Mary Balmanno's *Pen and Pencil* (1858). Simms was on friendly terms with Robert Balmanno and his wife, Mary (see note 116, May 28, 1852 [626]), and was one of the subscribers to her *Pen and Pencil* (see note 48, Feb. 27, 1855 [759]). Seven letters to Robert Balmanno are published in Vol. III of *The Letters of William Gilmore Simms*.

878a

[1]In the fall of 1857 Richards married Mary Anthony, daughter of Lorenzo Dow Anthony, of Providence, R.I. See letter to Mary Lawson of Oct. 27, 1857 (851).

[2]We have not located these letters.

different from our past habits, is due to a peculiar condition of things. You are aware, doubtless, of the death of my wife's father, after two or more years of Paralysis & partial loss of mind.[3] He succumbed to the final Fate at a period of considerable anxiety with us, my wife being absent in the city, for the purpose of accouchment, which was daily expected; and I with her the only member of the family. My daughter Augusta, with all the other children in charge, remained at the plantation with Mr. Roach. I had to keep the secret of his crisis from my wife, & the tidings of his demise, until her accouchement was safely accomplished;[4] and this, to me, torturous necessity was endured for two weeks. You can fancy the pain of keeping such a secret—the difficulty of guarding against its disclosure by thoughtless or ignorant visitors, &c. But all troubles of this order are now over. After Life's fitful fever, the old man sleeps well.[5] He was a most amiable, honorable & courteous gentlemen, and death came to him, no doubt, as a great relief, from a life in which he had survived all his susceptibilities of pleasure, & all capacities for thought. My family will remain in Charleston now, until October; while I shall dart at intervals from town to country through the summer, watching & regulating the plantation, until the same month, when we propose, with God's permission, to remove all once more to Woodlands. I shall be a resident here mostly, until the first of July, and any letter with which you may favour me, may be addressed me here. If next Spring, you are in the mood to visit the South, with your family, you will, I trust, find us at the plantation, where, I need not say, you will always be sure of a hearty welcome. I did not say that my wife had brought me another daughter. You may inform your wife, by way of hinting what is the true duty of a wife who loves her lord,[6] that this contribution makes the 12th. that I owe my lady. Of the 13 that I have had, I have, thank God, 8 living, four pair!

Yours very truly

W. Gilmore Simms

---

[3]Nash Roach died on Feb. 28.
[4]Harriet Myddleton Simms was born on Mar. 14.
[5]See *Macbeth*, III, ii, 23: "After life's fitful fever he sleeps well. . . ."
[6]See John Home, *Douglas*, I, i: "As women wish to be who love their lords."

881a : To Charles H. Gordon[1]

1858[2]
Charleston So. Caro. June 9.

Charles H. Gordon, Esq.
dear Sir:

There is no elaborate life of Sumter. I wrote the sketch of him in the collection published by Carey & Hart, entitled Washington & the Generals of the Revolution. Autographs of Marion, Sumter & Morgan[3] are exceedingly rare. They would readily command $100 each. I have but a single one of Marion, and know of but one other, & that is, or was, in the collection of Mr. Tefft of Georgia.[4] Fac similes of it have been taken, but even these are procured now with great difficulty.

Your obt servt.
&c

W. Gilmore Simms

889a : To James Thomas Fields

[July 17? 1858][1]

My dear Fields.

I enclose you a couple of trifles which I penned for the Editorial department of the Charleston Mercury. I trust that, in what I say

881a

[1]Not identified.

[2]We are unable to determine conclusively whether Simms or Gordon wrote this date.

[3]Francis Marion, Thomas Sumter, and Daniel Morgan, all generals in the American Revolution.

[4]In the *Catalogue of the Entire Collection of Autographs of the Late Mr. I. K. Tefft, of Savannah, Ga.*, p. 91, lot 890 is described as "Marion, Gen. Francis, *the 'Swamp Fox,'* A. L. S., 4to, 1788. Portrait inlaid. *Fine specimen.*"

889a

[1]The month and year are established by Simms' remarks about the sick members of his family at Sullivan's Island (see note 5, below); the day is probably the 17th, though the 19th is possible (see notes 2 and 5 below).

of the *unpublished* volume, I have not transgressed beyond the rights of a recipient.[2]—Is it possible to meet you in N. Y. I expect to visit that goodly city about the first week in August and to be there two weeks.[3] In a few days I run up to Augusta Georgia, for a week.[4] I have just returned from Sullivan's island where I have had some sick members of my family for two weeks.[5] I must visit my plantation before I go North; so that my feet will be busy, if not my fancies, to such a degree for the next month, as the last, as not to suffer me any liaison with any Muse.

Yours truly

W. Gilmore Simms

---

[2]In the *Mercury* of July 17 Simms published a review of John Godfrey Saxe's *Poems* (Boston: Ticknor and Fields, 1858), and under the heading "Unpublished Poetry" he wrote of Fields' *A Few Verses for a Few Friends* (Cambridge: Printed at the Riverside Press, [1858]): "We have before us a new and beautiful volume, just received, which is without title-page. No name designates the book; no initials even describe the author. On the cover is printed, gold on cambric, 'A Few Verses for a Few Friends.' On the fly leaf is written, in a well known hand, 'With the author's sincere regards.' The typography of the book is in the very prettiest style of the old English: quaint lettering, quaint bordering, with head and foot pieces of fantastic yet demure drawing. The paper is a delicate creamy vellum, 'worthy h.e [the] loving look of ladies' eyes,' and the verses, gentle as evening zephyrs, are just of the sort which should properly appeal to ladies' fancies, delicate, pure, graceful, and enlivened by a sweet, unpresuming fancy, that never trespasses beyond the slight ruffling of brown and raven ringlets, of course. We can make no further revelation, and must content ourselves with acknowledging this little proof of friendly preference, in which the modest writer distinguishes between ourselves and the public, and in our favor." On July 19 under the heading "Boudoir Literature" he published in the *Mercury* brief notices of a number of Ticknor and Fields' publications, including works by Longfellow, Leigh Hunt, Anna Brownell Jameson, and Sir John Bowring. Of these he remarks: "The beautiful editions of choice literature, issued in 'green and gold,' from the press of TICKNOR & FIELDS, in Boston, are just the sort of volumes that lie gracefully in the *Boudoir* of a graceful lady, to whom art and literature are as grateful as beauty."

[3]Simms left for New York City on Aug. 7 and returned to Charleston on Aug. 24. See note 258, Aug. 7 (895), and note 263, Aug. 19 (896).

[4]Simms probably left for James Henry Hammond's plantation, "Redcliffe" on July 23; he returned to Charleston on July 30. See letters to Hammond of July 16 (889) and Aug. 1 (891).

[5]Simms' son Govan, born on Sept. 1, 1856, was ill from teething, and Mrs. Simms also was unwell. They returned to Charleston on July 17. See letters to Mary Lawson of July 10 (887) and to Hammond of July 16 (889).

895a : To Nathan Covington Brooks[1]

New York, Aug. 11. 1858

Prest. N. C. Brooks.
Balto.
My dear Professor

Enclosed you will recieve a note to a committee of the Young Ladies of your College from whom I recently recieved a circular, which you will do me the favour to deliver. The Books will be sent to your address, through some one of the Booksellers of your city.— I trust, my dear Sir, that the Institution over which you preside so well, has been growing prosperously in your hands.[2]

Your obliged Servt &c

W. Gilmore Simms

895b : To D. Appleton and Company

[August, 1858][1]

Mess'rs D. Appleton & Co.
Gentlemen.

I enclose you one of my editorial notices in the Charleston Mercury which has reached me since my arrival in this city.—Should Mr. Burton, and yourselves, ever design any additions to his work,

---

895a

[1]Brooks (1809–1898), poet, historian, and editor, was born in Cecil County, Md., and was graduated from St. John's College. He began teaching at the age of sixteen, and was the first principal of the Baltimore High School. He later organized the Baltimore Female College, of which he was the first president. His most important book is *A Complete History of the Mexican War* . . . (Philadelphia: Grigg, Elliot, & Co.; Baltimore: Hutchinson & Seebold, 1849).

[2]The Baltimore Female College was founded in 1849 and closed in June 1890 when the state withdrew its support. We want to thank Richard J. Cox, Curator of Manuscripts, Maryland Historical Society, for sending us this information.

895b

[1]Dated by Simms' remarks about William Evans Burton's *The Cyclopædia of Wit and Humor Containing Choice and Characteristic Selections from the Writings of the Most Eminent Humorists of America, Ireland, Scotland, and England* . . ., 2 vols. (New York: D. Appleton and Company, 1858), reviewed under the title "Wit and Humor" in the Charleston *Mercury* of Aug. 12, 1858.

I should be able to suggest certain materials which are not generally known, and which might add something to the claims of the work in more Southern regions.

Very truly

W. Gilmore Simms.

911a : To Brantz Mayer

Woodlands, (Midway P.O.)
So. Caro. Jany. 31. 1859.

Hon. Brantz Mayer.
dear Sir:

I have suffered your letter to lie unanswered very long, but my life for the last three or four months, has been one of many distractions, and full of suffering and bitter griefs. Death has been in my household making fearful ravages during the last year. Early in the spring, I lost my venerable father-in-law, who had been endeared to me by the gentlest & most affectionate virtues for more than twenty years; and last autumn, the same cruel enemy of our mortal race, tore from me, in one day, two of the most noble little boys, while three other children barely escaped the same peril, having been sick with the pestilence that devastated our poor city last season.[1] Since then the marriage of my eldest daughter,[2] numerous guests all the time, the cares of the plantation, which were all suddenly devolved upon me, have combined to keep me from my desk, & to keep my mind in such a state of distraction that I could sit down to no performance that was not thrust upon me as an

911a

[1]Both Sydney Roach Simms and Beverley Hammond Simms died of yellow fever on Sept. 22. Chevillette Eliza Simms (see introductory sketch of the Simms family circle) became ill with the disease on Oct. 8. We do not know the exact dates on which Mary Lawson Simms and Govan Singleton Simms (see introductory sketch of the Simms family circle) also contracted yellow fever. See letter to James Henry Hammond of Sept. 24 (897) and following letters.

[2]Augusta married Edward Roach (see note 225, July 19, 1858 [890]) on Dec. 29. See note 205, July 10, 1858 (887).

imperative duty at the moment. And now that my house is once more free of guests, it is not free of care & toil and sleepless anxieties that scarcely suffer me to sleep. I cannot yet command my mind. My heart and head commune together only in a brooding vacancy and stupor. I have lost for the time all my wonted elasticity of spirit, and long for nothing so much as rest, even when I am most idle. To write even a letter needs an effort, and my correspondence has been neglected in great degree for months. This must excuse me to you for the seeming neglect of your favor, and in complying with your wishes now, I shall do so but feebly. I shall copy for you a few lines, and, at a future day, may send you something longer & more elaborate. I have no photograph of any value. Several portraits (so called) have been engraved from photographs or daguerrotypes, but my eyes are so sensitive—from coup de soleil when I was a boy—that they are almost shut up when I sit for a picture. Any intensity of gaze, or strain of light, causes the muscles to contract instantly. There is an engraved portrait of me, from a crayon sketch by Bounetheau, engraved by one of the best English artists, which illustrates my published poems in Redfield's Edition.[3] I think it likely that Mr. Redfield has some spare impressions & have written to him on the subject. If you will get some friend in New York, to call for you, in my name, upon Redfield, he will cheerfully let you have one, if he has it. In respect to other writers, I have no doubt, a good many letters in my collection, but that consists of many bushels, and to look them up would involve a degree of labour to which I am at present quite unequal. At some other day of more health, & peace & energy, I should be pleased to see for you & send what might seem worthy. But if you will write to Paul H. Hayne, William J. Grayson, Henry H. Timrod,[4] Prof. J. W. Miles, Mrs. King,[5] Mrs. Glover,[6] Mrs. Gilman,[7]—all of Charleston—under cover to Mr. John Russell, Charleston, you will procure pretty much all that that

---

[3]See note 2, June 10, 1853 (663b).

[4]The "H." in Timrod's name is obviously an error. For Timrod, see introductory sketch.

[5]Susan Petigru King. See note 38, Apr. 18, 1856 (806).

[6]Caroline Howard Gilman Glover. See note 104, June 16, 1854 (719).

[7]Caroline Howard Gilman. See introductory sketch of the Gilmans.

city can show of poets & literary people. A. B. Meek, A. J. Requier,[8] H. H. Caldwell,[9] Madame Le Vert, all of Mobile, you will no doubt find ready to answer such an application as yours. Wm. H. Simmons, of Charleston, also, must not be forgotten. He is the author of "Onea" one of the best *descriptive* poems ever published in the South.[10] If any other names occur to me, I will advise you. Excuse this languid epistle, and believe me,

Very truly Yours &c

W. Gilmore Simms

916a : TO ALEXANDER DALLAS BACHE[1]

Woodlands (Midway P.O.) S. C.
Feb 25. 1859.

[Profes]sor A. D. Bache.
My dear Professor.

I enclose you an editorial note, and [quota]tion, from the columns of the Charleston [Mer]cury, which I prepared for that paper.[2] I take [for g]ranted that you will feel pleasure in the con[vict]ion that you have friends & admirers at home, as [well] as abroad, who are solicitous of your fame, & [prep]ared to do you justice.

Yours Ever truly

W. Gilmore Simms.

---

[8]Augustus Julian Requier. See note 119, June 16, 1854 (719).

[9]Later this year Howard Hayne Caldwell, a native of South Carolina, was the editor of the Columbia *Courant* (see note 6, Jan. 18, 1860 [956]), so Simms may be in error in giving his address as Mobile.

[10]Mayer appears to have been collecting pictures and autograph letters and poems of southern writers.

916a

[1]Bache (see note 16, Jan. 20, 1859 [907]) was in 1859 superintendent of the United States Coast Survey. The left side of the manuscript is torn off.

[2]The *Mercury* of Feb. 23 reports that Bache has been authorized to accept a gold medal tendered to him by Sardinia and quotes the remarks made by Sir Roderick Impey Murchison on May 24, 1858, when he was presented the Victoria Gold Medal at the Anniversary Meeting of the Royal Geographical Society.

916b : To William Fuller[1]

Woodlands. Feb. 26. 1859

My dear Dr.

Do not give yourself any further trouble about the books. I sent you two heavy boxes, via Charleston & wrote to your factor at the time. I trust you have recieved, or will soon recieve them. I still further cherish the hope that you will find them all interesting or instructive, & most of them valuable. I aimed to give you a good variety. Of those that I picked out for you, there are ten or a dozen here, including a nice copy of Gibbon's Decline & Fall, which I could not get into the boxes, and did not wish to make a third box for so small a number. I failed, for the same reason, to put up the remaining volumes of the set of my own writings which I gave you. It is or was my purpose, to wait until I could select you a hundred volumes more, and wish you to count over those I sent & let me know how many you recieve. Before packing, I had selected & counted out more than 500, but before I got through packing, being called off, I lost the run of them, & was too tired to unpack to count. I preferred that you & Washy should have that trouble. When you have counted and will let me know, I propose, unless you should say otherwise, to bring the number up to 600, when I can be justified in making another box. The addition will help to make your library completer, and, as I told you, the money can be paid at your perfect leisure, and I shall leave it entirely to yourself to say when that shall be. I have been to town, unexpectedly. Tell Washy I found Augusta quite comfortably fixed & all well. The

---

916b

[1]Dr. William Fuller, of Pocotaligo, Beaufort District, S.C., married Mrs. Simms' cousin, Anna Washington Govan Steele (see note 56, Apr. 30, 1848 [426]) on Mar. 28, 1857.

In William Fuller's account and receipt book, 1852–1870, now in the South Caroliniana Library, is a document in Simms' handwriting dated July 21, 1863, which states that Fuller is to pay him $503.75 for a note "with interest," $350.00 for "cash lent, with interest from date [July 21, 1863]," and $450.00 "being the price of a collection of books bought in 1858 & 9" "with interest from date." The books, of course, are the ones Simms writes about in this letter.

Cuthberts were at W. R.'s and in a state of Bay tree flourishing.[2] Manly & Fishburne R. both doing the excruciating [?] to Miss Rosa.[3] Wm quite sick & looking very badly. But I suppose she will hear all about the parties from my wife or Augusta.—I am busy here with fencing, ditching, hauling out, scattering, ploughing in, breaking up, laying off—and smoking away care & anxiety. But the season is quite too warm for people & mules, doing the heavy labours which belong to it. Still we must hope, pray & work on. By the way, I must not forget to inform you that Edward Roach[4] is in a situation which will specially enable him to serve planters. He is in a miscellaneous auction establishment, where every thing is sold, and where the sales must be forced. The consequence is that things sell surprisingly cheap. I bought, for example, plantation fish, at 62 cents per barrel, which only two months ago, I paid $3.50 for it retail. Pickled & corned beef, and bacon, of good quality, sometimes sells at 3 & 4 cents a pound. I bought ale, at 1.12. a dozen pints—bottles & all—Scotch ale.—I also bought two boxes, one dozen each, of *Brandy*—labelled Dupuy & Co—*Otard*—at $2.50 per box of 1 doz Qts. very nicely & even handsomely put up. Of course, it is an imitation, but it is a better article than we pay $4 & 5 for on draught, and better than some of the hotels sell at 10 cents a drink. At $2.50 per doz., it is less than 21 cents a bottle. Now, if you will write to Ed. to buy for you certain articles, which you shall mention, in certain quantities, I have no doubt that you can save 90 per ct in feeding your negroes, & get articles for your own family use, of infinite cheapness, quite as good as you buy at retail. He sometimes buys for his own family.—One other subject: tell Washy, I am sorry to say that my wife has definitively settled to spend her summer in Charleston, *this season*. We both regret the necessity, but she considers it one. Believe me, neither of us would willingly go any where else than with you, & Washy,

---

[2]William Roach (see note 59, Feb. 28, 1859 [917]) was the brother of Edward Roach, Augusta Simms' husband (see letter to Tefft of July 19, 1858 [890]). The Cuthberts are the family of William Roach's wife, Fanny Cuthbert, of Beaufort.

[3]B. Manley Roach, brother of Edward and William Roach, and William Fishburne Roach, nephew of Nash Roach (see note 178, May 14, 1867 [1251]). Miss Rosa is probably Rosa Aldrich (see note 48, May 4, 1857 [845]).

[4]Augusta's husband.

if it were possible. I am not allowed to say why it is not possible, & you must tell Washy not to ask the why. [5] If the sickness breaks out in Charleston, I shall prove my regard for you both, by bringing Govan & Hattie[6] to spend the rest of the season with you. Enough for the present. We are all well, i.e. tolerably so. We spent Saturday with Mary Rivers,[7] as I had to go to Bamberg to pay taxes! I am hard pressed with labour, having to make up for lost time this winter. Augusta is to be up in May. I shall go down at that time. You & Washy had better take the route to Charleston, *via* Woodlands, & we can go down together. My horses can meet you at Bell's[8] whenever you notify me. Try & come. The world is too wanting in the society of true friends not to make us desire to profit by every opportunity for reünion. God bless you both.

Very lovingly Yours & W's

W. Gilmore Simms.

920a : To A. J. Smith[1]

Woodlands, (Midway P. O.)
South Carolina. March 15
1859.

A. J. Smith, Esq.
dear Sir:

It gives me pleasure to comply with a wish so modestly & gratefully expressed as yours; and I cheerfully subscribe myself,

Your obt & obliged
Servt. &c.

W. Gilmore Simms.

---

[5]Mrs. Simms was expecting a baby. Sydney Hammond Simms was born on July 21. See note 201, Aug. 11, 1859 (943).

[6]Govan Singleton Simms, born on Sept. 1, 1856, and Harriet Myddleton Simms, born on Mar. 14, 1858.

[7]Mary Govan Steele Rivers (see note 202, Oct. 23, 1846 [331] and note 95, c. May 6, 1849 [484]), wife of Christopher McKinney Rivers (see note 31, Feb. 25, 1860 [965]).

[8]Bell's Crossroads is about halfway between Midway and Walterboro, S.C.

920a

[1]Not identified.

933a : To William James Rivers[1]

Charleston, S. C. June 13. 1859.

My dear Mr. Rivers.

Your kind estimate of my volume, of course gave me the greatest satisfaction; for you are one of the few, whom I know, capable of following me along the route which I pursued.[2] You, perhaps, better than most persons, know the embarrassments of such a study, and have grasped, as well as this may be done, the whole extent of the province. You know its *element;* and had you pursued a department such as mine, you would probably have seen, with me, what are its *susceptibilities.* In this latter respect, my success has chiefly lain. I flatter myself that I have been the first to reveal the latent and romantic uses which lay in the soil. But I must not insist on these matters. It is enough if I congratulate myself on the favorable opinion of one so well knowing & ably judging as yourself. As far as I can hear, the book finds general approbation, though not because of the characteristics which specially commend it to you. Only as a story. In regard to yourself, let me say to you—do not suffer yourself to be discouraged. Your error has been in addressing yourself exclusively to a community which has neither the courage, the independence or the knowledge necessary to create public opinion. Here, we are mere provincials. Address yourself to the foreign, though it even be the hostile tribunal, and you will compel a secondary & reflective sentiment at home in your favour. As for giving umbrage in this or that quarter, if you suffer this to daunt you, you will never do any thing. Success, itself, will always offend somebody. Merit is always offensive to *some* nostrils. If I had been governed by what is called opinion here, I should never have gone beyond my first publication. Nay, if I had listened to those who claimed to be friends, my first page had been my last; I should never have published any thing. Your first work is excellent of its kind; more thorough than any thing in relation to the period chosen for

---

933a

[1] At the top of this letter someone (doubtless Rivers) has written "*Confidential.*"

[2] *The Cassique of Kiawah* was published in May. See note 137, May 23, 1859 (930).

historical exercise. It was well written and well arranged. I do not remember whether I advised you that the notice of it in the Mercury was written by me.[3] But, what did you expect? An octavo, with a copious appendix can never be made a school book; and, as a history it was only complete as an epoch. Were you to pursue so comprehensive a plan throughout, the Histy of a little State, like S. C., would swell beyond the dimensions of a History of Greece or Rome—150 years of an obscure people, occupying the space in a Library of the 1000 years of the most controlling & conquering of all the races of the world. You must beware of being copious, where the material itself lacks in interest for the *general reader.* The class is a very small one, throughout the whole union, which desires such a work. I warned Dr. Stevens of Geo. against this mistake, but, without comparing the quality of the respective material, he was ambitious of giving as many volumes to the 100 years of Georgia history which Prescott had assigned to the Conquest of Mexico

[3]The Charleston *Mercury* of Nov. 8, 1856, announces that Rivers' *A Sketch of the History of South Carolina to the Close of the Proprietary Government by the Revolution of 1719* . . . (Charleston: McCarter & Co., 1856) will soon be ready for publication; the same newspaper of Nov. 12 notes that the volume has been received but that a review of it will be delayed. Undoubtedly the delay was the result of Simms' being on his northern lecture tour. In the *Mercury* of Jan. 16, 1857, Simms published his review of Rivers's *History*, "a very valuable contribution to our Southern chronicles," though "in some of his generalizations, he has occasionally erred; but it is hardly possible that any one, living among us now, could have done better, if half so well." Most of the review is devoted to the neglect by the South, and especially South Carolina, of literary men: "We have already had occasion to draw the public attention to this valuable contribution of Professor Rivers to our local history, and to endeavor to awaken a public sense among us of the necessity of giving every encouragement to those individuals, who, laboring, as it were, against hope, have yet addressed themselves to the task of creating for us a local literature. When this labor contemplates our local history, it is especially our duty, and should be our pride, to give it the most loving countenance; and our sympathies along with our sixpences. It does not matter to us,—it should not,—that a work like the one before us does not aim at gratifying a mere popular taste. It is a work for study, consultation, reference; not for mere amusement,—such a work as every Southern gentleman should have in his library; such as he may well read at his leisure, such as he should counsel and commission his sons to read, as a duty; since every son of the soil, having any patriotism, should by all means, whenever it is possible, put himself in possession of all the facts relating to the history, the interests, the progress, the policy—nay, the very faults, blunders, mistakes, and even crimes, of his ancestry; history being designed as a beacon and a warning, no less than as a guide, a landmark, and a light." It is the duty of southerners "to find fitting recompense for those who write your histories, and, at

& Peru.[4] The consequence was that nobody bought his first vol. and after 10 years, the Hist. Soc. of Geo. is trying to raise the funds to print the second.[5] That you provoked certain parties by your vol. is no doubt true; and suffer me to say, as you yourself have said it, you have made some mistakes; but I do not think that anybody suspects you of doing so wilfully. I believe, had you given me but one hour in consultation I could have saved you from these mistakes; that I had clues in my possession for the study of the subject, which are not easily attainable thro' any other media. But, I fancy, there were sinister influences brought to bear upon your mind, chiefly meant to operate against myself. Several of the parties into whose hands you had fallen, were secretly hostile to me. Some of them tried to persuade Trescott to write a Histy of S. C. in order to supersede mine. They did not, in so many words, tell him so; nor did they tell you; yet these very parties were most active in regard to your work. Trescott refused; being pleased to say that he knew

---

great self-sacrifice, without the motive of emolument, assist your reputations, interests and renown, in the great arena of nations. . . . After a hundred years of politics, we are scarcely assured of one day of political existence. In truth, our capacity to live, as a free people, in the possession of our rights, has become a most perplexing problem; and we are constrained to think, that all this is due to the one melancholy fact, that, while we have *encouraged all sorts of politicians,* we have, as studiously, *discouraged all sorts of literature.* No writer of the South has ever earned *one* dollar by all his labors in behalf of the South." If we fail "in the great *mental* struggle," we will perish "in every other field of conflict." We should, if we are to survive, have "always at hand a strong cohort of able literary men. . . . In truth, we are to remember that literature is a new thing in the South, and especially in South Carolina. It has to make itself a beginning. It never had—never was suffered to have—an existence. We have been always more apt to sneer at our beginners, as rivals, than to stimulate them to proper performances, which would enable them to reach due rank as authorities, and they have, accordingly, usually abandoned it as a profession. It is necessary—and we begin to feel it so—that we should decree otherwise now, and have our own writers. Professor RIVERS is one of those who may be held to be inaugurating for us the new day. The old laborers, pretty well worn out, we suppose, have passed, or are passing, off the stage. If they did little in their time, we cannot complain; for we paid them never a stiver for what they did. We gave them neither pay nor praise, in their capacity of authorship." There can be little doubt that Simms had himself in mind when he wrote of the South's—and South Carolina's—neglect of its authors.

[4] Harper and Brothers, New York, published William Hickling Prescott's *History of the Conquest of Mexico . . .* in 3 vols. in 1843, his *History of the Conquest of Peru . . .* in 2 vols. in 1847.

[5] Vol. I of Stevens' A *History of Georgia . . .* was published by D. Appleton and Co., New York, in 1847; Vol. II by E. H. Butler & Co., Philadelphia, in 1859.

no one but myself who ought to attempt it.[6] Now, I mention these things, without going into particulars, and without caring one straw about them. Some of these parties went farther, and *opposed* the introduction of my little Histy into the public schools.[7] The *animus* of these people, or some of them, may be shown in the treatment which I recieved at the hands of the Hist. Soc. Think of this one fact. The same mail which brought me your letter, officially advising me of my election as one of the V. Press. of the Society, & kindly entreating my acceptance, brought me the Charleston Courier which reported the proceedings of the Society at a meeting that very week, in which, without waiting for my answer, I was superseded as V. P. by Mr. Trescott. Now, I had resolved *not* to accept & had so told Mr. Porcher; but certainly that could have nothing to do with the official necessities of the case. Should any opportunity occur for an hour's talk with you, I think I could show you how certain cliques in Charleston & Columbia rule society, by subsidizing, with cunning arts, the really able men, making use of them against one another. These never suspect the base uses to which they are put. Now, in this very Hist. Society, why should men be put into the chief offices who have never identified themselves with History or Literature? Why should men be selected, simply because of their social position, for the rule & the dignities of institutions, who can add no lustre or dignity to their authority; who are in fact grossly ignorant. What a wrong is this to the real honest workers in the province. The literary man, the student, recieves but little at any time from society. Why is he to be denied

[6]William Henry Trescot (see note 180, July 26, 1859 [941]), diplomat and historian, complimented Simms as an historian in an oration before the South Carolina Historical Society on Nov. 19, 1859 (in the introductory sketch of Trescot, 1857 is erroneously given as the date of this oration). Though Trescot used the spelling "Trescot" in his published works, Frederick Adolphus Porcher, recording secretary of the South Carolina Historical Society, spells it "Trescott" in the "Minutes" of the society (MS. in the South Carolina Historical Society). The Charleston *Courier* of Oct. 30, 1855, also uses the spelling "Trescott."

[7]On Nov. 23, 1841, a resolution was submitted before the S.C. General Assembly to subscribe two thousand dollars for Simms' *History of South Carolina* for distribution among the free schools, but it was defeated by a vote of 61 to 40. In an angry letter to James Henry Hammond of Dec. 19, 1841 (125), Simms blames the defeat on the "personal hostility" of Christopher Gustavus Memminger (see note 129 of that letter) and Albert Moore Rhett (see introductory sketch of the Rhetts).

the mastery in that very province which he has made his own. Why is he to play second fiddle always; to be tied, as a mere cannister, to the cat's tail of social position. Why should Mr. Petigru and Dr. Moultrie, the one a great lawyer, the other a great physician perhaps, but both of them grossly ignorant of our history, be put at the head of our Hist. Soc. You & I who have been *workers* in that field, & may claim to know something, are to give way to these![8]

---

[8]The "Minutes" of the South Carolina Historical Society record that on May 19, 1855, a meeting was held at the Medical College of South Carolina, in Charleston, preparatory to the formation of an historical society. The following men were present: James Louis Petigru, Mitchell King, Dr. James Moultrie, Dr. John Edwards Holbrook, Ogden Hammond, William James Rivers, Frederick Adolphus Porcher, Dr. Elias Horlbeck, Bartholomew Rivers Carroll, Dr. Thomas Lewis Ogier, George Seabrook Bryan, Dr. Francis Turquand Miles, and Dr. James Postell Jervey. At a second meeting, on June 2, the following officers were elected: President, James L. Petigru; First Vice President, Dr. James Moultrie; Second Vice President, Simms; Corresponding Secretary, William James Rivers; Recording Secretary, Frederick Adolphus Porcher; and Treasurer, Dr. A. Baron Williman. At a meeting on July 30 "the Secretary reported to the Society that W Gilmore Simms had declined the office of Vice President of the Society; whereupon it was resolved that Mr. Simms resignation be received and that the vacancy be filled at the next meeting." The society met again on Oct. 29 and elected Trescot the Second Vice President. (These same officers were reelected at later meetings, including that of May 19, 1859, the last held before the date of this letter from Simms to Rivers.) The Charleston *Courier* of June 4 reports the election of officers at the meeting on June 2, and Simms is listed as the Second Vice President. The *Courier* of July 31 in reporting the meeting held on July 30 does not mention Simms' declining the office, but in listing the officers of the society the vice presidents are given as "Dr. James Moultrie, ——————— ———————." On Oct. 30 the *Courier* in its notice of the meeting on Oct. 29 reports: "W. H. TRESCOTT, Esq. was elected a Vice President, in the place of W. GILMORE SIMMS, Esq. who declined." There is no way to reconcile the facts with the account Simms here gives Rivers. Probably Simms was both hurt and infuriated that his accomplishments as an historian had been honored with a mere second vice presidency rather than the presidency of the society.

For Frederick Adolphus Porcher, professor of history and belles lettres at the College of Charleston, see note 213, c. Nov. 1, 1849 (511); for James Louis Petigru, see introductory sketch. James Moultrie, Jr. (1793–1869), a native of Charleston, was graduated in medicine from the University of Pennsylvania in 1812. He returned to South Carolina and was president of the Medical Society of South Carolina during 1820–1821. He was influential in founding the Medical College of South Carolina and in 1833 was appointed to the chair of physiology. He was one of the delegates to the organizational meeting of the American Medical Association in Philadelphia in 1847 and was elected vice president of the association; in 1850 he was elected president. For an account of his career, see Joseph Ioor Waring, *A History of Medicine in South Carolina, 1825–1900* ([Columbia]: South Carolina Medical Association, 1967), pp. 272–275.

Now, if you have done me the honour to watch my course, you will have seen that I have always laboured independently, & would never sacrifice the dignity of my profession, to mere social authority. I could have had *patronage* enough, if I had consented. There were fashionable people, and pretentious people, to whose salons I might have had access; but the price was *death!* If I had been drugged by them, I had been emasculated. I am talking to you frankly. You are a young man still—very young to me—and there are paths open to you. And you are in a situation which is honorable & compensative, and can command leisure for literary asides. There is no reason for despondency; but you will need to exercise a certain *reticence.* Do not make yourself cheap. Let nobody know what you are doing, at least no one, who cannot positively, in some way, assist your studies. Columbia is just as corrupt and feeble a place as Charleston. Rely on your own honest purpose, manly industry, & youthful zeal. Go on with your work—to completion. Bring down the history, at all events, to the period of the Revolution & farther, if you please. Brought to that period, your work will be more in demand than when it included only the Proprietary. If you doubt, at any time, let me hear from you. Any how, when you come to the city seek me out. I have suggestive clues, which, I think, no man here possesses but myself. Believe me, in all this, to be above all considerations save those of justice, sympathy, & a true love for my profession & country.

Yours ever

W. Gilmore Simms

943a : To William James Rivers

Charleston, Aug: 18. 1859.

Professor W. J. Rivers.
My dear Professor.

You are aware that I am helping the Mess'rs Appleton in their Cyclopædia. You are also aware, no doubt, that I regard you as one of my legitimate subjects. Will you oblige me with such a brief narrative of your life, education, studies & performances, as you care to put before the reader. Dates are to be remembered where possible, & the full titles of the books you have published. Will you do me the favor to ask Professor La Borde to send me a similar report of himself.[1] Pray do these things as soon as possible, & oblige

Your friend & Servt.

W. Gilmore Simms.

Is Col. W. C. Preston in town,—or where? And who, in Columbia, would prepare me a notice of him?[2]

946a : To William James Rivers

Charleston, Sep. 12. 1859.

Professor Rivers.
My dear Professor.

Thinking it probable that by the time this letter reaches Columbia, you will have returned to it, or will soon return, I propose to just thank you for your satisfactory letter, of which I will try to make judicious use, by a brief and simple narrative, & not render you ridiculous by the employment of any superlatives. I wrote to Dr. Longstreet,[1] and sent messages to others, in Columbia, but have not yet been honored with any answer. Your mind seems to be in right tone, as regards as yourself and your relations with society. Keep it so. It is the wretched misfortune of most men, of any endowments, that they never get at any right notion of their true claims upon society. Their lives consequently are a long conflict with their own position, & a vain & miserable struggle after one

---

943a

[1]For Maximilian LaBorde, at this time professor of metaphysics at the South Carolina College, see note 52, June 17, 1842 (137).

[2]William Campbell Preston had retired as president of the South Carolina College in 1851.

946a

[1]Augustus Baldwin Longstreet (see introductory sketch) was at this time president of the South Carolina College.

which the world never suffers them to attain. In my labours & life, I have pursued a similar course to yourself; trying to do those things which I fancied I could do best, and never troubling myself about the result, so far as this contemplated human awards. I go on working, briefly, without much heed to the profit or the loss. Suppose me very hard at work at this moment, and only writing to acknowledge your prompt attention & to say that I am, as ever,

truly Yours &c

W. Gilmore Simms

949a : To Williams Middleton[1]

Monday Mg. Oct. 10. 1859.

My dear Mr. Middleton.

I have had left at the shop of Russell & Jones,[2] your copy of the Antiquitates Americanæ,[3] for the use of which be pleased to recieve my thanks. It will not, I suppose, be inconvenient to you to suffer your servant to seek it there. I am just on the wing for the plantation whither I remove to day. One word on a different subject. Some of my friends have been speaking of you for public life. They even felt disposed to nominate you for the mayoralty. While I would not commend to you such a place, it strikes me that, with your historical

---

949a

[1]Middleton (1809–1883) was the son of Henry Middleton of Middleton Place, near Charleston. He was educated at Brook Green in England and in Paris, and for many years was an attaché of the American Legation in Russia. On returning to South Carolina he resided at Middleton Place. He was a signer of the Ordinance of Secession and aided with laborers and materials in strengthening the defences of Charleston and repairing Fort Sumter. Union troops burned his house in 1864.

[2]The bookstore of Russell and Jones was located on King Street. For John Russell, see introductory sketch; for his partner, James C. Jones, see note 78, April 2, 1850 (529).

[3]*Antiqvitates Americanæ; Sive, Scriptores Septenrionales Rerum Ante-Columbianarum in America. Samling af de i Nor dens Oldskrifter Indeholdte Efterretninger om de Gamle Nord Boers Opdagelsesreiser til America fra det til 10de det 14d Aarhundrede. Edidit Societas Regia Antiqvariorum Septentrionalium* (Hafniæ: Typis Officinæ Schultzianæ, 1837). This work, relating to the discovery of America by the Northmen, prints the texts of sagas in Icelandic with Danish and Latin translations and copious notes by the editor, Carl Christian Rafn (1795–1864).

name, you should not withhold yourself from politics, seeking a proper field.[4] With best wishes for you every way, believe me Very truly Yours &c

W. Gilmore Simms

Williams Middleton Esq.
Excuse this spotted paper & hurried scrawl; but I am in the thick of packing up.

949b : To Williams Middleton

Woodlands S. C.
Nov. 2. 1859.

My dear Mr. Middleton.

I wish a brief biographical notice of Henry Middleton, author of a vol. on "The Government & the Currency." Will you furnish it to me in the course of a few weeks? The period & place of birth; the several writings, with their several titles;—these & whatever other details you may think proper to give; and with as few comments as possible. I wish these for a notice in the American Cyclopaedia.[1] Let me also remind you of your promise to give me a similar notice of Mr. Middleton, the artist, of whose performances

[4]Simms probably has in mind Middleton's grandfather, Arthur Middleton (1742–1787), signer of the Declaration of Independence, and his great-grandfather, Henry Middleton (1717–1784), second president of the Continental Congress. Williams Middleton's father, Henry (1770–1846), was also a distinguished public servant: he served in both houses of the state legislature, was governor of South Carolina, represented his state in Congress, and was for a number of years minister to Russia.

949b

[1]Henry Middleton (1797–1876), Williams Middleton's brother, was born in Paris. He was graduated from the U.S. Military Academy in 1815, but in July 1816 he resigned his commission. He began the study of law and was called to the bar in 1822. Soon afterwards he left for Europe and resided for a long time in England and France. He was the author of several works of a political nature, among them *The Government and the Currency* (Philadelphia: Printed for the Author, 1844; a new edition "with alterations" was published by C. B. Norton, New York, in 1850), which denied the right of the federal government to issue paper money. An account of him is included in Appleton's *Cyclopædia.*

you showed me such fine[2] specimens.[3] Now, pray you, do not show yourself careless on the subject. It is highly important, where one feels that he belongs to the human race at all, to show that great families maintain themselves, & assert faculties & endowments in various departments. Did you get a note from me some time ago?— in which I urged you to go into public life.—Do not despise the suggestion. I trust you are flourishing & all well. It is just possible that, if you keep in Charleston this winter, I shall look in upon you for a single hour, in my character as a backwoodsman.[4] Yours truly

W. Gilmore Simms.

Williams Middleton, Esq.

949c : To Edward Herrick, Jr.[1]

Woodlands, S. C.
Nov. 2. 1859.

Edward Herrick jr. Esq.
dear Sir:

I have been pretty nearly drained of all my autographs by some 3000 collectors or more. For twenty years, the demands upon me have been incessant, & it is now impossible to comply with them. In respect to Marion, he was more given to fighting than to writing, & few of his letters have been preserved. I have but one of his letters in my possession, and this cannot be parted with. The price asked for his autograph merely is $300. Judge for yourself how far

[2]Simms wrote *fine fine.*

[3]John Izard Middleton (1785–1849), Williams Middleton's uncle, was educated at Cambridge. He inherited the large fortune of his mother, Mary Izard Middleton (d. 1814) and spent most of his life in France and Italy. He was a talented amateur painter and archaeologist, the author of *Grecian Remains in Italy. A Description of Cycolopian Walls, and of Roman Antiquities. With Topographical and Picturesque Views of Ancient Latium* (London: E. Orme, 1812). An account of him is given in Appleton's *Cyclopædia.*

[4]Simms sometimes amused or outraged friends and acquaintances by acting the role of backwoodsman or of Indian chief.

949c

[1]Not identified.

it is now attainable. There are some lithographs of his autograph, but I can think of but one person who can supply these, & that is my friend Tefft of Savannah, Geo. one of the greatest autograph mongers in the world. From him you may procure it. I would oblige you if I could; the thing is impossible. With real regret that I cannot yield a more satisfactory answer, I am, Sir, Your obt Servt. &c

W. Gilmore Simms.

973a : To Augustus Baldwin Longstreet[1]

Woodlands, S. C. March 22, 1860.

Hon. A. B. Longstreet, Dear Sir: I owe to you the original MS. biography which you were so good as to send me, and beg you to accept my thanks for your polite attention. I did not previously answer your letter, as I desired to be able to report that the material had all been arranged and sent on to the publishers. This is now done. I have written to Messrs. Appleton to abridge as little as possible. In preparing your material, I separated the matter relating to William Longstreet and made that into a separate article preceding yours, as it seemed to me to merit a place for itself.[2]

Yours very truly and
respectfully,

W. Gilmore Simms

973a

[1]We have not located the original of this letter. Our text is from Oscar Penn Fitzgerald's *Judge Longstreet. A Life Sketch* (Nashville, Tenn.: Printed for the Author, 1891), p. 199. We want to thank Professor Mary Ann Wimsatt, of Southwest Texas State University, for bringing this letter to our attention.

[2]William Longstreet (c. 1760–1814), an important inventor, was the father of Augustus Baldwin Longstreet. In Appleton's *Cyclopædia* an article is devoted to each of them.

973b : To William Fuller

Thursday Night
March 22 [1860][1]

My dear Dr.

Since writing the accompanying scrawl, my wife instructs me to say that if you will send Wm. with the Horses to meet us on Tuesday next to Bell's, we shall be with you on Wednesday, starting early that morning, & making Bell's by 12.m. if possible, on Wednesday 28th. inst. Let me do my wife the justice to say that she has been greatly distressed at not being able to be with Washy; but this is the first day or two that the House has been free of guests this winter.[2] Mattie Steele has just left us hurried down by Express, as her husband is reported to be in perilous condition.[3] I am better. I shall only remain with you long enough to kiss the baby, a huge boy by the way, if not pair of them, & then go to Charleston to get money to pay taxes.

God bless you all four.

W. G. S.

P. S. Did you learn that my poor friend Lawson has lost his favorite son—my Godson—named after me, & a most lovely promising boy of 11. The good old man—it is the first child that he has lost—is almost distraught. My dear friend, set your heart on nothing mortal! The most precious things are the first to be taken from us!

973b

[1]Dated by Simms' remarks about the death of William Gilmore Simms Lawson, who died on Mar. 5. See letter to Lawson of Mar. 11, 1860 (971).

[2]Both Simms and his wife arrived at the Fullers on Mar. 28, the day on which Mrs. Fuller was delivered of a son, Middleton Guerard Fuller. See letter to Lawson of Apr. 9, 1860 (975).

[3]Martha W. Porcher Steele was the wife of Dr. Edwin Carroll Steele, who died on Jan. 29, 1861. See note 64, Mar. 21, 1860 (972).

But I must not moralize gloomily. You are young. Encourage faith & Hope in the young—and Humility. I will see if Frank[4] will go down with us. He spoke of going down with me.

Yours Ever

W. G. S.

976a : To Robert E. Earle[1]

Woodlands, *Midway* P. O.
So Caro. April 18. 1860.

Robt. E. Earle, Esq.

dear Sir: I feel greatly honoured by the complimentary election to deliver the next annual address before the Two Literary Societies of the University at Athens; but, as I learn that the period for the performance will occur in August next, I am compelled to decline the appointment, as—even should my health and leisure permit me to prepare the oration—which is somewhat doubtful,—I cannot possibly attend at that season, and shall probably be absent from the state, and in a region quite remote from your precincts.[2] I greatly regret this necessity as it deprives me of an anticipated pleasure. But it is a matter wholly beyond my control. Will you do me the

---

[4]Probably Dr. Francis Fishburne Carroll. See note 5, Oct. 21, 1861 (1060b).

976a

[1]Earle, a native of Elyton, Ala., was in the senior class at the University of Georgia in 1860. He was killed at the Battle of Chickamauga in 1863. The two literary societies mentioned in this letter are the Demosthenian, founded in 1803, and the Phi Kappa, founded in 1820; both are still in existence. It is thought that Earle was a member of the Phi Kappa. We want to thank Susan B. Tate, Assistant Special Collections Librarian Emeritus of the University of Georgia Libraries, for sending us this information.

[2]Simms was planning his annual trip to the North.

kindness to convey to your Societies the expression of my warm appreciation of their kindly compliment, and of my sincere regret that compliance with their wishes is impossible.

With great respect, I am,
dear Sir, Your obt. & obliged Servt.

W. Gilmore Simms.

999a : To William Fuller

[c. November 1, 1860][1]

My dear Dr.

Tomorrow, I will send you, via Charleston, a Box containing 30 pr. shoes. They are rough, but strong. There is a pair for Wm. for which I have not provided, my leather giving out, & you desiring a nicer pair of shoes than Edmund has made for the others.[2] I have just got back from a lecturing trip to Cheraw. Public feeling runs high. The blue cockade is every where to be seen. S. C. *will secede.* Take your precautions—make your preparations. Spend no money that you can avoid spending, and the money you keep in hand, *let it be in gold.* Get your crop out and send to market as fast as possible. Come up here, with your family as soon as you please. All well. Our governess has come.[3] Mr. Rivers[4] is better, though still in bed & very weak.

Yours ever

W. Gilmore Simms.

999a

[1]The year is established by Simms' remarks concerning the impending secession of South Carolina. Simms lectured at Cheraw, S.C., in Late Oct. (see letter to Lawson of Oct. 24 [999]).

[2]William and Edmund are, of course, slaves.

[3]Margaret Wilson served as governess for the Simms children from around Oct. 30, 1860, until Aug. 20, 1861. See letter to Lawson of Oct. 16, 1860 (995).

[4]Christopher McKinney Rivers.

1003a : To George William Bagby[1]

Woodlands, Midway P. O. S. C.
Nov. 9. 1860.

Dr. G. W. Bagby.
My dear Sir:

By the same mail which will bring you this letter, I forward a goodly package of proof sheets, segregated from a volume of my poems now in press. The volume will be large & uniform with the two volumes already issued by Redfield. It will contain all my hitherto uncollected fugitives, the productions of occasional moments during a period of thirty years. It will exhibit (no matter what the degree of merit) a sufficient & singular variety. I have endeavoured in the sheets sent you (with the consent of my publisher) to afford you an opportunity of estimating this variety. You will find song & sonnet; ballad and stanza; epigram & moral. You are at liberty to use these as you think proper; to detach & publish such as you prefer. They may afford you the subject of an article, and I confess I desire that they should.[2] The relations of the South with the North, are, in literary respects, as degrading as in political and commercial. We can never get justice or fair play in either province. Poetry, I hold to be my proper province; but I am not ambitious of writing the tinselly stuff which at this day, & in this country, is too commonly recieved as poetry; where a mere fancy is held to be a thought, & where a conceit passes for a beauty, if not an inspiration. Poetry, I hold to be winged thought. It must be fresh thought, winged by the Imagination, & coloured by the Fancy. The

---

1003a

[1]Bagby (1828–1883), a native of Virginia, received a medical degree from the University of Pennsylvania in 1849. His success as a writer of articles for the Lynchburg *Virginian* caused him to abandon the idea of practicing medicine. He was in the 1850s co-owner of the Lynchburg *Express* and a newspaper correspondent in Washington, D.C. In June 1860 he succeeded John Reuben Thompson as editor of the *Southern Literary Messenger.* He was briefly in the Confederate Army, but was discharged because of ill health and returned to his editorship of the *Messenger*, which he kept until Jan. 1864. He was the author of several pamphlets and books and was well known throughout Virginia as a lecturer.

[2]"Oh, the Sweet South!" published in *Simms's Poems Areytos*, pp. 9–10, was reprinted in the *Messenger*, XXXII (Jan. 1861), 5. Bagby did not write an "article" on Simms, but his volume was reviewed in the number for Feb. 1861. See note 2, Dec. 17, 1860 (1027a).

Northern Poets, the best of them, lack in Imagination. They are contemplative, and they possess Fancy in degree. The Imagination shows itself in the conception & the thought—the fancy in its decoration. Poetry, I hold to be an earnest thing—not a play thing; to be a living thing, not a set jewel, or filagree work from the hands of a goldsmith. It is only the living and earnest things in poetry that live. It is only the works of the jeweller that are fashionable. I have been earnest & honest, I believe, in all that I have written. The thought, I believe is always masculine, in my verses, though it may be that it shows the man, drowsing in reverie beneath the trees, as often as it shows him, manfully arrayed for battle in the thick of combat. In sending you what I have done, I omit the longer pieces, and confine my selections wholly to the Ballad, the Lyrical, the Sonnet or the Epigram. I have covered to you a few pieces of the moral & contemplative. I have sent you none which have ever appeared in your pages. And this is saying much; for I have been associated with the Messenger, as Contributor, more than 25 years—in the times of Poor White & Poorer Poe.[3] You can accordingly, use all, or any, of these extracts, freely, as they will all be new to your readers. I am the more free to send them to you, as I percieve that your mind (from your editorship) is fearless, earnest, and capable of piercing through the garments, to the core. Read what Macaulay says of the Italian Poets, & the characteristics of Poetry, & you will understand me.[4] I studiously address myself to a clear utterance of the thought, as energetically as I can make

[3]Thomas Willis White (1788–1843) founded the *Messenger* in 1834 and in Dec. 1835 asked Poe to join the staff of the periodical. Poe's editorial connection with the *Messenger* ceased in 1837.

[4]In two essays "Criticisms of the Principal Italian Writers," first published in *Knight's Quarterly Magazine* in 1824 and frequently reprinted, Macaulay attributes the evils of Italian poetry from Petrarch to Alfieri to the influence of Petrarch's sonnets: "Almost all the poets of that period, however different in the degree and quality of their talents, are characterized by great exaggeration, and, as a necessary consequence, coldness of sentiment; by a passion for frivolous and tawdry ornament; and, above all, by an extreme feebleness and diffuseness of style." He regrets that Dante rather than Petrarch had not been the poets' model. See Macaulay, *The Miscellaneous Works*, ed. Lady Trevelyan (New York: G. P. Putnam's Sons, [1898]), VIII, 60–105.

it—in good English, after the best models,—and leave the decorative matter to find place where it can. In confidence & Yours truly

W. Gilmore Simms

P. S. Several of these pieces, thus enclosed to you, have never been in print before—all of those which have been previously published, have been carefully rewritten and materially altered &, I trust, amended. You may safely assume that all of them are new to your readers. I will but add that the volume itself will hardly be published till late in December, or early in January.

Yours &c

W. G. S.

1026a : To Benson John Lossing[1]

Woodlands, Midway P. O.
S. C. Decr. 13. 1860

My dear Mr. Lossing.

I need not say to you that I wish every success to your labours, & would cheerfully contribute all the information in my power as respects the subject of your researches. It is hardly more necessary to add that I should at any time be pleased to entertain you in my country home. I cover to you a letter for Col. Arthur P. Hayne (who was a gallant aid of Gen Jackson during the conflicts in the Southwest), & to the venerable Dr. Johnson, both of Charleston & to Major Laval, either there or at Columbia. He, too, was in the war under Jackson.[2] But permit me to counsel you to forbear your visit at the present juncture. It would scarcely be pleasant to

1026a

[1]For Lossing, historian, journalist, and engraver, see introductory sketch.

[2]Lossing was doing research for his *The Pictorial Field-Book of the War of 1812* . . . (New York: Harper & Brothers, 1868), issued in twelve parts. Simms' letters to Arthur Peronneau Hayne and William Laval have survived and are included in Vol. IV of *The Letters of William Gilmore Simms* (1024 and 1025); we have not located Simms' letter to Dr. Joseph Johnson (see note 17, Mar. 15, 1843 [154]).

you, & might be annoying. The very researches you propose to make would invite military inquiries touching posts of defence, sites that have been & might be again needed for defence & assault, and every question you would ask would subject you to suspicion & finally to annoyance, in consequence of that vigilance which, at this moment, sees in every northern man making these inquiries, the emissary of an enemy. No personal character however high, no interposition of friends, however influential, though they might save you from personal danger, could serve you to elude suspicion, or to prevent annoyance. This would be even more likely to occur to you in the Southwest, than in South Carolina. Such is the exasperation of our *people* at large that they are no longer controllable by their politicians. It is a popular movement, the momentum of which has become irresistible, approximating the German landsturm, or a general rising of the people. In ten days more South Carolina will have certainly seceded; and in reasonable interval after that event, if the forts in our harbour are not rendered to the state, they will be taken.[3] I have no doubt that Georgia, Florida, Alabama & Mississsippi will follow S. C. in a month after, and Louisiana soon after. Judge for yourself from these facts, whether your visit would not be greatly mistimed, especially as, even were there no dangers, you would hardly find any citizens prepared to give his attention to remarks touching a war of 50 years ago, while he is preparing for one on the tapis. I repeat that I should be glad to welcome you at Woodlands at any period, but would not be your friend, nor a good adviser to encourage your visit just now to the South at all. Let 1812 wait, and devote yourself to the Schuyler papers, which you can study just as well in the security of home.[4]— I conveyed your regards to Miss Maggie,[5] who expresses herself grateful for them.

[3]The Secession Convention met in Columbia on Dec. 17 and adjourned the same day to Charleston, where on Dec. 20 the Ordinance of Secession was unanimously adopted and signed by the 169 delegates. For the attack on and surrender of Fort Sumter, see letter to Lawson of Dec. 31 (1031) and following letters.

[4]Vol. I of Lossing's *The Life and Times of Philip Schuyler* was published by Mason Brothers, New York, in 1860. This volume was republished together with Vol. II by Sheldon & Company, New York, in 1873.

[5]Margaret Wilson, who was serving as governess of the Simms children.

With the sincere hope that you will take my advice, for the present, and with the repetition of my sincere wish to serve you, believe me Very truly Yours

W. Gilmore Simms

B. J. Lossing, Esq.

1027a : To George William Bagby

Woodlands, Midway P. O.
Decr. 17. 1860.

Dr. G. W. Bagby.
My dear Sir.

Let me, *in limine,* thank you for your noble editorial essay addressed to Virginia in our present state of affairs. If such an appeal does not move your politicians (your people are sound) to the renunciation of the federal fleshpots, then their souls are not worth saving, whether by God or Devil. All here thank you.[1] I shall address this letter to you still at Richmond, though yours conveys the idea of your sojourn at Washington. I can write but few words

---

1027a

[1]In the "Editor's Table" of the *Southern Literary Messenger*, XXXI (Dec. 1860), 468–474, Bagby remarks that hitherto he has not "in this, a literary rather than a political magazine," discussed "the value of the Union" or called "in serious question the possibility of its speedy dissolution." "But the election to the Presidency of a candidate pledged to the ultimate extinction of a domestic institution which is the foundation-stone of a Southern society, and the domination of a party having no existence outside of the Northern States, and which denies the South its rightful share of the soil of the Territories, makes it the imperative duty of every citizen and especially of him who controls even the humblest organ of popular sentiment to speak forth his mind with the utmost plainness, to the end that the general opinion may be obtained and the proper course to be pursued in these the last hours of the United States of America may as quickly as possible be determined upon." He approves "the attitude of South Carolina" and declares "unreservedly in favour of a Southern Confederacy." The "heroic action of the Palmetto State" is extolled: "every Southern State" should "act in like manner, to join hands with her, to share her fate whatever it may be, and to throw heart and soul, mind[,] body and estate, into the righteous balance of Disunion." He rehearses past events and reaches the conclusion that dissolution is the only answer: the "Union" has been "not of love, but of the lust of lucre—a bestial, adulterous and unholy alliance." And he exhorts Virginia to join South Carolina immediately: "Will Virginia speak. She must speak. She must act, and that quickly. It is due to her ancient renown."

as my house is full of company and our hearts full of excitement. Even while I write at midnight, our Convention is probably giving forth our fiat of Independence for the South. *Laus Deo!* We will meet all the consequences. My book is out, but only in a Southern and a small edition, issued solely in Charleston. How can I address you a copy, and save postage. It is a heavy vol. of over 400 pages.[2] Can you give me the name of some M. C. to whom I can cover it? Write promptly & believe me,

Truly though Hurriedly,
Yours

W. Gilmore Simms.

1029a : To Simon Gratz[1]

Woodlands, S. C.
Decr. 19. 1860.

Simon Gratz, Esq.
dear Sir:

When I tell you that I have had to tear the enclosed letter out of a bound vol. of more than 500 letters of the Revolution (original) you will see that I have made no small sacrifice to oblige you. The letter though short is admirably characterisitic & interesting. Please return it to me as soon as you can accomplish the engraving.[2] Excuse

---

[2]Simms's *Poems Areytos* is reviewed in the *Southern Literary Messenger*, XXXII (Feb. 1861), 156–159. Though signed "A.," the review was possibly written by Bagby, since Simms in his letter of Nov. 9, 1860 (1003a), had asked him to write an article on the volume. Part of the review is quoted in note 299, Nov. 30, 1860 (1017).

1029a

[1]For Gratz, a prominent lawyer of Philadelphia and an avid collector of autographs, see note 259, Nov. 20, 1860 (1010), where we incorrectly give the date of his birth as 1838—he was born in 1840.

[2]Evidently a letter of "Baron de Kalb." See letter to Gratz of Nov. 20, 1860 (1010).

brevity, but just now, there are few South Carolinians who have time for comments and courtesies.

Yours respectfully

W. Gilmore Simms

You may use what of my article you please.[3]

1029b : To Thomas Hicks Wynne[1]

Woodlands, S. C. Decr. 19. [1860][2]

Thos. H. Wynne, Esq.
My dear Sir.

Be pleased to recieve my thanks for the copy of the beautiful volume of Virginia Revolutionary Documents, which you were so

[3]Simms' "The Baron DeKalb" was published in the *Southern Quarterly Review*, N. S., VI (July 1852), 141–203.

1029b

[1]Wynne (1820–1875), a native of Richmond, Va., was apprenticed as a young man to the Richmond iron foundry firm of Burr & Sampson. He later joined Talbot & Company and rose from the position of pattern maker to general superintendent. In 1855 he was elected superintendent of the Richmond gas works, and in 1859 he became superintendent of the Richmond & Petersburg Railroad, a position he held until the beginning of the Civil War, when he became treasurer of the Southern Telegraph Company. During the war he also served as president of the Virginia Iron Manufacturing Company and the Westham Iron Company and as chief agent for the Southern Express Company for Virginia. After the war he became owner of the Richmond *Examiner*, which he later merged with the Richmond *Enquirer*. He also founded the Richmond *Evening Journal* and the Richmond *Times*. Wynne served several terms in the Va. House of Delegates and the Va. Senate. For a number of years he was corresponding secretary and librarian of the Virginia Historical Society. He was the author or editor of several monographs, including *History of the Dividing Line, and Other Tracts. From the Papers of William Byrd, of Westover, in Virginia, Esquire*, 2 vols. (Richmond, Va., 1866), published as Nos. 2 and 3 of a series entitled "Historical Documents from the Old Dominion" (1860–1874). We are indebted to E. Lee Shepard, Editor of the *Virginia Magazine of History and Biography* for most of the above information.

[2]Dated by the clipping entitled "Virginia Revolutionary Documents" which is still preserved with Simms' letter. In his notice of *The Orderly Book of That Portion of the American Army Stationed at or near Williamsburg, Va., under the Command of General Andrew Lewis, from March 18th, 1776, to August 28th, 1776. Printed from the Original Manuscript, with Notes and Introduction by Charles Campbell, Esq.* (Richmond, Va.: Privately Printed, 1860), published as No. 1 of "Historical Documents from the Old Dominion," Simms thanks Wynne for his copy and remarks: "We are glad to welcome this volume. . . . It argues a revival of that patriotism which

kind as to send me. You will percieve from the paragraph on the next page, which I published editorially in the Charleston Mercury of this day, how much I appreciate your attention, and the value of your contribution to my library.

Very respectfully
Your obliged & obt.
Servt.

W. Gilmore Simms

1060b : To Anna Washington Govan Steele Fuller

Woodlands, Oct. 21. 1861.

My dear Washy.

We have been anxiously expecting a letter from you, and begin to feel all sorts of apprehensions lest the horrible disease may have, at length, penetrated your little family. May God, in his mercy, avert it! I wrote you a half playful letter when I was about to go to Charleston, telling you to meet me there, with a huge pile of your husband's money, & go up with me. It is just possible that you may have supposed, by my suggestion, that we were reluctant to send for you to Bell's. I write now to disabuse you of any such impression; for tho', no doubt, you would prefer to take the route via Charleston, yet I well knew that neither the Dr. nor myself could now afford the means for doing any shopping. We are quite prepared to send for you whenever you give notice. We have little or no domestic news to impart, & for the public or foreign, you get if just as soon as we do. Gilmore went to town on the 15th. to report himself for duty.[1] He is now at the Citadel, &, *Laus Deo!* he has the means to pay for his next quarter—a matter which I thought doubtful a month ago. Mrs. Whetstone,[2] who came up last

---

made and kept Virginia famous until her statesmen learned too greatly to love the honey and the dough of Washington City."

1060b

[1]See letter to William Gilmore Simms, Jr., of Nov. 7, 1861 (1061).

[2]Wife of John M. Whetstone (1809–1870), who lived near Midway.

night, sent us a message, saying that she had seen him, & that he was well. He carried off with him my last pistol & my Bowie knife, & Mr. C. Rivers got from me my pocket pistols. I am accordingly almost weaponless, especially as Edward Roach has my deer gun, Mr. Leland Rivers[3] my rifle, & Mr. C. Rivers, my new small shot-gun. Under these deficiencies let me beg you to bring up with you my duelling pistols, especially as I suppose the Dr. has no time for using them. I need something of the sort now, to assure myself of a weapon in the event of trouble. You may write to the Dr. that my expectations of a crop will, I fear, disappoint me. I have packed 36 Bales, but the Cotton threatens to run short. What with a change of seasons, and the effects of the storm, which was here severely felt, I can hardly calculate to make more that 70 bags, & will be well satisfied if it runs to 80. We shall have plenty of corn, meagre of potatoes, &c. Rice will fall short. We are drinking Rye coffee—so prepare yourself. I bought 6 lbs of Tea, but white sugar is now getting very scarce, and is selling, I am told, at 35 cents! Molasses has got to 55. Flour, fortunately is cheap. Candles & soap dear. Our young ducks are dying of distemper. Chickens few. I have been trying to make vinegar of may apples. *Nous verrons.* I have also tried at a bbl. of persimmon wine. Still,—*nous verrons.* Jamison has finished his new house—a very fine one; and now quite full with the addition of Mrs. Jenkins & 4 children.[4] Frank C. & wife[5] visit us occasionally, but spend most of their time at the Clear Ponds. Charles was over here a few mornings ago, & Aunt Sarah has paid us a visit.[6] Fishburne Roach has moved to Dr. F.'s where

[3]A. W. Leland Rivers, born on James Island, S.C., in 1826 and buried at Midway in 1892, is listed in the 1860 census for Barnwell District as a blacksmith. Perhaps he was a relative of Christopher McKinney Rivers, of Bamberg. We want to thank Margaret Lawrence of Bamberg for sending us this information about Leland Rivers.

[4]For David Flavel Jamison, see introductory sketch. His eldest daughter, Caroline Harper, was the wife of Micah Jenkins. See note 275, c. Nov. 23, 1860 (1013).

[5]Dr. Francis Fishburne Carroll married Julia Peeples Reynolds in 1861. See note 141, May 23, 1859 (930).

[6]Charles Rivers Carroll and his wife Sarah Fishburne Carroll. See note 147, Aug.? 1861 (1057).

he is to practice.[7] Mrs. P.[8] has got home. She makes a good crop as usual. In our immediate neighborhood all is quiet. There is no row, no scandal, no nothing. We stagnate. Mary, your sister,[9] was here last week. All with her as usual. Even Bamberg offers few or no subjects for gossiping. If there be any, my wife, who will write to you today, will tell you all. What has the Dr. done about negro clothes & shoes? I am about to tan leather to make our shoes. None can be bought, at present, in Charleston. Negro clothes, except domestics, are not to be had; and domestics, with a streak of wool in them, are 70 cents. We are about starting the old loom once more, and have bought yarn. What have you done with your wool? Better sell it, if you have enough to make a show, and buy cotton stuffs for the negroes. Give these hints to the Dr. I write them chiefly for his benefit. We have run through two club seasons, 16 weeks, this summer; and last Saturday, the last season was over. We killed a Beef for the negroes Saturday, saving a few rounds for ourselves, which were good. Yesterday, Sunday, we had fish from the river—trout & perch (Johnson) our own beef, & half a mutton from Jamison—Roast & boil. Never rains, says my wife, but it pours. Today, fresh mutton, beef & fish; tomorrow,—peas porridge hot—peas porridge cold,—& the other dish for the Duke of Hoppin John! But you will tire of this twattle. I leave my wife to tell you what else she finds in her budget, & am, as Ever,

truly Yours

W. G. S.

---

[7]Dr. William Fishburne Roach was the nephew of Dr. Francis Beatty Fishburne. See note 178, May 14, 1867 (1251), note 147, Aug.? 1861 (1057), and note 36, May 3, 1864 (1096).

[8]Probably Mrs. Hopson Pinckney. See note 34, May 3, 1864 (1096).

[9]Mary Govan Steele Rivers (Mrs. Christopher McKinney Rivers).

1067a : To John Reuben Thompson[1]

Woodlands, S. C. Jany 16. 1862.

I have been thinking of writing you repeatedly, my dear Thompson, but was kept in such blind ignorance of your whereabouts, that I was unwilling to expend my Poststamp, in a fruitless roving after you over a ravaged country. Now, that I see you spoken of as being in Richmond, and in hopes of a comfortable office under Govt., I assume the probability of your being *reachable* by letter.[2] I had written thus far when in the paper of today (18) I find it announced that you are about to edit a vol. of the patriotic poetry inspired by the Independence of Dixie.[3] This plan of yours chimes in with a measure of my own. My plan is to commence the publication of a "Library of the Confederate States", publishing a volume monthly, and, *seriatim*, representing the states severally. Thus I propose a collection of the writings of old Beverley Tucker, of Virginia, of Hammond of S. C. &c. The volumes to average 400 pp. each, & sold at 1.00 or 125 according to bulk. New works to be interspersed as prepared, and a wholesome variety to be sought in History, Biography, Statesmanship, Poetry & Fiction. I see that you have publishers in Richmond, disposed to make a beginning. Consult with them on the subject, & you & I may, perhaps better than any body else, put the machine in motion. I am now revising Hammond's Essays & Speeches for the press.[4] Tucker's Text Book

---

1067a

[1]Obviously this letter was written before Simms' letter to Thompson which we dated "January, 1862?" (1066), in which were enclosed copies of some of the poems Simms had published in the Charleston *Mercury*: "They . . . are, I think, worthy of publication in the projected vol. of Professor C." See note 3, below.

[2]Thompson was made assistant secretary of the Commonwealth of Virginia and as such had a share in the administration of the Virginia State Library, then under the direction of George Wythe Munford.

[3]In the *Mercury* of Jan. 18 under the heading "Richmond News and Gossip" (dated Jan. 15) is the following remark: "The songs of the war, many of which are well worth preserving, are being collected by Professor Chase, and Jno. R. Thompson of this city, and will ere long appear in book form from the active press of West & Johnston."

[4]Simms' revisions were probably used when the copy was prepared for *Selections from the Letters and Speeches of the Hon. James H. Hammond, of South Carolina* (New York: John F. Trow & Co., 1866). See note 12, Jan. 31, 1862 (1068).

on Govt.[5] would constitute a vol. *per se,* and be a proper book for schools & colleges. We should prepare Histories, in single volumes, of the several States, biographies of Washington, Jefferson, Randolph, Calhoun & others, with selections from their writings & speeches. These should be compressed into single volumes of portable size.[6] In respect to your proposed vol. of verse occasioned by the war, & occasioning it, you are probably not aware that I have been a frequent contributor to the Mercury. You will find also in my vol. called "Areytos &c." published in October last, a variety of things designed to stir up the soul of the South to the assertion of its independence. See for example, the poems at pp. 12—52—55—63—98—110—113—116 (which may be called The Battle of Manassas)—142—151—180—185—193 (To Maryland) 223—302—385—&c.[7] In the Mercury were pieces entitles "The Soul of the South," "Kentucky required to deliver up her arms", & several other things—song & sonnet.[8] If you have not got & desire them, I may be able to procure you copies. I sent a copy of my "Areytos" to the Messenger, & you may procure it from the Editor.[9] Or, if you will write in my name to Russell & Jones of Charleston & tell them that I request they will send you a copy, they will do so, by express, for which you will have to pay some trifle. Timrod & Hayne have both written some fine things on the occasion, the former especially.

---

[5]*A Series of Lectures on the Science of Government; Intended to Prepare the Student for the Study of the Constitution of the United States*, first published by Carey and Hart, Philadelphia, in 1845.

[6]Simms' plan was not carried out.

[7]*Simms's Poems Areytos or Songs and Ballads of the South with Other Poems* was published in 1860, not in 1861, as Simms here says. The poems he refers to are as follows: "Make Gay the Spear with Flowers," "Death, But Never Dishonor!," "Well, Let Them Sing Their Heroes," "Elegiac.—It Is the Cause," "Let the Bugle Blow," "Ye Sons of Carolina," "We've Sung and We've Danced," "Battle Ode.—A Tyrtæan.—For Music," "If Not Ready," "The Liberty Tree," "Battle Hymn.—Now Raise the Mighty Song!," "Battle Hymn.—Columns, Steady!," "Friends Are Nigh," "Forget Not the Trophy," "Joy! Joy! For the Day-Star!," and "The Spirit of the Land," pp. 12–14, 52, 55, 63–64, 98–99, 110–111, 113, 116–123, 142, 151–152, 180–181, 185–187, 193, 223, 302–303, 385–386.

[8]For "The Soul of the South. An Ode" and several other poems published by Simms in the *Mercury*, see note 1, Jan., 1862? (1066). "Kentucky Required to Yield Her Arms" was published under the pseudonym "Boone" in the *Mercury* of Oct. 10, 1861.

[9]George William Bagby.

I have been writing to this end for years, as perhaps you know.—I have almost ceased now to write. My domestic cares & troubles almost unfit me for any thing; and my sorrows of home seem destined never to cease. In the early part of 1861 I lost a fine little boy, and on Christmas morning, a noble little girl of Scarlet Fever.[10]—Write me, if you please. I feel the loss of such correspondents as yourself. What has become of Cook.[11] He, too, surely, has not gone over to the enemy, with his brother & Strother. These defections, are, I fear, due to the influence of J. P. Kennedy who has lost his head in this crisis.[12] But, I am sick of hearing & talking of the war, though the terrible anxiety forces all speech in this one direction. Once more, let me hear from you, & believe me

Very truly Yours &c

W. Gilmore Simms

P. S. You should suggest to your Richmond publishers[13] to send me their books, through R & Jones. I am one of few persons who make any regular reviews of them now in this section, & I write for the Mercury when I have a topic.

[10]Sydney Hammond Simms and Harriet Myddleton Simms. See letters to Lawson of July 4, 1861 (1056), and to Miles of Jan. 15, 1862 (1067).

[11]John Esten Cooke (see introductory sketch) was at this time "Captain of a gun in the Richmond Howitzers" (see letter to Miles of Jan. 31, 1862 [1068]). For his military career, see John O. Beaty, *John Esten Cooke, Virginian* (New York: Columbia University Press, 1922), pp. 76ff.

[12]Cooke's brothers, Philip Pendleton, Edward St. George, Henry Pendleton, and Edmund Pendleton, died before the outbreak of the war. Simms must have been thinking of his uncle, Philip St. George Cooke (1809–1895), a graduate of the U.S. Military Academy and a professional army officer, who was a brigadier general in the Union forces during the war (see Beaty, ibid., p. 4). David Hunter Strother (1816–1888), cousin of Cooke and of Kennedy, was an illustrator and writer who published under the pseudonym of "Porte Crayon." Under the influence of Kennedy he remained loyal to the Union, joined the army, and was assigned to the topographical corps. He resigned in 1864 and after the close of the war was brevetted brigadier general.

[13]West and Johnston. See letter to Miles of Jan. 31, 1862 (1068).

1068a : To George William Bagby

Woodlands, 25 Feb. 1862

Dr G. W. Bagby.
My dear Sir.

I send you a collection of verses designed by the Muse of Patriotism at least, which I fancy you may find deserving a place in the Messenger. The pieces entitled "Beauregard"—"The Border Ranger" and "Esperance", have already appeared in the Charleston Mercury. The rest have never been in print. I could wish that you would give them a place as soon as possible.[1]—I read "Hermes" with continued interest.[2] I fear that our govt. & officers & engineers—such as they are—as well as our people,—have been caught napping. We have been too confident from early successes, & have fallen into the grievous error of despising our enemies. But I trust that our recent reverses will not only serve to bring all parties to their senses, but to bring out all the steel & iron in our character—all the noble phrenzies, the enterprise, energy & will.[3] I have been too much oppressed by home cares, toils, & anxieties to do any thing at the desk, otherwise it would have given me great pleasure to have helped you in filling up the pages of the Messenger. Very truly Yours &c

W. Gilmore Simms.

Should you not need these pieces, or some of them only, hand over the rest to Professor Chase or J. R. Thompson.

1068a

[1]The following poems by Simms were published under the title of "Odes, Sonnets and Songs, for the Times" in the *Southern Literary Messenger*, XXXIV (Feb. and Mar. 1862), 101–105: "The Soul of the South. An Ode," "Sons of the South, Arise. Ode," "Morals of Party. Sonnet," "Beauregard. Song," "The Border Ranger," "On, Advance!" (the first line is "Esperance!"), "The Oath for Liberty," and "Shades of Our Fathers. An Ode." The same issue, p. 127, contains Simms' "The Ship of State. Sonnet," published under the pseudonym "Tyrtæus."

[2]"Hermes" was the signature of the Richmond correspondent of the *Mercury*.

[3]The fall of Fort Henry on Feb. 6 and of Fort Donelson on Feb. 16 dealt the Confederacy a severe blow in the West.

1068b : To George William Bagby

Woodlands, Midway P. O.
March 24. 1862.

Dr. G. W. Bagby.
My dear Sir:

My friend & neighbour, Gen. D. F. Jamison, the President of the S. C. Convention,[1] has, at my instigation, written a very elaborate work the interest & character of which you will readily gather from the title. It is "The Life & times of the famous Baron, Bertrand du Guesclin." It carries us back to the days of Froissart, the Black Prince, Peter the Cruel, &c.[2] The author has made it a labour of love, and has delved deeply among the old French chronicles. His style is clear & manly; simple & direct; without floridity, totally ambitionless, & with a touch of that quaintness which gives its flavour to Froissart. In the present condition of the country, it is hardly possible to publish the book *per se,* and I am trying to persuade him to suffer its publication serially, in a publication like yours. It will make some 350 of your pages, & might profitably run through a year; to be afterwards embodied in an independent volume. I can answer for it as quite suited to the Messenger, and as full of curious interest & instructive incident. A little persuasion from you,—provided that the matter is desirable to you,—would no doubt induce his consent. He requires no compensation, and would be content with 50 copies extra, for distribution among his friends. And, by the way, your publishers, West & Johnson, might well strike off an edition from your plates. Such a publication would be a novelty in the South, and would contribute much to its character for erudition. I am of opinion that such a

---

1068b

[1]David Flavel Jamison was elected president of the Secession Convention when it met in Columbia on Dec. 17, 1860.

[2]Bertrand du Guesclin (c. 1320–1380), one of the ablest captains of the Hundred Years War, supported Henry of Trastamara (1333–1379) against Peter "The Cruel" (1333–1369), king of Castile, and in 1366 helped put Henry on the throne of Castile. He was defeated and captured by Peter's ally, Edward the Black Prince (1330–1376), in 1367. Ransomed, he fought once more for Henry. In 1370 he returned to France and was for almost ten years occupied in fighting the English. Froissart is, of course, Jean Froissart (1337?–1410?), the chronicler.

work would be desirable to you, not only because of its real merits, & the novelty of its material, but in a lower respect, as it helps to make up a table of contents monthly, which, I feel sure is not easily done at a period like this, when most of our young writers, like our friend Cooke, have exchanged the pen for the Sword.[3] By the way, convey to him my loving regards. May he soon, like myself, get back to the old vocation. The war has ruined me. I take for granted that my plates & Copyrights, worth from 25 to 35000 Dollars are all confiscate—the brain-sweat of nearly 40 years. I derived from 1200 to 2000 per ann. from Copyrights. I am cut off from every copper of this; and Cotton can't sell; and I am prepared to burn in the event any of further progress of the enemy into our country. Tell Cooke to take notice and prepare himself for a future history of the war in Virginia, & elswhere, if he pleases. I will prompt him as to the facts in S. C.[4] Can you or he procure me a quart or two of Leaf Tobacco seed. I wish to give it my negroes in order that they may raise the article for their own consumption. If you can procure, send it by express to me, "Care of Leland Rivers, Express Agent, Midway Depòt, S. C." Whatever cost & charge you may be at, advise me, & it shall be forwarded. It is probable that I shall send you other articles, i.e. if you really need them: but I shrink from the task of copying, unless the matter be really wanted.—I do not despair of the Confederacy,—for the simple reason that I believe in God!—You will readily perceive the sequent relation in this logic. The curse of a democratic governmt. is and always has been, the incompetence of men in office. War, which purges society, through its instinct of danger, is necessary every thirty years, to every people who claim to rule themselves. Our govt. and army will be purged by its fiery processes in due season. Till then we may expect reverses. The opinion is gradually growing that Davis is one of those men who would be envious of a corporal's exploit, in

---

[3]Jamison's *The Life and Times of Bertrand du Guesclin: A History of the Fourteenth Century*, dedicated to Simms, was published in 2 vols. by John Russell, Charleston, in 1864. The copy Jamison presented to Simms is owned by Mary C. Simms Oliphant.

[4]John Esten Cooke did not write a history of the war.

capturing a spy: and be emulous of a man who should even be remarkable at push pin.[5]

Yours very truly

W. Gilmore Simms.

1071a : To George William Bagby

Woodlands in Ruins.
April 10. 1862.

G. W. Bagby Esq.
My dear Sir.

Thanks for your genial expression of sympathy. I am a great loser but do not despond.[1] Would cheerfully sacrifice all to make the country safe. Thanks also for the Tobacco seed. As soon as I can get a decent place from which to write, I will send you the *quid* for the Messenger, in some articles upon which I have spent much thought.[2] If there be no objection to the material itself, referring now to Gen. Jamisons "Life & Times of Du Guesclin," the copies which I required for him may be dispensed with. If authorized by you, I think I could procure for you the matter in instalments of 6 or 8 pages of the Messenger. Let me hear from you. Let us pray that our army in the West may continue & improve its victories. So may we escape the evils of feeble govt. As I write the tidings come of the bombardment of Ft. Pulaski.[3] We are anxious but hopeful.

Very truly Yours

W. Gilmore Simms.

---

[5]A children's game in which one player tries to push or fillip his pin over that of another player.

1071a

[1]For an account of the fire that destroyed Woodlands, see note 20, Apr. 10, 1862 (1070).

[2]Nothing in the *Southern Literary Messenger* after this date can be attributed to Simms.

[3]Fort Pulaski, on Cockspur Island, Ga., commanded both channels of the Savannah River. On Apr. 12 it was surrendered to the Union army, thus closing the port of Savannah to all vessels except blockade-runners.

P.S. I am writing from a corner of my Carriage House. Every other shelter is occupied by my family for whom I am now building a House of boards.

1071b : To Richard Yeadon

Woodlands, May 5. [1862][1]

My dear Yeadon.

I have been thinking, since I came home, that, if you have made no permanent provision for your daughters,[2] now is the time to do so; and property secured to them, would probably escape that danger of confiscation which would, in the event of the enemy's successes in Carolina, most certainly threaten yours. You occupy so conspicuous a position, & have taken so active a course, as well as so decided a stand, that you could hardly hope to escape the utmost penalties in the power of an enemy to inflict.[3] Your girls, however, might be made secure to a considerable extent, & in their security, your wife & even yourself, might find your future benefits. It is quite probable that you have already thought of these things, & made provision accordingly. But, as it is possible that you have not done so, it is only a friends duty to deliver his views & let you judge for yourself. With no children of your own, you have lived a great deal for the families of others. This I know. I take for granted that, now, your life & sympathies are inextricably bound up in the fortunes of your adopted children. Your wealth enables you easily, even at this juncture, to detach from the mass & variety of your

---

1071b

[1]Dated by Simms' remark about "our cabinned, cribbed, confined domain." See his other letters written during this year after the fire at Woodlands on Mar. 29.

[2]Yeadon adopted two nieces of his wife, Mary Videau Marion (a great-great niece of Gen. Francis Marion): Eliza Catherine Palmer and Mary Videau Kirk. See William Lee Thomas Crocker, "Richard Yeadon," University of South Carolina, master's thesis, 1927.

[3]Yeadon was a Unionist, but after the secession of South Carolina and the formation of the Confederate States he supported the Confederacy by buying large numbers of bonds and giving generously for the equipping of Confederate soldiers. Though he had retired as editor of the Charleston *Courier* in 1844, he continued to contribute editorials (the *Courier* of Aug. 30, 1862, in reporting that an Aiken Company had been named for him—the "Yeadon Blues"—calls him the "senior editor") and thereby also made himself conspicuous.

capital, a handsome independence for each of your daughters without seriously affecting your capital & resources; & a handsome support may be conveyed to them, either through stocks or real estate. But, after considering all the probabilities of the war, my conclusion is that you should invest for them, in real estate, at some point remote from the Seaboard. You might get for each of them a homestead, a fine farm, near Kalmia, if it so pleases you, though I should counsel a tract & settlements in the neighbourhood of Greenville or Spartanburg, or York. I do not know but that the latter place would be preferable. Here, or at either of these places, 10 or 20,000 dollars, invested for either of them, through the intervention of trustees,—and I recommend Petigru & Perry[4] for this purpose—would be a judicious investment of some of your surplus stock. Upon this place or places, you could place a few negroes, and they will probably be secure. The most important matter now is to gain time. *Charleston sacrificed, the State may be made secure;* & though you lose your *houses* in the city, you would save your stocks, which, I suspect, constitute the largest portion of your fortune. I fully believe that if we fight it out in Charleston, even to the utter destruction of the city, we shall save the State. In doing so, we save the money & the stocks. The Yankees have nearly exhausted themselves; but their superiority along the Seaboard will sustain them. When they find us in earnest, however,—even to the destruction of our cities, they must collapse. They will then despair, as they will see in our readiness to sacrifice our possessions, the determination never to coalesce with them again, but rather to welcome any fate than reunion. But, as I began this letter with the single purpose which is already stated, I will content myself with saying that I find all safe & well at home,—content with our cabinned, cribbed, confined domain, but with the hope of emerging

[4]James Louis Petigru and Benjamin Franklin Perry. See introductory sketches.

from it soon. Best regards to Madame, & the young damsels, Elisa and Tenella.[5]

Ever truly Yours

W. Gilmore Simms

R. Y.

1071c : To William James Rivers

Woodlands, S. C. May. 31. 1862.[1]

Professor Rivers.
My dear Professor.

In the perilous condition in which our country stands, it behooves every man of reflection, to put his house in order, & make his preparations for the worst. I have been thinking over this matter, and my mind involuntarily refers to you, as one of the few persons who might give me some succour. I will tell you how. Should our armies in Virginia, Tennessee & Mississippi meet with further reverses, and even should they not, it seems to be the general opinion that all our Seaboard, is to fall before the invader. Now, if Charleston be taken, the probability is that our Line of Defence will nearly approach Columbia & Augusta,—will, in fact, be only a little below these cities. In that event, all the country below & till we reach the Seaboard, will become a sort of debatable land, subject to the marauding incursions of both parties. My plantation will be exposed to these incursions, and there will be no security for property, especially if the war assumes a partisan character. I shall expect to lose terribly, but there are some losses which I might prevent, by a timely anticipation of the danger. I have, in my collection, a

[5]"Tenella" was a pseudonym used by Mary Bayard Devereux Clarke (1827–1886), of North Carolina, who published poetry in the *Southern Literary Messenger* and was the compiler of *Wood-Notes; or, Carolina Carols: A Collection of North Carolina Poetry* (Raleigh: W. L. Pomeroy, 1854). Perhaps Mary Videau Kirk used the same pseudonym.

1071c

[1]This letter is postmarked (by hand) "May 3." Either Simms or the postal clerk could have erred.

singularly large body of valuable Historical Documents, mostly of the Revolution, gathered from a variety of sources. These documents have been little used. I have made notes of them, & examined them carefully, but as yet have made few draughts upon their contents. They consist of papers of Marion, Gadsden, Maham, Henry & John Laurens, Rutledge[2] & a variety of other persons. There are four folio volumes, which I had interleaved & bound, with notes, and a large mass besides. I have thought of you as the properest custodian of these treasures, as you perhaps will better appreciate their value, than any other person I know. I shall be willing that you should examine & take notes of their contents; and it is my farther idea, and was long since, that you & I, at some future, more auspicious period, might jointly prepare them for the press. I had proposed Lives of Henry & John Laurens, for example, with selections from their correspondence & a running commentary, in which we might mutually engage.[3] And the collection will afford us other topics, in the brief biography, & papers for the Historical Society. The materials are very rich. There is a large body of the letters of R. H. Lee, Steuben, DeKalb,[4] &c. Now, have you room for these papers, and will you be willing to recieve & take care of them should the pressure of circumstances force me to send them off. Should the enemy penetrate thus far, I should be compelled to seek refuge for my family in the interior. I should wish to save my library & MS.S. The former will nearly reach 10.000 volumes, the latter, if published, would make 50. But my first regard is for these valuable old Documents. Can't you run down & see me? I can provide you with hog & hominy, & can shake down some fresh straw for you, as a bed, or procure you one at General Jamison's who is my next door neighbour, & has ample room. You are aware that my poor

---

[2]Gen. Francis Marion (c. 1732–1795), Gen. Christopher Gadsden (1724–1805), Lt. Col. Hezekiah Maham (1739–1789), Henry Laurens (1724–1792), Col. John Laurens (1754–1782), and John Rutledge (1739–1800), all soldiers or statesmen of the American Revolution.

[3]In 1867 the Bradford Club, New York, published *The Army Correspondence of Colonel John Laurens in the Years 1777–8: Now First Printed from Original Letters Addressed to His Father Henry Laurens, President of Congress, with a Memoir by Wm. Gilmore Simms.*

[4]Richard Henry Lee (1732–1794), Baron Friedrich Wilhelm Ludolf Gerhard Augustin von Steuben (1730–1794), and Johann Kalb, "Baron de Kalb" (1721–1780), Revolutionary soldiers.

old house is in ruins, and that I am living *al fresco.*—There is another matter. Mrs. Martin[5] has been gathering materials for a collection of Carolina Poets. She lately told me that she had transferred these materials to Professor Reynolds,[6] but that she doubted, if he had done any thing with them. I counselled her to secure you as a coadjutor of Reynolds. If this arrangement can be made, with your industry you might soon get the collection under weigh, and it might be published by subscription, the funds & sample copies being given to our soldiers.[7] Pray think of this. Let me hear from you as soon as convenient, as I greatly desire to be doing & to lose no time.

Yours very truly

W. Gilmore Simms

P.S. How does real estate sell in Columbia? Are houses to be bought, out of the corporate limits, in healthy situations, with a few acres of farming ground about them.

1104a : To Paul Hamilton Hayne[1]

Woodlands Sep. 5 [1864]

My dear Paul.

I am engaged, *inter nos,* in editing for Southern boys and girls, a new edition of the English Mother Goose. I am making it as original as possible, that is to say, adapting it to Southern life,

---

[5]Margaret Maxwell Martin, of Columbia, S.C., author of several volumes of religious prose and verse. See note 272, c. Nov. 23, 1860 (1013).

[6]James Lawrence Reynolds. See introductory sketch.

[7]This collection was not published.

1104a

[1]In *The Letters of William Gilmore Simms,* V, 11, we printed this letter from a typescript in the Duke University Library. The original, from which we here take our text, has the date "Sep. 5" in Simms' handwriting and the year "1867" in the handwriting of someone else. Whoever made the typescript now at Duke read the date as "Feb 5 1867" and typed it as Simms'; we, therefore, accepted it, though at the time we were dissatisfied with Simms' reference to Timrod's "boy forthcoming" in a letter so dated. The correct year is established by this reference (see note 3, below).

peculiarities, characteristics, &c. If you have ever manufactured any doggrel rhymes for your little boy,[2] or can *descend* to the effort, send me some. Bruns has done so, & sent me some very clever ones; and I write to Timrod to do some also in anticipation of the boy forthcoming.[3] Your reward shall be a copy of the new book for your boy.[4] Love to Mary, & best regards to your mother.[5]

W. Gilmore Simms

1110a : To Theophilus Hunter Hill[1]

Woodlands, 22 Nov. 1864.

My dear Sir:

It would give me great pleasure to comply with your wishes, but this is impossible. I cannot find time to write or revise my own verses, & must content myself with the simple pleasure of reading, very hurriedly, those of other persons. As for pausing to criticise,

---

[2]William Hamilton Hayne (1856–1929).

[3]Timrod married Katie Goodwin on Feb. 16, 1864; on Dec. 24, 1864, she gave birth to a son, William ("Willie"), who died on Oct. 25, 1865. See Edd Winfield Parks and Aileen Wells Parks, *The Collected Poems of Henry Timrod* (Athens: The University of Georgia Press, [1965]), pp. 11–12.

[4]Simms' "Southern Mother Goose" was in the press of Evans and Cogswell, Columbia, when the city was burned by Sherman's army in Feb. 1865 (see letter to the editors of *Southern Society* of Oct. 10, 1867 [1274a]). Two letters to Simms from Benjamin F. Evans dated "Sept. 3d. 1864" and "1864" indicate that the firm hoped to have the volume published before Christmas of that year (originals in the Charles Carroll Simms Collection, South Caroliniana Library).

[5]Mary Middleton Michel Hayne and Emily McElhenny Hayne. See notes 31 and 32, June 22, 1863 (1082).

1110a

[1]Simms addressed this letter to "Theodore H. Hill, Esq. / Raleigh,—N. C." Perhaps he misread Hill's signature to his letter to him; certainly he could not have been very well acquainted with him, if he knew him at all.

Hill (1836–1901), born near Raleigh, was a teacher and journalist and was also licensed to practice law. His main interest, however, was poetry. His first volume, *Hesper and Other Poems* (Raleigh: Strother & Marcom, 1861), is reviewed (probably by Simms) in the Charleston *Mercury* of Jan. 17, 1862: "This is the title of a modest little volume of fugitive poetry, by Mr. Theo. H. Hill, of Raleigh, N. C. . . . We have glanced over some of Mr. Hill's verses, and find in them abundant marks of poetic genius, as well as polish and good taste. This is the author's first book, and the fact that he has ventured to publish it in revolutionary times like these, certainly argues that he is full of zeal for the advancement of Southern literature, and of confidence in the success of that great cause." Hill later published two more volumes of verse: *Poems* (New York: Hurd and Houghton, 1869) and *Passion Flower and Other Poems* (Raleigh, N.C.: P. W. Wiley, 1883).

even in my own mind, without giving utterance to the criticism, I might as well attempt to gather the crops which I have not planted. I have no overseer, & this is harvest time, tything time, tax time, and to gather for the tythe & find money for the tax, is a problem of time & temper that leaves me little for patient walks & wanderings to the Illissus or the Aganippe.[2] The poem published in the Courier is not in my possession, and I do not now remember how it was published, whether with or without my introduction. This was simply complimentary, & possessed no value as criticism.[3] In regard to the poem which you send me now, I would not advise its publication in its present state. As a specimen of very *felicitous versification,* it is highly creditable; but as a creation, a conception bold & original duly worked out,—you have done nothing with the subject. It is still, as you found it, a naked statement of fact—viz: that Narcissus, a beautiful youth, became so enamored of his own beauty as to pine away to death in consequence. In your effort at musical effects, you have been content with giving this history in a happy collection of rhymes, but the only moral which you work from it, is to be found in that very portion which your friend urges you to omit. I, myself, do not see the necessity of making a poem to illustrate a moral; but every poem must embody *thought,* conception, & a poem of this class should show design. The earlier efforts of all young writers in Poetry, are designed to acquire mastery in utterance. They naturally strive to make language deliver itself in rhythm. Until this faculty be acquired, thought cannot become malleable in language. Now, it is not unfrequently the case that, after a while, the young writer continues his practise, *seeking musical* effects only. He forgets that these musical *effects* are only means to an end, and that rhyme & rhythm are only agents for utterance in Poetry. Poetry is *winged thought,* and flies like an arrow to its mark. Having, as you have done, acquired a sufficient mastery of rhythmical utterance, your aim must be now embody your *thoughts* in this

---

[2]Ilissus, the river in Attica, and Aganippe, the spring on Helicon sacred to the Muses.

[3]We have examined five years of the Charleston *Courier* prior to this date and cannot find any poem with Hill's signature or his initials. Most of the poems in the *Courier* are signed with names, initials, or pseudonyms, and none of these or

mode of speech. You are not merely to rhyme, however musical the rhyming may be—you are to design, concieve, think, seek, find & deliver. You are to *extort* from every subject its inner secret—for the Poet is a Seer. Whatever of problem there be in the story of Narcissus you are to find out—the moral of himself and story, which is its vital principle. Narcissus was passionless. He had no earnest passions. He loved himself only. He could not love women. He had no blood for it. He was probably an onanist, and his story, probably founded on a fact, was a satire. Hercules, poisoned by the shirt of Nessus, was doubtless a victim to Syphilis, imparted by his wife who had been previously ravished by the Centaur; and so the Greeks disguised the satire in a fable or allegory.[4] That Poetry which is simply graceful & harmonious verse, has no vitality. Nothing lives long in literature of any sort but that which is informed by vigorous original thought; & it must be thought beyond the time. The poet who too readily enters into the general sense, cannot long survive. The generation which he perhaps has taught—up to a certain point—goes beyond him, leaves him while he remains stationary. It asks for more than he can give. Milk for babes—meat for men. In degree with his fullness, depth, power of thought, will he endure, as in the case with Shakspeare, Dante, Milton—all the great masters. It will need 300 years of ever advancing civilization, before any approach will be made to the depths of Shakspeare. Poe & others, who aimed at nothing more than musical effects, & pretty surprises, have materially injured the present growth of Poets. Even Tennyson, exquisite master as he is, is working injurious effects upon thousands, who might succeed as original writers, yet are content to fail & blunder as his Imitators.—Beware of this. Use rhyme only as the organ of thought. Make yourself the master of your art, only that you may work out original designs. As I have said, your verse, as verse, *per se,* is happy & spirited; and yet numerous faults occur even in this respect. In the 1 paragraph, you have the rhymes day, away, day & stay, occurring too closely together. So we have vain, swain, strain, refrain within four lines of

---

the few unsigned poems are prefaced by complimentary remarks which can be identified as by Simms.

[4]Simms is obviously a euhemerist.

each other.[5] So on page 4, the line "Scarce perceptible decline," finds its rhyme only in the next paragraph where you begin a new proposition.[6] This is wholly inadmissable, &c. You exhibit a good deal of fancy, but must remember that fancy is a decorative, an augmentative agency, which must have its basis in original & solid thought. Your friend was right, in one sense, in suggesting the exclusion of your last paragraph. It is a foreign grafting—an excrescence—has no proper connexion with the subject.[7] Study now

---

[5]Hill apparently ignored Simms' suggestions—perhaps his Muse was inadequate to the task. In the published versions of "Narcissus" in *Poems*, pp. [1]–9, and *Passion Flower and Other Poems*, pp. 90–97, the poem opens:

Pining for the beauty he
In himself alone could see,
Wan Narcissus, day by day
Wasted wofully away:
Love-lorn Echo, all in vain,
Sought the self-enamored swain,—
Calling on his name again,
And again, until the woods,
In their wildest solitudes—
Grown familiar with the strain—
Syllabled the sad refrain:
"O Narcissus! where art thou?
Dost, in frolic, hide thee now?
Ah! tis cruel thus to stay
From thine Echo, *all* the day. . . ."

[6]In the version in *Poems* (as doubtless in the manuscript) this passage (revised for *Passion Flower and Other Poems*, though without altering what Simms found objectionable) is as follows:

Still more futile his essay,
Who would vividly portray
Scarce perceptible decline,
Where the substance and the shade,
Interfused—*together fade!*
Metaphor may not define
Stealth of gradual decay—
Toying with its tortured prey—
Growth of shade, decrease of shine,
Narcissus, in those eyes of thine!

[7]Neither Simms nor Hill's friend convinced him to discard his "excrescence" in either published version. In the last paragraph of "Narcissus" Hill drops his narrative and addresses a nameless "Maiden" and thus points his "moral":

Shouldst thou, like Narcissus, guess
Half of thine own loveliness;
Though his fate were surely thine!
Echo's never would be mine!
Shouldst thou half thy charms discover,
Maiden, peerless as thou art,
Hope would droop within thy lover,—

for concentration. Study the old English Dramatists—Ben Johnson, Shakspeare, &c. Poetry is the profoundest philosopher. Philosophy is a younger sister. Music is more naturally allied to mathematics. Poetry is intellectual—music is sensualistic. You have fancy, and you have shown that you can master the flexibilities of verse. Study now for the pabulum of thought. Read the masters, & see by what art they evolve all the secret in a subject. You are young. You have time. Do not rush too hastily into print. Your true object is self-development. Find out the secret in your own soul & you will find out the secrets in other souls. Excuse haste. I give you all the time I can spare.

Yours truly

W. Gilmore Simms

1112a : To William Gregg[1]

Woodlands, Midway P. O.
5 Jany. 1865.

Hon. Wm. Gregg.
My dear Gregg.

I am sorry that your rules do not permit you to oblige me in regard to the bale of Cotton. If I understand your letter, however, you will take it & pay in the currency at the rate of $1.40—353

Die upon his loyal heart;
Love, though mine, with hope would perish;
I, with life itself would part,
Sooner than survive to cherish
Thee, as other than thou art!
Knowing all thou wert before,
Self thou learnedst to adore;
Seeing what thou then wouldst be,
I no more could bend the knee:
Love, *though mine*, would not retain
Fond regret for one so vain. . . .

1112a
[1]For Gregg, the leading southern cotton manufacturer of his day, see note 142, Sept. 14, 1848 (444).

lbs @ 140—$494.20. If my assumptions be correct please forward the money by Express, and oblige

Yours, truly but hurriedly

W. Gilmore Simms

1137a : To [Correspondent Unknown][1]

Columbia, S. C. Oct. 5. 1865

I fully concur in the opinions expressed and the recommendations made, by the several distinguished gentlemen in the preceding pages. I have known Mr. Janney's position in society for twenty years, and known him personally for a very long time. He is a most worthy, industrious & enterprising citizen, of great business habits & experience, & most exemplary morals. As a Hotel Keeper at Glenn's Springs, and in Columbia, he proved himself singularly capable of conducting such an establishment, and in the prosecution of this business, had realized a fortune. His interests in Columbia are still large and valuable, his energies are still vigorous, the prestige of his House is undiminished, & I see no reason to doubt that once re-established, his Hotel can be made to yield him once more, as

1137a

[1]This letter is one of several letters or notes signed by various prominent South Carolinians recommending J. C. Janney "to the capitalists North and South." Janney's hotel, according to a letter signed by Benjamin Franklin Perry and C. P. Sullivan, "was destroyed by the fire which desolated so large a part of the City of Columbia S. C at the time of the occupation by the army of Genl. Sherman. . . . In lending money for this purpose [the rebuilding of the hotel] or in uniting with him in such an establishment an opportunity is afforded to capitalists of making a judicious and profitable investment." Attached to the letters of recommendation is an affidavit signed by D. B. Miller, "Clerk of the Court of Common Pleas and General Sessions, and Register of Mesne Conveyance from said district [Richland District]" that there is "no Mortgage or any other lien on the real estate of James C Janney, John S. Leaphart, & Sherard L Leaphart located on Lady Street, between Richardson and Assembly Streets in the City of Columbia . . . that I believe it to be of value at least Twenty-five thousand dollars, that I know said James C Janney his Son-in-law John S Leaphart and his brother Sherard L Leaphart to be the actual and bona-fide owners of said property, the said Janney owning one half, and the said Leapharts the other half."

large an income as ever. I know no interest in South Carolina which, to my mind, seems to promise more profitably.

W. Gilmore Simms

of Woodlands, S. C.

1141a : To Orville James Victor[1]

Charleston S. C. Decr. 17. [1865][2]

O. J. Victor Esq.
My dear Mr. Victor.

Had I known where to seek you while in New York, I should certainly have sought you out; but it was only the day before my departure from your city that I recieved your note, and at that late moment my time was too extremely occupied to suffer me to do so.[3] I greatly regret that we could not meet, as there are many topics of interest between us, upon which we might have discoursed with mutual profit. But I hope to see N. Y. again early in the Summer, if in the meanwhile, we do not all here perish of starvation. We are dreadfully desolate here. I have lost, with more than $100.000 of other property, my whole collection of books more than 10.000 vols. All my *pictures* are gone. If you have any spare sets of your Art Journal,[4] send me a copy, & any thing besides, of the publications of the last five years. Write me, "Office of the South Carolinian",—where I do some small labours for the present.[5] Write soon, I pray you[.][6] My best regards to Mrs. V.[7] Yours in haste, but very truly

W. Gilmore Simms.

1141a

[1]For Victor, author, editor, and publisher, see note 181, July 26, 1859 (941).

[2]Dated by Simms' remarks about his losses during the war and his request for "the publications of the last five years."

[3]Simms went to New York City in Oct. and returned to Charleston on Dec. 4. See letters to Dawson of Oct. 2 (1137) and to Lawson of Dec. 5 (1141).

[4]The *Cosmopolitan Art Journal* (1856–Mar. 1861).

[5]Simms was associate editor of the *Daily South Carolinian* (Charleston). See note 147, Dec. 19, 1865 (1142).

[6]The MS. is torn.

[7]Metta Victoria Fuller Victor. See note 181, July 26, 1859 (941).

1141b : To James A. H. Bell[1]

Charleston, S. C. Decr. 18. [1865][2]

James A. H. Bell, Esq.
My dear Mr. Bell.

Very many thanks for the little volume which you sent me of the Lives of the Pirates,[3] & for the pretty copy of Landor. Do you know that I once edited a collection of the fine things from Landor, which was lost in the hands of a Publisher.[4] He was one of my favorites.— I have no doubt that I shall be able to glean something from the Pirates, for the work I have in contemplation.[5]—

I very much regret having missed seeing you before I left your city. But my time was terribly occupied, & my frequent absences up the river, materially abridged that which I might have given to society. Let me hope that I shall be better able next summer (D.V.) to seek & see the friends to whom I owe so much kindness. With best wishes for your health & prosperity believe me

Truly yours

W. Gilmore Simms

1141b

[1]The *Brooklyn City Directory* for 1865 lists Bell as the owner of the James A. H. Bell White Lead Works at the corner of Hicks and Nelson Streets. After 1870 he is no longer listed. During the 1860s Brooklyn produced more white lead than any other city or town in the United States, and this industry was one of the leading commercial activities of the city. We would like to thank Anthony Cucchiara of the Long Island Historical Society for this information.

[2]Dated by Simms' remark about the work on pirates which he has "in contemplation." See note 5, below.

[3]On Oct. 29, 1869, Simms wrote to Duyckinck (1377): "With enough money in hand, to my credit, please see [Henry] Kernot, pay him for the copy, put aside for me, of Johnsons Lives of the Pirates. . . ." Capt. Charles Johnson's *A General History of the Pyrates* . . ., 2 vols. (London: T. Warner; T. Woodward, 1724–1725), therefore, could not be the book which Bell sent him. We are unable to identify it.

[4]For Simms' proposed edition of Landor, see letters to Baird of Mar. 17, Apr. 14, June 9, July 17, 1854, and Oct. 14, 1855 (705, 708, 716, 725, and 792).

[5]For Simms' unfinished romance, "The Brothers of the Coast," see note 118, Sept. 9, 1865 (1133).

1142a : To E. J. Mathews[1]

Charleston, S. C
Decr. 28. 1865.

E. J. Mathews, Esq.
dear Sir:

Your note, addressed to me at Columbia on the 28th of last October reached me but two days ago; the delay resulting from my removal from Columbia to my plantation, and, subsequently, from my prolonged absence from the state.[2] I now hasten to comply with your wish, adding my own,—that you may enjoy, what is not permitted to us here,—'A merrie Christmasse.[']

Your obt. Servt.

W. Gilmore Simms.

1142a

[1]Not identified.

[2]Simms wrote from Columbia to Dawson on Oct. 2 (1137) that he had resigned the editorship of the Columbia *Daily Phœnix* and planned to visit Woodlands "this week" for about ten days before returning to Columbia "to proceed to N. Y."

1190a : To George W. Ellis[1]

78 Dean Street, Brooklyn
15 Augt., 1866

My dear Mr. Ellis:

Have you received the photographs I sent you from Yonkers, & do they satisfy you. The head and face are those of an ourson[2] of the antique, and all that have ever been made of me are villainously like—yet unlike. My eyes being very sensitive to any light or strain upon them,—in consequence of my being sun-struck when young—at once contract themselves & all the muscles about them, the moment the machine is brought to bear upon them. The engraver should be instructed to do some "eye-opening" while working on the picture. Verily I am always shocked to see what a grisly bear I present to the world, with every picture made by the instrument. You might get a more amicable, &, I think, quite as natural & true a portrait, by adopting that which accompanies my poems, in Redfield's[3] Edition.[4] So again, you will find an excellent profile likeness,

---

1190a

[1]The manuscript of this letter (in the Philhower Collection of the Rutgers University Library) cannot be located. Our text is from Herbert Smith's "An Unpublished Letter of William Gilmore Simms," *Journal of the Rutgers University Library*, XXIX (Dec. 1965), 26–28.

Simms had become a Freemason during the Civil War and was a member of Orange Lodge No. 14, in Charleston. In 1865 the Masonic Lodges of Columbia appointed him the head of a commission of three to go North "to try & make collections for the relief of the Fraternity in this place [Columbia], the restoration of their paraphernalia & buildings." The Freemasons of Columbia were to pay his expenses, and in Mar. 1866 he was made an honorary member of Richland Lodge No. 39, in Columbia (see letter of B. Mendel to Simms of Mar. 6, 1866, original in the South Caroliniana Library). He left for New York City on June 7, 1866, and returned to Charleston on Oct. 8. See letter to Lawson of Sept. 9, 1865 (1132), and following letters.

Ellis was a Freemason, a member of Trenton Lodge No. 5. When he received his Master Mason degree on June 12, 1865, he was in the U.S. Navy and was thirty-one years old. He died on Oct. 20, 1908. We are indebted to Edward Rainey, Grand Secretary of The Grand Lodge of the Most Ancient and Honorable Society of Free and Accepted Masons for the State of New Jersey, for this information.

The contents of Simms' letter indicate that in 1866 Ellis was a member of the publishing firm of Chapman and Co., 116 Nassau Street, New York City.

[2]Smith reads this (evidently somewhat illegible) word as "ourson," French for "cub-bear."

[3]Smith prints "Newfields'," an obvious misreading.

[4]See note 2, June 10, 1853 (663b).

published in Griswold's International Magazine.[5] These were made 20 years ago, & are thought to be very good presentments of the subject at that date. As respects my appearance, I am free to say, I am quite indifferent (which I ought *not* to be) but it is your policy to exhibit your bears, or lions, under the most favorable aspects.—When will you commence your "Sunny Side Series." I think you do wisely in choosing that title.[6] I shall be glad to see you beginning and shall rejoice to learn that you succeed. This will depend wholly upon the degree of dash, novelty, and general ability which you employ. It will be in my power, I modestly think, to prepare as soon as the Summer is over,—and I think of doing it—a series of novellettes, which shall be unique and fresh—distinguished by passion [*illegible*] and, perhaps, fun & frolic.[7] You may think it strange, but my penchant for humor, fun & gaiety, is always more active when my sadness is most pressing; so that, I tell my friends, if you find my letters lively, you may conclude that I am at my saddest. But this is sorry egotism.

I think, my dear Mr. Ellis, that you and Mr. Chapman are both perfectly aware of the importance, to me, of realizing, from my poor brain all the pecuniary results possible, and that you will take care to let me have my *quid,*—in part, at least—before I depart for the South. Will you be so good as to say in what manner this shall be done? You were to pay me $100 by the 20th Augt. and the remaining $100 by the 20th Sept. How, & on whom, shall I draw? Advise me, if you please, of all necessary particulars.

[5]This engraving accompanies a biographical sketch of Simms in the *International Magazine*, V (Mar. 1, 1852), 433–435 (see note 50, Mar. 10, 1851 [570]). It was made from the same daguerreotype by George S. Cook that was engraved for *The New American Cyclopædia* (see note 1, Jan. 1, 1858 [856b]). This engraving of Simms is reproduced facing p. 198 of Vol. IV of *The Letters of William Gilmore Simms*.

[6]"Sunny Side" is of course the name of Washington Irving's home.

[7]The only work Simms published in the series is *The Ghost of My Husband. A Tale of the Crescent City* (New York: Chapman & Company, [1866]). It had earlier been published under the title *Marie De Berniere: A Tale of the Crescent City* (Philadelphia: Lippincott, Grambo, and Co., 1853).

I shall be pleased, if possible, to visit Trenton, and as it is not unlikely that I shall return South by the land route, I may have a chance to look in upon you & our brethren of the Mystic tre[8] when you least expect it. Present me gratefully to yr. *medico* (Dr. C.), our medical brother.[9] I may need a potion at his hand. Commend me to him expressly, to the fraternity generally, and hold me as ever

very truly yours,

W. Gilmore Simms.

P. S. Brady, by the way, has taken several portraits (photographs) of me for a large quarto work of the publisher, Johnson.[10] He has also made some *cartes de visite*—all frightful—more so than those I sent you, since they were taken when I wore all my fearful wilderness of beard. But it may be well to look in at Brady's & see them.

W. G. S.

---

[8]Smith remarks that this word is "Illegible in the MS." but that it is "apparently a Masonic symbol of some kind, from the context meaning something like 'assembly' or 'company.' " He was unable to identify it, nor can we.

[9]*The Trenton Directory, 1867–68. Containing a List of the Inhabitants, Together with a Business Directory* . . . (New York: Webb & Fitzgerald, n.d.) lists three physicians whose last names begin with "C": James Chamberlain, James B. Coleman, and Thomas J. Corson. Edward Rainey writes us that the only one of these who was a Freemason, a member of Trenton Lodge No. 5, was Thomas J. Corson, who died on May 10, 1879.

[10]The firm of Johnson, Fry and Co. (Henry Johnson and William H. Fry) was the publisher of Duyckinck's *National Portrait Gallery of Eminent Americans* (see note 80, Mar. 15, 1861 [1047]). The engraving of Matthew Brady's photograph is reproduced in Vol. V of *The Letters of William Gilmore Simms*, facing p. 104.

1200a : To Orville T. Smith[1]

[October 5, 1866]

Orville T Smith, Esqr.
Brooklyn, L. I.
dear Sir:

Cheerfully complying with your desires, I am

Your obt Servt

W. Gilmore Simms.

Brooklyn, Oct. 5, 1866

1200a

[1]Anne M. Gordon, Librarian of the Long Island Historical Society, writes us that Smith is not listed in the Brooklyn directories for 1862, 1864, 1866, or 1868 or in the *New York Directory* for 1866.

1867–1870

1221a : To Henry Barton Dawson[1]

Charleston Feb. 1. [1867][2]

My dear Mr. Dawson.

You will see from the enclosed editorial that your last issue has been recieved, examined & favorably reported on. Much might be done for your magazine in the South, but for the terrible deficiency of money. Our people are literally on the verge of starvation, & from the lack of money & labour, one half of our planters will be compelled to forego any attempts to make a crop of any sort. I met half a dozen this morning, trying to borrow the means with which to resume their corn & cotton planting. They have not money to buy the ordinary implements of labour to buy mules, or the corn to feed the latter. Such is my own condition. With 2600 acres of prime land, with son & son-in-law[3] to manage, I am unable to make a single step forward. With $2000 I could probably make 100 bales of Cotton. As it is, I can hardly make my bread,—and by the plantation I do not. We are literally, in great numbers, dying by inches & in silence! One planter today said to me "I have 20 in family. I yesterday sold one of the few remaining articles of value, my watch, a family watch, that cost $120 for $30. to get food for my family. They have been living for months on similar sacrifices, which yet enabled me to buy for them nothing better than common corn hominy, without butter, and occasionally a bit of fat bacon.

1221a

[1]Dawson, the historian, was at this time editor of the *Historical Magazine* (New York). See note 274, Oct. 16, 1858 (900).

[2]Dated by Simms' reference to his review of the Dec. 1866 number of the *Historical Magazine* in the Charleston *Mercury* of Feb. 1, 1867, and by his account of conditions in South Carolina.

[3]Gilmore and Chevillette's husband, Donald Jacob Rowe (see note 21, Feb. 10, 1866 [1147]).

I have tried to get some employment, but in vain." And this is a common story. But the subject is too painful & humiliating.

Yours truly

W. Gilmore Simms

1229a : To [Correspondent Unknown]

[March 1, 1867]

My dear Sir.

I comply with your request, and send you a good natured epigram from the Portuguese.

Your obt. Servt.

W. Gilmore Simms.

Within her breast, more fair than snows,
Sweet Amaryllis plants the rose;
Not that the flower should fix your eyes,
But the rich garden where it lies.[1]

South Carolina, 1 March 1867.

1238a : To Paul Hamilton Hayne

Charleston, March 21. [1867][1]

My dear Paul.

The writer of the within is a most amiable gentleman of New York, a devoted admirer of men of letters, and a fast friend of mine.

1229a

[1]We are unable to identify this Portuguese epigram.

1238a

[1]On the MS. of this letter someone (probably Hayne) has written "1867." The year is undoubtedly correct: William Hawkins Ferris (see introductory sketch) had asked Simms' help in making a collection of autograph poems of southern writers, and Simms wrote to him on Mar. 21 (1239) that he had "already executed all your commissions, & have written a letter on one page of yours, to each of the

Let me second his request and beg you to send him one of your best sonnets, or such other poems as you prefer. Should you go to the North, at any time, Mr Ferris will welcome you, as he has welcomed or entertained me. "Win golden opinions from all sorts of people," is the wise counsel of Shakspeare.[2] The literary man can readily do this, for he has power, if he is sufficiently amiable. With best regards to Mary, and your mother, and blessings on the boy, believe me ever truly Yours

W. Gilmore Simms

1247a : To Charles Warren Stoddard[1]

Charleston, S. C.
May 1, 1867

Mr. Charles Warren Stoddard.
My dear Sir:

You will see from the enclosed, published Editorially in the Daily News of this city, this morning, what use I have made of the several very graceful poems which you sent me. I need not add any thing of comment to what I have said in this article.[2] I shall be pleased

---

parties." Actually in the case of Hayne, Simms had enclosed a note from Ferris that is not preserved with this letter: on Mar. 27 Hayne wrote to Ferris that he had received Simms' letter enclosing Ferris's note of Mar. 18 and is sending Ferris two short poems, a song and a sonnet. The original of Hayne's letter to Ferris is in the Ferris Collection, Columbia University Library; it is printed by McKeithan in *A Collection of Hayne Letters*, p. [209].

[2]Simms misquotes *Macbeth*, I, vii, 32–33: "I have bought/Golden opinions from all sorts of people. . . ."

1247a

[1]For Stoddard, poet and prose writer, see note 280, Oct. 24, 1866 (1206).

[2]Under the title "California Poetry" Simms writes: "We gave, some time ago, in the columns of the NEWS [of Dec. 25, 1866 (see note 16, Jan. 23, 1867 [1219])], some very happy and fresh specimens of poetry from the pen of CHARLES WARREN STODDARD, a young poet of San Francisco, California. We commented briefly at the time upon the felicity of the verses—their general grace, fine taste and frequent beauties. In the additional specimens from the same writer, which we give below, the same general characteristics will make themselves apparent. . . . Mr. STODDARD belongs legitimately to the school of TENNYSON, who blends, with the contemplation of WORDSWORTH, the metaphysical subtlety of SHELLEY, and the graceful abandon of KEATS, and, as in TENNYSON, Mr. STODDARD shows himself a peculiar master in the felicitous choice of phrase and epithet." He then prints several of Stoddard's poems and has few faults to find in them. He concludes: "We

to hear from you when you are disposed to write. I thank you for your kind & friendly expressions, and shall always be happy in your case, as in that of all other young writers to give every encouragement to the claims of merit. Excuse the brevity of this note. My time is greatly occupied at this moment & my head is not in good order.[3]

Yours very truly

W. Gilmore Simms

1253a : To John Esten Cooke

Charleston, S. C. June 4. '67

My dear Cooke.

There is a demand for your "Wearing of the Grey" in this market & not a copy to be had.[1] I have had to give up to a friend the copy

---

shall always be pleased to welcome to our columns the contributions of a writer of poems such as these. The reader will readily see how very superior they are in originality of thought, feeling, fancy, and expression to the average verses of our newspapers and magazines. We beg to assure Mr. Stoddard, to whose favor we owe these articles direct, that he shall always be sure of a place in our columns, when his offerings are of so choice a kind. . . ."

[3]For Simms' difficulties at this time, see letter to Duyckinck of May 1 (1247).

1253a

[1]*Wearing of the Gray; Being Personal Portraits, Scenes and Adventures of the War* (New York: E. B. Treat & Co.; Baltimore: J. S. Morrow, 1867) is noticed in the Charleston *Courier* of May 22—almost certainly by Simms, who appears to have written most (if not all) of the reviews published in the *Courier* at this time. *Wearing of the Gray* is called a "lively and sketchy publication . . . a valuable as well as pleasing contribution to what may be entitled the Anecdotical History of the War." Of Cooke as a writer, the reviewer comments: ". . . it is generally known, and acknowledged, that he is one of the most versatile, prolific and genial of all the living writers of Virginia. He has probably made larger contributions to the history and biography of the war and its heroes, in and out of his native State, than any other writer of any State; and the wonder is that, writing so much on one theme and in one province, he has succeeded so invariably and so happily in making his works several, distinct, various and individually attractive. This, alone, is in high proof of his versatibility of genius, the vitality of his fancy, and the various constituents in his mental nature, for evoking the picturesque from his subject. He has impressed his own individuality upon his themes, and this individuality equally displays itself in his works of art and fiction as in his history." He continues to discuss Cooke as novelist, in particular his *Surry of Eagle's Nest* . . . (New York: Bunce and Huntington, 1866): "In 'Surry,' the mere story was one of a simple, direct interest, not implying much complication, and not marked

sent me. Now, I can sell 25 copies for you. Get your publishers to send me that number, on *your* account, at *Colporteur* prices, and send them to me, addressed to the care of "Wm. Roach, Com-

---

by any particular invention; and this, perhaps, was the result of one of Mr. COOKE'S defects, or, we should say, faults. His narrative, which is wonderfully full, free and flowing, runs away with him, and makes him too little heedful of his characterization. He does not individualize his persons of the drama, with sufficient sharpness of outline; does not choose them with sufficient care and consideration, and too many of them are, accordingly, of a single and uniform type in society. From the uniform, or ordinary types of society, however respectable they may be in the social world, you can rarely hope for any very distinctive or heroic traits; and it is a contradiction in the art-moral, to conceive of a large and beautiful invention, implying novelty, where the characterization itself does not imply the necessity for its development. When you select your *dramatis personæ*, you do so with regard to the development of individuality in character; since this individuality must imply such situations as will force the several parties into action, each according to his own nature and the peculiar gifts with which you endow him. These parties, among the great masters in the drama and in fiction, are types of humanity, rather than society; and, accordingly, their passions are employed, along with their morals and intellect, and made earnestly alive and active, by being brought under the operation of coercive and external influences. All these types, even when they represent the mere humors of men, must be drawn with an earnest brush; which must dip for its coloring into the very heart's blood of the subject; and these are the only paintings that ever exist enduringly under the corroding operations of time. The dashing cavalier, in the impetuous charge, makes an impressive picture for the moment. We hear him shout, we see his gallant onset, and he goes from sight, and we forget him. The hot blood of youth—the *Hotspur*—must not be suffered to be seen only when his heroism is on horseback; for, in such a situation, we lose sight of the *man*, in the contemplation of the *centaur.* In this sort of sketching Mr. COOKE excels. He has done some admirable battle pieces—the word-painting being singularly felicitous. But he suffers these scenes to take undue proportion of space upon his canvas, and so will, in time, incur the imputation of monotony. . . . We have hinted that the free flow, the eager impulse of Mr. COOKE'S composition, his ready command of language, the ardency of his fancy, and the quickness with which his enthusiasm rises—however admirable and beautiful at times—however spirited and forcible—are yet among his greatest dangers; leading to amplification, which, already, is one of his chief defects, and to diffusion; and so to the enfeebling of his style, and the danger of a confirmed mannerism. He must guard against these, as among the influences which may tend, but too rapidly, not only to lessen that popularity which he possesses as an author, but to limit, in still greater degree, the claims which he should establish upon the future."

Simms was probably also the author of a review of a book that has established its claims "upon the future," John William De Forest's *Miss Ravenel's Conversion from Secession to Loyalty* (New York: Harper & Brothers, 1867), published in the *Courier* of June 4. Here his southern bias kept him from recognizing the very considerable merits of the novel: "It is the embodiment of all the brutal malignity Northern writers have ever conceived, or reported, to the slander and misrepresentation of the South. With none of the art-faculty of Mrs. BEECHER STOWE, the writer endeavors to *outbeecher* her in his gross and infamous disparagement of the characterisitics and the people of the South. His book is remarkable for nothing mission & Shipping merchant." Have the Bill sent, at *Colporteur prices*—remember that—and the draft for the money shall be sent to *you,* as soon as the books are recieved. It will be so much *cash* in your pocket. Do not delay, but write & send promptly.[2] I have neither health nor leisure to write you more. I have just got back from the plantation & elswhere, & am hors de combat from a wretched catarrh, besides finding my desk covered with letters, all of which say *work,* and many of which cry, as the voice to John in Patmos—"Write."[3]

Àdios. Yours

W. Gilmore Simms.

---

but the intense malignity, which has blackened every page with a slander, and pointed every paragraph with a lie.

"But the venom is baffled by the unmitigated dullness of the volume. It consists of a long string of lugubrious dialogues between very silly or very stupid people; only spiced by the malignity which poisons all its pages. There is no story, no art, no invention. There is no decent characterization. The heroine (Miss RAVENEL) is a silly and vulgar chit, who is converted from secession to loyalty, by appetite rather than argument; her father is a raving and ridiculous blockhead; one of her lovers is a blackguard, the other a snob; which is being a peg or two below the English standard of snobbism. Briefly, with the exception of a good masculine style, and a smart epigrammatic facility in rounding a period with a sting, the book is wholly without merit. As a work of art in fiction, it is bald, utterly and below criticism; as a narrative, pretending to facts, it is as false in its design throughout, as an ingenious malice and a viperous hate could make it, in the hands of one whose morals suggest no scruples when slandering a whole people, either for the gratification of a passion, or the earning of a penny. Why such books should be put forth now, with what object and to what good end, it is difficult to conceive. They are in direct conflict with the avowed desire of the Northern people to conciliate rather than to stab or wound. They are in conflict with the avowed policy of the Government, they are in conflict with the needs as well as the morals of society, and they are utterly damnable in the sight of Christianity. In such publications as this, the press becomes a panderer either to the greed of gain, or to the roused malignity of individual hate, which is too strong equally for public policy or private morals. We trust that the HOLMES' Book Store will keep its counters unpolluted with all such writings."

[2]Cooke sent Simms' letter to his New York publisher, E. B. Treat on July 11: "The within note from my friend Mr Simms is sent as connected with 'W. of G.' I do not feel myself at liberty to adopt Mr Simms' suggestion—and only forward his note to show that copies could be sold in Charleston, and for your information." Treat replied: "We have sent Mr Simms a case of 22 books & requested him to recommend the right man as an agent." (Original in the Clifton Waller Barrett Library, University of Virginia Library)

[3]Revelation, I:10.

1255a : To John Bostwick Moreau[1]

Charleston, June 18. [1867][2]

John B. Moreau, Esq.

My dear Sir: Absence from the city, much labor & no little indisposition have combined to delay my answer to your last letter; but I acted upon the matter of most import in it, as soon as it was recieved. The Photographer Cooke[3] was quite unwilling to part with the negative of Laurens, but I do not suffer myself to be baffled, and succeeded finally in procuring it. I have it now in my possession, paying him $5 for it. I know not whether the charge is high or not; but such was the demand & I paid it. I do not suppose that you need it immediately, & accordingly do not send it; but propose to bring it on with me when I next visit New York. This (D.V.) I propose to do early in July, when I hope to enjoy the gripe of yours & other friendly hands, & to find you & all other friends in better flesh, faith and condition generally than is the case with myself. We are all in wretched case here, pecuniarily, politically and socially. The country is destitute of money & provisions & the grain crops will not be available till late in August. In Haste, but

Ever truly Yours

W. Gilmore Simms

1255a

[1]Moreau was secretary of the Bradford Club, New York City, which published Simms' *The Army Correspondence of Colonel John Laurens in the Years 1777–8* . . . (1867). See note 169, July 28, 1866 (1182).

[2]Dated by Simms' remarks about the negative of the picture of John Laurens. On Mar. 21 Simms wrote to Duyckinck (1240), enclosed "two photograph impressions of the brooch miniature of Col. Laurens," and remarked that he had "sent two other impressions to Mr. Moreau in order that if the mail should fail with either, the loss could be at once supplied." On Mar. 31 he wrote to Moreau (1242) that he trusted "that before this you have been put in possession of the two photographs of Laurens, sent directly to you." Apparently Moreau had also wanted the negative, though an engraving rather than a photograph illustrates *The Army Correspondence of Colonel John Laurens in the Years 1777–8* . . . (see note 129, Mar. 21, 1867 [1240]).

[3]George S. Cook.

1256a : To William Hawkins Ferris[1]

Charleston,
June 27. '67

My dear Ferris.

Enclosed I send you two photographs of Mary Lawson. One of these for Mrs. Ferris, & the other for Mrs. Bockee.[2] Mrs. F. will take her choice, &, this done, send the other to Mrs. Bockee. I have no time to write, being up to my eyes in toils, mostly for other people. But you shall be advised duly when I have decided upon our departure.[3] Five Northern mails due.

Yours &c.

W. Gilmore Simms.

1266a : To Mary Lawson Simms

Brooklyn, 23 Aug. [1867][1]

My dear Baby.

Since writing you yesterday, I recieved another letter from your sister,[2] the contents of which will interest you. The precarious condition of Mary Rivers is painfully evident, and in these repeated

1256a

[1]See introductory sketch.

[2]Isabella Smith Donaldson Bockee, wife of John Jacob Bockee. See introductory sketch.

[3]Simms and his daughter Mary Lawson sailed for New York City on the *Manhattan* on July 13, arrived on July 16, and went almost immediately to visit the Lawsons in Yonkers. On Aug. 1 they removed to the Ferrises in Brooklyn. See letter to Duyckinck of July 6 (1260) and following letters.

1266a

[1]Mary Lawson Simms accompanied her father on his visits to the North in 1867, 1868, and 1869, but the date of this letter is established by his reference to the illness of Mary Rivers (see note 3, below). On July 29 Simms had written to William Gilmore Simms, Jr. (1263), that on Aug. 15 he and Mary Lawson were "to proceed to the Sherwoods & Kellogg's at Berkshire. There I propose to leave M. L. for some weeks. . . ." The letter is addressed to Mary Lawson, "Care of Wm. Sherwood Esq. Great Barrington, Massachusetts."

[2]Chevillette Simms Rowe, the wife of Donald Jacob Rowe. See introductory sketch of the Simms family circle and note 7, Jan. 8, 1867 (1217).

attacks, I see the proofs of a rapidly failing constitution. That she has temporarily rallied is due to her natural vigour & comparative youth; but that she will permanently recover, I think very doubtful. The probabilities are quite great that she will succumb under a renewal of the attack, & we may possibly lose her this very season.[3] Do you take care of yourself, and avoid damp cold air, avoid exposure, see that your clothing is warm & adapted to the season, and write me fully as to your health & general feelings. Do not fatigue yourself in the attempt to do too much in the way of exercise. You are to remember that you have had no experience in tall hill or mountain walking, and must get on, as Boys go through College, by *degrees.* I am still in tolerably good condition, but the weather is dreadfully inauspicious here. Nothing but rain storms, & winds from the East. It has rained all day, and the night is raw, dark, drizzly, & diabolically offensive. Make my best regards to the Ladies Kellogg, and to Mr. Sherwood.[4] Mr. & Mrs. Ferris send love; but the former came home today, quite sick.[5] No news, other than what I send you.

Your affec. father

W. Gilmore Simms.

---

[3]For Mary Govan Steele Rivers (Mrs. Christopher McKinney Rivers), Mrs. Simms' first cousin, see note 202, Oct. 23, 1846 (331), and note 95, c. May 6, 1849 (484). In his letter to Mary Lawson Simms of Aug. 29 (1267) Simms writes, "I rejoice in the improved condition of Mary Rivers." We do not know the date of her death, but she is mentioned by Simms in his letter to William Gilmore Simms, Jr., of Aug. 1, 1869 (1361).

[4]Simms must have met William K. Sherwood and his wife, Frances Kellogg Sherwood, before 1837, when he, Mrs. Simms, and Augusta stayed at their home in New York City; the families became close friends. The "Ladies Kellogg" are Mrs. Sherwood's sisters, Sarah, Mary, and Nancy. See letter to Lawson of June 26, 1837 (49), note 11, Mar. 28, 1838 (65), and note 223, Sept. 15, 1866 (1193).

[5]Simms was visiting the William Hawkins Ferrises.

1271a : To the Editors of *Southern Society*[1]

New York, Sep. 20. [1867][2]

Gentlemen.

Yours of the 17th. reached me yesterday. It finds me about to run up the north river to day, in compliance with a previous invitation. I shall accordingly be able to do nothing to day, and another engagement, for tomorrow, will equally serve to keep me from the desk. I have besides the completion of another literary labour on hand, which I had calculated to conclude next week;[3] and my farther plans contemplated my departure for South Carolina, by the 5th. proxo. You will see from these details, that I can only accomplish any thing for you, before reaching home, by a *tour de force.* Even when I shall reach home, I have unavoidable duties which will somewhat embarrass, if not impair the value of, my efforts for your paper. Still, I hope to do you justice & contribute duly to the satisfaction of your readers. On Monday next, I shall begin to work for you, and I shall probably send you day by day, sufficient matter for successive days to your printer. Something may be sent you on Monday.[4] Before I can fairly lay myself out for your work, as I could wish, it will need that I should be at home, at

1271a

[1]Eugene Lemoine Didier, chiefly remembered as a biographer of Poe, founded *Southern Society* (Baltimore), a weekly which ran from Oct. 5, 1867, through Mar. 28, 1868. Since Simms in this letter speaks of "the Editors of Southern Society," apparently William J. McClellan had already joined Didier as coeditor and coproprietor. With the issue for Jan. 4, 1868, Peter Morse joined the firm. See note 214, c. July 6, 1867 (1261).

[2]Dated by Simms' remarks about *Southern Society.*

[3]"Joscelyn: A Tale of the Revolution," published in the *Old Guard,* V (Jan.–Dec. 1867), 1–17, 91–103, 161–176, 241–260, 321–339, 401–421, 481–500, 561–567, 668–681, 731–745, 822–834, 897–935.

[4]Sept. 23. Before leaving for South Carolina on Oct. 5 Simms sent *Southern Society* the following editorials: "Southern Society," I (Oct. 5), 4, "What of the South?," and "A Republic of Letters," I (Oct. 12), 12. He also sent some "book notices," probably those published in I (Oct. 5 and Oct. 12), 6, 15, and at least one poem, "Among the Ruins," I (Oct. 19), 21. See letters to Didier and McClellan of Sept. 26 (1271b) and Oct. 2 (1273).

ease, and free from these excitements, whether of business or society, which now distract my mind & absorb so much of my time. You do not give me the name of your firm, and I can accordingly address you only as the Editors of Southern Society; but does this address reach your Publisher & Proprietors also? Please advise me.

Yours respectfully

W. Gilmore Simms.

P. S. A few of your prospectus's might be sent me here, but it will not be much in my way to do any thing with them here. When I shall reach Charleston, I will cheerfully undertake the distribution of them. Your cohort of contributors is sufficiently strong for success.[5] If contributors do their duty to themselves & the Publishers to the public, there can be little doubt of your success. The chief embarrassment in your way will [be] the great lack of means among our unhappy people, who may well be permitted to ignore the claims of literature, while goaded by the want of bread!

1271b : To the Editors of *Southern Society*

New York: Sep. 26. [1867][1]

Gentlemen.

I send you the accompanying article, as an introduction, & to see how you will like it.[2] I shall possibly send you something more tomorrow, and will do what I can for you, under the circumstances in which I find myself at present. I am preparing to return to South Carolina & propose to depart on Saturday, the 5th. Oct. in the Steamer Champion for Charleston. Closing rivets up here, packing up, seeing friends & paying last visits will consume a great deal of my time, and I shall not be prepared to harness myself fully for your

[5]The "Prospectus of Southern Society" lists among its contributors Simms, John Esten Cooke, Paul Hamilton Hayne, Henry Timrod, John Reuben Thompson, Henry Lynden Flash, Augusta Jane Evans, Sidney Lanier, and Oliver P. Baldwin.

1271b

[1]At the top of the MS. of this letter one of the editors wrote "a. Oct. 5/67."

[2]"Southern Society," published in the first number of the periodical. See note 4, Sept. 20 (1271a).

or any other labour, untill I shall be quietly settled down at home—if I may be said to have a home. In the meantime be pleased to write me as soon as you recieve the within article & say how it suits you. As it is not easy to know what you design or desire clearly, and as I can not conjecture how far you are willing to go in Politics, and what you think & what you wish said, I necessarily speak more vaguely and with more caution than would be the case under better advisement. Address me here before my departure; and be pleased to give me your names. Simply to write as "Ed'rs of So. Society" is rather too mythical. You will also be so good as to state in what manner you would prefer to make your payments. My needs, as in the case of most of our wretched people, render it important that the *quid* should be equally prompt and certain. It will be *your* policy as well as mine, that the Editorials which I may write for you should, in no wise be coupled with my name.[3] I myself will attach my name to such pieces as I design should bear it. Yours truly

W. Gilmore Simms

1273a : To James Lawson[1]

Oct. 5 1867

dear Lawson.

I should have been greatly glad to see Mr. Verplanck[2] in person, & tried to meet him. Had I done so I could have told him much of Cardozo, which my present limit of time will not permit me to write. J. N. Cardoz*o*, not Cardoz*a*, is a Jew of *liberal* character.—His favorite province as a writer was political economy. He wrote for the Southern Review on subjects of this description. He was for some 40 years an Editor (newspaper) in Charleston & elswhere in

[3]"Southern Society," "What of the South?," and "A Republic of Letters" (see note 4, Sept. 20 [1271a]) carry no signature.

1273a

[1]This letter is written on stationery with the following letterhead: "Office of Lawson & Walker, Average Adjusters & Insurance Brokers No. 62 Wall Street. New York ———— 18." We want to thank Professor Thomas L. McHaney, of Georgia State University, for bringing this letter to our attention.

[2]Gulian Crommelin Verplanck (1786–1870), of New York City, was a teacher and author. He was a member of Congress during 1825–1833.

the South. Has recently published a small vol. of sketches descriptive of the City of Charleston. Was also considered a good writer of Dramatic Criticism. He is now somewhere about 80 years of age; is feeble of health & very poor in fortune. I saw him several times this summer. He came frequently to see me & I counselled him about some literary ventures. He is very much respected; is *moral*, though unmarried; moral, perhaps, with a caveat—the usual *qualifications* of bachelor life being understood. His present address is Charleston.[3] Whether he is related to Judge Cardoz*a*, I can not say.[4] Please convey my respects to Mr. Verplanck, whom I very much esteem, and whom I should have been very much gratified to have seen this season.

Yours ever in great haste

W. Gilmore Simms.

James Lawson, Esq.

---

[3]Jacob Newton Cardozo (1786–1873) was born in Savannah, Ga., but moved to Charleston in 1796. In 1817 he became acting editor of the *Southern Patriot* and six years later bought the newspaper and remained its proprietor and editor until 1848. In 1845 he founded the *Evening News*, which he sold two years later, though he continued as commercial editor until he moved to Savannah in 1861. During the Civil War he edited newspapers in Atlanta, Ga., and Mobile, Ala. He wrote for the Savannah *Morning News* until a year before his death. His book which Simms here mentions is *Reminiscences of Charleston* (Charleston: J. Walker, Printer, 1866).

[4]Probably Francis Louis Cardozo (or Cardoza), (1836–1903) a freeborn black, who was reputed to be the son of Jacob N. Cardozo and a woman who was half black and half Indian. He was graduated from the University of Glasgow, studied theology in London, and became a Presbyterian minister. An imposing man of elegant manners, he held several important administrative offices in South Carolina, including those of secretary of state (1868–1872) and treasurer (1872–1876). He was asked to leave the latter office, was convicted of fraud, but was pardoned. He left South Carolina and went to Washington, where he became a clerk in the editing department of the U.S. Treasury. His father was probably not Jacob N. Cardozo but Jacob's brother, Isaac (1792–1855), a customs officer in Charleston: the matriculation albums for the Faculty of Arts at Glasgow University for 1858–1861 give his father as Isaac, a customs officer in Charleston. We are grateful to Jean S. A. Robertson, Reference Librarian, University of Glasgow Library, for examining these records for us.

1274a : To the Editors of *Southern Society*

[October 10, 1867]

Ed'rs Southern Society.
Gentlemen.

Poor Timrod is dead. In a day or two I hope to prepare for you an editorial on the subject,—something like a biography, &c. Keep space for it.[1] How would you like a Juvenile Dept.? I can send you, weekly, a few things, suited to the young, having prepared a "*Southern* Mother Goose" during the war—all fresh & original, & illustrative of objects & interests in the South chiefly. It was in press at Columbia, & more than 25 illustrations made for it, when Sherman destroyed the publishers & press together. I saved the M.S. & some of the illustrations.[2] Please forward me *two* copies of each of your issues from the *first.* I have not seen your first. In haste, but truly. Your obt. servt.

W. Gilmore Simms.

P.S. (Over)

P.S. I left N. Y. on Saturday last, and am for the present in Charleston. Next Saturday I shall probably run up to my plantation for a few days. My address for some time will be Charleston, S.

1274a

[1]Timrod died on Oct. 6. Simms did not wait "a day or two" to write an editorial on his friend: "The Late Henry Timrod," published in *Southern Society*, I (Oct. 19), 18–19, was sent to the editors the same day that he wrote this letter (see note 276, Oct. 10 [1275]). On the MS. of this letter one of the editors wrote "a Oct. 12."

[2]Simms' "Southern Mother Goose" was in the press of Evans and Cogswell, Columbia (see note 88, Nov. 8, 1864 [1107]), when the city was burned by Sherman's army. From Dec. 1865 through the first part of 1867 Simms with the aid of Duyckinck tried unsuccessfully to find a publisher for the work, then called the "American Mother Goose" (see letter to Duyckinck of Dec. 19, 1865 [1142], and following letters to Duyckinck). The MS. of at least part of it is in the Charles Carroll Simms Collection, South Caroliniana Library.

C. Pray take heed of this. For awhile, my contributions to your paper, must be irregular, if not spasmodic. It will take some time to clear my decks for proper action.

Yours &c

W. G. S.

Oct. 10. 1867.

1276 : To the Editors of *Southern Society*[1]

Charleston, Oct. 11. 1867.

Gentlemen.

Yesterday, I sent you by mail an editorial on Henry Timrod. I now enclose you a column of matter for the Juveniles, which I trust you will approve.[2] In all probability I shall send you something tomorrow.

Yours truly

W. Gilmore Simms

Be sure & send me several copies of your paper. I may be able to do some thing for your circulation.

1279a : To the Editors of *Southern Society*

Charleston, Nov. 23. 1867.

Editors of Southern Society.
Gentlemen.

Returning from a week's absence in the interior, I was very much surprised to learn from my New York correspondent that you had

---

1276

[1]We earlier printed a fragment of this letter from a copy made by James Hungerford (see note 24, Mar. 6, 1868 [1292]). We here print the complete letter, which obviously was addressed to the editors of *Southern Society* rather than to Eugene Lemoine Didier, as we then thought.

[2]"The Melodies of the American Mother Goose," published as "By Grandfather Gander," *Southern Society*, I (Oct. 26), 27.

declined the payment of my last draft on you for fifty Dollars. I have waited a week since that information was recieved in the hope to have some explanation from you on the subject; but I have waited in vain. Meanwhile, I have your letter proposing to me a new arrangement for future contributions & compensation. In respect to the length of my articles, I have only to say that when you desired particular subjects to be treated, it was to be inferred that you wished them to be handled as thoroughly as possible. I have sought to do so, in the hope not only to exhaust their leading ideas, but to obtain credit for your editorial chair, for its authoritative expositions. Short paragraphs may be written & substituted for these, and I only wait for some explanation touching the protest of my draft, to answer your subsequent communication. Let me add that "Southern Society" for the last ten days, has not reached my address.

Very respectfully &c.

W. Gilmore Simms.

1285a : To the Editors of *Southern Society*

Charleston, S. C. Jany. 10. 1868[1]

Editors Southern Society.

Gentlemen. I very much regret that there should be any difference between us, or any misunderstanding needing explanation. In my first correspondence with you and when I thought you desired some serial fiction at my hands, I told you that I would contribute for $50 weekly, and that my contributions would make probably from 4 to 6 columns. As I was liberal in quantity of matter usually, I well knew that I would be able to provide 4 columns, and simply wished to convey the idea that you might possibly have to find

1285a

[1]Simms wrote *1867*. The correct year is established by his discussion of his contributions to *Southern Society*. See his letters to the editors of the periodical written in 1867.

space for one or two more. But my terms were $50 per week, no matter what was published, two or ten columns, and I think you must have understood that as I answered several applications, at the same time, to this very same effect. I certainly never engaged for payment by the column, though had you published all that I sent you each week, the four columns would have been supplied down to & beyond the period of my last draft for $50 (unpaid)[.] My contributions begin with you Oct. 5 and conclude with Nov. 30. including 9 weeks.[2] Of these 9 weeks, I find, upon examination, that my articles average *more* than 4 columns for 6 weeks, and over 2 ½ columns for the last 3 weeks. You have paid me for four weeks only. Now were you to count these 5 weeks for which no payment has been made at the very rates you subsequently proposed, viz: $25 per week for 2 ½ columns,—and each of these weeks having more than the required quantity of matter, the sum due me will be $125, and clearly this is the sum to which I am entitled by the arrangement with which you superseded our original contract. Had you written me, in season, frankly, of your embarrassments, and proposed the new arrangement, before my draft had been dishonored, I should cheerfully have entered into the new arrangement with you, having a real solicitude for your success, and being anxious to promote your & the public interests equally in the establishment of a noble organ of Southern opinion, sentiment and society. That I laboured faithfully for this object you will probably admit. I had laid out plans for a series of elaborate papers, contemplating these objects which would have included a full consideration of the characterisitics, susceptibilities, capabilities & performances, as well of our people as our country; and such labours required much more effort & study, involving a vast variety of topic in history & morals, than would be the case in any work of serial fiction.—When you wrote me making the new proposal, I was in possession some hours before of the dishonored draft which was promptly returned to me. In your letter you made no reference to it, nor for a long time after did I recieve any further communication; yet, for fully five weeks

[2]For Simms' contributions to *Southern Society*, see note 30, Mar. 6, 1868 (1293), and letters to the editors of the periodical of Sept. 20, Sept. 26, Oct. 10, and Oct. 11, 1867 (1271a, 1271b, 1274a, and 1276).

after did you continue to publish my articles, editorially & otherwise, without intimating to me a single word as to payment, whether under the original contract, or that subsequently proposed. Did I deserve this treatment?—I can very readily concieve your embarrassments, and do not write to add to them. I forbear all comment upon your proposal to pay me now for *two* columns, and refer you to your own files for the verification of my count, even of columns, in the summing up of my contributions, running, as you will see for 9 weeks from the 5th. Oct. to the 30th. Nov. inclusive. If, after paying me $50 weekly, for the first *four* weeks, you then, of your own head, proposed to me $25 weekly, for 2 ½ columns of matter—each week,—and if, during the ensuing 5 weeks, you actually did publish more than 3 ½ columns per week of my writing, you clearly owe me for those 5 weeks, at the rates which you yourself proposed, and the sum total will be $125. Submit the proposition to any disinterested party, and I do not see how he can escape the conclusion.—I confess to being much pained by the misunderstanding between us, but sincerely hope that your Journal will succeed & that better auspicies for our country, will enable you to secure that patronage which you undoubtedly deserve.

Very respectfully

W. Gilmore Simms

P. S. I am willing to discharge all claim beyond, if you will honour my draft for $100.[3]

W. G. S.

---

[3]In his letters to Hungerford of Mar. 6, 1868 (1292), and to Gayarré of Mar. 13, 1868 (1294), Simms discusses his problems with *Southern Society*. Simms had not collected from *Southern Society* when he wrote to Hayne on Mar. 6, 1869 (1348); whether he ever did we do not know.

1293a : To Henry Barton Dawson[1]

Charleston, March 9. [1868][2]

My dear Mr. Dawson.

Friend, between us, is still I take it Constitutional:—i.e. It does not violate any provision of the Constitution, unless impliedly, & by a strained construction. You must have failed to recieve one or more of my friendly letters, whether long or short. With laborers like ourselves, who have need to be writing all day long with cramped fingers, by feeble fires, and in wintry weather, it is no policy with them to be long winded in our epistles. We condense naturally, dealing with one another, however copiously we may indulge in our addresses to the pleasant public.—You ask me what I am doing. Alas! Alas! Little to profit or pleasure. I am a sort of actor of all work. I scribble paragraphs for newspapers, which give me daily allowance of tobacco & *uisquebaugh.* You know our hard whiskey is Irish in origin, and *uisquebaugh,* the water of life, is simply an equivalent to the French "eau de vie," and the Spanish aguardiente, and the redman's Firewater. I write poesies and proses for periodicals which sometime forget to pay for them; and I am now engaged on a Border Romance, the scene laid in the Old North State, from which I hope (?) to derive the porridge for my self & children for the next six months.[3] Briefly, my life now, is one long & almost sleepless drudgery. It requires incessant labour, not simply to find the porridge but to boil the kettle, with coal here now at $16 per ton. I do not *edit* any paper, though I contribute occasionally to several, & in the Editorial character.[4] I do rotate between Charleston and my plantation at Woodlands, where I am now seeking to rebuild *one of the wings* of my old dwelling house, four

---

1293a

[1]Dawson had begun a 2d series of his *Historical Magazine* in 1868. For Simms' contributions, see note 55, Feb. 12, 1867 (1226).

[2]Dated by Simms' remarks about the rebuilding of Woodlands and the death of his granddaughter (see note 5, below).

[3]Simms was writing "Voltmeier" for the *Southern Home Journal* (Baltimore). It was published in the *Illuminated Western World* during 1869. See letters to Gayarré of Mar. 13, 1868 (1294), and to Victor of Oct. 3, 1868 (1324).

[4]Simms was contributing to the Charleston *Mercury*, the Charleston *Courier*, and the Charleston *Daily News*. See his other letters written during this period.

rooms in a single story, and for this even, my funds threaten premature collapse. It is a matter of duty with me to bestow upon my children all the shelter I can, while the strength is still left me to do so. My pressure of troubles and afflictions do not seem to lighten—as yet I see no silver lining to my cloud. Two weeks ago, I was called upon to bury a lovely little grandchild, which up to the moment when it was taken sick with membraneous croup, was one of the fattest, cosiest, healthiest little creatures in the country. The little life was reft from it in two brief days of illness. The poor mother, my eldest daughter, suffering from night watching, exposure, anxiety & finally prostration, being *enceinte*, was threatened with premature accouchement. That danger has been temporarily averted, but she is still very feeble & still keeps her chamber.[5] Yet, through all this, my brain is not suffered to be idle, let the pangs of the heart be what they will. I am now writing harder than ever, in the hope to avert a foreclosure of mortgage upon the house in which my son in law & daughter reside, and in a room of which I find my temporary shelter now. You see from all this that I can hardly be said to get along at all.—I am surprised that you too should have reason to complain. Your success, I had supposed, considerable, if not complete. Your desire for a more genial climate is expressed in very like language to that of a Boston friend who recently wrote me on the subject, and I answer as I did to him[6]—"If you have no dread of the frequent prospect of the reign of mongrelianism in our miserable country, then you can find no more grateful or advantageous region in which to invest capital. There is no money here. Every body is bankrupt, and there is any quantity of rich and beautiful lands sold daily for a song. Fine houses and excellent farms can be had for the merest trifle. Good lands in healthy districts are sold daily at 50/100 to $3.00 per acre. There is now one farm of 70 acres, in a pretty country, one of the most salubrious, contiguous to several villages and to one large city, well situated in a small hamlet where a few excellent families reside,

---

[5]Esther Singleton Roach died on Feb. 8; Annie Tefft Roach was born on Apr. 6. See note 83, May 2, 1868 (1301).

[6]We have not located Simms' letter to his Boston friend Arthur Williams Austin (see introductory sketch).

which can be had for $3000 to $4000 at private sale. The region is admirable for grapes & peaches, figs & other fruits. The proprietor of an adjoining farm has sold more than $10,000 in peaches, to New York, in a single year. The proprietor of this place, besides giving away large quantities, has realized in one year from $2000 to $3000 from peaches in New York, and this with no sort of experience as a farmer. Large quantities of wine are produced here annually. The dwelling, with all necessary outbuildings including a fine conservatory, is a handsome edifice, frame, of two stories, and comparatively new. The owner, a retired lawyer, who during the War was worth a quarter of a million has, in his old age, been compelled to resume his profession, but his once immense practice is not recoverable, and he finds it difficult to live & pay his taxes on real estate in Charleston. To pursue his profession, he has had to leave his suburban [home], and return to that city.[7] Were I able, I should take all risks, and buy this property myself. But I am helpless. When I add that the region of this farm is singularly healthy, & the resort annually of hundreds of invalids from the North, you will readily concieve the degree of sacrifice which will be made of the property by any such price." You ask touching an opening in our region. The question, in reply, is what do you propose? Such a work as yours, not depending upon the great city or the caprices of fashion, may be conducted—no matter where issued from the press—from any editorial location you may choose. You know Derby, the Publisher.[8] He has bought in this very neighbourhood. See him & enquire. When you tell him that the property in question is at Kalmia, two miles from Aiken, a mile or two from Graniteville—a large successful manufacturing village—two or three miles from Kaolin, another manufacturing village, and but 12 or 13 miles from the city of Augusta, you may concieve, & he describe, the advantages & attractions, as well as the susceptabilities of such a place. When, in addition, I mention that Redmond[9] told me that he had sold (living fifteen miles off) in one season, more

[7]Richard Yeadon. See Crocker, "Richard Yeadon," p. 31.
[8]James Cephas Derby. See note 231, Dec. 10, 1860 (1022).
[9]Dennis Redmond. See note 279, Oct. 22, 1866 (1205).

than $250 in strawberries alone, to the one city of Augusta, you will appreciate the value of such a place. Our own miserable people, are every where compelled to sell, for the absolute means of life—can no longer afford the enjoyment of the otium cum dignatate, or that *rus in urbe*[10] which constitutes the charm of Kalmia. There, my friend, you have a long letter, and Heaven give you patience for its perusal.

Very truly Yours

W. Gilmore Simms.

P. S. As for lightening my burdens, my good friend, God forbid that I should tax any friend, while God allows me the soul for resolution, & the strength for work. I have, thank God, many friends who succour me in a small way. They give me shelter when I go North, give me generous welcome, sometimes send me some grateful little token of affection & sympathy—books, paper, a knife, a pipe, and in one or two *cases,* some good wine, and English Porter, and this too with the expression of sympathies the purity of which I can not question. My girls are not forgotten in their gifts, and my loss of fortune, ease & possibly of comfort, in no degree lessens my courage to do, and my firmness to endure. My chief mental want is books, and I am sorry to tell you that, with one or two exceptions, the Publishers do not seem to consider my need, even if they remember my existence. I write *stans pede in uno,* quite chilly, with no sunshine in the sky and no fire in my grate.

À Dios.

W. G. S.

P. S. My Plantation, Woodlands, by the way, is fifty miles from Kalmia, the Rail Road passing directly through it, conducting to the very foot of the Kalmian Hills. At Aiken and Kalmia, as at Augusta, & the whole precinct there is a considerable number of highly intelligent, intellectual and scientific men, experienced as farm-

[10]Simms failed to underline "in urbe."

ers, vinegrowers, chemists and art workers. I mention these details, not with the view to persuade you to any step, but to possess you of all necessary facts. You are also within 8 or 9 hours by Railway of Charleston. Let me advise you to see Derby, late Publisher, in New York. He has bought, as I say, in this very neighbourhood, & can go more into detail than I do. And he has bought, I understand, with distinct reference to the superior sanitary & salubruous character of the region. I have been told that he proposes the cultivation of the grape, the peach and other fruits. Rid us of mongrelianism & the Negro, and this would be as healthy & happy a region as Tempé in Arcadia as in the days, or nights, when Diana came down to Endymion.

1315a : To Arthur Williams Austin[1]

New York August 14 1868

Hon. Arthur W. Austin.

My dear friend. You see by this that I am almost within handshaking distance of you—700 miles nearer at all events. I write simply to mention the fact & to remind you of my continued existence, & my continued & grateful remembrance. Of my plans for the summer, I can say nothing specifically just now. I am now, with my daughter Mary, a guest of my old friend, Lawson, at Yonkers. Towards the close of the month my daughter proposes to visit some of our old friends at Great Barrington, Berkshire. I shall take her there (D.V.) and after a day or two, there leave her till some time in September. My hope is also to be able to run for a week to Boston, or rather Roxbury;—i.e. if all is well with you. Let me hope that such is the case.[2] Meanwhile, it is not impossible that

1315a

[1]This letter is written on stationery that carries Lawson's letterhead (see note 1, Oct. 5, 1867 [1273a]); Simms tore off all but "New York ———— 18."

[2]On Sept. 5 Simms took his daughter to Great Barrington to visit William K. Sherwood and the Misses Kellogg. He left her there, went to visit Austin at West Roxbury, near Boston, and returned to New York City on Sept. 16. Mary Lawson went to Boston to visit Austin and his daughter, Florence, in late Sept., and she and her father returned to South Carolina in Oct. See Simms' other letters written during this time.

you will be occasionally visiting New York. If so, you will hear of me, perhaps see me almost daily at Lawson's office 62 Wall Street;—Mr. Lawson begging me to assure you that he will not only be glad to welcome you there, but, at your pleasure, at his seat at Yonkers. Commend me gratefully to Mr. & Mrs. W. to Mamselle Florence, and the young gentlemen.[3]

Yours as ever faithfully

W. Gilmore Simms.

1315b : To Joseph Henry[1]

Yonkers, New York.
Augt. 25. 1868.

Professor Joseph Henry.
My dear Professor.

I trust that the terrible events of the last few years have not totally obliterated me from your memory, or, in any way, altered the grateful relations that once existed between us. In this hope, amounting almost to conviction, I presume to commend to your attention & that of your family, my friend, Mr. Thomas Sandford, of New York, and his graceful and amiable wife, the daughter of one of my oldest friends, who are about to pay a brief visit to Washington.[2] They will stay but a few days, & will naturally desire

[3]"Mrs. W." is Harriet Whiting Willard, the widowed mother of Austin's late wife, Ellen Maria; "Mr. W." is doubtless one of Ellen Maria Willard Austin's three brothers, Sidney Algernon, Paul, and Timothy Whiting (see note 172, Sept. 17, 1868 [1320]).

1315b

[1]Henry (see note 1, Jan. 9, 1858 [858]) was at this time director of the Smithsonian Institution. On the back of this letter is a note signed "Leech?": "This gentleman called and wished me to express his regret at not being able to see Prof Henry; his wife did not accompany him." In his letter to Henry of Dec. 5, 1868 (1331), Simms again recommends the Sandfords if they pay "any future visit to Washington."

[2]James Lawson's daughter Mary had married Thomas Sarjeant Sandford on Oct. 26, 1865. See *The Letters of William Gilmore Simms*, IV, v–vi.

to see all the sights of the capital, & especially the treasures & curiosities of the Smithsonian Institution. I can safely commend them to your courtesy, from their large intercourse with society, and the training which they have recieved, in what must now be considered, its ancient circles. In commending these friends to your care & courtesy, I am not regardless of our own relations. I shall be especially grateful to you to make my respects to Mrs. H. and to the fair daughter, whose efforts in plaister I had the pleasure to appreciate when I was last with you.[3] Let me hope that all are well with you, prosperous and happy. Nothing will afford me greater pleasure than to know that while the globe seems to be swinging, every where, awry from the centre, you at least maintain your position on the plane, which you have so meritoriously won. With most affectionate regards, believe me ever truly, Your obliged friend & servt.

W. Gilmore Simms.

1335a : To Emily Timrod Goodwin[1]

Charleston, Dec. 25, '68

My dear Madam

One of the Baltimore Publishers to whom I had written for information says—"If we were allowed, under the Editorial head, to draw attention to the fact that the widow[2] and widowed sister of a distinguished Southern Poet are in destitution, we have no doubt that effectual help would come forth." If you will permit me to have this done, it shall be done, without any name being given, and I

[3]Mrs. Henry was the former Harriet L. Alexander (see note 3, Jan. 9, 1858 [857]). Mary was the name of the Henrys' daughter.

1335a

[1]Emily Timrod Goodwin was the widow of George Goodwin and the sister of Henry Timrod. Our text of this letter is from a typescript made by the late Edd Winfield Parks of the original in possession of the late Katherine Dearing Goodwin, of Athens, Ga. The dots (apparently indicating omissions) are Parks'.

[2]On Feb. 16, 1864, Timrod had married Katie Goodwin, George Goodwin's sister. See note 41, May 8, 1864 (1097).

concur in the belief of this editor that effectual relief would follow. . . . Another matter: The same Editor made a suggestion which prompts me to ask if you own a sewing machine? You will need one if you have to derive any substantial support from taking in needle work. The Editor says—"We have an arrangement with Glover & Baker, by which they engage to furnish us their $55 machine for $22.00 cash, & $33 taken out in advertising. If the $22 can be raised, we will, with pleasure, give to Mrs. Timrod's benefit the $33 advertising."[3] . . . Did you recieve the $8 I had sent you from the Courier's office. Please advise me of your wishes in respect to the preceding matters. In haste, but truly, your friend & servt.

W. Gilmore Simms

Mrs. Goodwin.

1344a : To William J. Widdleton[1]

Woodlands, Feb. 6. 1869.

W. J. Widdleton, Esq.
dear Sir:

Please pay to the order of W. Hawkins Ferris, Esq (Cashier U. S. Treasury in New York) whatever sum you may have to my credit on your books, and oblige

Your obt. Servt.

W. Gilmore Simms.

P. S. Mr. Ferris proposes to visit me shortly, & will bring any package that you may send for me.

---

[3]Two periodicals were being published in Baltimore at this time: the *Southern Home Journal* and the *Southern Review*. Since Simms was a contributor to the former and apparently not to the latter, it was probably John Y. Slater, editor of the *Southern Home Journal*, who had written to Simms. For these two periodicals, see note 248, Sept. 1, 1867 (1268), and note 38, Mar. 13, 1868 (1294).

1344a

[1]Widdleton had taken over Redfield's publishing house. See note 207, Oct. 20, 1860 (996).

1352a : To Paul Hamilton Hayne

Woodlands, S. C.
May 13. 1869.

My dear Paul. I do not know whether I owe you a letter or not; but I think not. Still, I have been so great a sufferer from severe illness at four successive periods during the last eight weeks, that I can be certain of nothing, especially as I have had to write so much & to so many.[1] I have terribly overworked myself, having written since the 22 Oct. last, two elaborate prose fictions of the usual dimensions,[2] to say nothing of smaller pieces, and of a monstrous correspondence. I saw your boy[3] in town for a little while, and heard about you, all that he knew I suppose; though I was little in the vein for making a cross-examination. He told me, and I had learned something of your writings for the periodicals, most of which have cheated you, I take for granted, or paid you so little that compensation was only another name for mockery. I knew that such would be the case with Southern Opinion, & I presume that Southern Society & Home Journal, have all treated you as they have done me. I told your son, repeating counsel which I have often given to yourself, to address your pen to prose writing as that province alone which might properly compensate you. Poetry, no matter how good soever, holds forth no attractions to the Magazine publisher in America, unless coupled with some notorious name. But if you would write a series of sketches like your Skepter Jogul (?) or rewrite that, you could sell to Putnam, Lippincott & Harper very readily.[4] Short tales, & sketches of that class are always popular.

1352a

[1]Hayne had written to Simms on Apr. 25 saying that it has been more than six weeks since he has heard from him. Hayne's letter is printed in McKeithan, *A Collection of Hayne Letters*, pp. 213–215, from the original in the Ferris Collection, Columbia University Library.

[2]"Voltmeier" (see note 3, Mar. 9, 1868 [1293a]) and "The Cub of the Panther," published in the *Old Guard* (see note 191, Oct. 29, 1868 [1327]).

[3]William Hamilton Hayne.

[4]Professor Rayburn S. Moore, of the University of Georgia, writes us that Hayne's "The Skaptar Yokul," a Poesque short story, was first published in *Russell's Magazine*, I (Apr. 1857), 55–63, and that it was revised and shortened and published in *Appleton's Journal*, VIII (Nov. 23, 1872), 567–570. The three magazines to which Simms here refers are *Putnam's Magazine* (New York), *Lippincott's Magazine* (Philadelphia), and *Harper's New Monthly Magazine* (New York).

Verb. sap. For myself, I barely live, & to do so, have not an hour to spare in any aside from my daily tasks. I have rebuilt one wing of my house, but 4 rooms, designed to build 6, but exhausted my resources in building 4. My son & son in law are trying to make a crop, but with small capital, & I have so far resumed planting as to take 2 acres under my charge for gardening purposes. I have probably the finest garden in all this precinct. I have set out 1200 cabbage plants, have been eating radishes, lettuces, green peas, snap beans &c. have squashes beginning to bear, corn in tassel, beans in any quantity, sweet corn for the table, tomato, cucumbers, Irish potatoes, okra, onions, white & red, eschelots, turnips, beets, carrots, parsnips, and most of the herbs, most of these in large quantities, as I hope to supply the table of my daughter in town,[6] as well as our table here, where we never seat less than 10 persons, 3 times per diem. With these vegetable supplies, a little meat will suffice. I hope you are pressing your labours in the same direction. Potatoes will pay better than poetry. I have four large beds of them, planted at different periods. You could also find a market in Augusta doubtless for much that you can raise. But if you will write for the magazines try the prose. Your prose is fully as fine as your verse. Sam Lord told me that he had hopes, *by compromise,* to secure $4,500 at least, on your Mother's Insurance Case. Fortune grant it be so, if you can do no better.[7] Write me when you can & expect as little of me as possible. Remember I am an old man, 63 last month, & that in my old age I am required to begin all the labours of life *de novo,* & work as I never had to do before. From John

[5]Gilmore and Chevillette's husband, Donald Jacob Rowe.

[6]Augusta.

[7]Hayne's father, Lt. Paul Hamilton Hayne (1803–1831), of the United States Navy, died while on duty aboard the U.S.S. *Vincennes.* His widow declined a pension at the time, but after the war, when she had lost most of her property, she applied for one (see McKeithan, *A Collection of Hayne Letters*, p. 216). In his answer to Simms' letter Hayne wrote on May 17 that Samuel Lord, Jr., a Charleston lawyer and lifelong friend of Hayne, had recovered $2,500 for his mother. Hayne's letter is printed in McKeithan, pp. 216–219, from the original in the Ferris Collection, Columbia University Library.

Bruns I hear nothing. What of Dick Michel.[8] My best regards to your wife & mother. Keep your boy at his books.

[*Close and signature cut*]

1366a : To Chevillette Conyers Roach[1]

Great Barrington,
Massachusetts
Augt. 1869.[2]

My dear little Grand Daughter,

I recieved your pretty little letter, sometime ago, and was quite pleased to see how much you had improved in writing, spelling & composition. I would have answered it before this, but Grandpa has been travelling about, & has been frequently quite sick, so that he could not write conveniently and did not feel like writing to any body. I am sick now, and feel quite weak, but hope to get better soon, and to go to New York, next Saturday.[3] I hope your Mama will be able to take you & Annie up to Woodlands, by the first of October. It will do you all good. Carroll now rides on horseback, and he & Govan will show you every thing. I think you will all be quite happy up there, and I hope that Mamer & Grandpa will come home soon after you get there.[4] Be a good child & believe that Grandpa loves you very much.

Your affec. Grandfather

W. Gilmore Simms.

---

[8]Richard Frazer Michel, Hayne's brother-in-law. See note 297, Nov. 29, 1866 (1211).

1366a

[1]For Chevillette (born on Dec. 8, 1859), the eldest child of Augusta Simms and Edward Roach, see note 76, Apr. 9, 1860 (975).

[2]This letter was probably written around Aug. 23. See Simms' remarks about his plans for travel in his letter to Gilmore of Aug. 11 (1365).

[3]Aug. 28.

[4]Mary Lawson Simms had accompanied her father on this trip to the North.

1379a : To Henry Barton Dawson

Charleston, S. C.
Nov. 9. 1869.

Henry B. Dawson, Esq.
My dear Sir:

I regretted not seeing you in New York. Lawson writes me touching some papers in respect to the capture of Ft. Sumter, which (he says) I had promised to furnish you. If so, I really remember nothing about it, and just now, I can see to nothing & hunt up nothing. I am seriously ill, & painfully suffering while I write. Pickens is dead. Of his widow, I really do not know the whereabouts.[1] But as soon as I get able to do any thing, will enquire & if any thing is to be had, get it for you. I witnessed the scene, and know something of all the parties.[2] In pain & haste, but very truly Yours

W. Gilmore Simms.

1404a : To Sallie F. Chapin[1]

Woodlands, S. C.
March 19. '70

My dear Mrs. Chapin.

I fully expected to have been with you on the night of the 14th. but the fates were adverse. The day opened with a rain storm from the North East, and, as if in sympathy with the external, my internal

1379a

[1]Francis Wilkinson Pickens (see note 120, Dec. 30, 1842 [148]), governor of South Carolina during 1860–1862, died on Jan. 25, 1869. In 1858 he had married (as his third wife) Lucy Petway Holcombe, noted for her beauty, charm, and accomplishments. A regiment of South Carolina troops was named the Holcombe Legion in her honor, and her picture was engraved on Confederate currency. After the death of Pickens she continued to live at Edgewood, Pickens' plantation near Edgefield Court House.

[2]On Nov. 15 Dawson wrote Simms that he planned to write "the story of Sumter, *as it really was.*" Simms replied to Dawson's letter on Nov. 25 (1386).

1404a

[1]For Mrs. Chapin, the wife of Leonard Chapin, see note 140, June 30, 1868 (1312).

elements painfully & strenuously opposed my leaving close quarters. I have been suffering from an acute attack of my miserable malady ever since, and write you now, under a sense of constant uneasiness and with frequent twinges of pain, if not of conscience. My hope is, if the weather moderates, to get down next week. But here, it has been intensely cold. Black frost, if not ice, daily, and the ice sometimes ¼ inch thick. It is still cold, though more moderate. Here, I have abundance of fuel, & warm fires night & day as I require, free of cost, and a more close & comfortable chamber. Shall I exchange these, for a bleak chamber, no fire, no carpet, and many desagréments. My poor children[2] are assiduous in making me comfortable in town, but their resources are very limited, and I check them in every expenditure as long as I can endure. But I prefer to endure up here, untill Spring shall more decidedly put forth its nose in despair of the North winds. My hope is that, with this very severe cold snap, the reign of Winter is over. But this last stroke has been a severe one. We have fears that every thing in the garden has been killed. Such is the fear this morning. My hope is that the green peas, of which we had 3 fine beds, have escaped.— Of course, you are wrapped up in furs & philosophy. How comes on the satirical romance.[3] *Festina lente.* There is abundance of material. Only, do not *contract* yourself. It is one of the mistakes of young writers, that they do not sufficiently *unfold* themselves. You remember what the Knight of the Faerie Queen read over each of the doors in the Enchanted Castle? "Be Bold! Be bold! Be bold!" Over *one* of the doors only was it written—"Be not too bold!"[4] All this means only,—be bold with judgment. Let judgment qualify audacity. Excuse this brief scribble—I am still under suffering, and a half an hour at the desk, makes me very wretched. I have des-

[2]Augusta and Edward Roach.

[3]*Fitz-Hugh St. Clair, the South Carolina Rebel Boy; or, It Is No Crime to Be a Gentleman* (Philadelphia: Claxton, Remsen & Haffelfinger; Charleston: J. M. Guer & Son, 1872).

[4]Book III, Canto xi, Stanza 54. This quotation was one of Simms' favorites.

patched several letters this morning, & have several more,—*ex necessitate*—to write, before the day closes.

Let me hope, my dear Lady Samaritane that you, my Lord, & all the juvenile sprigs of nobility are well, and rejoicing in fields of clover.

God be wi' you in mercy.
Yours truly

W. Gilmore Simms.

1419a : To William Hawkins Ferris[1]

Charleston 27 May. [1870][2]

dear Ferris.

I spent a couple of weeks very gratefully at Woodlands, and felt quite a physical improvement there; came to the city last Saturday,[3] was quite well that day & Sunday, but Sunday night had one of my atrocious paroxysms & have been suffering ever since. For two successive nights I never slept a wink. I am better today—i.e. easier;—but I am still under the action of medicine & quite feeble. All are well save myself. I write simply to tell you that I still live. God bless you & yours.

W. Gilmore Simms

1419a

[1]This is the last letter written by Simms which we have located. He died on June 11.

[2]Dated by Simms' remarks about his health and his arrival in Charleston on Saturday. See letter to Edward Roach of May 17 (1419).

[3]May 21. Since before the discovery of this letter we were uncertain on what date Simms left Woodlands for Charleston for the last time, we conjectured in note 78, May 17 (1419), that he may have left at a later date and that a letter in the Charleston *Courier* of May 27, dated "South Edisto, May 24, 1870" and signed "*," was possibly written by him; it was almost certainly written by his son Gilmore and revised by Simms.

APPENDIX
Letters of Uncertain Date

1420 (1a) : To Israel Keech Tefft

Woodlands, Nov. 23. [1842–1850][1]

My dear Tefft

I see by the papers that you are in Charleston, and hasten to invite you to see us at Woodlands.[2] We are just 72 miles from the city. Our post town is Midway, which is 1 ½ miles from our residence. Have you leisure enough to partake of our hog & hominy, and let me assure you how very truly, I am,

Your friend &c,

W. Gilmore Simms

I. K. Tefft Esq.

1420b : To John J. French[1]

Woodlands S. C. Decr. 15 [1845–1849][2]

dear Sir:

I regret that I cannot comply with your wishes. I do not keep autographs myself & have readily yielded the letters of my corre-

---

1420 (1a)

[1]This letter sent to Tefft "Politeness Mr. S. Hart Sen." must have been written after Hart took over the bookstore of J. P. Beile in 1841 (see letter to Carey and Hart of Aug. 2, 1841 [113]). Simms saw Tefft in Charleston in late Oct. 1841 (see letter to the Griffins of Nov. 3 [122b]), so it is unlikely that it was written in that year. Since the handwriting appears to be early, the letter must have been written during 1842–1850. We have checked the Charleston newspapers for these years (and, in fact, for a few years earlier and a few years later) without finding the notice Simms saw of Tefft's being in Charleston.

[2]Simms wrote *Woodland*.

1420b

[1]Not identified.

[2]There is nothing in this letter by which we can determine the year in which it was written. It appears to have been written after Simms' meeting with James Fenimore Cooper in 1843 (see letter to Cooper of Sept. 27, 1843 [*174a*]), and before the death of Calhoun in 1850.

spondents to the collections of my friends, whenever the letters themselves were of such a nature as to permit their publication. Those of Mr. Cooper and Mr. Calhoun which I yet retain, are of a character which do not permit of this.[3] I repeat my regret that I am not able to serve you as you desire.

Very respectfully
Yr obt servt. &c—

W. Gilmore Simms

John J. French, Esq.

1423a : To James Chesnut, Jr.

Woodlands, Jan 16. [1848–1850?][1]

Col. James Chesnut
My dear Sir.

There is a gentleman, a Mr. George Hopkinson, and Englishman of excellent character & education, living at present in or about Camden, in the capacity of a private tutor. In this capacity, he proposes the private study of the Law, and is, I am told, but little in the way of procuring the requisite facilities. I have been applied to by a friend in Charleston, whom I am anxious to oblige, to write to some friend in Camden, & solicit for this young stranger, the usual facilities; and I have been able to think of none to whom I could so confidently refer in such a matter as yourself. I have every reason to believe, from what I hear, that Mr. Hopkinson is a worthy & proper gentleman, of excellent & even distinguished connexions

[3]Only one letter from Cooper to Simms, dated Jan. 5, 1843 [1844], is known to be extant. It is printed in James Franklin Beard's *The Letters and Journals of James Fenimore Cooper* (Cambridge, Mass.: Harvard University Press, 1960–1968), IV, 436–439. In a footnote to the letter Beard says that the manuscript had been given by Simms to Israel Keech Tefft. No letters from Calhoun to Simms are known to be extant.

1423a

[1]If the George Hopkinson of this letter is the same as the George Hopkinson who was admitted to the bar in Charleston in 1852 (see Belton O'Neall, *Biographical Sketches of the Bench and Bar of South Carolina* [Charleston, S.C.: S. G. Courtenay & Co., 1859], II, 601), this letter was perhaps written in one of these years.

& education, reduced by circumstances, but deserving of the most favorable consideration. I feel sure that I shall need only to draw your attention to the matter. Mr. H. is dwelling at Wm. Kennedys[2] either in or near Camden, and will, I doubt not, be grateful for your attentions, as will be most certainly

Your obliged frd & servt.

W Gilmore Simms

1428a : To William H. Sweetzer[1]

Charleston, So Caro. June 23. [1850–1860][2]

Mr. Wm. H. Sweetzer.
My dear Sir:

It gives me much pleasure to comply with your request.

W. Gilmore Simms

---

[2]William Kennedy, a native of Scotland, came to the United States in 1822 and was naturalized in 1827. He first settled in Charleston and was employed by Douglas, Kirkpatrick, and Haile, commission merchants. He later settled in Kershaw County, married Mary, the daughter of Benjamin Haile, and operated his wife's plantation on West Wateree and a fleet of pole boats between Camden and Charleston. In the late 1860s he moved to Texas.

1428a

[1]Not identified.

[2]The handwriting of this letter appears to belong to this period.

1431a : To William James Rivers

Woodlands, S. C.
March. 13. [1862–1864?][1]

My dear Professor.

I shall probably be at Hunts or some other Hotel[2] in Columbia, on Sunday night—shall probably stay but a single day. For 'auld lang syne' I shall be glad to see you. Will you do me the honour to find me out.

Yours Ever truly

W. Gilmore Simms.

Professor Rivers.

1431a

[1]Since during these years we do not know where Simms was in Mar., any one of them is possible.

[2]The United States Hotel, run by A. M. Hunt.

INDEX

Note On The Index

This index is divided into two parts: a general index and an index of Simms' works.

The general index includes the names of all people, firms, clubs, societies, periodicals, and newspapers mentioned in the letters, in the footnotes, and in the introductory material. The titles of all books, articles, tales, plays, and poems, with the exception of those mentioned only in the biographical notes, are entered under the name of the author. If the author is unknown to me, the work is entered under its title. Periodicals are entered under their titles, newspapers under the city of publication.

The general index also includes some topics (such as secession) and the names of battles and wars and of countries, states, and cities when Simms has commented about them or when, in the case of cities, he has delivered a lecture there. I have not attempted an exhaustive entry under South Carolina: the whole of Simms' letters are to a considerable extent concerned with his native state.

There is an entry under William Gilmore Simms, but it is by no means complete. It consists of several topics relating to Simms which might be useful to scholars, but any scholar seriously working on Simms will, of course, find it necessary to read the letters.

In the index to Simms' works I have entered each work under its title. Even unpublished or unfinished works to which Simms gave titles are thus entered. When Simms gave a title to a review (e.g. "Topics in the History of South-Carolina"), the review is entered under the title and also under the general topic of Reviews and Notices, which contains largely his shorter, untitled reviews. There are two other general topics: Biographical Sketches and Projects. This last comprises unfinished works and ideas for works and for volumes of collected works which were never carried out.

T.C.D.E.

GENERAL INDEX

INDEX OF SIMMS' WORKS

MARY C. SIMMS OLIPHANT is the granddaughter of William Gilmore Simms and is known in South Carolina for her revision of the Simms history of the state, which has been used in public schools for more than a century. She has been called "South Carolina's First Lady of Letters," a title earned largely by collecting and coediting the five previous volumes of *The Letters of William Gilmore Simms.* She also served on the editorial board of the Centennial Edition of the Writings of William Gilmore Simms and the executive committee of the Caroliniana Society.

T. C. DUNCAN EAVES is Professor of English at the University of Arkansas in Fayetteville. His specialty is English and American literature, with emphasis on, in addition to Simms, the eighteenth-century novel and modern poetry. He was coeditor of the published five volumes of the Simms *Letters*, and coauthor of *Samuel Richardson: A Biography* (Oxford, 1971).